MW01140864

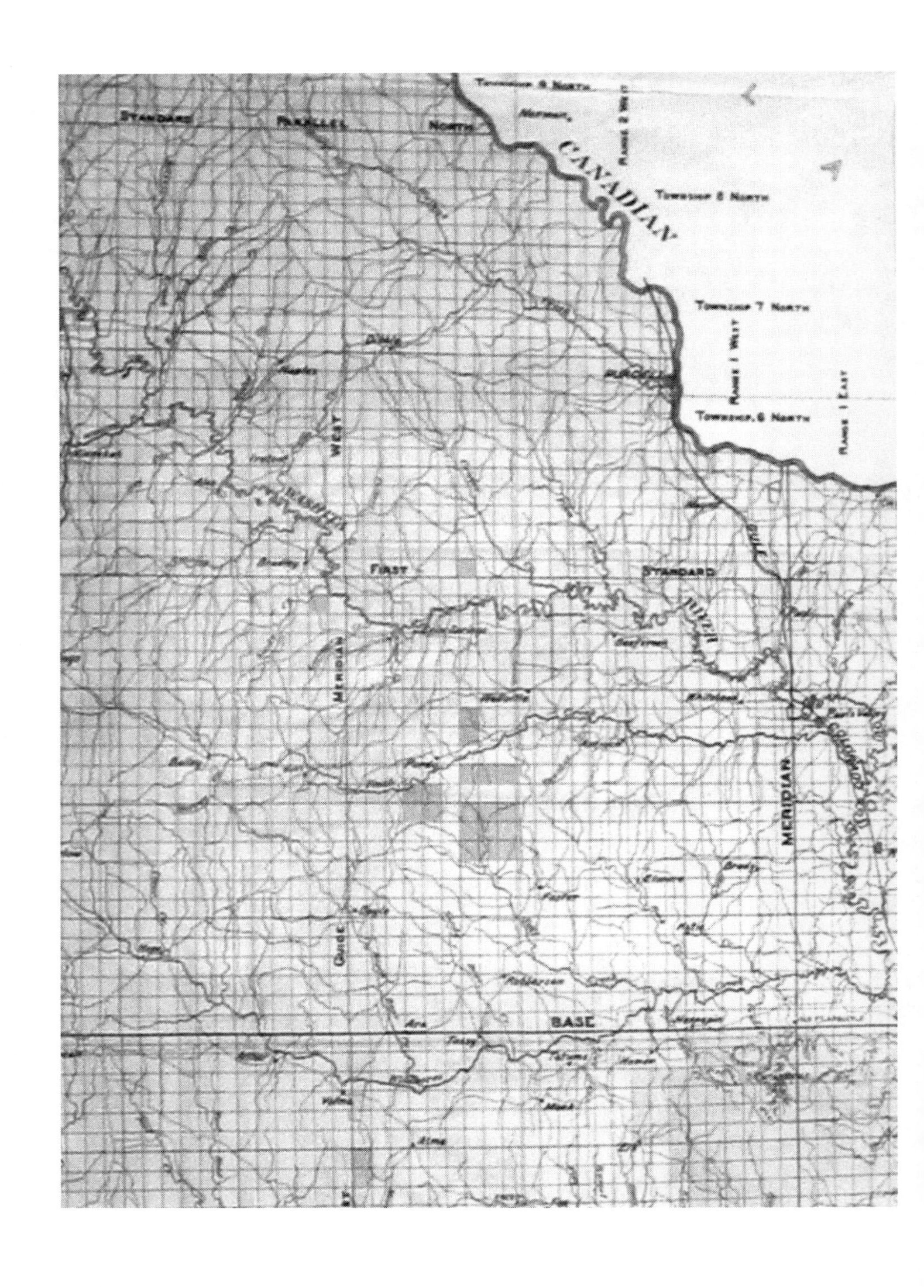

STANDARD PARALLEL NORTH
CANADIAN
Township 8 North
Township 7 North
Township 6 North
Range 1 West
Range 1 East
WEST
FIRST STANDARD
MERIDIAN
GUIDE
BASE

COMMISSION TO THE FIVE CIVILIZED TRIBES
MAP OF
CHICKASAW NATION
INDIAN TERRITORY
COMPILED FROM OFFICIAL RECORDS OF
THE UNITED STATES GEOLOGICAL SURVEY
SCALE OF MILES
The Pontotoc
Conspiracy
RIVER
PARALLEL
NORTH
LINE
Phillip M. Swatek

For information address
435 Brevard Avenue
Cocoa, Florida 32922
website: www.pontotocconspiracy.com
email: questions@pontotocconspiracy.com

Manufactured in the United States of America
ISBN 1-886104-12-3

Published by
The Florida Historical Society Press
435 Brevard Avenue
Cocoa, Florida 32922
phone: (321) 690-0099
website: www.florida-historical-soc.org

Dedication

Until I met Margaret Harris I had given little thought to Indian Territory or the vibrant early days of Oklahoma, not that she witnessed either one personally. She came along much later, but the Western spirit remains with her undiminished, unchanged by eastern education or world travel. Our marriage was rewarding to me in many ways, including an awareness of the curious history of her hometown—Ada, in Pontotoc County. This book was born from that awareness and I am grateful for that—along with countless other things, starting with our four children: Phillip Jr., Maui, Hawaii; Randall, our elder daughter, Wilton, Connecticut; John, Houston, Texas, and our younger daughter, Shelby, Los Angeles. It is only right this book is dedicated to Margaret and our children.

- Phillip M. Swatek

KANSAS
ARKANSAS
TEXAS
Canadian River
Guthrie
Muskogee
Oklahoma City
The Corners
Saloon
Sasakwa
Canadian River
Pauls Valley
Center
Ada
Red River
Ardmore
Red River
Red River
Fort Worth
Dallas

With ready-made opinions one cannot judge of crime. Its philosophy is a little more complicated than people think.

Fyodor Dostoyevksy

White shall not neutralize the black
nor good
Compensate bad in man, ablsove him
so:
Life's business being just the terrible
choice.

Robert Browning

THE PONTOTOC CONSPIRACY

Prologue

Steady night rain turned to drizzle, then ended as mist in the hollows. To the east, under a heavy cloud deck, there was a watery grey streak along the horizon. Dawn of a new day, Monday, April 19, 1909, a day in Ada, Oklahoma, that outraged the Governor and shocked the nation.

There was enough first light to make out a dozen or more bundled figures walking around a flimsy barn a hundred yards down the track from Ada's Frisco railroad depot. The figures would stop and peer through cracks between boards of the barn wall, then move to another opening, as if the dark inside might be more yielding there.

Their talk was muted. Most of the voices were mens', though there were at least two boys outside the barn to hear them. They were excited and exasperated with the dark, not being able to see what they feared to see.

"I can make out four of 'em!" one of the boys announced to his friend in a strangled whisper.

Two men came over to see if somehow the boys had found an opening big enough to actually see anything in the barn, or if it was young imagination and excitement at work. Then, from the other side of the barn, a deep voice, "there's four of 'em alright."

The barn door was closed, heavy latch in place, but no sign of a lock. There was nothing to keep the boldest of the intense band around the barn from pulling the door open and looking inside…nothing except by being there as the night ended, they knew they were already trespassing on a grave conspiracy.

The sun couldn't break through the gloomy overcast, but minute by minute a shadowless light came over the scene, seeped into the barn. Bundled figures kept going from one gap in the boards to the next, trying to get the best look, though it was agreed by now there were four men hanging by the neck inside, lifeless, hands wired behind them. Only a white horse, Old John, moved once in a while looking for the best hay.

A one-horse buggy came up at a trot. The town photographer had arrived with his equipment. He searched quickly for a place to poke his camera lens through the boards for the picture he wanted. He couldn't find the right spot, then, without much trouble, pulled a board aside for his historic photograph.

A wagon with three men aboard arrived. The men were Ada's chief jailer and his two assistants. They swung open the barn door on squeaking hinges, filed inside, pulled the door closed behind them. Orders were given urgently, in such hushed tones nobody on the outside could understand. Five minutes passed. The barn door opened again.

The crowd outside gathered around the door. Four men, hands no longer bound behind them, no rope around their necks, were stretched out on the barn floor side by side, ready to be put in the wagon. The chief jailer and an assistant hurried outside, jumped up on the wagon bed. The chief said to the assistant still at the barn door , “Gi’mme the hands.”

Two of the bodies dragged from the barn then hoisted into the wagon were those of fit-looking, middle aged men; another looked like that of an overweight accountant. The last appeared to be the body of a church deacon in a dark suit with a black fedora hat still on his head.

“Who done it, Walter?” an onlooker squeezed against the door frame asked the chief jailer. The chief jailer kept pulling and lifting lynch victims and wouldn't answer.

“Walter– who done it?”

“How the hell would I know!” the agitated chief jailer finally shouted.

Oklahoma's first Governor, C. N. Haskell, demanded an answer to the same question when he got news of the Ada tragedy. He swiftly organized a Blue Ribbon grand jury and charged jury members in the strongest official language to identify those involved in the lynching and bring them to justice.

Governor Haskell based his successful political campaign on a promise to bring law and order to a new state that had just emerged from eighty years as Indian Territory. Law and order were historically thin in Indian Territory. The supporting judicial system was for many years in Arkansas, three days away on horseback. Justice was often regarded as a personal responsibility, as it was by tribal custom for the Chickasaw Indians.

In 1908 – one year after statehood – there were thirty six homicides in Pontotoc County, the last remaining part of what had been Indian Territory since 1830. Statehood hadn't done anything to improve the staggering record of violence, despite Governor Haskell's campaign vows to bring needed reforms. The Governor was deeply angered that the Ada lynching focused nationwide attention on his state's continuing problem.

The Governor's Blue Ribbon grand jury started hearing the first of twenty eight witnesses April 27, 1909. Two and half days later, the grand jury gave up. Not one of the witnesses provided the first scrap of information to help answer the question – who did it?

Nearly one hundred years after the lynching on a rainy spring night in Ada, not a single member of the mob who took the lives of four men has ever been identified, much less indicted for the crime. No single member has ever said a word about it publicly. None of them left in papers or in a diary the first clue about who the conspirators were.

What would move so many citizens–including community leaders of standing and consequence–to commit an act so violent and on such a scale?

Why would none of them ever try to explain what they did? Why wouldn't one of them ever express doubts, or remorse?

The Pontotoc crime and conspiracy sounded not only the last melancholy echo of Indian Territory, they brought a convulsive end to a half century of the Wild West, all in a prairie town where the Main Street water trough once read, "Ada not a lady, but a dandy place to live."

The Way West

Most Oklahomans as old as I am started out somewhere else–Alabama in my case, right after the War Between the States. I was three years old when the family left Alabama in a big wagon with four mules pullin', so I didn't have much to say in the matter. Just as well. From what I heard prospects looked brighter most anywhere else–anywhere but the southern plantation states with nobody to work the cotton fields.

My name is John Harris and I was the youngest member of the family when we left the plantation, headed for Illinois, which might seem like an odd place for a southern family to go right after the war. Certainly we weren't headed here–Oklahoma was Indian Territory then–but that's where I ended up.

Most of the Alabama families who pulled up stakes after Appomattox headed straight for Texas, just like there weren't any Yankees out there. What they saw in Texas was opportunity, only it wasn't as easy as it looked when they got there, particularly for young people starting out.

Many of these young Texas newcomers decided they would have to go north across the Red River into Indian Territory to find the life they dreamed of, generally a ranch of their own. Gus Bobbitt was one of them. So he and I followed different trails to Indian Territory. Anyway, I'm glad we both made the trip, because Gus and I became good friends.

I'm eighty-eight years old now, and while they claim I sometimes forget things, I sure haven't forgotten Gus Bobbitt. Fate dealt unkindly with Gus. He deserved better. What fate our town deserved, isn't all that clear. It's not easy to decide. Maybe it will be for you—

Gus and I were both born on small cotton plantations on the Tom Bigbee River in Western Alabama. He was born in the middle of the War Between the States–'63, I believe. I came along right after the war, February 15, 1866.

The Bobbitt place, from what he later told me, must have been about fifty miles upstream from us in McClaren County. Our folks didn't seem to know one another in Alabama.

Gus said they had a half dozen field hands before the war, so theirs wasn't an outfit to be ashamed of. We had about the same number, plus Mammy, who stayed with us after the war and helped bring me along like she did my older brother and sister.

The Bobbitts left Alabama right after the war and headed for Sherman, Texas, north of Dallas, all of them, in two big wagons. They had kin in Sherman. Gus said he didn't really remember much about the trip, he was so young, but from what he heard at family gatherings through the years, he knew at least one story for every mile.

Neither the Bobbitt property nor ours was damaged in the fighting. No big battles or anything like that way down in Alabama. Well, there was the Navy battle in Mobile Bay in '64. That was south of us. Nobody around our place was hurt by gunfire, though Admiral Farragut ordered his Marines to burn five hundred bales of our cotton on the Mobile dock, and that hurt our family financially.

After the war, none of the landowners around us knew how to run their plantations without help, from what everybody said. They sure didn't have the money to pay field hands.

Our family was in this fix, my mother told me years later. She remembered our fields looked good all during the war though. They didn't go to weeds with Papa away. Even if they did look cared for during the war years, there weren't many workers you could count on to chop and pick cotton when the fighting stopped.

Two of our people, Sam and Luke, did stay on for several years, not sure at all that freedom would provide food and shelter. Two field hands can't make a real cotton crop of course, but they kept the vegetable garden up and tended the livestock, our pigs and two old cows. All our horses went to the war. Papa rode off to battle in style on our big Morgan. I wish I could have seen him.

Mammy stayed. She told my mother she didn't have anywhere to go. So my mother said, "stay put."

My father told me one time he thought about taking us to Texas after Appomattox, but he never was the kind to do what everybody else was doing. He had to find his own way.

Papa was a tall, strong-willed man, who put great faith in the Bible, word for word. He had a thin, curved mustache and a little goatee, favored by many Confederate cavalry officers. My father was a major in most of the war, and a good-looking man. I never got to be tall like he was, though I wasn't short. I took after my mother's family, I guess. I grew a mustache as soon as I could.

I called my father Papa all of our lives. It was customary in our part of the world. But I didn't call my mother "mama." I remember she told me when I was about five, "I am your mother. If you wish to speak to me, say 'Mother.'" Even my father called her "Mother" sometimes. She usually called him "Mr. Harris"–or around us children she did.

My father rode through more than three years of the war unhurt. The last eighteen months of the fighting he was under General Nathan Bedford Forrest's command, and he was very proud of that.

When Papa came home, he was still wearing his tan tunic and floppy cavalry hat, his pistol still strapped on his right side, saber on the left, Mother remembered. "He didn't look like the war was over," she said.

In addition to the wonderful good fortune of being unhurt, my father was still riding Big Dan, our Morgan, who wasn't wounded in the fighting either. Lucky as they were, both of them looked thin and tired to Mother.

I have no doubt thousands of Yankee cavalrymen came home thin and tired, too, but they had victory to boost their spirits. My father didn't, and Mother recalled he was very grim, vowing he would not stand by and see the Yankees take our farm. No Yankees even came to see it, from what I was told.

Papa simmered down two or three weeks after he came home, Mother said. Sam and Luke had the garden hoed and weeded and had already started planting. We had more pigs than we knew what to do with. One of our old cows had died but the other was doing fine.

Papa helped with the farm work of course, though his heart wasn't in it. He wasn't a farmer. With the family safe at home and doing better than most of our neighbors, he decided he had to go out into the world and make his fortune, wherever that took him.

At this time there was heavy recruiting of southern planters to go down to Brazil and produce cotton with slave labor. That's what planters in our part of the country knew how to do. I'd say the recruiters did very well. Twenty thousand Southerners did go to Brazil and lived in six colonies.

My father didn't like the idea of living in a colony and growing Brazilian cotton, but one of the recruiters happened to tell him foreign prospectors were finding big emeralds in the mountain streams feeding the Amazon River, if you had the nerve to get up there.

Picking up emeralds from Peruvian riverbeds must have seemed like the solution to war-stricken and poor Alabama to Papa. Plantation life as he knew it was gone. He had to take action. Emerald hunting, dangerous as it might be, suited him.

Mother said she understood why my father wanted to go to the Peruvian mountains. She said she understood, anyway.

My father got to the emerald country all right, true enough, as far as you can go up the Amazon River. He found some stones, but sure no fortune. He brought us all a little emerald when he came back two years later. I still have mine. It's really pretty small, but I liked that he remembered us.

I was more than a year old when Papa got back from South America. Nothing much had changed for our family, except for my arrival. Mother said we always had enough to eat while Papa was away and no carpetbaggers or any one else threatened us. Still, it was an unhappy time in our part of Alabama. It was easy to understand why so many families went to Texas, like the Bobbitts did, or were planning to go. The cattle business in a huge, sparsely populated part of the country offered hope, Yankees and all.

Maybe if my father had thought of going to Texas first, we would have gone right after the war. But with so many going ahead of us by the time he returned from South America, he thought he had to do something different. He decided to beat the Yankees at their own game–commerce.

Papa thought he could run a store because he was good at numbers. He didn't want to try it in Alabama, though. Money was scarce. It had to be in the North. That's how we got to Albany, Illinois, across the Ohio River. Papa had enough money from Brazil to start a small grocery store.

From his cavalry scouting missions he came to believe the people in southern Illinois were sympathetic to the South in many ways, and even talked about the same way we did, though they were technically Yankees. So off we went, north across the Ohio River to do business with the Yankees. That was 1869.

Sam and Luke agreed to help us on the long wagon trip. From what I read later, some stretches of the South were unsettled in those post-war years, even dangerous for a family traveling alone. I'm sure Mother was glad to have Sam and Luke along. They both knew how to shoot, and they were both good at handling our mules.

Once across the Ohio River, they planned to go farther north on the railroad as far as they could get. Papa agreed to their plan and when we were in Illinois, he bought their tickets on the Illinois Central to Chicago.

My years in Albany, Illinois, were all right. Boys in school tried to make fun of what they called my "Rebel accent" at first. That didn't come to much. They sounded more Southern than I did. Until I heard them talk, I was never sure what a southern accent was.

I was able to graduate from grammar school without half trying. I learned more at home from my mother, who was smart. She was a Rodgers, niece of our Lieutenant Governor in Alabama, and even had tutors when she was a girl. Papa was big on the Bible, as I said, and he drilled me on that. Mother knew about books and history.

When I was thirteen years old Papa gave up the grocery store business and we finally went to Texas–Weatherford. We had Alabama friends who moved there right after the war and they were doing well enough on their farm. They sat down together three times a day to eat at their kitchen table. That's doing well enough I thought.

My school days were over when we moved to Texas. Papa, my older brother, Edward, and I had to work, and that's when I started tending cattle for nearby farmers. The year was 1878. I got more promises than pay at first, but I did learn something about the cattle business.

After a couple of years I was getting pretty good at handling cattle. I could out-fox most of the cows anyway. Having a smart cattle horse–they call 'em quarter horses now–makes the job easy enough. A dumb horse and smart, ornery cows take time. One day I got an offer from a cattle buyer to come down to South Texas and do the same kind of work for two dollars a day guaranteed, cash.

Two dollars a day wasn't bad pay because we didn't have any place to spend the money we got and the Triple R–the ranch where I ended up–supplied the food and horses. They were decent folks at the Triple R, but it didn't take long for me to know I wasn't meant for a life in the cattle business.

Gus Bobbitt was just the opposite. After I got to know him, he told me he decided he was going to be a rancher when he was in the second grade at Lettellier's Academy in Sherman, not that Sherman was ranching country or even close to it. I think there must be something about being in Texas that makes some people want to run cattle. Gus was one. For sure he wasn't any more interested in growing cotton than I was.

The Bobbitts may have come through the war better off than we were. Both Gus and his older brother Isador–they called him Izzy in the family–had several years at Lettellier's and that was pretty expensive for those days. Maybe relatives paid for that much education for the boys. I'd say it paid off.

Isador became a railroad contractor in New Orleans and, from what I heard, he had a lot of political connections. Government officials in Washington considered him an expert on the West since he went to school for a while in Sherman.

Gus said Isador was older than he was, but they were close and very much alike. They were both big talkers, Gus would admit with a grin. You could call them both glad handers, too, quick to laugh and slap you on the back. I figure Isador must have been really good at it, having influence all the way back to Washington.

Gus did speak well, I thought, and he sure never lacked for something to say. You never had trouble hearing what he had to say, either. He had a voice that carried. His laugh too. Where the big voice came from, I'm not certain. He wasn't a big man, not tall anyway, but he did have a kind of barrel chest. Maybe that was it.

Most people really liked Gus. Not many people passed him on the street here in Ada without a "Howdy, Gus." He certainly was important in the Masons in the early days. A good many people, even those who liked him, said he was a natural politician, and I suppose he was. That's not generally a compliment in our part of the country, then or now.

For all his jokes and easy talk, Gus was a determined man, determined to get what he wanted, and what he wanted was to be a rancher. Except for political office maybe, I don't think he ever considered any other goal.

Of course that's easy for a young man to say, that he wanted to be a rancher, but if his folks don't have land enough for a ranch, and he doesn't have any money to buy his own land or stock, it might be a long time coming. A determined man can do it though, if he's willing to take some risks, put up with some hardship, and maybe do some things he'd rather not do.

Gus was willing to do all the hard things, at least for a while. He wasn't willing to stay on the family homestead and help with the farm work. So he left home and worked for a couple of small ranchers on the Texas side of the

Red River. He could see pretty fast he wasn't going to get a ranch of his own that way. He decided to cross the river into Indian Territory.

Remember that even in the 1880's there didn't look to be many people in Indian Territory, at least not along the north shore of the Red River. It was mostly open prairie country with patches of woods–Chickasaw hunting grounds.

To begin with, there weren't many Chickasaws anywhere, something like six thousand in 1890, counting every man, woman and child. And the Chickasaw Nation covered about seven thousand square miles. There weren't even two thousand Chickasaws in all of Pontotoc, one of four districts in the Nation.

Gus Bobbitt knew, like most Texans knew, you couldn't just cross the Red River and set up ranching in Indian Territory like you owned the land, or that you could ever own it like you might in Texas, no matter how unsettled it looked. The land belonged to the Chickasaw tribe in severalty by law. It was community property. One Indian couldn't sell you a piece of the tribe's Nation.

Pressure from white ranchers to settle permanently on the great pastures in Indian Territory was beginning to build up, though there were already a few white newcomers who could own land when Gus first crossed the Red River. Those few who could own property married a Chickasaw and were taken into the tribe.

Some of these "intermarrieds," as they were called, ended up with huge tracts. That's how some of the biggest ranches in Oklahoma were started. Joe Roff started his big ranch about twenty miles south of Ada that way.

Gus Bobbitt wasn't interested in the intermarried approach. Leasing land in Indian Territory was what interested him. Leasing, not having to buy the land, would make it possible for Gus to start his ranching career, though leasing took money, too. No where near as much as buying though.

Champions of the Indian cause thought terms for leasing tribal land in Indian Territory were scandalous, the Indians got so little out of it. That was probably true, though the acreage and value of land Gus Bobbitt thought he needed cost more money than he had starting out. What he had in mind was property with a steady water supply and good grass somewhere near the Red River Valley and Texas. Most of the newcomers were thinking along those lines, so leases were expensive there. It wasn't as easy getting started as it sounded back home.

To get the straight of it, Gus took a day off from the ranch where he was working and rode up to Tishomingo, the Chickasaw capital, south of Ada. He found an Indian land agent willing to lease him four hundred acres near Center, west of Ada, at a price he could afford.

The leasehold was a good seventy miles north of the Red River Valley and the Indian agent admitted it was "lonesome up there," but promised it was good pasture land. Gus decided to compromise, to gamble, and signed up.

Gus never told me what the lease cost him. Of course I didn't ask, even when we were friends, but the most common rate about that time was $30 to $60 for two hundred acres of prime agricultural land. Leases most often ran for fifteen years. Some ran for life, despite the Chickasaw law, if the Indian agent could be hornswaggled or given enough whisky.

While there wasn't outright cheating in most transactions, it was clear to wiser Chickasaws land leasing would be the ruination of their Nation. Actually, they passed a law in 1867 prohibiting leasing land to non-residents for more than a year, but by the time Gus came along so many tribesmen were involved, offering contracts on any terms that brought them a few more dollars, the Chickasaw courts wouldn't punish anybody. The law never did work.

When the U.S. Congress passed the Curtis Act of 1889, stating it was the policy of the government to abolish land held in severalty in the future, immigrants knew sooner or later they would be able to buy land in Indian Territory. That would be a great opportunity for those who had the money. Since buying takes more money than leasing, it wasn't the opportunity Gus was looking for in the beginning.

Gus didn't want to start his ranch alone. He already had that figured out, so he went back to Texas and persuaded Tennessee Stanfield to become his wife. Tenny, as she was called, was one of a range of Stanfield kids, most of them boys.

Tenny was spirited and quick to speak her mind. I suppose a girl raised with a bunch of brothers gets that way, and she was that way as a lady in Ada. The Stanfield and Bobbitt farms, both in Grayson County near Sherman, were no more than an a half hour's buggy ride apart. Family members were all friends.

Starting a ranch without any capital behind you was a tough business and the young Bobbitts were just getting by. One good thing, while there weren't many people around up north, as the Indian agent admitted, those few who had come earlier were mostly young couples starting out, scraping by as the Bobbitts were. So that must have helped a little, everybody being in the same boat. It wasn't an easy life.

While Gus was starting his ranching career, Isador Bobbitt was expanding his construction business in New Orleans and political contacts in Washington. Through his new political friends, he was able to get Gus an appointment as U. S. deputy marshal in the Southern District of Indian Territory, which included Pontotoc. The year was 1894, start of the second Cleveland Administration.

Being a deputy marshal in Indian Territory was a very hazardous job. Many were killed. Even so, appointments were prized, hard to get, as if they were some kind of political plumb.

Getting his appointment in the Cleveland administration made Gus a Democrat, beholden to the Democrats anyway, though I never heard him talk about political parties. Being tagged a Democrat wasn't necessarily a drawback in any case. Many of the early settlers in Pontotoc came in the 1870's and 1880's and crossed the Red River on rafts from Texas. Most had ties to southern states and were natural Democrats.

Deputy marshals didn't get much government money in any administration as dangerous as the job was, but some additional income came with the appointment–a big help to the Bobbitts for buying tools, fence, medicines, things you have to have for any ranch, even a small one. Most of these law officers went on ranching or farming in addition to handling their government duties. Gus was one of them.

Rewards for capturing fugitives were an important part of Gus's income. Certainly he wasn't the only lawman or bounty hunter going after rewards, but he did have an advantage in Indian Territory–his friend Christian Harding, a big Chickasaw who was an Indian Police officer. With help from his Indian friends, Harding could find anybody.

Some of the fugitives were no smarter at hiding than an ostrich. They'd hole up in a cave, go out to rob for food or money, and come back to the same cave. Made a regular trail, back and forth. Smarter ones always went to a new hideout after a robbery, a new cave, or maybe they'd hide in the woods for a while. It never mattered. The Indians might take weeks to find the smart ones, but they never failed to find anyone they were looking for.

I first met both Gus and Christian Harding at Harding's cabin near Roff, which had become a settlement near Joe Roff's big ranch. By that time I had left Texas and the cattle business and had become a snuff salesman. I traveled around Pontotoc County once or twice a year when the weather was good, maybe in late spring or fall.

Pontotoc was in the Chickasaw Nation part of Indian Territory and the Chickasaws had it divided up in districts, just like they organized things back in Mississippi before they came west. Pontotoc was one of four districts, though most of the white newcomers around here called it Pontotoc County anyway. With statehood, Pontotoc District was divided up into several counties. Pontotoc County was one of them.

Marketing in Indian Territory, whatever you called the political divisions–district or county–wasn't my main job, though. My real job was selling Appalachian Gold snuff in Oklahoma Territory up north. My boss, Frank Rutgers back in Blackbyrne, Virginia, wanted me to develop the Indian Territory market when I had the time. He said that would take "commercial courage." I don't know about that. I enjoyed traveling in country that looked pretty much the way Indian hunting parties saw it.

The Santa Fe had pushed their tracks down from Kansas, through Oklahoma Territory to Pauls Valley on the western boundary of Pontotoc, then on to Ardmore and Texas. There still weren't any railroads in the middle of Pontotoc. You traveled on a horse or in a wagon or buggy to get to the settlements.

Pauls Valley was about as close to the middle of Pontotoc as you could get on the train, and I had stopped there before. I made a friend of the owner of the livery stable near the depot and he rented me just the rig I needed, a small, four-wheel buggy, and one big, patient horse who could manage it.

I avoided getting a team. Why have to take care of two horses if one can do the work? Of course I tried hard to make a friend of the one horse I got. Let 'im know what was expected but never asked too much in rough going.

On the trip when I met Gus Bobbitt and Christian Harding, I was pleased to get Loredo again, a solid, ten-year-old bay gelding who knew his job. We headed east, away from Pauls Valley and the railroad, stopping at the settlements. Sometimes it was no more than a crossroads store, not even a settlement. I always got some sort of order, all of them small, in keeping with the shelf space. Size of the order never mattered to Mr. Rutgers. He said that's how you develop a market.

In most of those little places I was the only salesman they ever saw. Usually they had to take a wagon over to the railroad for supplies they ordered. Some storekeepers seemed surprised I had the nerve to make business calls out in the country by myself.

I was mostly alone once I rode away from the Triple R ranch buildings and pens, and there were a plenty of rustlers operating in south Texas then. Being alone was nothing new for me. I usually had with me a heavy old Navy Colt .44 revolver my father gave me. He had it in the war.

My father said General Robert E. Lee carried a Navy Colt in his saddle bag, though it might have been a .36 caliber model. I never did make a display of the pistol…never had to use it anywhere. Just as well. I couldn't hit anything with it. That's harder than it looks.

Having any salesman call was surprise enough for some store keepers, but a snuff salesman was more than they could figure out. I guess they didn't realize how much snuff people used in other places, or how it got into stores anyway. Flour and coffee they could figure out, but not snuff. It hadn't occurred to me, either, until I saw a little ad in a torn up magazine in the Triple R bunkhouse.

The ad said this Virginia tobacco company, Appalachian Gold, was looking for enterprising young men who wanted to make a lot of money selling snuff. I never thought about selling snuff. I didn't use it, never even tried it, but this was the end of a long day in the saddle and I was sure ready to do something besides tend cattle.

I wrote to Papa in Weatherford and asked him what he thought about it. He wrote back and said I might as well try, but I was so late, I better just go there and he sent me thirty five dollars. I drew my pay from the Triple R and spent three days on a train getting to Blackbyrne, Virginia, headquarters for Appalachian Gold.

When I got to the Appalachian Gold office–it was on the second floor and not much bigger than a shoe store–I showed the ad I had saved to a lady sitting behind a desk near the door.

"But that was last year," she said.

"Well, things don't get out to the Triple R in Nueces County very fast. I got here when I could."

The lady looked at me in my boots and rumpled coat and then said, "I'm afraid those positions have long since been filled, but wait a minute, the sales manager happens to be here today. I'll tell him you've come all the way from Texas to work for him."

She was gone quite a while then she came back, trailing a fat fellow who stuck out his hand and said he was Appalachian's sales manager. He asked what he could do for me.

I told him–Mr. Rutgers, as it turned out–I was enterprising, like the ad said, and I wanted to sell his product. I also told him I had sales experience, though I didn't mention it was on the Illinois Central depot platform selling apples when I was six.

Mr. Rutgers was a smart man and I'm sure he knew right off I was cowhand from somewhere out west and a young one to boot. I'm glad he didn't ask me any more about my "experience."

He told me all the positions he advertised the year before were long since filled and there was nothing available. He added he was impressed I would come all the way from Texas to apply for a job and that he would certainly keep me in mind when he had an opening.

"You probably couldn't get word to me in Nueces County in time, Mr. Rutgers," I said. Then I proposed an idea Papa suggested in his letter because I hated the thought of more twelve-hour days in the saddle on the Triple R.

"What if I worked for nothing, only a commission on what I sell, and we tried that for six months?" I asked.

Mr. Rutgers seemed a little surprised, and then answered, "Well, we could try that, but I'll tell you now, our sales representatives work in districts and all of the established markets are represented."

He thought for a while then said, "There are areas back up in the mountains none of the men want to tackle–no hotels, not even many places to get a decent meal, as I understand it. If you want to try that for a couple of months, I'll go along."

There weren't any hotels in the far pastures of the Triple R either, so sleeping out when I had to wouldn't be anything new for me. Well, sleeping out in the mountains in winter would sure be something new, but I figured I'd face that when the time came. I told Mr. Rutgers I was ready to start right then.

It wasn't part of the arrangement, but he gave me five $10 bills and told me to get a suit, some lace-up shoes and a hat to make me look more like an Appalachian Gold salesman. I'm not sure I looked like an Appalachian Gold salesman in my new suit. I did look different. In the overcoat I bought with my own money, I looked very different, felt like an Eskimo papoose. How I looked didn't matter. That overcoat was a lifesaver.

Things went very well for me. Most storekeepers seemed impressed anyone would come into the mountains to call on them, particularly in cold weather. I never did have to sleep out, though. In every one of the little settlements there was at least one family that would take a traveler in for the night. It would be hard to imagine nicer people.

Nobody seemed to have much money back in the mountains, even the storekeepers, so the sales I made were very small. That didn't keep me from writing optimistic progress reports to Mr. Rutgers, though. I told him I expected an upturn in business when the weather turned nice and visitors came for the scenery.

I was looking forward to springtime myself, but in four months Mr. Rutgers wrote and told me to come back to Blackbyrne, I was going to be a regular Appalachian Gold salesman. That meant I'd get $50 a month in addition to sales bonuses.

I was really surprised when Mr. Rutgers told me he had been reading about Indian Territory and what great opportunities there were in this undeveloped part of the West. I didn't think many people in the East ever heard of Indian Territory.

"I want you to be Appalachian's man in Indian Territory, John, since you're from that part of the country and you don't demand hotels and fancy restaurants. I've never been out west, but I'll bet snuff would go over as well out there as it does in the mountains."

Maybe Mr. Rutgers was impressed that I tried hard and lasted as long as I did in the cold mountains. My sales volume was certainly not impressive. Whatever it was that led to my promotion I'm not sure, but I was pleased to become a regular Appalachian salesman. I was sorry not to see spring come to the mountains, but I was anxious to get started on my new assignment.

It was 1888 when I arrived in the Cherokee part of Indian Territory on the Santa Fe, wearing the suit Mr. Rutgers bought for me. The railroad people told me that part of Indian Territory would become Oklahoma Territory in 1890, and Guthrie would be the capital. So I went there first and expected to stay.

The railroad folks were right. The whole region became Oklahoma Territory and Guthrie was made the capital. I can tell you though, it wasn't much of a town in those days –mostly tents.

It wasn't part of my plan, but I was in Guthrie in time for the big land rush in '89. The rush was for two million acres of what the Federals called Unassigned Lands, land taken from the Creeks and Seminoles. Land was also opened for settlement in the Cherokee Outlet and on west in '93.

The government decided these were "Unassigned" because of the pressure brought by the "Boomers," white settlers from Kansas who kept pushing down into Indian Territory illegally in wagon trains. The Army turned the Boomers back many times through the years.

The standoff with the Boomers was settled when the government made Unassigned Lands available to them and anybody else who raced out to claim it after twelve o'clock noon, April 22, 1889.

The starting line was anywhere back of the border of the Unassigned Lands, though rushers did bunch up nearest the most valuable land. Soldiers were stationed every mile all the way around—it may have been one hundred miles around—to make sure nobody left early. At noon April twenty second, soldiers shot their guns in the air, and that's how the rush started officially.

It would be nice to say it was a fair start with all the soldiers on hand, but there are always people who feel the rules aren't for them. The "Sooners" you hear about sneaked out on the land the night before the soldiers fired their guns and staked their claims in the dark.

That's where the Boomer Sooner name they have for Oklahomans comes from. I guess I'm a Boomer Sooner too, even though I came to Oklahoma on the Santa Fe and started the land rush when I was supposed to.

Driving a buggy over rough ground was nothing new for me and I got to Oklahoma Station, south of Guthrie, as fast as about anybody except the riders, and the Sooners. Never did see a Sooner.

Farm land didn't interest me and I staked out several lots in or near the planned city, not having any idea of how the town would grow. Oklahoma City, as it would be called, started growing fast right from the beginning. It was nearly in the middle of the Territories and had good train service. I decided to make my home there, even if Guthrie was the capital.

I worked Oklahoma Territory mostly and Mr. Rutgers said he was pleased the way things were going. It was nice of him to say that. Really, it was slow going. Snuff wasn't in demand, and there were very few store owners interested in leading the way. I kept trying though, getting to most of the new towns on the railroads, pushing out over the prairie, bringing settlers with them.

All of Oklahoma Territory was growing with the railroads, not just Oklahoma City, and I had enough to do trying to build a market there. There was little pleasure in it for me. Hours and hours rattling along in a railroad car with other traveling salesmen was boring. That's one reason I went south into Indian Territory when I got the chance, rough as it was. I didn't have to hear the same stories all the time.

The other reason, the important one, Mr. Rutgers liked for me to travel in Indian Territory, if I could do it without neglecting Appalachian's main market up north. He said Appalachian Gold was "at the frontier, leading the pack," and things like that. I'm sure for anyone sitting in an office on the East Coast it sounded like real adventure, the "Indian" part, I mean. Anyway, it wasn't boring, like riding those trains.

There were darn few hotels of any kind in Indian Territory settlements in the early days, and on some of my adventures in "commercial courage," as Mr. Rutgers liked to call it, I had to spend the night in a space I cleared in the buggies by pulling out the driver's bench. Even then I couldn't stretch out and it made for a long night. It was out of rattlesnake range, though. In warm weather, out on the prairie, that's important.

Sometimes a leasehold farmer, or even an Indian, had a small barn or lean-to I could see from the road, and if it was rainy, and I couldn't get to the next town, I would ask if I could sleep there. Nobody ever turned me down.

On this particular trip, I was planning to get over to Roff and then hit a couple of new settlements on the way north to Ada, which was beginning to grow. I got pretty close to Roff in the buggy when I started to hear thunder back of me. It was early summer and afternoon thunderstorms were becoming fairly regular, so it wasn't a surprise.

Before long I could see mountains of dark clouds in the west, beginning to block the sun, and lightning flashes. The storm, a really big one, was still a way off, but there was no doubt it was going to be long, wet night.

I had hoped to get on up to Ada–there was a new hotel there, the Brown–but with the storm coming closer, I figured it might be smart to change my plans. I saw an unpainted board cabin with a small barn back of it and decided to stop.

I knocked at the cabin door and in a minute, this big, square-faced Indian, mahogany skin and black eyes, was looking out at me. He was a very strong looking character, not somebody you'd want to rile.

Behind him I could see in the dark cabin a woman and little kids chasing around. I could also make out a white man inside, sitting on some sort of short bench.

I told the Indian who I was, a snuff salesman from Oklahoma City, and that I had hoped to make it to Ada, but the weather didn't look good. A chance to get in the hay loft for the night would be appreciated, I explained.

The Indian backed up a step, pulled the door open wider. He didn't actually say anything. It just seemed like he meant for me to come in. I stepped through the doorway and the white man stood up. The woman and the kids melted back against the wall.

"The name is Bobbitt, Gus Bobbitt," the white man said, sticking out his hand, "U. S. deputy marshal, Southern District. This is Chief Harding, Indian Police."

Gus Bobbitt wasn't a big man like the Indian, no taller than I was, though he was husky enough. He had a trim mustache, not the big droopy kind some of the lawmen favored. Just to look at Bobbitt, you'd never think he'd be the kind to wear a badge and carry a gun. He didn't have that hard look about him.

While they were looking around for a place for me to sit down, there was a blinding flash and then what sounded like an explosion. Thunder, of course, but I don't think I had ever been that close to a lightning strike before.

Christian Harding turned to the wall and took down a rain slicker hanging on a nail, and a big hat beside it.

"…get your horse. Put 'im with mine," he said and disappeared through the door.

I started to protest, but Marshal Bobbitt put his hand on my arm.

"He's a Chickasaw. They care more about horses than people, I think. He'll just run your horse into the corral with my horse and his. There's some sort of shelter for them."

Christian Harding came back in, dripping. "He's near spooked…all right with others," he said, hanging his coat back over the nail. "Horses need others when afraid…can't run…all right now. Anything on buggy need dryin'? Rainin' hard."

"No, nothing thanks. I always expect it to rain sometime on a trip and everything is under a tarpaulin."

The Indian found another wooden bench for me and put it over by Gus Bobbitt. We sat a few feet from each other in the gloomy cabin. It was late afternoon but nearly dark outside, the clouds were so close and heavy. The woman, Mrs. Harding, I learned, went over to the fireplace and started a little blaze, though it was certainly not cold. The fire looked cheerful anyway. I was soon peeled down to my shirt sleeves. Rain drummed on the roof.

"I heard you say you were sellin' snuff to the stores around here," Gus Bobbitt said. "I wouldn't have guessed they'd buy enough to make it worthwhile to you. Lot of folks chew. Not many use snuff. I don't know any. It's kind of an eastern habit, isn't it?"

I admitted to him it might be fair to say more men, and more women, too, use snuff in the East than in the Territories.

"That's why Appalachian Gold, my company, sent me here," I explained, "to change that.

"Snuff has all the advantages of chewing tobacco–leaves your hands free to work, don't need matches, don't need to make a flare at night. That's important to lawmen, isn't it?"

Marshall Bobbitt looked at me, a little puzzled. "Well, you mean when we're trailin' someone at night? Sure it's important. There's no point in sending signals. It's surprising how far you can see a match flare in the dark. Maybe a quarter of a mile."

"The big thing about snuff though," I said, "you don't need to spit all the time. Ladies are particularly pleased about that."

Marshal Bobbitt smiled. "For sure my wife wouldn't put up with spittoons in the house. So I don't chew. Pull on a pipe some winter nights, sittin' by the stove. That's all. So don't count on me as a customer."

We sat for a while, listening to the rain and thunder drifting off to the east. Marshal Bobbitt then said in a friendly way, "I hope you find some stores to take your snuff, Mr. Harris. Don't count on it. Don't be disappointed. Folks around here have been chewin' for a long time. Hard to change that sort of habit. And...I'm not sure travelin' around here by yourself is such a good idea anyway."

"Maybe not, Marshal Bobbitt, but I was alone half the time on a South Texas ranch. And then I traveled alone all through the mountains back east, sellin' snuff. Met a few Cherokees, too," I added with a glance at Christian Harding. His eyes were fixed on the fire.

"Well, let me put this straight," the lawman said. "Indians don't cause harm to travelers. Chief Harding sees to that. It's the white trash that comes into Indian Territory with the settlers, often as not because the law is after 'em.

"We get rough men drifting back from railhead towns in Kansas, towns from the big cattle drive days. Things were gettin' just too dandified for some of 'em out there. They think they can get back to the old ways in Indian Territory.

"Down here in south Pontotoc we get fugitives runnin' from the law in Texas who think if they get across the Red River into Indian Territory, nothin' matters, like there's no law here.

"Chief Harding can't help with those people," the marshal added. "Light Horse police–Indian Police now–were set up some seventy years ago to deal with Indians, just Indians. Indians were about the only ones out here then, so it made some sense."

The marshal stopped. Then, looking at Harding he said, "It's one of the biggest problems we've got, not near enough officers of the law for this much territory. We need Indian officers and Federal officers to work together. If they can't manage to do that on their own, maybe we need them in one organization, if there's no other way, maybe two divisions."

Chief Harding nodded his head gravely, and Bobbitt went on: "Politics, and the crazy notion some people have about Indians, all Indians, keep that from happening. And it's not just new settlers, either. Chief Harding and I work together anyway.

"You come through often?" Marshal Bobbitt asked suddenly. It took me by surprise, like I could have been wanted by the law for something. Then I saw he wasn't being a stern lawman. And I could see he wasn't much older than I was.

"No, I couldn't sell enough snuff down here in Pontotoc to make a living," I answered. "I work Oklahoma Territory mostly. It's more built up and I can get to most of the bigger towns on the train now. I live in Oklahoma City."

We sat for a minute then Bobbitt said, "Well, Pontotoc is beginning to grow. And it's pretty country. Great ranchin' country. Besides that, they claim cotton stalks jump right out of the ground, not that I want to grow cotton."

I grinned at him. "Neither do I. I'm from Alabama."

That started the stories about how we got to Indian Territory from the middle of Alabama. Chief Harding might not have been that much interested, but it was still raining, not pounding down like it did when the storm was right over us, but raining. We all sat. It wouldn't make sense to travel if you didn't have to. We pretty much filled up the Harding cabin.

After close to two hours, Marshal Bobbitt said, "My ranch is a two or three hours north of here and then another half hour west of Ada. I don't know if I want to strike out for either one. I might ask the Chief if I can spend the night in his hay loft, too."

The Indian nodded. His wife started moving some kitchen pans around near the fireplace. I announced I had bread, honey and apples in the buggy, some coffee as well. I said I was prepared to fix my own supper in the open if I couldn't get to Ada, but if Mrs. Harding would take it all and let us eat together inside, I would be pleased.

"I also have an orange and some candy for the youngsters," I added, glancing at the three solemn brown children who had never taken their eyes off of us. They never once peeped.

There weren't enough cups for water and coffee but it was a good, plain meal, some kind of pork and collard greens. I was pleased my contribution seemed to add to the occasion. Chief Harding never did say much, and Mrs. Harding didn't say anything at all. It was just as well. Marshal Bobbitt talked most of the time.

Daylight was about snuffed out when we finished eating, and the last of the thunderstorm was rumbling away off to the east. Getting to his feet, Gus Bobbitt suggested since we were both headed for Ada, we might sleep early and get going at sunup. He said he had to stop at his chief deputy's office in town, then check up on his Mason friends.

"Mrs. Harding, ma'm, much obliged for the fine supper," Gus said, heading to the door.

"I want to thank you too, Mrs. Harding, for taking us in and making such a good supper. It was very kind of you," I added, following Gus.

Harding had a lantern going by now. He went out the door and led us around the bigger rain puddles in the black night to the small barn. Inside the barn there was a wheel barrow, a big scythe hung on the wall, pitch forks, shovels and other tools leaned against the wall. Except for the work and storage area near the door, hay pretty much filled up the rest of the barn.

"This'll do fine," Gus said to Harding. Gus suggested we get the tarpaulin from my buggy since the rain had stopped. "Sleep on that, then we won't have to pick hay out of our ears all mornin'," he added with a wink.

Having the tarp between you and the hay is a good idea, a practice I followed, so Harding, with his lantern, guided us back outside and around to the corral. I pulled the harness off Loredo, turned him loose in the corral, and got the tarpaulin. Gus took the saddle off his horse and let him walk over to the other horses.

We went back into the barn. Harding turned the wick down and put the lantern in the wheel barrow to keep the flame away from the hay. It made just enough light to move around.

"Rattlers come in huntin' mice," the Indian explained. "If you get up in dark, better you don't step on 'em."

Harding left, pulling the barn door shut behind him. Gus and I looked at each other, then got busy moving hay around. We leveled off a place for the tarpaulin pretty much in the middle of the stack, as far away from the barn door as we could make it. We agreed it was unlikely rattlesnakes would go through that much hay after mice.

It had been a very full day for me, getting on the Santa Fe before sunup, and a tiring one. Even so, sleep didn't come easily, though I had no trouble lying there on the tarp–carefully in the middle of the haystack–until first light of the new day.

Gus woke up early, too, and we decided to get going, without saying anything more to the Hardings. They would have wanted to give us something for breakfast and we didn't want to impose any more. We got hitched up and saddled up and on the road with the sun yet to appear.

Gus said he would ride alongside, but after a half hour he tied his horse at the back of the buggy and we rode together on the driver's bench.

From that time on, I considered Gus Bobbitt a friend. I liked him and found him good company. He never did stop talking, as I said, but he had something to say.

Sometimes Gus sounded like he might consider politics in the future. He knew all kinds of people for miles around and seemed to like most of them. And he had what I considered very good, business-like ideas about what was ahead for the country we were riding through–Pontotoc County.

The Lawmen

The thunderstorm that drove Gus Bobbitt and me into Christian Harding's hay barn for the night was gone without a trace in a bright blue morning sky. The air was crystal clear after the rain. It was like you could reach out and touch everything stretching to the horizon. Patches of live oak stood like islands in a sea of tall blue stem grass, waving in puffs of chilly northern air. There wasn't a house, barn or a fence anywhere.

Gus and I were perched on the driver's bench of my little buggy, jostling comfortable enough over the road north to Ada, maybe more muddy than my horse, Loredo, would have liked pulling two passengers. For all the rain, the road wasn't washed out anywhere.

Gus was unusually quiet as we clopped along. He was busy taking in the view, one side, then the other. I suspected he was dreaming about his ranch.

"This what you had in mind for your ranch, Gus?"

He turned and grinned. "Yeah, this will do—

"I've come by here before. It's just perfect...good bottom land for alfalfa, what looks to be some good timber near that little stream over there, fine pasture. I even like the ridges runnin' off into the distance. 'Picturesque,' my wife would say. Yessir, this will do."

It was pretty country, I agreed to that easy enough, a lot prettier than anything I saw in South Texas. It wasn't exactly flat down there, of course–there were arroyos and mesquite trees–but not much to see lookin' out. Whether the hills and woods in Pontotoc would make ranching difficult, I didn't know exactly.

"Be lots of places for your stock to hide, Gus, like maybe in those woods," I said, pointing at the oak and hickory trees he was looking at. " Mor'n enough wood for fence posts. You'll have to have a bunch of Alabama boys to keep tabs for you."

Gus laughed. "Oh, I might need some help, but I'll manage in any case. Maybe I could even afford some barbwire by then. I like fenced pastures.

They look like somebody cares. The open range is pretty much a thing of the past…maybe it's just as well. Lots of problems come with herds runnin' together.

"I heard they put barbwire around the whole Bell Ranch out on the Panhandle, something like one hundred and forty miles of it. Can you believe that? I don't doubt it's true. Foreigners own it, Englishmen, I think. They have money to do that."

I told Gus I had read a lot of stories about foreigners buying up the best ranch land both in West Texas and eastern New Mexico. I knew they had whole towns on the Bell.

"Oh, It's true enough," Gus said. "Guess I can't blame 'em. But it does make it tough on people startin' out to compete. I hoped to ranch out in West Texas in the beginnin', maybe west of Abilene, then I heard about these Englishmen with all the money they got and figured I better find a different trail.

"Maybe that's one good thing about the Chickasaws' common-hold land. Foreigners can't buy it, either. Or up to now they can't. Hope I'm ready when the law changes."

Gus was right about that. Non-residents"–only Indians were residents–still couldn't buy Chickasaw Nation land in the ordinary business way. There were more exceptions all the time, though, and not just for intermarrieds.

Railroads were getting big grants of Federal land after the Railroad Enabling Act of 1866. Besides the right of way, they got alternate sections forty miles deep along the route. That was later made to fifty miles deep, far more land than they'd ever need just to run their railroads. The important thing, they could sell the land to farmers, ranchers and businessmen who wanted to establish towns, all future customers.

The Act was meant to encourage railroads to move on out west and develop the country. It worked just that way. The railroads brought thousands of immigrants into the Territories on the new tracks. That was going on mostly up north of Pontotoc in the '70's and '80's, country that became Oklahoma Territory in 1890, where I lived then.

Changes for Indian Territory were clearly in the wind, though there was nothing to make most non-residents think land could ever be theirs without paying for it. There weren't any homestead grants proposed for Indian Territory like they had in Oklahoma Territory. Gus would have to buy his ranch land even if Chickasaw tribal ownership was abolished.

"It's good you know exactly what you want, Gus, even if you don't know right off how to get it. Having a goal is necessary for accomplishment, Mr. Rutgers always tells me. He even has us write it down, our goals. I'm sure you'll find a way."

Gus nodded and smiled a little. "Yup, John. You're right. My brother says things like that. 'The time is coming,' he says. 'You better be ready. ' What he doesn't tell me is where to get the money.

"Course for somebody like Izzy it's not a problem. He makes money just talkin' to people. I'll have to stick up a bank or something..."

Nothing Gus said gave me a clue about how he really expected to raise the money. His small leasehold ranch couldn't produce much more income than what it cost the Bobbitts to live, and I didn't know how much being a deputy marshal helped.

Years later I read a book by an Oklahoma writer, Glenn Shirley, who wrote the average marshal in Indian Territory in the 1870's and '80's made less than $500 a year. They didn't get a salary. What they got was two dollars for serving a warrant or arresting someone on the "wanted" list, from a down-and-out horse thief to a bank robber, all the same, two dollars. And they got per diem.

From what he said, Gus did work at getting rewards for capturing outlaws, and with Christian Harding's help, made rewards an important part of his small government income. Being a Federal lawman, he usually had a jump on bounty hunters who might have to wait to pick their targets from pictures on the Post Office wall.

If I had to guess, the morning Gus and I were in the buggy, I would have guessed marshals made a little more than $500 a year, but not much. Most of them did some farming or ranching in addition to their law enforcement duties. Gus was not unusual in that way.

"Gus, I don't think Alabama boys were cut out for robbing banks. You may have to find another way. Maybe being a lawman is not the answer...Mr. Rutgers always says–"

"Well, I got my ranch goin', too," Gus interrupted. "...makin' some progress. We're living fair enough. It's getting ahead to where I'll be able to buy the land I want. That's the problem."

I nodded my understanding. "I'm not sure I'd think what the government pays would be worth it, particularly if it means collaring any of the killing types, and from what I hear up north you've got more than your share in Pontotoc County."

"Well, we got some ornery cusses around, for sure," Gus answered. "I'm not a foolish man, though. If I know I've got to deal with somebody quick on the trigger, or if I know they're ridin' with someone, I wait until I get a pardner, sometimes Christian Harding, or one of the other marshals.

"Mostly, though, I deal with a sorry bunch," Gus went on." I don't turn my back on 'em and I let them know I don't get much pleasure out of the job, particularly if I have to haul them into court. I tell 'em it would be a whole lot easier for me just to shoot them. I guess they think about that."

We plodded along, Loredo still going along pretty much as he started, only I had to cluck at him more, talk to him. It was beginning to get warm under that bright sun. Not a cloud.

I turned to look at Gus. "Talking about hauling fugitives into court, you don't have to take prisoners over to Arkansas–Fort Smith–anymore do you? Just to the new Federal court in Muskogee?"

"That's right, and with all the railroads comin' into Oklahoma Territory, I got a lot easier time of it. Have to get up there though…north from Pauls Valley. There's no trains in Ada. Guess you and your horse know that.

"The way it is now, if I have a prisoner from down around here, say, and I have to get him to Muskogee, I take him first to the Ada jail. If I want to see my family, I got to ride fifteen miles out to the ranch, back to Ada the next morning. Then, with my prisoner, I got to double back–pretty close to the ranch–about twenty miles to Pauls Valley to get the Santa Fe north.

"If I miss train connections up north, it might take a day and half. Still, it's a lot easier than sittin' on a horse for three days–and getting shot at in the woods.

"For a while I took 'em back home for the night and shackled them to a big oak log I had in the storage room. Saved me from having to go back and forth to Ada.

"My wife got so she couldn't stand that. Didn't want them around the children, she said. 'Take them to the jail in Ada! That's where they belong!' I can hear her now. Course she didn't have to ride the extra thirty miles.

"Oh, I never did bring any really dangerous man home. Or anybody I knew had a gang around. Most of 'em were really sorrowful. Luck all run out. And hope about run out, too. Some just kids."

"I guess you're glad you don't have to get any of the hard characters in Pontotoc all the way over to Arkansas on horseback, eh, Gus, like in the old days?"

Gus laughed. The buggy lurched a little. Gus was a solid man. You're sure right about that. It was dangerous work. Judge Parker, he was the judge at the Federal Court in Fort Smith, he told Congress sixty-five of his officers got killed escorting prisoners from Indian Territory to his court from 1876 to 1896.

"You heard of Judge Parker?" Gus asked. "That's Judge Isaac C. Parker, called the 'Hangin' Judge' by some of the newspapers back east. Called him a 'tyrant', too."

I said with all the newspapers I read, and I read them from start to finish, I probably had seen his name.

"Well," Gus started—I knew right away this was a matter close to his heart—"Judge Parker did order one hundred seventy-two prisoners brought in from Indian Territory hanged. And seventy-eight of 'em really did hang.

"Judge Parker never would apologize for that record, no matter what the newspapers back east wrote about him. He said the men who came before him were only the worst of a 'depraved lot' in Indian Territory."

That was a surprise to me, sixty-five court officers getting killed in twenty years transporting prisoners. Maybe my expression gave me away.

"Oh, it's true all right," Gus said. "Remember, goin' through the Kiamichis with a prisoner is a mean job. A lawman wouldn't have any friends at all and it's slow goin' over the mountains. Well, they're not like the Rocky Mountains. Still, it's pretty rough country. That's exactly why a lot of men wanted by the law go there. They've been driftin' in since the Civil War. They hole up there. Come out in gangs to rob."

Gus also told me the outlaws living in the mountains, called "border ruffians" by some of the newspapers, were one of the strong arguments Texas cattlemen made to Congress for getting the railroads out to Kansas. With tracks out on the Kansas prairie they could drive their herds straight north through Indian Territory to the railheads and miss the Kiamichis.

"The first of those Texas herds gettin' to Missouri railheads really had it hard," Gus pointed out. "It was right after the war. They called it the Sedalia trail. They didn't drive the cattle straight over the mountains, of course, only through the foothills. But it was rugged country. And then they had all those bandits waiting to take their herd. Lots of Texas cowboys never got back home from there.

"Texas trail masters naturally started moving away from the Kiamichis. Went west of the mountains goin' north, then turned east. They still had to get to Missouri–at least for a while they did. So that became the Shawnee Trail. That's how Shawnee town started up in north Pottawatomie County, providin' for the Texas drovers. A lot of those herds right came through here. Maybe east a little.

"They might'a come through right where we're goin', John!" Gus said, sweeping his arm across the prairie ahead of us. Fortunately, we had a grassy path and wagon ruts to follow. I tried to imagine what it would be like having twenty five hundred head of cattle walking alongside.

"That would be quite an experience, Gus. I would have liked that."

"Yeah. It was a special time out here. It didn't last long though. Both Union Pacific and Santa Fe got railheads set up in Kansas to serve the market, Union Pacific's Dodge City bein' the most famous, I suppose.

"With railroads in Kansas, most of the big Texas herds went straight north through Indian Territory, first on the Chisholm Trail after '67. The Chisholm ran just west of the Pontotoc County line. After a couple of years, a lot of the drovers went west another hundred miles–the Western Trail. Millions of cattle made those two trails on the way to the eastern markets."

We clopped along, the path and ruts looking more like a real road closer to Ada. Both of us were quiet, looking out over the prairie, bluish hills in the distance. A hawk was wheeling overhead, so high he looked like a dot on the blue dome.

"Do you think he's watching us, Gus?"

"Naw. He's looking for some kind of varmint, maybe a gopher…maybe a snake."

"Looking for a snake from up there?"

"Sure. Some scientist figured out they can see eight times better than we can. And once he spots something he circles down lower and lower, swoops up from behind, and whap. It's all over. A Red Tail Hawk. Common around here. They've seen a lot of things in time."

"You mean like the big cattle herds coming through?"

"Well, the cattle, sure. There used to be buffalo here, too. Not like the giant herds on the High Plains, though. All kinds of wild animals around here before the Tribes started comin' out in 1830. There were a lot of trappers. Most of 'em worked east of here.

"Then a good many of the prospectors goin' to California in the '49 Gold Rush came through, travelin' from Fort Gibson up north, down to Fort Washita on the Red River. Homesteaders came this way, too, but there wasn't any palavering about leases in those days. They knew it was Indian land, knew they couldn't settle down. I'm glad of that."

I agreed–glad they didn't settle down to build barns, houses, fences, roads, maybe even towns where we were driving. Sure would have been closer than Oregon though.

"This country will change anyway," I predicted. "Always does, but I like seeing it the way it was for Indian hunting parties. I really like being right on the place with history, thinking back…"

Gus straightened and said gravely, "Yeah, this is great country–"

The sun was beginning to bear down now. Gus shifted around and tugged his coat off. He unbuckled his holster and put it with his revolver inside on the floorboard.

"I guess you don't let that get far away," I said, looking down at the gun.

"Nope. Not if I'm wearin' the badge, I don't. Keep it handy. Just seein' a lawman sets some people off. I don't want to be on the short end.

"And there are 'depraved' people in these parts, as Judge Parker likes to say. They're not all up on the Canadian River.

"Up to a few years ago, a half dozen marshals from Paris, Texas, would cross the river with a big wagon, carryin' a bunch of 'John Doe' warrants. They'd arrest Texas fugitives 'till they filled the wagon. Chained 'em down. Then they'd take them back to Texas. Course they couldn't get 'em all."

Gus looked over at me and said, "John, it may not be my business, and I sure don't want to offend, but I think you ought to try and protect yourself, travelin' around here alone in your city clothes.

"If you don't mind me sayin' so, you'd look to be easy pickins' to some of the tough hombres we get. There just aren't many lawmen in Pontotoc County to help and there never were. It's not like back east," Gus added.

I'll have to admit, I was a little put off, even though I knew he was being friendly. I knew I didn't look like a gunfighter, didn't even want to, but I didn't like to think I looked that easy a mark.

"Gus. I appreciate your concern. I do have my father's Navy Colt .44 in the bag behind. He carried it in the war. I'm not going to let anyone just walk over me."

"No, of course not, John. But that big hog leg pistol in a bag behind you may not answer. Colt has been makin' guns right along since the war and they're makin' some now a lot smaller and lighter and effective enough. A .38 revolver like the police use in the cities back east would do it.

"You ought to get a .38 and have it up here somewhere. Maybe not strap it on, if that's not good business practice, but have it where you can reach it fast while you're drivin'."

Gus's story about the fugitives in south Pontotoc being hauled back to Texas by the wagon load, and how few law officers there were, white or Indian, got me thinking about the future of Pontotoc County. The future didn't look all that promising seen that way, no matter how pretty the landscape was. I asked Gus about that.

"Well, we got ten times more whites than Indians here now and Indian lawmen can't touch 'em. There aren't anywhere near enough Federal officers to take care of all this." He waved his arm across the horizon.

"Well, you and Christian Harding work together. Why can't that happen all the time? Take advantage of what few lawmen you have, no matter what kind?"

Gus paused. "There have been times when Light Horse officers and our men worked together, some well known.

"One of the famous cases happened a few years ago now, 1880 I believe. Federal lawmen in Little Rock wired Light Horse Captain Peter Conser in the Choctaw Nation–the Choctaws are just east of the Chickasaw Nation, I guess you know–they asked for help in locating a particularly dangerous man who got away from them and disappeared in the Kiamichis.

"Captain Conser put his men on it and in a week they located this 'dangerous' fugitive in a cave. Since the fugitive was white and a non-resident, Captain Conser's men didn't know exactly what they should do about it. They got word back to their chief, asking for instructions.

"Captain Conser wasn't sure about the rules either, so he sent orders, 'shoot him.' That they did. Then Captain Conser wired authorities in Little Rock they found the fugitive dead."

Gus was quiet for a minute looking out, then went on. It wasn't all so good, though. There was a real tragedy in Tuskahoma, the Choctaw capital, later that same year. Indian Police had arrested an Indian suspected of murdering a white man and had him on trial in the regular Choctaw court room.

"While the trial was goin' on, a bunch of marshals from the Federal court in Little Rock, Arkansas, came in and demanded the prisoner be turned over to them. The Indian police captain in charge said he couldn't do that since his job was to handle Indian lawbreakers, and this was an Indian lawbreaker on trial. The judge backed him up.

"Words got uglier and gunfire broke out. Seven of our people got killed, six Indians died, including the judge. It was a sad time."

"I can see working together after that would be pretty hard."

Gus nodded agreement. "Yeah. There wasn't much workin' together before, a lot less after. One good thing goin' on now though. Some towns are hiring constables–city marshals. That's good for the towns. It doesn't do much for out here."

"Can't your famous 'Hangin' Judge' do something about getting more Federal law enforcement out here if the Indian Police can't really help much?"

Gus nodded. "Well, sure, he has tried to help, but you have to remember it's all kind of political. Take me," he said, pointing to the badge on his chest, "I got my job through politics as part of President Cleveland's administration. Izzy's doin'. If a new crowd takes over the government in Washington, I lose out. I'm gone. There's just so many jobs and you know every Federal court in the country is crying out for more officers.

"Not many people back east understand you can't operate in Indian Territory the way you can most anywhere else," Gus declared. "Judge Parker calls the facilities 'primitive'. And that's just where there are any "facilities" at all…not counting hay lofts."

Gus said Judge Parker also tried to get Congress to set up a small salary for the Federal lawmen, but the politicians wouldn't go along. The politicians pointed out there didn't seem to be any problem getting them, so why offer a salary.

While Gus didn't sound very happy telling me about how Washington treated marshals in Indian Territory, he didn't sound bitter, either. I think he really liked wearing the badge and would keep on doing it whether he got a small salary or not, and no matter what the per diem rates were. These men were generally looked up to, appreciated by most people.

There's nothing like being appreciated. I learned that from Mr. Rutgers. Gus was no different than the rest of us, liking to be recognized. Wearing his badge in the train depots and around the towns he visited must have been important to Gus. It's just natural.

Gus wiggled, and the buggy wiggled, too. It really wasn't easy going for two people. With obvious pride Gus then recalled Judge Parker telling a Congressional committee he couldn't hold court "a single day" without his officers. "Indispensable," was the word he remembered.

Judge Parker's tribute seemed a good place to back away from talk about Gus making enough money to buy his ranch when the time came. It didn't sound promising from what he said. I thought we could talk about Christian Harding easier.

"That was mighty nice of your friend Harding to put us up, Gus," I started. "Is he really a Chickasaw chief?"

"Naw, not really. I just call him 'Chief' because a lot of the Indians around here think that way about him.

"He was in the Chickasaw legislature down in Tishomingo, and he went to Washington with a delegation of Chickasaws once to get the government to keep some of the promises they made when they moved the tribe west in 1837."

Gus thought a moment, then went on. " Ol' Andy Jackson promised they'd have their own laws, own schools, court and police, 'as long as the grass grows and the waters run', or somethin' like that…a long time anyway. This was to be their country. But newcomers now don't care what Andy Jackson said back then."

I did know something about the beginning of Indian Territory. I found out about it when Mr. Rutgers asked me to be Appalachian's man out here. I knew there were five tribes moved from their old lands east of the Mississippi to Indian Territory, starting after 1830. Some Cherokees left earlier–1817–the

Cherokees West. They left because they wanted to, more than ready to leave the white settlers behind.

Chickasaws were one of the five Civilized Tribes. They're some kind of cousins to the Choctaws east of here, still in Oklahoma, near the Arkansas border. Spoke the same language. They're smallest of the Civilized Tribes and come from the northern Mississippi area, on the river.

One thing I learned about the Chickasaws surprised me–they were well known for their horses, very unusual for a tribe east of the Mississippi. The Plains Indians were maybe better known for horses, particularly the Sioux and Comanche.

Western Indians got to be famous horsemen, all right, but the Chickasaws had horses first. They got their first stock when Hernando DeSoto came through in 1541, headed west, looking for gold. DeSoto and his exhausted soldiers treated the Chickasaws like slaves, demanding food for his soldiers and grain for the horses. It was a big mistake.

The Chickasaws couldn't long tolerate the conquistadors and they attacked the flimsy Spanish barricades one night. They killed twelve soldiers and more horses. Horses were a strange new animal for them. All the Chickasaws knew about horses was that they belonged to the Spaniards, good enough reason to kill them.

Fortunately, more horses escaped in the woods during the attack than were killed. In the following days, the Chickasaws saw many of the horses didn't run away like wild animals. They decided to capture them and learn to ride like the Spaniards did.

Not only did the Chickasaws learn to ride, they learned the value of their horses in trade. They became excellent breeders and through the years seized every opportunity to improve their stock.

Nearly two hundred years after the Chickasaws got DeSoto's horses, they ended up with their own breed, the Chickasaw breed, a kind of showy, bigger horse. I never did see one. Somebody told me most of them were stolen or killed in the Civil War.

When the Chickasaw Trail of Tears started in 1837, the tribe left with four thousand of their horses. That drove the Federals in charge of the move crazy, all those horses. But the Chickasaws said they were not going to leave them behind.

The Chickasaws hadn't caused a big rumpus about moving west up to then, so the government officials thought it might be a good thing to give in, and they did.

Only about half that big herd got out here. Some never got across the Mississippi River, some strayed away in the Arkansas woods. Rustlers in Arkansas got hundreds of them.

"Too bad the Chickasaws lost so many of their horses in the move out here," I ventured. " I'd like to see one of the Chickasaws."

"Me, too" Gus agreed, "I think most of them really were lost in the Civil War. Just about everything else the Chickasaws had was lost, more likely stolen. Not everybody thought the Chickasaws had the best horses though, despite their size and looks. A lot of people thought the smaller Choctaw ponies had more endurance... 'bottom' as the breeders say."

It had been a long morning and we had only stopped once for a few minutes. The bench was getting pretty hard and we were both hungry.

"Gus," I admitted, "I'm afraid I gave away all my food last night. I don't have a thing to offer you. I'm sorry."

"Well, John. I didn't expect food on your stage," Gus said. "Tell you what. I've got some beef jerky in my saddlebag. Maybe that will get us through to Ada."

Gus jumped down and walked around to his horse tied at the back. He pulled out an oilcloth package from a saddlebag behind his rifle holster and opened it up. I was standing beside him, glad to be doing something beside sitting.

"Much obliged." I took a piece of the dried beef. It didn't look like something I'd choose to eat ordinarily, I'll have to say in all honesty, but it sure tasted good. Of course it made us thirsty but I didn't have any water either.

"That's all right, John," Gus said. "There's a runnin' creek not far ahead. We can drink there. Your horse will like it too."

We got back on the bench with some care and started on the last stretch to Ada. It must not have rained as much up north of the Harding place, or the sun baked it out already. The road was about dry and Loredo had a little more pep, like he thought he was headed for the barn.

There was a little farm road, or maybe a trail, leading off from the Ada road, and a wagon full of Indians was stopped there. Counting young and old, there might have been eight of them, a very large family. They didn't move so I drove on by them. I guess they were going to Ada, though it was pretty late in the day for that. Indian families generally open up the stores in the morning.

"Howdy," I called out to the wagonload, and gave a little wave. They just sat there, didn't say a word.

"Golly, Gus," I asked when we were past them. "Are they unfriendly? Is that how they usually act around here?"

"Nah. They're just not sure...probably don't see many white men out here in the country. They're farmers. Full Bloods. They're the kind that would do anything for Christian Harding."

Gus gave a quiet laugh. "And you look like you might be some sort of Indian Affairs official. They're on their guard."

I wouldn't blame the Chickasaws, or any other the other of the Five Civilized Tribes for being suspicious. The agreement they got from the Federal government for moving out to Indian Territory didn't hold up after the Civil War. The army of settlers that came after the war swamped the Indians.

"Seems like the Chickasaws only got part of what they were promised, I said. "Only half their horses got here and from what you say, their police can't help much."

Gus didn't answer at first, then he started, "Well, I'm not one to say the Indians got a fair shake with their police or anything else. You have to remember though, seventy years ago the plan was to have mostly Indians in Indian Territory. There were only a few trappers and missionaries who weren't Indian.

"So the policy might have made sense to Washington politicians then. The Indians' police–called 'em the Light Horse–kept busy tryin' to keep whisky out of the Territory, that and catchin' runaway slaves. The policy didn't make much sense after the Civil War," Gus concluded.

"Well, if Christian Harding is Indian Police, what happened to the Light Horse? I like the name."

"Nothin', really. They still have Light Horse officers in some places. Now they've got Indian Police as well. Indian Police were set up by Federal Territory agents in 1880, and they appoint officers. It's a hand picked group. Many of them appointed came from the Light Horse, though. Having the Federals pick the recruits eliminated some tribal politics anyway.

"Indian Police get a small salary, can move anywhere in Indian Territory, any of the Nations, if they're after somebody. Got some mighty good officers.

Maybe more 'professional' people, would be the way to say that…like Harding.

"They didn't solve the big problem though. Indian Police can't touch white lawbreakers any mor'n the Light Horse could. That's the trouble. The whites are the ones breakin' the law."

Police work is not my field, but I do hold great store by tradition. Light Horse sounded like something out of the past, like a tradition, something to hold on to, though I didn't know why the Indians called their police Light Horse in the first place. I asked Gus if he knew.

"Well, the Cherokees who came west here in 1817 set up the Light Horse. They called 'em Light Horse Police after the Revolutionary War hero, Light Horse Harry Lee, a cavalry general. The general believed speed was an important–gettin' to the battle before anybody expected him.

"So, speed being important, the general's troopers carried only carbines in their saddle holsters, a lot lighter than the big 'ol smooth bores the infantry carried. That's where the 'light' comes from. And from what I read about the War of Independence as a kid, they did move fast.

"When it came time to name the police out here, somebody thought General Lee's ideas would be perfect–well mounted, lightly armed troopers, able to cover a lot of ground in a hurry. It did make sense in the early days of Indian Territory."

Gus thought a few moments and then added, "In the early days a Light Horse company had a captain, a lieutenant and twenty-four troopers. A couple of companies did sign up with the Confederates in the Civil War. Never did any fighting. Just signing up caused the Indians a lot of grief, though.

"The Federals never forgave the Chickasaws for siding with the Confederates. Took half the Chickasaws' western territory after the war because of it. Really, the Federals needed the land to relocate more eastern tribes. They just called it 'justice'."

I had looked at the big rifle Gus had in his saddle holster while we were eating the beef jerky. "That's no carbine you're carrying. You not set up for Light Horse speed?"

Gus grinned. "Naw. I'm not usually in that big a hurry. You got a good eye though. That's the biggest rifle Winchester ever made…thirteen and a half pounds of it. I have it for the range. If I get holed up somewhere, I don't want any outlaw able to drop rounds in on me and me not able to drive him back. I wouldn't carry anything else."

I could understand why Gus thought more law enforcement officers of any kind would be welcome in the remaining part of Indian Territory. A mule-headed tradition of settling disputes personally had grown up with so few peace officers around. "Take care of it myself," was how a lot of people looked at it. And they did take care of it, often as not shooting first and maybe not talking at all. Shooting was the first and almost natural response to problems for a good many early citizens.

Just as serious as sparse law enforcement, there wasn't a civil court system to handle ordinary grievances among white settlers for many years, problems that you would expect to be settled in court, rather than shooting–cut fences, strayed cattle, water rights, that level of dispute. The Chickasaws had their court at Stonewall, but again, the Indians weren't the problem.

"How do you and Christian Harding work together if he has no authority over ninety per cent of the people?"

"Well," Gus started, "Say some Texas bandit escapes across the river and starts robbin' the Indians for food, stealin' their cattle for money. They got to eat. It happens all the time. The Indians ask Harding to help them. They ask Christian Harding himself. The Indian Police have no jurisdiction if the bandit is white and non-resident.

"Harding can track anything," Gus said. "Maybe it's a skill he got from his ancestors. The Chickasaws were great hunters back east.

"Anyway, Harding, or his friends, can usually find the stolen cattle, but then he's in a spot, not having jurisdiction over whites, which the rustlers usually are. If there's time, he gets me and we get the cattle and the rustlers all at once.

"A lot of the time, there's some kind of reward out for the rustlers and I get in on that," Gus added with some satisfaction. He already told me rewards were important to him. He didn't tell me exactly what that meant and it didn't seem fitting I should ask for dollar amounts.

Christian Harding's name interested me and I told Gus I got to know a few Indians in the mountains, one family named Applewhite, the other Smith. So I knew they didn't believe they had to stick with their Indian names.

"How did Harding come by his name?"

"Oh, somebody at the orphanage the Methodists had down in Lebanon, south of Tishomingo, suggested that for him," Gus said. "He was only five when they took him in, as I understand it, and he thought Christian Harding was a fine name. He told me once his Indian name was Chi-ke-na-niew–something like that. I don't know what it means."

"Well, names don't matter all that much, I suppose," I agreed." There's Frank Byrd at the mill south of Ada. I'm sure you'd know him. If he got his name from his father, he didn't get much else. He looks pure Indian to me, a real copper color."

"Yeah, sure, I know Frank," Gus said. "He's a mixed blood and I suppose that was his father's name. They're an important family around here–the Byrds. His brother William was Governor of the Chickasaw Nation.

"Frank is smart in business, 'cept he carries around more money than makes sense. He doesn't mind shown' it either. Everybody knows he's got a wad of bills big enough to choke a bear. I half expect to hear he's been shot and robbed one day, but it doesn't seem to bother him.

"He makes money off that mill and maybe land leases," Gus said, "but, I'll tell you, the land he's got, with that big spring is going to be worth a lot more if Ada grows. It's good water and there's a lot of it flowin' out. Mor'n enough to run the mill. Could supply Ada, too. Byrd said Indian hunting parties always stopped there before white men came."

On a ridge we were crossing, we could see some buildings off in the distance–Ada. From there–and it was miles away–Ada didn't look much different than the first time I saw it, not any different than a half dozen other settlements around. Since Gus lived out near Center, not in Ada, I felt I could say without causing offense the town didn't seem to have made much progress.

"Well, I don't know about that. We're getting ahead. More people comin' every day," Gus replied, like he was going to run for mayor." All the little towns–Center, Byng, Stonewall–oh, there's a bunch of 'em all about the same.

"It depends on where the railroad goes. If the tracks come into town, there's a future. If they don't, it's hard to see how the town would grow. Ada people know that and are workn' hard to bring the Frisco down, like I told you.

"It's all movin' fast," Gus went on." You have to remember, there wasn't anybody livin' in Ada until 1890, not just passin' through, I mean nobody livin' there. Not a soul. I don't think there were even any Chickasaws, unless you count Byrd, and he's south of town.

"You ought to stop by and see ol' Frank Byrd again," Gus advised." You're talkin' about investing a little here and there. He's tellin' people there's oil south and east of Ada, that it's comin' out of the ground in some places.

"Frank said Indian hunters told him about it first and he went to see for himself. He didn't see any oil–like a puddle of oil–but he said the ground was greasy in spots, a sure sign like it was back in Pennsylvania when they got oil there."

I have to admit I never thought of investing in oil wells. I knew they found oil in Western Pennsylvania in 1878, but Pontotoc County is a long way from there.

"Well," I told Gus, "I'm just a snuff salesman. I don't have enough money to invest in oil wells. All I can do is buy little pieces of property in towns I think will grow and where I can get some kind of title, then hope that it ends up on main street."

Gus thought for a moment. "You don't have to have a fortune to get mineral rights on a few acres, particularly now. Not many folks know what Frank's talkin' about and some who have heard Frank just shrug if off. Oil's not somethin' they think about much, not around here.

"You could talk Frank into giving you quite a lease. I don't know how legal it would be or anything. But I hear he's willin' to do it. Maybe that's where some of the money comes from, not just land leases and the mill."

Since Gus brought the subject of money up, and I didn't have to appear nosey in another man's business, I asked, "Well, I guess you've taken advantage of the opportunity?"

"Me?" Gus laughed. "Good Lord no, man, I'm just scrapin' by haulin' in crooks. If I had any money right now I'd put it in pastureland somewhere, maybe across the Canadian. I don't know there's any oil around here, no matter what Frank says. I'm interested in cattle."

"Why didn't they start the town near the spring and the pond where Frank Byrd has his mill, Gus? That would have been pretty, really nice."

"Well, I wasn't here and don't know, but this was Chickasaw land remember. Settlers weren't supposed to come in and set up anywhere they felt like. I had to get a lease for my ranch land. But just for building a cabin and settin' out a vegetable garden, probably nothing was said. The Chickasaws had about given up trying to protect their land, from what I heard.

"Or, if they wanted to be on the safe side, being on Indian land, the settlers could have worked something out easy enough, maybe got a lease from Frank Byrd. He goes to Tishomingo all the time and he's sharp enough in business. Maybe Byrd didn't want white settlers any closer."

"That's right. I keep forgetting about whose land it was."

Gus thought a moment about the water and then said, "Well, it doesn't matter that much where the water starts out. Byrds Mill water runs down toward Ada naturally anyway. It's not like some little creek. There'll be plenty of water even if the railroad comes and Ada grows fast.

"However they worked it out with the Chickasaws, and I never heard how they worked it out, the first Ada settlers moved up from Red River County, Texas, in 1890 and built themselves log cabins. They knew about Byrd's spring but dug their own wells anyway. Plenty of water.

"They were the Daggs brothers and then Jeff Reed. He's still here. They called the place Daggs Prairie for a while then Reed opened a little store and got a post office set up inside.

"He wanted to name the place Sulfur Springs, but the government decided there were already too many places with Sulfur in the name. He tried a whole bunch of other names, like Eagle Flat, but none of them would do. He gave up. 'All right,' he said, 'name it for my daughter, 'Ada', and they did."

"What about 'Pontotoc'? Whose idea was that?"

"Well, the Chickasaws brought that with them from Mississippi. That was the name of the district where most of them lived in Mississippi. So for them, when they do tribal business, this is Pontotoc District. For most everybody else, it's Pontotoc County.

"Pontotoc is a Choctaw and Chickasaw word. Has something to do with bulrushes on the prairie. I guess I'd like that name better for a town than Ada."

It was early afternoon now and I could see there were maybe twice as many houses than there were on my first visit, more than I first saw from a distance. More stores on the main commercial street, too. It was beginning to look like a real town and I said so.

"Oh, I think it's comin' along pretty good," Gus agreed." They got people in Ada who want to get things done. The railroad's the main thing, like I said. They're promising all kinds of things to the railroad. They seem to know how to do it.

"The Masons were going to put up their new hall in Byng and the Ada folks got busy and got us to build it in Ada. I think Ada's going to be the place in a few years."

I could see a sign on the commercial street ahead that read, Brown Hotel. It appeared to have two stories but otherwise, it wasn't very impressive. Still better than last time. There wasn't any hotel.

"Well, Gus, I think I'll try to get a bath and spend the night in a bed before I take the rig back to Pauls Valley. It was good talking to you. Take care of yourself, dealin' with the outlaws. Hope you get the ranch you want."

Gus was at the back of the buggy unhitching his horse. "Well thanks, John. Best of luck to you."

"I got some people to see here, then I'll get on back to the ranch by night-fall. Tenny will be wonderin' what happened to me. She worries a lot."

Gus mounted, then said before he headed up the street, "Next time you're back this way, look me up."

Making the Stake

Gus Bobbitt was right about westerners being set in their ways when it comes to tobacco. A plug or a chaw is what they were used to, and my efforts to have them switch to Appalachian Gold snuff was not the success Mr. Rutgers or I expected. I thought not having to have a spittoon nearby would be enough of an argument in favor of snuff right there. It turned out it wasn't.

Mr. Rutgers was very kind the way he expressed his disappointment, telling how many days it took to build Rome and how things usually turn out for the best. I guess we both realized the market wasn't there. I *s*ent him a nice letter thanking him for everything, including my first business suit and shoes, and resigned.

Actually, it was a good thing for me like Mr. Rutgers said it would be, not being able to build a big snuff market in the Territories. I got married and my wife, Emma, a schoolteacher in Oklahoma City, didn't approve of snuff, tobacco or anything like it. She said it was a "disgusting habit."

I got so I could use snuff if I had to. I'll have to say, it was no sacrifice for me to give it up. Emma also said I should get a real job in one place, go to work in the morning, come home at night, and do something constructive. Being a traveling salesman is constructive in a way, and a demanding job, but I couldn't argue with her about opportunities right there in Oklahoma City, it was growing so fast.

Watching buildings going up in every direction made me think I might do something in the construction business. I ran across an old man in the south end of town who was making bricks as fast as he could all by himself, trying to keep up with the demands builders were making on him. He didn't like to be hurried or badgered by them. You'd think he was making glazed pottery.

When I asked the old man about his business, he just about gave it to me. He put his hat on, walked to the door of the shed that was his office and said, "Send me somethin' fair when you get going." He took a train east, back home, and disappeared.

I didn't have to start the business from scratch–just close to it. I fast hired four men to do the heavy work and I took the sales end. Really, it was more taking orders than selling. We couldn't make enough bricks. It still took many hours every day just to keep the paper work straight.

Being the kind of family man Emma had in mind took at lot of hours, too. Her vegetable garden was almost a full time job for me. She was from Missouri and believed every year without fail she had to fill long shelves of Mason jars with green beans, peas, tomatoes, turnip greens–things that are "good for you."

It was a very busy time and I was pleased both family and business seemed to be doing well. You could hardly go wrong in the building business in Oklahoma City then. There was talk about moving the capital down from Guthrie, which wasn't keeping up with Oklahoma City at all.

Besides the demand for my bricks, I was feeling pretty good because one of the lots I got in the Land Rush of '89 was on a street that was bound to be in the commercial center of the city. I figured it would be really valuable some day.

With all that was happening, I didn't have time to travel south in Indian Territory any more. There was no real business reason to go either. I couldn't haul bricks down there and I wasn't selling snuff. When I resigned I told Mr. Rutgers I would show his new man the ropes, especially important in Indian Territory. Mr. Rutgers never did send anyone else, as far as I know.

While I had nothing to sell in Indian Territory, I still liked the country around Ada and the country south of town. Besides, I was curious to find out if the little pieces of property I bought years back in the other little towns were worth anything. It all depended on how the towns might grow, or maybe not grow at all, if the railroads didn't run through.

When spring finally came in 1904, I decided I could get away from both business and family for a few days, and take the Katy south to see what was happening in Atoka, Stonewall and Ada. The Katy—the Missouri, Kansas & Texas Railroad—was Ada's second. The Frisco—the St. Louis and San Francisco Railroad—was the first and got to Ada in 1900.

A good place for me to start finding out what was happening, I figured, would be to talk to my friend Gus Bobbitt. If he was still around he'd know everyone in town and probably have more ideas than ever about the future.

April sometimes brings our worst weather, a late sleet storm or maybe a twister out of the first thunderstorms of the year. To make up for it, April brings us days made in heaven–calm, clear, a cheerful sun to take the morning chill off. On one of those mornings, I got the early Katy train southbound.

When the train stopped at the Ada station, I jumped down to the platform before the conductor got his step box in place, and walked fast down to the end at Main Street. My first look west on Main, I saw the town was growing fast like Gus said it would if the railroad came through. There were two-story buildings for three, maybe four blocks.

A big new hotel not far the from the Katy depot on Main was going up, too. A fellow standing in the middle of the street watching the work told me it would have sixty rooms, really something for a small town. I didn't have any doubt commercial men coming in on the railroads would fill it up.

The new hotel wasn't close to being ready, so I walked on down Main and paid for a night's lodging at the old Brown hotel. I say "old." They were still working on the back rooms on the second floor when I first saw the place, and that wasn't more than five years before. The Brown did have a bathtub on the first floor, and I appreciated that.

Finding Gus Bobbitt was the most important reason for my trip to Ada, and I thought I might have to go out to his ranch. I knew his ranch was near Center from what he said. That's all I knew, and there's miles of prairie out there. I didn't know if I could find him or the ranch.

So I decided to take a quick look around town to see if there was any promising property for sale, property I could afford, and try to find out about Gus while I was going along.

Lending money to new businesses is always important to a bank, particularly for banks in new towns, and I passed right by the Tennessee-Western National Bank on my way down Main. They would know about commercial property.

I must have been the first person to walk in that morning. There was a neatly dressed young man, white shirt, proper stiff collar, tie and a button sweater, just sitting down at a desk near the door. They didn't have anything you could call a lobby. We exchanged "mornin's" and then I told him I wanted to see the officer in charge of commercial property.

While we were talking a tall young fellow dressed in an eastern business suit with a vest–with a vest, mind you, in the middle of Indian Territory–came out of a cubby hole office at the back. He came over to us by the door and said to me, "Good morning. I am Dwight Livingston, president of our bank here in Ada. How can we help you?" The man I first talked to told him I was interested in looking at commercial property.

"Well, good," this Mr. Livingston replied. "I think we can help. Ada is just booming these days and there couldn't be a better time to invest in the town's future."

I quickly told him no matter how good a time it was for investing in Ada, I was trying hard to build my business in Oklahoma City and wasn't in a position to make any sizable commitment. "Just a small lot in the right place that may have a future."

"That's interesting," Mr. Livingston observed with a smile. "You come all the way down here from Oklahoma City to make a modest investment in Ada? I wish some of the businessmen in Ada could hear that. They don't seem to realize what we've got here. I think you are very wise."

"Please, Mr. Livingston," I protested, "I'm not in the real estate business. It's just that I used to come through here in a buggy, before you had any railroads. I like the area.

"I've seen the growth and expansion that followed the railroads up north. The same thing seems to be happening down here, now that you've got rail service."

"Exactly! Mr. Harris, exactly! Just what I believe," Mr. Livingston said.

I told him I read in the Oklahoma City paper the Frisco shipped more bales of cotton out of Ada in the last year than any other town in their Red River Division.

"It must be happening now," I pointed out, "like it did up north. I'd like to have a stake in that kind of growth, if I can afford it."

I must have been saying things about growth and the future he had been preaching there in Ada. He seemed pleased to hear that kind of Chamber of Commerce talk from someone else, particularly someone from out of town. He asked if he could inquire about my business in Oklahoma City. I told him.

"You make bricks?" he asked. "That's wonderful. Why don't you come down here and make bricks? We've got one manufacturer who is thinking about retiring and he has his plant sitting on a deposit of first-rate clay that will last forever, as I understand it."

I told him I was happy enough, and doing well enough in Oklahoma City, and that my wife enjoyed her life in the city. "I'm not sure a move would be welcomed in some quarters."

That was the start of a business discussion Dwight Livingston and I had that would run on over the next several years. He said he would make very causal inquiries about the existing brick plant in Ada, and when it seemed like a good time to buy it, he would get in touch with me. That was also the start of a fine friendship.

"We need your kind of forward thinking down here, Mr. Harris," he said. I told him to call me John and he told me to call him Dwight. That's what we did from then on.

I asked Dwight if he knew Gus Bobbitt. "Heard the name, John, but I really don't know him. I can ask around if it would help."

I told him not to bother, I would take that matter up when I concluded my business, my "modest" investment. He smiled. "I don't care how modest it is, John. I'm glad you are taking that first step toward being part of the community. Let me get Ralph here to take you around to see what's available now. Then you'll be hearing from me on the other matter in the coming weeks."

Ralph, the first one I spoke to in the bank, steered me around to the back of the building and we got into a small, one-horse buggy.

"Something in the growing commercial district on Main, or maybe Twelfth Street, I imagine?" he asked.

No, I told him, what was prime commercial property one day might not be the next. I told him I wanted something I could afford somewhere near the Frisco train depot.

"They aren't going to be moving those tracks anytime soon. Anything that has to do with the Frisco is what I want. They're doing very well."

Ralph seemed a little disappointed with that. He said the town was already moving east away from the Frisco tracks and the "Old Town" environment.

Old Town was where the original settlers built their cabins in1890, fourteen years before. That's how "old" it was. The Frisco station was a block or two away.

"Growth is going to be on Main Street and on Twelfth Street," Ralph stated, "Not in Old Town. There isn't much down there I would recommend."

He was right, there wasn't much to be recommended. Still, I went ahead and put a down payment on an old livery stable barn near the tracks. I don't know how it got be so old looking and still be standing. Well, I do. It must have been thrown together like all the first buildings. You could see right through the cracks in the walls, which were nothing but boards. It wasn't worth much, but it didn't cost much, either.

There was no way I could have known that shoddy little barn would be famous in a few years. Or maybe famous isn't the word. It was just that's where an awful thing happened. I wasn't in town the night it happened, and maybe I should be grateful for that.

While we were riding back up Main Street, I asked the young banker if he knew where I might find a man named Gus Bobbitt.

"Gus Bobbitt?" he asked. He shook his head slowly. "Sorry. Never heard of him. Was he in real estate here?"

I told him he was a former deputy marshal here, not in real estate.

"Sorry," he said. "You'll have to forgive me. I've only been in Ada six months. Maybe the sheriff would know. Or ask the newspaper people. They seem interested in law enforcement, police officers...people like that."

I saw a sign for the *Ada Weekly Journal* down a side street when I was walking to the bank from the train station, so I thought I would follow his suggestion.

The *Journal* didn't have much of an office. It was no more than a small wooden box of a building, but there was nothing at all on that side street a few years before. I was told they started up in a tent, so it was an improvement.

A tall, thin older man was alone inside, setting type. There was just one room with two desks on one side and the press on the other, up front near the window.

Ben Franklin spectacles perched on the typesetter's nose, an ink-blackened leather apron hung from his neck. He turned his head for a good shot at the spittoon and saw me.

"Howdy. Hep ya?" he asked.

"Much obliged if you would. See you're busy," I answered. "I'm looking for Gus Bobbitt. Thought the newspaper might know where I can find him."

"Gus Bobbitt. Gus Bobbitt," he mumbled. "Remember the name. A lawman in the early days. City alderman for a while. But it's been a couple of years since his name came through here.

"Editor's not in yet, but as far as I know Bobbitt's still workin' in a saloon up on the Canadian–The Corners saloon," he said.

"Working in a saloon?"

"Yup. Workin' with Jesse West and Joe Allen. Those two left for Pottawatomie some time ago now. Guess Bobbitt joined 'em. That's what I heard. Never been up there. Not likely to go neither. Heard it's a rough place."

The typesetter seemed friendly, so I said, "Well, I don't know Gus Bobbitt very well. Met him when he was a marshal. Guess I'm surprised he ended up working in a saloon."

"Yes sir," he answered, "workin' with Jesse West besides. I hear he's a difficult man, that Jesse West."

"What's so difficult about him?" I asked since I was planning to go up there.

"Actually, I've never seen him. He was gone, up to Pottawatomie before I got here. People who did know him say he's kind of wild eyed and quick to take offence at the smallest thing. I don't know he's hurt anybody around here. It's just that he looks like he might easy enough."

"Well, I'm obliged to you," I said. "Goin' up to the river may be a better bet than trying to find his ranch. Do you know if he still has his ranch…out near Center?"

"Far as I know, mister. Like I said, he hasn't been in the news lately. Good luck to you."

It was coming up on nine o'clock when I left the newspaper office and got a one-horse buggy of my own for the day. I was still in my business suit but I wanted to get started. There were a lot of miles to cover. My job now was to find Gus Bobbitt up on the Canadian River.

Hurry or not, I didn't want to miss Frank Byrd if I could help it. I never forgot Gus telling me Byrd reported oil was oozing out of the ground southeast of Ada. If Byrd really was selling leases, like Gus said, it might be worth talking to the old Chickasaw.

My problem was Byrd lived a little way south of town and to find Gus I needed to get up north to the river. Fortunately, the roads were dry, almost powdery. Fast enough. Still, it was going to be a long day. I got a little trot out of the livery stable horse and we headed towards Byrd's mill. I didn't expect that old mare to go very far at a trot, but with a little coaxing, she did pretty well.

I had no idea whether Mr. Byrd would be at the mill. I figured every hour that went by would hurt my chances of catching him. I wanted to ask him if he knew, really knew first hand, if anybody planned to drill for oil anywhere around Ada. People were not just talking about oil up around Tulsa, they were drilling. Just in case you forgot, they brought the first well in little more than a year later–1905.

When I got close to the mill, there was a sign by the road with an arrow pointing to a big, unpainted wood building with a tar paper roof about one hundred yards away. I could see a woman bustling around. She was dressed in overalls. Black braids hung below a heavy pink sweater. When I got closer I could see she was a forceful looking woman, not big, just strong, her black eyes bright in a brown face.

"Mrs. Byrd?" I asked. She stopped but didn't say anything. She just looked at me. I said who I was and that I was hoping to talk to Mr. Byrd for a minute. Gus Bobbitt suggested I do that, I added, hoping it would make Mrs. Byrd less suspicious.

Mrs. Byrd didn't seem to recognize Gus Bobbitt's name and she still looked suspicious. She finally did tell me Mr. Byrd left for Tishomingo at sunup. She said she didn't know when he'd be back either, she was so busy trying to keep the flour mill going she couldn't worry about it. I realized it would be a long time before she told some strange white man anything about her husband worth hearing, so I thanked her and left.

It was early afternoon when I finally got up to the South Canadian. It didn't look like much of a river, which was fine with me. It was mostly sand. A few long pools of water, sparkling in the sun, were stretched along what was the channel in rainy times. There were dry paths of sand leading to the other side, so I clucked my horse out onto the riverbed. She didn't like it much and stopped dead in her tracks.

There was a little whip in a socket there in the buggy, but I didn't want to use it. I flapped the reins hard over the horse's rump and shouted "Git!"

Before I could shout again, two characters in beat up hats and dirty short coats rode out from behind a willow-tree clump and came onto the sand with me. Without so much as a "howdy," one of them reached down and grabbed my horse's bridle.

"We'll get you across, mister," he called back.

The other rider pulled up alongside me and said, "You're damn lucky we're here to help you."

They were a pretty sorry pair to look at, though they had good looking mounts. I couldn't help thinking they stole 'em. Their coats and hats didn't go with the horses.

I was surprised at how old looking these two were, as old as my father, though they sure didn't look like my father. They hadn't shaved lately or it might have been they had scraggily gray beards. When the little breeze stopped, I could smell whisky on the rider next to me.

"That's kindly of you," I said in a loud voice to the rider in front, though I made it as friendly as I could since there were two of them. They looked ornery. I couldn't see any firearms under their coats but I didn't doubt they had them.

"I cross a lot of streams worse than this!" I declared.

"Git!" I shouted and flapped the reins hard.

The rider in front grabbed the bridle harder and pulled the mare's head over.

"Hey! Wait a minute, young fella'," the rider next to me said. "We're just tryin' to help you.

"Here you are, all dressed up in that fancy city suit. You're goin' to get out there, get yourself stuck in the quicksand, then have to wade through the mud!" he predicted. "We'll give you a hand and if you want to give us a couple of dollars on the other side, we wouldn't mind."

I wished then I'd taken the time to put my jacket on instead of the suit coat after visiting the newspaper office. Sitting there in a buggy in my business clothes, going nowhere, I must have looked like a plucked chicken to those two tramps. No rancher would have them around.

I hated to get robbed that way and ideas for escape raced through my head. None of them made any sense. They had my horse by the bridle, and she didn't want to go anywhere anyway. And there were two of them, probably armed. I sat back.

"Well, it doesn't appear I have much choice," I said. "Don't carry much money travelin' alone through the country, but I guess I could give you both two dollars."

The rider in front turned to look at his partner next to me. They both shrugged. The lead rider turned and pulled straight ahead on the mare's bridle. The buggy wheels ground through the sand but didn't sink in more than an inch. I've driven through a lot of places worse than that.

"You lookin' to buy some good whisky cheap?" the rider next to me asked when we were about half way across.

"No. I'm not lookin' for whisky," I answered. I didn't really want to talk to him so I left my answer there. We went on, around the end of a long pool of water.

"You're 'bout the only one crossin' the river not lookin' for whisky," he finally said. "Sometimes there's a half dozen a day crossin' here for whisky. And a lot more on Saturday."

As much as I didn't care to be indebted to him for anything more than the toll I agreed to, I had to ask directions from someone and he sure was close enough.

"Well, I'm not looking for whisky, but I am looking for The Corners saloon. Where would that be once we get across?"

The tramp next to me thought a minute, then said, "Oh, maybe an eighth of a mile upstream. Conner's place is about the same distance downstream…and they'd treat you a whole lot better there.

"And, like I said, if you're lookin' for some good whisky cheap, I got some stashed under a tarpaulin not far from where we're headed."

"No. I'm not lookin for whisky. I am lookin' for a man, Gus Bobbitt. They said back in town he's probably at The Corners."

"The tin horn deputy?" the tramp hooted. "You hear that, Will? He's lookin' for Gus Bobbitt!" The lead rider turned and grunted. He didn't say anything.

"Oh, yessir," the near tramp said to me. "He's probably up there, him and that crazy Jesse West. Let me give you some advice since we're travelin' across together…don't get mixed up with Jesse West. He's crazy. Just as soon shoot you as look at you."

We pulled up out of the river sand onto a rough road, or maybe it was no more than a path running beside the river. I fished in my pocket for a money clip that had some folded paper dollars. Really I had some more money but it was in a pouch I carried on a belt around my waist. When I counted out four dollars from the clip, there wasn't much left to look at and I was glad about that.

"Much obliged," I lied, handing them each two dollars. They grunted and headed down the path along the riverbank, downstream. I flapped the reins, clucked at the mare and headed upstream.

There weren't many people around. In fact, except for the two old bandits that took my four dollars, I never saw anybody along the river. I kept going and then on the other side of a poplar thicket growing out of the sand at river's edge, I saw an old building.

Chunks of tar paper on the roof flapped with a little gust of wind. There was one door, half open, and two windows on the side I could see. The rough milled boards under the roof weren't painted. About fifteen yards in back, there was a one-hole outhouse, built the same way.

There were no more than thirty or forty yards of sand and tufts of lank grass between these two dismal buildings and the river. If the two bandits were right, this had to be The Corners, though there was no sign saying that or anything else.

Three saddle horses were tied to a hitching rail near the door. I pulled up and looped my reins around the rail. Then I heard some loud voices inside, a shout, but nothing angry. Still, it made me wary. For the second time that afternoon, I wished I had stopped somewhere long enough to get my old jacket on. There was no doubt in my mind I wasn't going to fit in very well.

In the doorway I stopped a second or two to let my eyes adjust to the gloom inside. It was just one room but the windows were so dirty there wasn't much daylight coming through. For someone walking in from the sun, it was pretty dark.

All the talking stopped and I could see two young farm hands or maybe cowboys wearing their hats, on one side of the bar and a heavy set man with a black mustache on the other. He was about my age.

"Howdy," I said taking a few steps inside. "I'm lookin' for Gus Bobbitt."

The two country fella's turned away from me and looked at the man behind the bar. He stayed looking square at me.

"I'm Gus Bobbitt. Who's askin'?"

I took a couple more steps inside, gave my name, and said to Gus Bobbitt, "I met you in Christian Harding's cabin down near Roff on a stormy night five or six years ago. Rode up to Ada with you next day…"

"Good Lord! I remember you now. You're the Alabama snuff salesman!"

He came out from behind the bar, stuck out his hand.

"Good to see you. Have a drink. Go sit down there. I'll be right with you."

There was splintery old table with four chairs around it under one of the windows. I went over and stood there. Gus came back with a bottle and a couple of glasses.

"Sit down. Sit down," he said, pouring some whisky in the glasses. We both pulled a chair out and sat down. "Are you still sellin' snuff?"

"Nope. Gave that up a couple of years ago. I'm makin' bricks in Oklahoma City. Got a wife and a little kid. Another on the way."

"Makin' bricks..." Gus muttered. "Never thought of that."

"Well, I never thought of it either. My wife did," I admitted. "She's very practical. A schoolteacher. Likes things you can use to good purpose. Snuff didn't measure up in her opinion."

I told Gus Ada was beginning to grow just like he said it would if the railroad came through, and I had been thinking it would be good to be in on its future. I told him I bought a little piece of property down near the Frisco depot that very morning and was thinking about maybe buying a brick plant.

"Oh yeah," Gus replied. "That'd be smart. Ada's going to grow. They're already talkin' about getting another railroad, makin' it three comin' into Ada, if it comes. You better be in on what's happening."

It was puzzling to me that Gus was not only aware of the commercial activity in Ada, was so enthusiastic, but still ended up in this claptrap saloon. It seemed to me he could do better with his life.

"A newspaper printer in town told me you were a city alderman, Gus. That's great," I said. "You'd be good in politics, I have no doubt of that. Are you still in office?"

Gus laughed. "Nah, I'm not interested in Ada politics. I bought a little house on South Broadway so we'd have a place to stay in town if it was too late to get back to the ranch. They were lookin' for people to run for alderman. I agreed and won. Didn't even campaign. Nope, that's not for me."

"Well, that's too bad. I thought sure you'd be mayor one day. If city politics don't interest you, how about one of the business opportunities that are coming with the railroads?"

"Oh, I'm not a businessman, John. I'm a rancher. I don't have a business head like you do. I want a ranch on my own land.

"I'm homesteading a section over in Seminole County not far off from here. It's just over the county line. If I 'pioneer' it so it pleases some government inspector, I can own it some day. I can't in Indian Territory. I guess you know that."

"From what I read, Gus," I advised, "that may change pretty soon. There's been talk for years, I know, but I really think severalty may be ending soon. Lots of folks up in Washington are sayin' the Indians would be better off with private property, even in Indian Territory. Senator Dawes must have convinced most everybody. Maybe it'll be just like Oklahoma Territory. I'd bet you'll be able to buy Chickasaw land before long."

"Well, I hope you're right, but now it doesn't make much difference. I don't have the money to buy what I want anyway. That's why I'm here in this place." He looked around the shadowy room with a sorrowful grin.

Gus made no effort to cover up the dislike for what he was looking at, though he didn't say anything more. He might not have been a businessman, but it seemed to me he could make more money with a little store in town, if money was the goal, more than he could tending bar on the Canadian River. My thoughts must have shown on my face.

"I don't own this place," Gus volunteered. "Jesse West and Joe Allen do. They're old friends from Center, west of Ada. We all came up from Texas and leased land more'n ten years ago.

"Then, a couple of years ago, they came up here to Oklahoma Territory so they could homestead," Gus went on. "But they had the same problem most of us do–gettin' the money to operate a decent ranch whether the land belongs to us or not. Jesse came across this place and took it over.

"Took it over?" I asked. Comments about how fierce Jesse West was came to mind.

"Well, it was peaceable enough, from what I heard. There are different stories how he managed the deal. Anyway, I don't pry into it. I've known Jesse a long time… he's not one you want to question. The old man who built the place was ready to walk away. He all but gave it to Jesse…"

Gus waggled his head slightly over this remarkable business transaction, and then added, "I'm not just a bartender, you understand. I come up here as much as I can to help, usually on the way over to my Seminole County section. I fill in for certain when Jesse and Joe both have to be away. They got a ranch operation goin' too…We've got our differences, but we're workin' it out.

“We don’t have anything down in writing. Maybe that’s not smart…anyway, nobody’s complaining. I let them pasture some of their herd on my stake over in Seminole. Got good grass over there. Jesse gives me a cut from the business here every month. I’m savin’ some money.”

Talking low so the two at the bar wouldn’t hear, I ventured, “I’m glad it’s workin’ out. I heard back in town Jesse West is a boisterous character…best I should avoid him if I came up here lookin’ for you.”

“Oh, I don’t know that’s fair. Jesse’s all right, I suppose, but he does get agitated with things around here. Those people down at Conners’ place are enough to aggravate anyone. They’re always spoilin’ for some kind of fight. I don’t know why. There’s enough money for everyone sellin’ whisky.”

Gus paused and I told him abut the two old bandits who “helped’ me across the river. Gus laughed.

“That’s right! Remember I warned you first time we met about lookin’ too prosperous travelin’ alone. Sure, they got a bunch of people down at Conners’ place like that. That’s why Jesse asked me to help out here. They know I was a deputy marshal. We let ‘em know they better not fool with me. So far it’s worked all right.

“Nobody’s come here lookin’ for real trouble. There’s some tough talk along the river…on the road to Ada. Even in Ada, down on West Main. So far, it’s just talk.”

“Well, Gus, I hope it stays that way. Don’t appear to be many lawmen around to help out.”

Gus laughed. “You’re sure right about that. Never have seen one.”

Gus might not have been interested in business, but he was smart enough to be good at it. He’d do fine with a hardware store–saddles, guns, ammunition. Whatever arrangement he had with his old friends, the two ranchers, must have seemed worth it to him, though. He wasn’t complaining. It sure would take a lot of money for me to work in that ratty place.

The afternoon was wearing on, so I told Gus I’d have to start to town if I wanted any daylight for my trip back.

“I’d ride down to the crossing with you John, so you don’t have to pay any more tolls,” Gus said, smiling, “but I’m the only one here now, and I told Jesse I would handle things.”

“Aw, I’ll be all right, Gus. Those two old coots are probably lyin’ drunk by now. One of ‘em had a pretty good start when I came over.

"I don't know when I'll get down to Pontotoc again. Maybe pretty soon if I decide to get that brick plant. Maybe later if I don't. Anyway, whenever it is, I'll sure look you up." I got up and headed for the door. Gus walked out to the buggy with me.

Just then a rider came up at a lively trot, hitched his horse and went to the saloon doorway. He turned and gave a quick wave to Gus. Didn't say anything.

"That's Jesse West," Gus said when the rider disappeared into the saloon.

From all I'd heard, I had expected to see someone different, bigger maybe, or menacing, wild looking, all but breathing fire.

Jesse West was about my size, and he looked fit enough. Really a nice looking man, wearing a light jacket and regular ranch hat. Dressed up, he'd fit right in at church. I suppose women would consider him handsome. Anyway, I was surprised that a man with a reputation like his looked so ordinary.

It was getting late in the day when I crossed the Canadian on the way back to Ada. Crossed without any help, I'm pleased to say. Didn't see a soul and my horse went right out onto the sand.

My short visit to The Corners saloon was a success I thought. I found Gus Bobbitt and got to talk to him. He still had the same enthusiasm for Ada and the community, and that was reassuring to me.

It was also what you might call an interesting visit. I've ventured into some pretty rough saloons in Texas and the mountains. I didn't stay long but I saw them, and from my experience, The Corners could match any of 'em for awful. I got to see it in broad daylight, too, most likely the best of conditions. I'm sure it would have been a lot more interesting on Saturday nights.

Gus had survived years as a deputy marshal in Indian Territory, truly a hazardous job, so I wasn't going to start worrying about him. Still, the Corners Saloon looked like trouble to me.

The Corners

Some horses are smarter than others and I've known that for a long time. What surprises me though, is how every last livery stable horse anywhere in the country seems to know when he's headed back to the barn. It's like they had a map and a timetable. However my old mare figured it out I don't know, but once across the river, headed for Ada, she started a little trot. I didn't even cluck at her.

My trip up to the river and visit with Gus in The Corners was both pleasurable–seeing Gus again–and disturbing. Maybe the worry started with those two old villains who took me over the riverbed to the north shore. It was hard to get them out of my mind. I was angry with myself for letting them take my money so easy.

Bad thoughts kind of melted away though, clip clopping along in the late afternoon sunshine. Blue stem grass on the prairie was showing signs of green through the winter straw color. First of the wild flowers were popping up – Indian Paintbrush, Blue Bonnet. Texas doesn't have all the Blue Bonnet, I can assure you. Trees along the road were coming alive, too…miniature pale green leaves showing on the branches.

The scene put me into a kind of trance, and I decided I would like to sell my business in Oklahoma City and go on making bricks in Pontotoc County. I like making good bricks. They're an important part of strong and pretty houses, churches, office buildings, schools.

For me to decide on a late afternoon buggy ride that I wanted to move my business down to Pontotoc County and live there was one thing, to have it happen was another. First, with the account books open in front of me, I would have to be sure the move would make good business sense. Things were going very well in Oklahoma City.

Then I would have to convince Emma it was a good thing to do for her and the children. That would not be easy.

I could see Ada would probably never be really big like Oklahoma City. There were too many towns like it out on the prairie, none of them on a navigable river, or lake. Pretty much the same really. It would be all right with me if Ada never became a big city. It would be big enough in years to come to have good hospitals and schools. A nice place to live and raise a family. Well, maybe it would be a nice place to live.

For all the new businesses and people coming in, Ada still had the old West Main crowd. They weren't going anywhere. Those two scruffy old robbers on the river would fit right in. It was no wonder commercial activity was moving away from them. Ralph, the young banker, was right about that.

Ada seemed to me to be at some kind of crossroads. It wasn't clear to me what kind of town it would become. If Gus Bobbitt didn't want to be an alderman, didn't want to get involved in Ada politics, who would? I had no doubt there would be some strong candidates from West Main if Ada prospered. It would be just like those big cities back east where gangs of rough citizens took political control, ran everything for their own profit...different scale, of course.

I figured I could take care of myself no matter who was making the decisions, but what about Emma? She read stories about the shootings in Pontotoc County in our paper all the time. It didn't worry her. To her it was like it all happened in Bolivia. What would she think about actually living in Ada?

Would she shy away from walking down Main Street, fearful about going to the stores in her own town? I thought about how pleased Emma was with her garden club and friends in Oklahoma City. Would her life be anything like that in Ada?

I had no answers of course. It depended on the kind of people who were leading the way in years ahead–hiring police chiefs, setting up the schools, setting the social standards, making clear what was acceptable behavior and what wasn't. The high homicide rate in Pontotoc County, year after year, made that a real concern to me. Would tomorrow's leaders have the stomach to bring change? That could be dangerous.

The bootleg whisky business on the Canadian River was another part of it. I was glad I took the time to go up to the river and find Gus Bobbitt. Seeing The Corners saloon and encountering the old tramps from Conners' saloon, gave me a feeling for the place...an uneasy feeling. Those two rattlesnake dens so close to Ada kept the West Main scene going and were surely part of the explanation for all the shooting in Pontotoc.

Most of the river people came into Ada every week or so to make whisky deliveries, go to a café and order the food they wanted, maybe go to the stores for a new hat, or boots. From what I heard, part of the routine was to show up in the pool halls to drink and talk tough. Newcomers to Ada arriving on the Frisco would sure get a bad impression. They'd pretty near have to pass right by a passel of rowdy characters, particularly late in the day.

I went up to the river to find Gus Bobbitt, not to see The Corners saloon. I didn't even know it existed. Wouldn't have been interested anyway, though when it got to be famous in a way, I was glad I saw it. I had even less interest in seeing the other saloon, Conner's place, which was actually the first one up there.

Bill, or William Conners, one of the earliest white farmers in Pontotoc County, must have thought selling whisky would be an easier way of making a living than farming. He didn't waste any time getting into the saloon business after Congress passed the Organic Act of 1890, establishing Oklahoma Territory.

The southern boundary of Oklahoma Territory was the South Canadian River. Selling whisky was legal north of the river. It wasn't legal south of the river, in Pontotoc and Indian Territory, and hadn't been from the start in 1830.

Lawmakers in Washington decided hard spirits would be bad for Indians and made prohibition the law throughout Indian Territory. Maybe they were right, but it was a bonanza for bootleggers and a law enforcement problem to the very end.

Less than a year after passage of the Organic Act, Conners gave up farming and built his rough-board saloon. He built it in a Sycamore tree thicket maybe two hundred feet north of the river, as though he wanted to hide it. Why I don't know. It was legal enough to sell whisky there after 1890. Anybody bent on buying whisky, or even a revenue agent, would sure find it.

Having the first, and for a while, the only saloon on that stretch of the river was very profitable for Conners. Sure enough, he soon had competition. The competition came from a new saloon upriver, The Corners, the place Jesse West took over later on.

Both saloons were built on what was called a "fraction" of land, small parcels left over after the surveyors laid out sections as straight as they knew how with transits. Their straight lines didn't provide for bends in the river however, and there were little chunks of land left over. Those were the fractions.

Fractions of land were in the public domain. Anyone on them could stay on them, but could never own the land. They were squatters. Bill Conners and Jesse West were squatters. It was their business that was valuable, not the real estate.

I told you what The Corners looked like. From what I heard, the builder must have copied it from Conners' place. Both were just big wooden boxes with a couple of windows and doors and a tarpaper roof.

It wasn't what you'd call a family business for either Jesse West or Bill Conners, though regular customers were nearby farm or ranch people. They were agreeable enough when sober. Full of whisky, some got aggressive and difficult to deal with, the younger ones most often.

The bootleg part of the business–supplying the illegal Indian Territory market–brought a different kind of character on the scene, including hard-eyed drifters, men not intimidated by threatening competitors, or by the law.

Some of these drifters were already wanted by the law, before they did any bootlegging. Saloon proprietors had to be able to take care of themselves dealing with them. Having a few stern, unsmiling regular employees around was a good idea. Gus Bobbitt filled that role at The Corners, though it's hard for me to picture it. He just didn't look ornery enough.

The festering whisky trade along the river in the far southeast corner of Pottawatomie County–that's where "the corners" came from–wasn't all that unusual. A series of saloon settlements sprang up along more than a hundred miles of the north bank of the Canadian after passage of the Organic Act.

A retired Army colonel by the name of Charles Mooney wrote a history of Pottawatomie County before statehood in 1907. He reported eleven saloons popped up at Young's Crossing after passage of the Organic Act. Keokuk Falls was home to what they called the "Seven Deadly Saloons."

For anyone wanting to make money in hurry, the whisky business, both legal and illegal, was a powerful calling. Not only could you make a lot of money, you really could turn a profit fast. Didn't need to wait for crops to grow, or calves to join the herd. That suited Jesse West just fine. He could become a successful rancher quick.

There was a saloon at Violet Springs near where Jesse West and Joe Allen settled, but the proprietor was a big, burly fellow with three brothers who promised trouble for anyone trying to horn in. Jesse and Joe decided to steer clear.

Jesse didn't give up the idea of solving his financial problem by pushing into the whisky business, though. What he needed was a location that didn't stir up a hornet's nest. On cattle searches he made every month or two, looking for cattle cheap from disheartened ranchers, or maybe unbranded cattle, he also searched for an abandoned old house or barn near the Canadian. He could make that into a saloon.

It was on one of these expeditions Jesse ran across The Corners, about twenty miles down river from Violet Springs. The proprietor was sick to death of the threats and violent behavior that were part of the whisky trade, and had let his stock go way down. He was ready to walk away, though he was the one who built the saloon only a few years before.

It was a perfect set up for Jesse and he seized the moment. He didn't have any money, so he made some convincing promises about future payments. That was good enough for the proprietor, more than ready to abandon the place anyway. Jesse took over.

Colonel Mooney wrote The Corners was "the worst 'hell hole' of them all…the roughest, toughest and most infamous of the saloons in the entire Old West.

"It was here," the Colonel declared, "…men were killed and ungloriously dumped into the Canadian River only fifty feet away, and where they were found mysteriously floating down the river, never to return home again." That was Jesse West's new business.

The Pottawatomie County census of 1900 counted Jesse West as a saloonkeeper, not a rancher which he was trying to become. I never did get to know Jesse West, but from what I understand, he wouldn't have gotten much pleasure being identified as a saloonkeeper. Joe Allen wasn't counted at all.

Competition between Jesse West's saloon, The Corners, and Conners' place never let up, and sometimes it was threatening. Despite that, there is no record of any of the many casualties Colonel Mooney wrote about coming directly from competition between those two saloons. There was tough talk, but that's all it amounted to. The Ada newspapers took it very seriously, however, and warned of a shootout on Main Street between the two neighboring Canadian River "gangs."

Conners considered any new arrival at Jesse West's saloon a "gun slinger" recruited in preparation for the armed showdown he feared was ahead. It was this kind of worry Conners grew tired of and decided he had enough. He knew that while farming was more work, it was also less stressful. He sold out to Dave Hybarger from north Oklahoma Territory up near the Kansas border, a man new to the Canadian River area.

Well, it didn't take Hybarger long to know he had gotten himself deep into a very hazardous trade, and he didn't like it. He suffered a loss, but sold out to James McCarthy, an East Side New Yorker who knew what was going on and wasn't put off by conflict.

McCarthy was in fact starting to build his own saloon the river bend when Hybarger came to him with a proposition to sell. McCarthy quickly accepted, stopped building, and gave full attention to the contest with West and Allen.

I got to know McCarthy years later when he was a jailer in Ada. He might not have been the smartest man in the West, but he wasn't timid. To get ready for the worst, he hired two employees who usually had guns, one carried a holstered revolver everywhere, the other always had a lightweight Winchester rifle nearby. They weren't really "gun slingers," men who made their living shooting people, but men who looked like they'd welcome trouble.

The newcomers were Frank Starr and George "Hooky" Miller. Miller got his nickname after he lost part of his right hand in an Abilene, Kansas, saloon. Hooky had been a cowboy. He made two long trails from the middle of Texas to Kansas, got his fill of that hard and risky work and hired on as a guard at the North Star saloon.

Hooky tried to talk a drunken cowboy into giving up his revolver. When the talking didn't work, Hooky reached for the gun before the cowboy could get it out of his holster. He was late.

After the accident, Hooky couldn't grip his pistol right handed and couldn't hit anything left handed. To make up for the handicap, he practiced hard and got to be very quick and good with his rifle, never far away from him. He cradled the rifle with his left hand, operated the lever action and pulled the trigger with his maimed right hand. McCarthy thought he would be useful in the showdown he saw ahead.

Hooky would have been a good one to have on your side in a showdown. He looked like a pirate with glinty blue eyes, lank grey hair and grey stubble on his chin. He had a voice to go with his appearance. It was kind of a cackle. Hooky worked for McCarthy a couple of years.

Hooky's first job for McCarthy was typical of the shenanigans that went on along the Canadian then. One little dustup was started by Joe Allen at The Corners when Jesse West was away for the day. A government revenue agent happened to be making a routine inspection at The Corners, so Joe sent a twelve year-old boy over to McCarthy's saloon with enough money to buy a jug of whisky. It was a simple entrapment plan.

Government revenue agents had a reputation for being very tough on saloonkeepers who sold to minors along the Canadian. They didn't feel any responsibility at all for what grown-up men were doing to one another.

The scheme was to have the revenue agent see the twelve-year-old struggling back from McCarthy's place with a jug of whisky, pretty heavy for a youngster. McCarthy would have to be the one catering to children. There was no other saloon around. McCarthy would have to be the culprit.

Just outside the door at McCarthy's saloon, Starr and Miller stopped the boy and asked him where he got the money for the whisky. The frightened youth told them. The men took the money and sent the boy back to The Corners. Then they saddled up and rode within shouting distance of Jesse West's place.

"Here's your jug!" Starr shouted, and threw the jug down. It hit in sand and didn't break. So they backed their horses away and waited. The story goes there was no sign of the boy, a government agent or anyone else. Just quiet. The pair gave up, wheeled their horses and went back to the McCarthy camp. Nothing to it. Just more poison for the river air.

When McCarthy decided the whisky business wasn't worth it to him either, he rode away from the saloon, leaving most of the Indian Territory trade in Pontotoc to Jesse West. Hooky Miller was without a job. He had nowhere to go.

A man who looked like Hooky did, who couldn't hire out as a cowboy or ranch worker with his bad hand, would have trouble finding a regular job. That's why Hooky moved over to The Corners to work for Jesse West after years of threatening games and squabbles–nowhere else to go. He belonged on the Canadian River shore, one saloon or another, not in any town.

When Nettie West finally talked Jesse into moving back to Texas and away from the dangerous bootlegger's life on the Canadian, Gus Bobbitt took over The Corners. There was a legitimate basis for Gus's move. He believed he had become a partner of Jesse's working in the saloon as much as he did, and sharing his Seminole County pasture. However, the arrangement was never spelled out in writing anywhere.

Jesse did not see the "partnership" the same way. He was resentful and angry that Gus simply took over when he left, rather than buying him out, the way he got The Corners. Naturally Joe Allen left with Jesse.

I know from Gus himself, he regarded Jesse's departure as a very mixed stroke of fortune. Gus didn't like the dingy saloon or the people around it, but he did need the money. The Indian Territory market was more rewarding than ever with settlers coming in all the time, and Gus had no close competition any more. The money was good.

Gus was happy enough to get the owner's share of the profits, but like in most opportunities, there were drawbacks. One of the drawbacks was some of the people who then called him "boss," including Hooky Miller. The former deputy marshal–Gus–used to smile about that. "Never would have believed it," he'd say.

You couldn't claim Hooky ever got to be a real friend of Gus's, though he did take Gus's side in the days when there was bad blood in the saloon between Gus and Jesse West. It would be pretty hard to line up with Jesse before he left for Texas. He was angry most of the time.

"What in the world did Hooky Miller do for you?" I asked Gus once, partly joshing him. I knew very well Gus thought he might be some kind of lunatic.

"Well now, John, you'd be surprised," Gus explained. "Hooky was very helpful keepin' the peace around here. Sometimes when those young bucks got liquored up and wanted to take on the world, Hooky would get a bottle, put it under his right arm, get a stack of glasses in his left, go over to the buckaroos and say, 'Let's have a drink.' No one ever turned down a free drink. I learned that fast enough.

"Then Hooky'd spin a yarn about the Chisholm Trail back in '67, about all the trouble he had on the trail, or maybe tell about all the trouble he'd seen as a saloon guard. 'Don't need no more trouble,' he'd say. "

In a couple of months everybody knew Hooky was at The Corners, Gus recalled, grinning. People rode for twenty miles just to get a drink and see him.

"They could have seen him over at McCarthy's place before," Gus pointed out. "Maybe they kept him out of sight. Couldn't blame them much.

"Anyway, everybody got to know Hooky was at The Corners as a kind of sociable guard–out in front, talkin' to people–maybe like a side show at the fair, which was just fine with me. "

Where else in the world could George "Hooky" Miller get such a job, and be a big help, I don't know. It was a particular time, and not a long time either, between 1890 and 1907. And there was just one place, along the Canadian River.

I never met this Colonel Mooney, but he did write a good history of Pottawatomie County, as far I know. I don't think he exaggerated conditions along the Canadian in that period. There were a lot of saloons up and down the river, and of course they were all bootlegging. That's why they were there.

I'm told that's where the word "bootlegging" came from–riders buying a flask before they crossed the Canadian into Indian Territory and jamming it down into their boot.

Dead men did float down the Canadian regularly, as the Colonel stated, but nobody kept count and usually nobody followed up. Pottawatomie officials didn't want to take responsibility, and neither did Indian Territory people.

Most often these unfortunate folks were never identified. Nobody wanted to get involved. A number of people around The Corners, and maybe even more at McCarthy's place, were going to some trouble to cover up their own identities. The last thing they wanted was a long, drawn-out conversation with a lawman about some poor stranger. There never was a body count either.

Every once in a while, a body was pulled from the river and was identified. Exactly that happened in the second year Gus was in charge at The Corners. Gus found out about this one victim when he learned he was being sued by the widow. The victim turned out to be an unlucky itinerant cattle buyer from Kansas City.

The cattle buyer was apparently new to the area and just happened to stop at The Corners. Nobody could remember ever laying eyes on him, so it was probably a one-time, and unforgettable, visit.

Some time before his death, the cattle buyer wrote home to his wife and described The Corners. There's no doubt he was there. He described it in some detail, perhaps a little exaggerated. The truth would have been bad enough, but he chose to make a good story better for the Kansas City urban dwellers and made the grim facts worse than they really were in his letter.

The widow didn't charge Gus or any of his customers with killing her husband in her lawsuit. Perhaps she was persuaded he could have been killed in any one of several saloons, or by robbers along the riverbank. Her husband was found face down in the river with a number of bullet holes in him, not far but up river from The Corners. Reports were that he had been in the water a while.

The widow's suit, based on what her husband wrote, charged that Gus was running a wildly disreputable and dangerous public place. He must bear some responsibility for the death of her husband, she insisted, whether or not he was guilty of homicide.

Gus was permitted by the court to submit a deposition answering the widow's charges. In his sworn statement, Gus didn't try to hide the fact that some undesirable people, maybe even some wanted by the law, came into The Corners from fifty miles around.

Rather than being defensive, Gus argued in his deposition that until 1890 Pottawatomie County was still part of Indian Territory. Law enforcement had been sparse and uncertain in Indian Territory since the Civil War, Gus pointed out. Being a part of the new Oklahoma Territory a few years hadn't changed things.

As a result of thin and sometimes non-existent law enforcement, and an even weaker judicial system, Gus wrote, social order was slow in coming to remote areas, such as along the Canadian. He stated with pride that he was a former deputy marshal in Indian Territory and had first-hand knowledge.

Gus argued that history and very specifically legalization of whisky in Oklahoma Territory, just across a shallow river from "dry" Indian Territory, were responsible for the turmoil around the big river bend, not any shortcomings in his management. He won the day.

It is possible the judge was influenced by Gus's service as a marshal. Those who understood law enforcement problems in Indian Territory were generally grateful for the very few marshals they had.

Gus was never apologetic about being proprietor of The Corners saloon. Certainly he wasn't to me. He hadn't found any other means of providing for his growing family, while at the same time putting enough money aside to buy the ranch land he wanted. His small ranch operation out at Center didn't generate that kind of income.

Nor was the Seminole County homestead he was "pioneering" much help, except that it gave him bargaining chips with Jesse West when West needed more pasture. Gus could never have bought Lightnin' Ridge–what he named his ranch–without the money he made from The Corners, most of it after Jesse West left.

Gus was aware there were people in Ada who disapproved of his business on the Canadian. He was philosophical about that. His many loyal friends among the Masons didn't seem much bothered by it. The business being in Pottawatomie County was helpful–provided a buffer for the moral problem, though it was just across the river. Pottawatomie County did not have a high standing in Ada at that time.

Most important, the Canadian River enterprise didn't appear to reflect poorly on Tenny or the children in Ada. They were highly thought of everywhere, including church circles, an increasing population in Ada.

While Gus was never defensive about the saloon business, he was ready to forgo the whole thing with the coming of statehood in 1907 and statewide whisky regulations. The Canadian River didn't matter in the whisky trade after that. Regulations were the same, one side of the river or the other. Operating The Corners had been a stressful time in his life, while Jesse West was there and after he left.

Having Jesse West back in Texas made life some easier for Gus. The bickering and angry exchanges with West were in the past, leaving only the routine disputes of aggressive customers for Gus to deal with.

It was an improvement, but now Gus had to guess what Jesse was thinking about and that was no comfort. Gus had put up with West's dark suspicions for years and knew very well a return to Texas wasn't going to make him forget the treachery he believed was done to him.

In his rare gloomy moments, Gus wondered how West might try taking his revenge. Whatever was ahead, Gus always concluded that it had been worth it. He had made his stake.

The Spirited Rancher

Horace Greeley, founder of the *New York Tribune*, advised: "Go west, young man! Go west!" and a lot of them did, a good number of them wanting to be ranchers. Not all were from the East Coast either. There were a lot of Europeans, mostly Englishmen, caught up in this dream of a home on the range.

The westward surge of ambitious young men lasted from the end of the Civil War for thirty years or more, until farms, fences, railroad tracks and towns dimmed the romantic visions.

Hundreds of young men already in the West wanted to be ranchers as well, and they were largely free of romantic notions. They liked the outdoor excitement of ranching, the swaggering independence they thought came with being a rancher. Most of them knew for sure they didn't want to be tied down to farm drudgery.

Never would you find two young men more perfectly drawn to fit this description than Gus Bobbitt and Jesse West. Gus never even considered any other calling, as far as I know. His work in law enforcement and ventures into politics were all in support of his ranching goal. I didn't get to know that much about Jesse West's ambitions first hand. From what I did learn through the years, they were about the same as Gus's.

I can't think of anything besides this single-track determination to be ranchers would bring them both to spend years in that dismal Corners saloon. The money they made there, legally and illegally, made it possible for them to become ranchers as they saw the role. Sweating over a small herd on leased acreage wouldn't do it.

Many of the young men who came west had no idea of what it takes to get a ranch or to be a rancher. Most of them weren't equipped to do anything more than tend cattle, about my level on the Triple R. A couple of winters in the wind and summers in the sun for what little pay they got discouraged a lot of them.

A surprising number of these disappointed newcomers to the cattle business decided it would be easier to use the guns they practiced with hour after hour either to enforce the law or break it. Many did both at various times.

William Bonney–Billy the Kid–was the most famous of those who gave up being a cowboy for faster rewards. He started out as a teen-age cowhand in Lincoln County, New Mexico, and was both a famous outlaw and dead at twenty two years of age.

Just how far either Gus Bobbitt or Jesse West would go in skirting the law to reach their objective, the ranch, was never put to a crucial test. Both were from good, solid farm families, both were churchgoers and both were married to women of high principles.

Selling whisky illegally might have been more of a problem for Gus, since he had been a deputy marshal, sworn to enforcing the law. Even so, I can't imagine he would have done anything more clearly against the law than The Corners operation. However, there were people in Ada who thought selling whisky legally was plenty bad enough.

The fact that Gus and Jesse West both wanted to be ranchers is not surprising, but that was only the beginning of what they had in common. Just to glance at them and their backgrounds, you'd think they should have been brothers, not enemies. Actually, they were great friends for a while when they both lived near Center with their young families.

To begin with, Jesse West and Gus Bobbitt had their ages in common. They were both forty-six when the curtain came down on the last act. Jesse was born January 8, 1863 in Montague County, Texas, on the Red River. Gus was born in Alabama later the same year, then went to school in Sherman, Texas, as I told you.

Along with a lot of other young Texans, they crossed the Red River into Indian Territory to make something of themselves. Neither was expected to stay home and work on the family farm. Neither would be content very long to be a hired farmhand or cowhand. They wanted to be in charge.

The Texas side of the Red River was pretty well settled a few years after the Civil War. The best land was occupied, anyway. On the Indian Territory side of the river, there were stretches of scrub oak woods, a scattering of massive granite or limestone outcroppings, but mostly it was open, rolling prairie. Signs that anybody lived there were few and far between.

Texas drovers who went north to the railheads through Indian Territory on the Chisholm Trail and later on the Western Trail told of vast and good pasture land all the way to Kansas. Tall grass didn't peter out just beyond the Red River Valley. You can see why young men who wanted to be ranchers were willing to go up there, isolated or not, if land in the Valley was beyond their financial reach.

Jesse West crossed the river from Montague County and entered what was then called Western Indian Territory. It had been sliced off the original Chickasaw Nation by the Federal government as a punishment for the Chickasaws siding with the Confederates in the Civil War.

Jesse needed to work and signed on with the old Addington outfit, which was set up before the Civil War without the benefit of any lease. How Old Man Jeremiah Addington survived the Comanches back then, I don't know. This was Quanah Parker's country. He was the fierce warrior chief who never lost a battle to the whites. Jesse Chishlom survived as a wandering trader, but he was half Indian.

The Comanches were very warlike people, not like our Five Civilized tribes. You can understand why the Choctaws were willing to let the Chickasaws settle on the western half of their Nation in 1837. The Chickasaws would be between the Choctaws and the Comanches. In 1855 that buffer zone would become the Chickasaw Nation.

After a year on the Addington, Jesse, then 18 years old, went back to Montague County and married Docie West, August 30, 1881. She was a second cousin, born in Newton County, Mississippi.

Jesse went on working for the Addington family for about six months after he got married, then saw being a hired hand with a pretty new wife on somebody else's ranch, with nothing but lonesome men around for the most part, and always miles from any town, was not a good idea. He was also smart enough to know there wasn't any way he could become a rancher in the Red River Valley with no more money than he had. Leasing inexpensive Indian Territory land up north was his only path. He had to go north but vowed to return to the Valley some day.

While he was working at the Addington, Jesse learned there was good pastureland available in the Center area at a lease rate he could afford. Gus had learned the same thing the day he rode up to Tishomingo from the ranch where he was working. Jesse signed with a Chickasaw agent and with his bride, Docie, headed for Center. Gus was on his way with Tenny.

When the young Wests and Bobbitts first settled on their leaseholds, there weren't many people around, so they got to know each other, got to know each other's children in a few years, too. Joe West, Jesse's eldest son, was to say Jesse and Gus were "particular friends" in those days.

To understand how their friendship, which had such a strong start, could have ended the way it did takes some looking back. Jesse was a little bit different from the beginning.

R. T. Anderson, sheriff in Montague County for many years, and a proud boyhood "chum" of Jesse's, was later to acknowledge Jesse was a "spirited" youth growing up, and was "the bravest man I ever saw." That's what he told the newspaper out there.

The sheriff would not believe Jesse would ever be guilty of any wrongdoing behind somebody's back. The sheriff agreed Jesse might be difficult to deal with if provoked but he wouldn't do anything sneaky.

"Jesse West was always quick to face any challenge," the Sheriff remembered.

The sheriff's loyalty aside, there was something more than spirit and bravery in Jesse as a young man. That spirit had a cutting edge to it. Ned Warren, a cowboy pioneer, experienced it first hand, an experience vivid enough so he remembered it in detail nearly a half century later.

Mr. Warren, as he was usually called by everyone in his later years, survived to become one of the last of the classic Western cowboys, the kind you see in the movies. He was interviewed at great length in the 1930's by a Federal government writer in a W.P.A. program to preserve first person American history.

Mr. Warren told the W.P.A. writer he first met Jesse West when they were both new hands on the Addington ranch. Ned wasn't even as old as Jesse, but he had already survived a couple of long cattle drives from Texas to the Missouri railheads, back in the days when some of the herds went through Pontotoc County. Warren was young but experienced.

Jesse was pleased with the range he had leased. There was good grass and a couple of creeks that could be impounded when he had the time. What he needed was stock for his ranch.

A few months after the Wests arrived and built their little house, Jesse was able to buy a scrawny herd of about twenty-five head from a sick rancher near

Weatherford, Texas. He then had to get the cattle across the Red River and up to his new place up north here. It wasn't much of a herd, not much of a drive for those days. Most of the herds up from Texas had something like twenty five hundred or three thousand head. One had twenty thousand, so big it had to be divided into three parts.

Small as his new herd was, Jesse still couldn't make the trail by himself. Somebody had to be at the lead, somebody had to ride the flanks. He remembered Ned Warren.

Mr. Warren recalled the herd, besides being small, wasn't much to look at either. The cows were mostly bone and horn. They were alive though, and Jesse could afford them. They were the start of Jesse West's herd.

"My father didn't like for me to go," Mr. Warren told the W.P.A. writer. His father warned him, "Well, if you're bound to go, be careful, for West will kill you if he gets the chance."

"Across the Red River we went through Kiowa, Comanche and Apache reservations because it was too much trouble to go around," Mr. Warren remembered.

"The government had built houses for the Indians, but they didn't live in them. They lived in their teepees. They put grain for their horses in the houses, and put the horses in them, too.

"We finally got to a ranch owned by someone they called 'the Dutchman.' Either the fence he put up was knocked down before we got there, or maybe our herd knocked it down. Anyway, some of our cows were on his property before I could do anything about it.

"The Dutchman had some big dogs and he must have sicced them on our cows. The dogs came racing out at us. Jesse just shot them down.

"Then," Mr. Warren told this writer, "West galloped toward the house, jumped off his horse and banged on the door. We could hear him shouting for the Dutchman to come out.

"The Dutchman wouldn't come out, and we could see West kick the door in. We really don't know what happened in that little house. There weren't any gunshots. We never did hear anything more from the Dutchman.

"I really wasn't afraid of him, " Mr. Warren said of West, "but after that I didn't like to work with him."

Ned Warren wasn't the only pioneer cowboy who remembered Jesse West. When D. N. Doak, another pioneer was interviewed for the W.P.A. program, he said "Andy Pickett was the first man killed in Duncan. He was killed by Jesse West and three others. "

I was told there were few signs of this fierce side of Jesse during the early years on his Center ranch, at least nothing the people in the community could see. Or maybe nobody wanted to cross Jesse. Maybe they kept things to themselves.

The first ranch years were a difficult but rewarding time in Jesse's life. Work was hard and long, but he was his own man, doing work he liked. He became knowledgeable about animal husbandry–improving his stock.

During the years he was starting his own ranch operation, Jesse became convinced Hereford cattle were the best suited for this part of the West, though there's usually enough water in Pontotoc County for European breeds, including Shorthorn and Angus. Herefords just look right, Jesse used to say according to his son Joe, and he was proud as punch when he saw a new "white face" in the herd.

There were troubles beyond hard and long work. A real tragedy struck the family in 1894. Jesse was away, negotiating for more bargain cattle. Docie was home alone with their four children.

The *Ada Weekly News* reported fire broke out in the West's small frame house shortly after a very cold midnight, January 14. It went up like a big bonfire…the whole thing. Docie managed to save all four of the children. She was badly burned in her heroic efforts and died the next day, leaving Jesse to raise the children.

Jesse was a demanding father, but a loving one, the children remembered. At least Joe did. I got to know Joe in later years. They all stayed loyal to him in the tragic days ahead.

You can imagine the domestic routine and the care of four children was not for Jesse. He really needed help. Joe Allen, a friend and neighbor who had also come up from Texas, had the answer.

When Joe Allen crossed the Red River to better his lot in life, he left behind his young sister, Nettie. She was very young–fifteen years younger than Docie, though she had already been married and widowed and was back home.

Joe Allen jumped at this opportunity to be matchmaker and arranged for Jesse to meet his young sister, then Nettie Venable. They had need for each other and were quickly married in 1901, six years after Docie's death.

Nettie had inherited a big job with the West children. She was not a beauty, but she was vigorous and direct and won over all the children. She also had children of her own with Jesse.

With his home life settled again, Jesse turned with new determination to get ahead. He was making progress with his herd, though it seemed like slow going for anyone of Jesse's temperament. Of course there was nothing he could do to speed up the calving cycle, and he didn't have the money to expand the whole process with more cows and more bulls.

One thing he could do though. He proposed to his new brother-in-law, Joe, that they combine their herds and create a bigger operating base. Joe accepted and they were partners in everything from then on.

Progress developing the herd, slow as it was, pleased Jesse though that couldn't make up for the fact the ranch was on leased land. He considered the progress temporary. I'm sure he had a good lease. Everybody else did.

Every week or two newspaper stories in that time would come out saying the national policy guaranteeing the Chickasaws would always own their land as a tribe was going to change. It hadn't changed, though. The future was still unclear to Jesse West and the homestead programs being advertised in Oklahoma Territory across the river sounded better and better.

What a homesteader had to do to acquire the land in his own name was stay on the tract he signed for and "prove it up." Proving it up meant building a house of some sort, living there and working the land, farming or ranching.

From what Joe West told me, Jesse made a couple of exploratory trips into Pottawatomie County, Oklahoma Territory, and decided that would be the next move. The two families, the Wests and Allens, pulled up stakes at Center, packed their wagons and crossed the South Canadian River with their children and small herd. They settled on their homestead land near Violet Springs, an agricultural village close to the river near Lexington.

While homesteading was a step in the right direction, it didn't solve Jesse's other problem–a lack of money. "Money on the hoof," as the expression goes, didn't help in buying equipment, fencing, tools, medicines, or in getting more and better stock. He didn't even have anything to mortgage as a leaseholder, no way to secure a loan.

The money problem was so pressing that Jesse took a job as a clerk in a small store in Violet Springs. That's really something to think about, Jesse West being a store clerk. It was an act of desperation for man with a fuse as short as his. Of course he didn't last long, and he didn't make much money, either. The good thing was that nobody got hurt.

Jesse West should be given credit for doing anything he could, such as being a store clerk, to earn some money honestly. It was hardly surprising the effort failed. He was a vigorous "outdoor man," and he quickly got back to the outdoors. That's when he started combing the countryside for bargain cattle near the Canadian River, and found The Corners.

Gus Bobbitt was a step behind getting his own ranch. He was still on leased land near Center and never did find a way to replace the income he got as a deputy marshal, small as it was.

Whether Gus would really try working in a store like Jesse did, I don't know. I doubt it. He never once expressed any interest in any activity in town except the Masons.

Gus wasn't asleep though. He decided to cover his bets like Jesse West did and started "pioneering," or homesteading, his own section of land in Seminole County. Seminole County is the next county east of Pottawatomie, also in Oklahoma Territory. It was a hedge. He never did figure to live there.

How long it would have taken Gus to prove up the Seminole County section, one square mile of land, was a guess even he wouldn't take seriously. He acknowledged it was no more than a safeguard against the possibility Chickasaws would hold their land in severalty forever, never selling it.

Gus figured he didn't have much to lose, pioneering the Seminole section. His was a one-man operation and he wasn't on the land very long at any time.

As infrequent as his trips north across the river to Seminole County were, it was on one of them he learned Jesse West and Joe Allen, had taken over The Corners. Gus told me when I went up to the river to find him in 1904 how he started working in the saloon, and how he let Jesse run some of his herd on his Seminole pasture.

That arrangement held up for several years, and never with a written agreement. Maybe something in writing would have helped prevent the crisis ahead. Probably not. Reasoning with Jesse would become more and more difficult.

Looking back at Jesse's life you can see he was always on the edge of trouble. Maybe not always of his own doing, like the house fire. Trouble kind of trailed after him.

His marriage to Nettie was going well, though being innkeeper at The Corners was enough to make any man edgy. Angry disputes between the customers, and threats from the saloon down river were just part of the atmosphere, not that he was personally dragged in very often. Jesse West was not one to cross. His reaction was quick and promised danger.

Actually, Jesse West was something like that when he and Sheriff Anderson were boyhood pals back in Montague County, except trouble didn't nettle him as much when he was young. He kind of liked the excitement. That was changing.

What may have pushed Jesse too close to the edge was the death of his thirteen-year-old son, Martin. As I got the story–some of it was in the Oklahoma City newspaper–Martin was shot by Cephus Brunner, an eighteen-year-old "Seminole black" on a dusty road not far from the West home in Violet Springs. It was a late November afternoon in 1901.

Brunner shot Martin once in the stomach with a .38 caliber revolver, for reasons that were never clear to me, and then fled for the hills. He was quickly captured and put on trial. In less than thirty minutes, the jury concluded Brunner was guilty, though he insisted the shooting was accidental. The judge sentenced him to life in prison. He was pardoned two years later.

Getting shot in the stomach is a miserable thing, of course. There was nothing they could do for the hole in Martin's stomach and he suffered a long and painful death. It was a very sad, difficult time for the rest of the West family as well. Martin died the day after Christmas, 1901.

Jesse organized an impressive funeral for Martin in Ada. Naturally the Bobbitts attended. Gus was working with Jesse and the two families had been good friends back in the early days.

After the funeral service, with people standing around in front of the L. T. Walters Funeral Home, talking low and sad, Jesse West said something to Gus about "siding" with Cephus Brunner following his capture.

Gus was dumbfounded by Jesse's comments. He had known Martin as a little tad back in Center and wouldn't be "siding" with anyone who shot him. He also had a son, Bailey, who he thought the world of, about Martin's age. He had no reason to take up Cephus Brunner's cause, and he certainly understood how Jesse felt.

To make it worse, Jesse then came close to charging Gus with stealing his cattle from the Seminole County range, Gus's homestead section. You could understand how that might have come up. The property wasn't fenced. Neither of the homesteaders had money for a major investment like that.

The cattle–West's and Bobbitt's–mingled of course. Nobody was tending the herd on a regular basis. Some of the stock might have strayed off, some might have been stolen. Accounting for missing stock, if any were missing, would be difficult for people who saw the herd no more than they did.

It wasn't just a matter of stock ownership though. What really bothered Gus was the loud way Jesse talked about it in front of all the people at the funeral. He didn't understand the accusations, nor why they were leveled at him so angrily, but he didn't want to argue about it out in the open at Martin's funeral.

Whether the charges made any sense, the bitterness was clear enough to Gus. Knowing Jesse like he did, knowing how bad tempered he had become, Gus was alerted and concerned.

Neither Gus nor Jesse could just walk away from a tattered friendship, however. Jesse needed help at the Corners and needed pasture for his growing herd. Gus, without government pay, needed money for the ranch he hoped to buy. The two old friends went on with the routine, but everybody could see their relationship was very different.

In the coming year, there were times around the saloon Jesse and Gus wouldn't talk to each other directly. They had to talk through Joe Allen. Joe was usually where Jesse was so it wasn't a big problem. It was just odd for two grown up men.

Regulars around the saloon couldn't help but take sides. Most people took up for Gus. They didn't really believe the things Jesse was saying and he was getting more difficult to deal with every day. He was surly much of the time, anger ready to boil up.

Oddly enough, since both Jesse and Gus were at The Corners, the talk stoked older rumors about a feud between regulars at the two different saloons. You'd think war was about to break out along the river. The *Ada Evening News* was certainly concerned, envisioning a "shoot out" on West Main.

Those saloon people wouldn't have to come clear into Ada for a shootout. They could have had it right there along the river. Of course that wouldn't do. They wanted everybody to know about it. Maybe they could get famous. That's the kind of people most of them were, kind of left over from the Old Wild West. Gun play on West Main would suit them fine.

From what Gus told me, these were difficult years for everyone around The Corners, not just for him and Jesse. The only good thing to happen was when McCarthy finally had enough and just walked away from the old Conner's saloon he bought, leaving all the business to The Corners. Even more money came in. Many of the new homesteaders settling in Pontotoc were used to getting whisky if they wanted it. They were ready customers. If bootlegging didn't bother you, The Corners was a real money maker.

Maybe Jesse would have stayed on to make some more money, except that Nettie was determined the family would leave the whisky business behind. Operating The Corners was a very stressful job, as Colonel Mooney made clear in his book, and I suspect Jesse's wife could see the damage being done to Jesse's emotional state. She wanted to go back to Texas and be a proper ranch family–nothing to do with whisky.

I saw Jesse West only the once I told about, and didn't talk to him then, so I can't shed any light on his emotional condition. I don't know if he was some kind of Dr. Jekyll and Mr. Hyde, though there were clearly two sides of him. His two wives and children seemed genuinely devoted to him. Joe Allen was surely a steadfast friend.

There had to be something hidden in Jesse's mental or emotional state to explain his deep antagonism toward Gus. Nothing that deep was apparent to anyone in Ada, though none of Gus's friends ventured up to The Corners very often.

It was early 1906, after years of urging, Nettie finally got Jesse to move back to Texas. That included the Joe Allen family as well. Jesse decided not to fight about the value of what he was leaving behind for Gus Bobbitt and his "gang" to take over, perhaps because of Nettie's worries, which had become intense.

The saloon building itself was worthless except to field mice and barn owls. Nothing had ever been done to it. And it sat on public land. What Jesse was leaving behind was a thriving business.

Most of the West-Allen herd was sold off. They did ship three of their prize Hereford bulls out to the Panhandle, to Canadian, Texas, in Hemphill County. From there they drove the animals to their new ranch on Gageby Creek.

For Jesse West, The Corners saloon days were over. He thought they were, anyway. Joe West, the eldest son, told a reporter for the *Ada Weekly* years later that within months after his Dad and Joe Allen left Pottawatomie County, Gus Bobbitt sent two men out to Hemphill County to kill his father.

"They were suspected," Joe said, and they left Texas. He didn't explain how he knew they were Gus's men. And I don't know why Gus would want to do that anyway.

Jesse never did go back to The Corners. He did come into Ada every once in a while to check on leases and deeds. Joe West also told an *Ada Evening News* reporter his father and Joe Allen were in the Pontotoc County courthouse two years after they left The Corners when "the gang" caught up with them.

"Guns were leveled," Joe stated. "My father and Mr. Allen were only saved by the intervention of impartial Federal officers." That's what the newspaper quoted him as saying, anyway. It was in the May 6, 1909 edition.

I never think of Gus Bobbitt being the worrying sort. To see him in town with his Mason cronies you'd think he didn't have a care in the world. There was always a lot of laughing in any group where Gus was.

I'm sure Gus, happy working on his new ranch, would have liked to put Jesse West and the Corners out of his mind forever, except he was too smart for that. He knew it wasn't over. After his death, Tenny Bobbitt found a notice in his papers he kept at home in a box, that anyone who identified his assassin was entitled to a $1000 reward.

Ambush

Gus Bobbitt's life was turned around by Oklahoma statehood–turned for the better, too. First, he got out of the whisky business. Statewide liquor laws eliminated the very profitable bootleg arrangement for saloons north of the Canadian River.

Second, the end of tribal severalty in the Chickasaw Nation made it legal for Gus to buy the ranch land he dreamed of. The money it took to buy the land came from The Corners profits.

I wasn't in Ada November 16, 1907, when Teddy Roosevelt made Oklahoma a state by proclamation. I still had my brick business in Oklahoma City, though Dwight Livingston kept telling me I would be able to get the Ada brick plant "any time now."

There wasn't a big hurry about it as far as I was concerned, though I still thought it would be a good thing to do. Life was pleasant for us in Oklahoma City and I hadn't really talked seriously with Emma about moving down to Ada. There never seemed to be a right time. *The Daily Oklahoman's* correspondent in Ada always produced another detailed story about somebody being gunned down just when I was thinking of bringing the matter up. Emma doesn't like poor manners, swearing or shooting.

Dwight told me there was a real celebration in Ada when news of the statehood proclamation came through from Washington the morning of the sixteenth. Church bells were rung, those with cars tooted their horns, they even got a Frisco engineer to toot his locomotive whistle. The famous Ada Merchant Band performed on Main Street featuring "Dixie" over and over, though there were more Yankees moving into town all the time.

I don't doubt there were some Chickasaws unhappy about the end of Indian Territory. "Resentful" might be closer to it, resentful that the guarantees President Andrew Jackson gave them for peaceably leaving their homeland in Mississippi never amounted to much, though the monthly allotment the Chickasaws received was more than any other of the Five Civilized Tribes.

All tribal allotments were discontinued during the Civil War because Union authorities were afraid the money would fall into Confederate hands. In addition to that sudden financial blow, the war was particularly difficult for the Chickasaws because the Yankees plundered their Nation from the north, the Confederates from the south.

The Chickasaws did their best to hide harvested crops, feed and livestock. Mostly it didn't work. It's no wonder I never could find one of their famous bred horses.

Rebuilding was slow after the war. When tribal allotments were restored, the Chickasaw allotment was cut way back because, again, Washington believed they had sided with the Confederates. Then came the railroads with so many white settlers the Chickasaws were soon a small minority in their own Nation.

Of the Five Civilized Tribes forced to go west to Indian territory, the Chickasaws were the last to go, except for a few bands of Seminoles rounded up in Florida later. Some of the Chickasaw mixed bloods had become very successful cotton growers in Mississippi by 1837 and were shrewd businessmen. They became shrewd negotiators with Federal officials organizing the Chickasaw's forced removal, and arranged for the higher tribal annuity.

Getting more money from the government isn't usually considered a problem, though it was for the Chickasaws. Compared to the other Five Civilized Tribes, the Chickasaws were well off. They didn't have a struggle to survive. The annuity cushion–which wasn't very much really, but nobody ever gave the tribe anything before–plus uncertainty in the earliest days dealing with the Choctaws over what was to become the Chickasaw Nation slowed transition to their new prairie home.

Having more money than other tribes was a mixed blessing in other ways, as well. The Chickasaws became prime targets for whisky dealers up and down the Red River Valley before the Civil War. The bootleggers even had small, shallow-draft whisky steam boats to serve the market–the Chickasaws and the tribal nations north of them.

Despite these problems, many of the tribesmen, especially the mixed bloods, adapted easily and did well in Indian Territory. Coming of statehood didn't make much difference in their lives. "Mixed blood" and "full blood" are terms the Chickasaws use in a very matter-of-fact way. It was all right to be either one.

The long awaited–or for the Indians, the objectionable–land allotment program had gone well starting in 1903. Officials in charge of the program thought it did anyway. Each tribal family head received one hundred sixty acres of homestead land, which they could never sell.

In addition to the untouchable homestead land, they were given additional acreage for farming or ranching, which they could sell. The average total allotment made in 1903 was three hundred twenty acres, bigger–up to six hundred and forty acres–if much of the land was rough, less if it included prime bottomland.

Dividing up tribal land was against all the things the Indians believed in, but the Chickasaws went through it calmly enough, long since resigned, I think. I guess it made Senator Dawes of Massachusetts happy, anyway. As the Senator saw it, the Chickasaws, now with private property, would be real Americans.

Chickasaw farmers might well have been satisfied with three hundred or so acres. What Chickasaw hunters thought about having three hundred acres was another story. Three hundred acres would be big farm, but to a hunter, three hundred acres would be more like a backyard.

By statehood, Indian schools which the Chickasaws were promised, had long since been replaced, or largely so, by white schools, like the Sacred Heart Mission north of Stonewall. Chickasaw Indian Police had become less and less useful because they couldn't deal with the invasion of immigrants–couldn't touch most of the newcomers no matter what they did.

Many Chickasaws thought they, and everybody else, would be better off with one effective police force, even if it wasn't their own. Lawlessness was a big problem for everybody. Gus reminded me Christian Harding felt that way and said so the rainy night we all met.

Some bootleggers along the Canadian were no doubt sorry to see the end of their bonanza with statehood, as difficult a life as it might have been. Gus wasn't one of them. He was happy to get out the business. Tenny was even happier to have it end with her husband intact.

Whatever Tenny thought about the years Gus put in at The Corners, that's where he made enough money between the time Jesse West and Joe Allen left for Texas, and Oklahoma statehood, to buy the ranch land he had in his sights for years. The ranch, Lightnin' Ridge, was about seven miles southwest of Ada.

The morning Gus and I drove up to Ada from Christian Harding's place we passed right by it. It was just open country then. No houses, barns or fences. Grass three feet high. Nice rolling country. I could see why Gus thought it was perfect, though I never did want a ranch anywhere. If someone was to give me a ranch though, that would be a good one, just so I didn't have to tend the cattle.

Lightnin' Ridge was close enough to town so Gus could get in, maybe a couple of times a week. He sure liked working on his new ranch, but he still liked hobnobbing with people in town as well. Tenny came in with him maybe once a month. Stayed over with her church friends until Gus's next trip when he brought a buggy.

One reason Gus could be away so much was that he had Bob Ferguson working for him. Bob had a little piece of property not far from Lightnin' Ridge and he built a small frame house on it. More of a shack, really. Whatever it was, it suited Bob, and he got over to Lightnin Ridge before sunup during the winter months, working away before Gus had breakfast.

Bob was the slow, methodical kind. Didn't say a lot but you could count on what he did say. He always wore about the biggest hat I ever saw, pulled way down, summer or winter. All you ever saw looking at him coming toward you was hat and mustache, the big droopy kind of mustache.

Gus more than liked Bob. He trusted him all the way. He'd just ride off from Lightnin' Ridge and holler at Bob when he thought he might be back. Bob was in charge–except for Tenny, of course. She didn't say much about the stock, or putting up alfalfa, things like that, but when something happened to put her off, everyone knew it.

I had seen Gus a couple of times in town after he got out of the saloon business and started ranching. After years of fretting over it, I had made up my mind to go ahead and sell my brick plant in Oklahoma City and buy old man Potter's plant in Ada as soon as I could. So I was in Ada every two or three weeks, getting my plans laid out. Often as not, I'd bump into Gus somewhere, on Main, in the bank or maybe the Broadway Café.

Dwight told me Potter talked about leaving all the time–going back to Ohio where his daughter lived. Whenever he mentioned to him he had buyer waiting, that seemed to make Potter want to stay. He couldn't make the decision to give up the business he started, Dwight said. It was getting awkward between me and the old man.

I can understand how Mr. Potter felt. I didn't actually start my business in Oklahoma City, but I sure built it up, hours and hours, seven days a week except for church Sunday morning. It's hard to just walk away from something you've put so much effort and time into.

Mr. Potter made good enough bricks. If you've got good clay, it isn't that hard. What he didn't know was how to sell the bricks, or even let people know he had them for sale. He'd sell you a load if you came and asked him for a load. He just sat there.

So I called on Jake Potter every month or two to "compare notes." He was a great coffee drinker and we spent hours in the Broadway Café drinking coffee and talking. I can't say I learned much, except what one Yankee thought about the War Between the States. The Civil War he called it.

The Broadway Café was a good place for me to meet businessmen and to catch Gus when he came in from the country, so I didn't mind sitting there too much. With Gus in town, Bob Ferguson was usually back at Lightnin' Ridge, so I didn't get to know him until later.

When I moved to Ada and got to know Bob, he was willing to tell me the whole story of Saturday, February 27, 1909. It was certainly the worst thing that ever happened in his life. He hadn't forgotten a detail. He even remembered colors of the sunset.

This is his story as I remember from our talks off and on through the years. Bob never did talk much at any one time, so I got the story piecemeal:

To start at the beginning, Bob said Gus had decided they would take two wagons into town–his and Gus's–and get cotton seed meal for the herd. Bob knew it would take all day, not just because both teams were used to the slow, steady pace pulling the alfalfa mower or rake. Mostly it was because Gus always had to palaver with his Mason friends at the Broadway Café at noon, and then make his political rounds in the courthouse before they could leave.

Bob was quick to say he didn't really mind having to wait for Gus. Once in town, he'd go about his business, on this trip getting the wagons full of cottonseed meal. With the wagons loaded and the horses watered, then he'd just mosey along Main Street, mixing in with all the farm and Indian families making their rounds of the stores, the usual Saturday routine. That's about as much socializing as Bob ever did, though he did go along with some of the ranchers on hunting trips in the Kiamichis to cook for them.

Bob remembered this was a perfect day for February–bright sun, not much wind, a day that brought everyone who was not laid up into town. The Ada Browns baseball season hadn't started so the only sporting event was the horse racing down Main, from the Frisco tracks to Broadway, and that went peaceable enough, Bob said. There was the usual hollering and gunshots in the air. Nothing unfriendly.

"Warn't never in a hurry to get back to the country," Bob acknowledged, "but I knew Miz Bobbitt was a big worrier and come nightfall, if Mr. Gus warn't home, she was fretful. Mr. Gus was always tellin' her thar's no reason to worry…same time he bought one of them lightweight Winchesters and had it under the wagon seat, full loaded."

It was well after three Saturday afternoon before Bob saw Gus striding down Rennie Street toward the Southern Cotton Gin. That's where they always linked up. Bob had parked the wagons one behind the other, headed toward Main, where they'd turn right and then cross the Frisco tracks on the way home. The sun was still bright, but a little breeze from the north had an edge to it.

"Howdy, Mr. Gus," Bob said when he came up. "We best get a move on. Miz Bobbitt will soon start a' worryin' and she'll blame me for bein' late."

"No she won't, Bob. She knows better," Gus answered back, cheerful like always. He untied the reins for his team from the wagon brake, looked under the driver's bench to check on his rifle, jumped up on the bench, flapped the reins, cried 'gee haw!' and we started back to Lightnin' Ridge."

There were some other farm wagons on the road at first, all headed out of town. Then, about five miles out, they were pretty much alone, Bob said. "The sun was still up but the shadows were gettin' long."

"Maybe a mile and a half from the ranch there was a lone rider up ahead of us…too far to tell anything 'bout him," Bob remembered. "Anyway, he wheeled his horse and went on, fast out of sight.

"I was some been forty or fifty yards back of Mr. Gus most of the trip, but we were gettin' close to home now–less than half mile–and I began movin' up. The sun jus' sunk under the horizon but there was still plenty of light, all kind of reddish."

As Bob described it, ahead of them on the left hand side of the road was a clump of brush with a big elm tree growing out of the middle, a couple of saplings sprung up around the trunk. The ranch house wasn't yet in sight. That was just around the bend. Gus was going by the elm tree.

"Two flashes of light came out of them bushes," Bob said, and then two explosions.

"Everything was so quiet on the prairie, and I was so close behind Mr. Gus by then, it sounded like a cannon goin' off."

Bob said he can't ever forget how Mr. Gus cried out, "Oh Lord!" then fell off the driver's bench into the dirt on the side of the road. His team bolted and galloped off down the road, pulling the wagon, heavy as it was.

"Mr. Gus was layin' in a heap, not movin', groanin' n'er anything. I knew he was either dead or hurt real bad, but I didn't dare pull my team up, or go up to help him…I'da been 'bout fifteen feet from the bushes where the shots came from. Whoever shot Mr. Gus would have an easy time of it shootin' me too.

"I locked the wagon brake, held tight to the reins–the team was skitterish and 'bout to run off. I climbed down with the wagon 'tween me and the bushes. I couldn't figure out what to do. I wanted to help Mr. Gus, but there warn't much use both of us layin' there in the dirt, dead.

"Maybe two or three minutes went by–it seemed like an hour–this rider came out from behind the bushes. He didn't have a 'kerchief up, no mask–nothin' over his face. Had one of those foreign hats on…wearin' ordinary town clothes, not ranch clothes.

"He walked his horse over to where Mr. Gus was layin' and looked down at him. He had a shotgun or somethin' jus' like it in a long white cover. I thought he was goin' to shoot Mr. Gus again. He didn't. Instead he turned his horse and headed back down the road toward town.

"Everything was kind of reddish, but there was still enough light for me to get a good look at this bushwacker with the shotgun. He rode right by me on the other side of the wagon. I never laid eyes on 'im before, anywhere. Course I'd never forget 'im after."

Bob said once the rider got by the wagon, he put his horse in an easy canter down the road. Soon he was gone.

With the rider out of sight, Bob ran up to where Gus was lying. Bob said he could see even in that light there was blood all over Gus' clothes along the left side. "His face was all right, though.

"Mr. Gus? I said, leanin' down over him. He opened his eyes. Then he said so quiet I could hardly hear him, 'you better go tell Tenny.'"

"I will, I said, and then added on, because I thought he would sure want to know, I saw the man that shot you. Don't think he's from around here. Never saw him before.

"Mr. Gus was havin' trouble gettin' words out but I heard him say, 'never saw him before either…I just lay still so he wouldn't shoot me again. Hurry…'"

Bob ran back to his wagon and galloped the team down to the ranch house, no more than an eighth of a mile. "It was gettin' dark," Bob said, "but I could make out Miz Bobbitt standin' just outside the front door. She would have heard the shots.

"Mr. Gus got shot! I called, getting the team stopped in front of the house. I think he'll be all right! I talked to him. Com'on up here. We'll go back!

"We galloped back down the road, the wagon lurchin' this way and that but stayin' on the wheels. Miz Bobbitt hung on to the wagon bench hard. In a couple of minutes we could see a mound on the side of the road. I yanked the team to a stop and Miz Bobbitt jumped down to the ground and hurried over to Mr. Gus.

"I unhitched one of the horses, jumped on and called to Miz Bobbitt that I was goin' to ride into Fitzhugh, tell Doc Sutherland to come right away and telephone the sheriff. And that's what I did.

"By the time I got back there wasn't any daylight at all but the moon was risin' and there was silvery light, enough for me to see both Mr. Gus and Miz Bobbitt huddled together on the side of the road. Miz Bobbitt was on her knees leanin' back a little. Mr. Gus's head was in her lap.

"Doc Sutherland said he'd git here as fast as he can, Miz Bobbitt," I told her when I got down from that tired plough horse.

"In a low mournful voice, Miz Bobbitt said, 'It's too late...Gus is dead.'

"I didn't know what to say and I just stood there, I guess," Bob admitted. "I remember how quiet it was and how empty the prairie seemed. No lights, nothin' moved.

"Miz Bobbitt," Bob finally got out. "I'll go get the team back together and we'll take Mr. Gus home.

"I drove the wagon over close to Mr. Gus, then pulled him up on top of the load of feed. Miz Bobbitt climbed back on the wagon bench and we slowly headed for the ranch house.

"I stopped the team by the house, went around to get Mr. Gus off the wagon. I dragged him over to the front door. Miz Bobbitt held the door open and said, 'Put him on the sofa.'

"There was so much blood on Mr. Gus's clothes I must have hesitated," Bob recalled.

"'Over there, Bob,' Miz Bobbitt told me, pointing to the sofa. So that's where I put him. Miz Bobbitt seemed like she was in a trance and just stood there lookin' at Mr. Gus. No tears left, I guess, but I never saw anything so sad and mournful."

Bob remembered he tried hard to find the right words to tell her how sorry he was, but nothing came. Finally he said in his slow, respectful way, "We don't know who did this, Miz Bobbitt. We don't know they ain't out there now. We should draw the curtains…not stand near the window 'til the sheriff comes.

" Don't you worry, Miz Bobbitt. There'll be justice… as certain as I'm standin' here. There'll be justice."

Photograph courtesy: Denzil. F. Lowry Family/Oklahoma State Bank, Ada.

Cotton harvest was a busy time in early Pontotoc County. Farmers brought wagons loaded with "seed cotton" to the gins in Ada starting at dawn. Then, with "cotton checks" in their pockets, they would return to the Main Street stores. There were no traffic or parking ordinances, as the picture taken in 1903, suggests.

Photograph courtesy: The History & Genealogical Society of Pontotoc County.

The St. Louis and San Francisco Railroad–the Frisco–reached Ada in 1900, the first to arrive. Shown above is a Frisco 4–4-2 Baldwin locomotive at the Ada station with one passenger car and two freight cars. Cattle cars were usually part of the train mix.

Photograph courtesy: The Museum of the Great Plains

When the Five Civilized Tribes were forced to leave their ancestral homeland east of the Mississippi River for Indian Territory, they were assured of having their own police force. Three of their Indian Police officers–originally called Light Horse Police–are shown above.

Photograph courtesy: The Historical & Genealogical Society of Pontotoc County

Four Texans were hanged in the early hours of April 19, 1909 in a dilapidated barn near the Frisco depot in Ada. Between thirty and forty citizens from Ada and the surrounding countryside, including many community leaders, were thought to be guilty of the crime.

Photogragh courtesy: The History & Genealogical Society of Pontotoc County
Augustus O. Bobbitt–"Gus"–and Tennessee Standfield–"Tenny"–were neighbors in the Sherman, Texas, farming area before they were married. The picture above was taken on their wedding day.

Photograph courtesy: Denzil F. Lowry Family/Oklahoma State Bank, Ada.

Bob Ferguson, left, was Gus Bobbitt's loyal ranch hand. Above right, Gus Bobbit is shown prepared for his Masonic duties.

Photograph courtesy: The History & Genealogical Society of Pontotoc County.

Tribal ownership of land in Indian Territory ended with Oklahoma statehood in 1907. Settlers and newly arrived ranchers could then buy land–if they had the money. Gus Bobbitt made enough money to buy the ranch he dreamed of. He called it "Lightnin' Ridge," seven miles southwest of Ada. Shown is the original ranch house

Photograph courtesy: Margaret Harris Swatek

John Harris arrived in Indian Territory in 1888 when he was twenty two years old. The picture, left, was taken in Oklahoma City soon after. He had already been a Texas cowboy and a snuff salesman in Virginia.

Photogrpah by Phillip M. Swatek

John Harris started manufacturing bricks in Oklahoma City not long after his arrival in Indian Territory. He moved his business to Ada to be part of the future of Pontotoc County. He is shown here at the Ada Brick Plant in 1954.

Photograph courtesy: Mrs. Karen West Scott

Jesse West, above, was one of many young Texans who started their ranching careers on leased land in Indian Territory. He moved his family to Oklahoma Territory after passage of the Organic Act of 1890 to homestead. He then became owner of the Corners saloon.

Photograph courtesy: Bill James

Jim Miller met Sally Clements, shown here with Jim, when he went to work as a hired hand on her father's ranch in McCulloch County, Texas. They were married soon after Miller left the Clements' ranch and became a deputy sheriff in Pecos City, Reeves County, Texas. Miller was a devoted husband.

Photograph Courtesy: The Western History Collection, University of Oklahoma.

Jim Miller was highly thought of in his first two years as a deputy sheriff in Reeves County. Townsmen were impressed with the fearless way he handled hardened troublemakers, though he was only twenty four years old.

Photograph courtesy: Bill James

Jim Miller had aspirations far beyond being a gunman and assassin. His goal was joining mid-level entrepreneurial ranks in Fort Worth as a cattle buyer and real estate broker. He is shown here, in 1904, suited up for the role.

Photograph courtesy: Denzil F. Lowry Family/Oklahoma State Bank, Ada.

Robert Wimbish, above left, seven years out of law school in Texas, was elected Pontotoc's first county attorney in 1907. He came to Ada in 1903. The picture above right shows Wimbish many years after the lynching tragedy. He became a highly respected community leader. "Judge Bob," died in 1950.

Photograph courtesy: Denzil F. Lowry Family/Oklahoma State Bank, Ada.

Joe Deckert, above left, was owner of the O.K. grocery store in Ada in Indian Territory days, though he looked more like a cowboy on occasion. Many Ada businessmen also had small ranch operations. A number of newly arrived businessmen, such as the young banker shown above right, preferred bicycles to horses for getting around town.

Photograph courtesy: The History & Genealogical Society of Pontotoc County.

U. S. deputy marshals were the only effective law enforcement officers in early Indian Territory. Indian police were not permitted to deal with non-residents–white settlers mostly. City marshals appeared later. Bob Nester, shown above, was one of the first deputy marshals in Pontotoc County.

Photograph courtesy: Denzil F. Lowry Family/Oklahoma State Bank, Ada

Merchants of Ada's Twelfth Street, above, were determined to supplant Main Street as the town's commercial center before statehood with this impressive array of two story buildings. Twelfth Street was the first Ada street to be paved, the first to have electric lights. The pedestrian shown on the street lost his leg in the War Between the States.

Photograph courtesy: Denzil F. Lowry Family/Oklahoma State Bank, Ada.

Ada's first post officewas in the small store of Pioneer Jeff Reed. Ada's first regular post office in "Old Town." Mule teams pulled it up to Main Street in the middle of the night.

Photograph courtesy: Denzil F. Lowry Family/Oklahoma State Bank, Ada.

Having a hotel was a matter of pride for any town in Pontotoc County in the 1880's and '90's, but a hotel of two stories, such as this one on Ada's Main Street, was particularly notable. Early travelers in the county had to be prepared to sleep under the stars.

Photograph courtesy: Denzil F. Lowry Family/Oklahoma State Bank, Ada.

Flow from Byrds Mill Spring was dammed in 1869 to create a small lake or pond and a mill race. The area was a favorite picnic site for Adans until the 1930's. The area is now fenced off for security reasons.

An Early Break in the Case

Gus Bobbitt's assassination happened too late for our newspaper in Oklahoma City to get anything into print Sunday and the *Ada Evening News* didn't have a Sunday edition. So I didn't know anything about the murder until I read an Associated Press dispatch from Ada on Monday. We didn't have radio news then.

The AP stringer sure got the feeling of community outrage in his dispatch, though there wasn't a word about who did it, or who was suspected–nothing. I don't fault him for that. Nobody in Ada had any solid knowledge about the killer when he was writing Sunday. He did know, however, a tracking party had been at work since sunup.

I knew without reading it in the paper Ada would be in an uproar with another ambush murder. Zeke Putnam, the town marshal in Allen, sixteen miles northeast of Ada near the Canadian River, got gunned down from ambush in January, and most of the community leaders had been yammering at the sheriff to do something since then.

You can't really blame the people. The new year was starting out with the same kind of violence that had plagued Ada for years. It's bothersome to live in a town with a bad reputation. It's also worrisome for someone thinking about moving his family to such a town. People talk about property values being affected by a community's reputation, but nearly as important, people like to be proud of where they live.

Ada's reputation, already bad, was getting worse, and not just with my wife. Politicians up in the legislature were saying a teachers' college was obviously needed in the south, in old Indian Territory. There was no doubt about that. Ada wouldn't be the place however–too dangerous. Of course they wanted the college in their own town. Atoka or Ardmore would've been mighty pleased to get the college.

I had been talking to Dwight about how Ada's future might be stunted if everyone in the whole state came to believe the town was lawless and dangerous. It would have to effect growth, and that would matter to me and a new brick business.

As strong a promoter of Ada as Dwight was, he never sugar coated the problem. He would agree there was a big job to do and then say—"We got some public officials with regular state government who are going to come forward and meet this head on."

"They're really going to make big medicine, eh?" I asked. Maybe it sounded like sarcasm.

"John, I know you are needling me, and I know you are concerned," Dwight would say. "You have every right to be concerned, to approach such a big change in your life with caution. And I sense from what you say, your wife is happy where she is.

"You haven't met Bob Wimbish, the county attorney yet, have you? He's going to make a difference. He's young, smart as a whip and believes it's a critical part of a county attorney's job to fight lawlessness, critical for the county attorney to be involved personally, not just wait for the sheriff to act.

"John. He thinks just like we do. He thinks Ada is already in trouble, and it will get worse unless we act. Bob wants more than just to be Pontotoc County's first attorney. He wants to be the best one, the one who set the standards. I believe he will do that."

It was true I hadn't met Bob Wimbish yet. I had heard good things. You know how that is. Hearing good things is fine. The fact of the matter is nothing much had changed, and now one of my Ada friends, a well-known citizen, was murdered.

All this was running through my head that Monday morning. I was half sad, half mad. My final decision to move to Ada wasn't so final anymore. I decided to use my new telephone at the office, call Dwight and ask him what he thought about the future now. The bank had a telephone of course.

"Well, John," he said when the operators finally got us connected, "I'll be direct with you. People are very upset. Gus Bobbitt was a popular figure. His wife has just as many friends as he did. People are demanding Sheriff Smith do something or resign. There are calls for vigilante action, but, we don't know for sure who we're lookin' for."

I caught that "for sure" and asked what he meant by that.

"John, I can't say any more. All I can tell you is there is some progress. It's not as hopeless as most people think, including the newspaper people.

"I don't want you to be discouraged about Ada," he added. "I think Jake Potter is finally ready to go back to Ohio.

"The funeral is Thursday. I know you and Mr. Bobbitt were friends. You'll want to go to the funeral. Why don't you come down Wednesday? We can talk about settling on the brick plant, I think. Maybe there'll be more to say about the Bobbitt tragedy by then."

I had no idea what Dwight was driving at. I did know him well enough by then to believe it must be important. He knew just about everybody in town–well, all the business people. He never did talk about being a friend of the sheriff's, so I guessed he was getting information from somewhere else. After Dwight told me all the wonderful things the county attorney was going to do, Bob Wimbish would be a good guess.

Gus Bobbitt's assassination Saturday night was the big story for the *News* on Monday as you might expect. It was their first edition after the murder. They had time to straighten out some of the things the *Oklahoman's* correspondent wired in Sunday, such as talking to Sheriff Tom Smith about how he was going to track the killer. Sheriff Smith was in Ardmore for his father's funeral when Gus was killed and didn't get back to Ada until Monday. He didn't know anything about the murder Sunday.

What the editors lacked in real information, they tried to make up for in a big, dramatic headline Monday, March 1, 1909:

GUS BOBBITT, PROMINENT CITIZEN, ASSASSINATED

Former Bad Man Hunter and Alround Vigorous Western Character Meets Death While Performing the Labors of Quiet Modest Farmer

This Rugged Character of the West, Feared and Hated by Many Bad Men,if not by a Few Honest Men

As Gentle and Regardful as a Woman Among his Friends and Loved Ones.

The story with the headline had the time and place of the ambush right, and the fact that George Culver, Ada city police chief, led a tracking party all day Sunday. The absence of Sheriff Tom Smith was noted as the reason the city police chief was working out of his jurisdiction.

The sheriff's chief deputy, Ben Snow, was part of the tracking party. He would become a good friend in the years ahead, and it was from him I got the real story of that "tracking party." It wasn't exactly the miracle it appeared to be.

News editors were fair enough to mention the fact that Sheriff Smith was attending his father's funeral in Ardmore, though references to the sheriff would become hostile. The editors' admiration for Chief Culver, on the other hand, would become increasingly clear. The chief did do a good job during the community crisis.

People who can track a horse would find the first part of the trail easy enough, out on to the road from behind the bushes, by the spot where Gus had fallen off the wagon, by the wagon where Bob Ferguson was, and then down the road toward town. A number of men, already calling for a vigilante force, did start tracking that Monday afternoon after the story came out. They didn't get far when the shoe marks on the road petered out–just went off into the grass.

Sid Higgins was the other sheriff's deputy in the search party that started out Sunday morning. He was already out at the ranch. Bob Ferguson and, I later found out, Christian Harding, were the other trackers. Chief Culver wanted at least five men, not knowing what they might get into if they found the assassin. Bob Ferguson said he saw only one killer. There might be others riding with him.

News reporters had their hands full Monday covering the assassination Saturday night and then the search Sunday. Of course they wanted Chief Culver to tell them what progress he and his posse made Sunday trying to find the killer.

Reporters claimed "everybody" in town seemed to know the trackers found a pair of wire cutters near a new-cut, barbwire fence on Old Stonewall Road Sunday. And most people knew, they said, the trackers weren't just wandering around, that they seemed to have direction, basically north from the ambush site. Why couldn't Culver tell the straight of it?

Chief Culver acknowledged they had found a pair of wire cutters, but declared he couldn't say anything more until Sheriff Smith got back in town later in the day. The sheriff would be in charge of the investigation, he explained.

I heard later a number of people, starting with the newsmen, were unhappy with the police chief for not saying more about what he had done, but Culver wouldn't budge. All the disgruntled citizens could do was try to guess where the assassin might have gone from where they found the wire cutters–a near hopeless exercise. Discovery of the cutters did, however, confirm that the assassin traveled north from the Bobbitt ranch and went through the pastures, crossing roads and cultivated fields only when he had to.

Even in winter, grass in our pastures can be two or three feet high in the bottom lands. It's kind of a golden wheat color, not green, but still thick. A couple of minutes after a horse travels through, any trampled grass would go back the way it was, or so close to it there wouldn't be anything to notice. Hooves wouldn't get down to the soil to make a print.

Tracking a horse from Lightnin' Ridge, east around Ada and then north to Jim Williamson's farm where the trail ended–it might have been twenty or thirty miles–would have been close to impossible, even if the greatest Indian tracker in the world was helping. Finding the wire cutters would be a small piece of a very large puzzle.

The sheriff got back to Ada on Monday afternoon and was briefed by Chief Culver and Ben Snow. The next day, the *News* carried a report that a horse had in fact been tracked from the spot where Gus Bobbitt was killed, all the way to a small farm in northeast Pontotoc County, a farm belonging to Jim Williamson. No mention was made of how remarkable a feat this was. However, more critical, the story did break the news that Williamson was a nephew of Jim Miller, a well-known Texas gunman and assassin for hire.

The young farmer had acknowledged to the lawmen that it was his horse they tracked and that his uncle had borrowed it. With nothing more to go on, the *News* headline demanded to know, "Where is Jim Miller?"

Developments were coming so fast those first few days, none of the newspaper people followed up on how it was possible for the lawmen to track that far, from Gus Bobbitt's ranch to Jim Williamson's farm, and do it so fast. Well, in just one day. You'd just have to know there was something missing in the story. There was.

Missing was any mention of a routine telephone call made to the sheriff's office Saturday morning, February 27, the day of the assassination. The call was made by Peter Tompkins, owner of Tompkins Livery on Johnston Street. Tompkins, and other livery service operators, hotel men, railroad people and hardware store owners–merchants stocking guns and ammunition–participated in the sheriff's "alert" program. Those in the program were asked to tell the sheriff if they picked up any information about the comings or goings of individuals law enforcement officers would be concerned with, men pictured on the Post Office wall for example. The sheriff called it a community service.

Jim Miller's picture wasn't on the Post Office wall. He was free on bail, after a grand jury in Johnston County, south of Ada, indicted him for murder of Ben Collins three years before. When Jim Miller was in their jurisdiction, southwestern lawmen, and particularly those in Oklahoma, came to full alert.

Deputy Sid Higgins took Tompkins' telephone call Saturday morning. The message to the sheriff, as Sid interpreted it, was: "Your Texas friend paid his bill, saddled up and left a half hour ago. Said he wasn't coming back."

With the sheriff on his way to Ardmore, Ben Snow was in charge of the office. Sid got up from his desk and put the carefully penciled message in front of him. Ben read the message twice, frowned, and said:

"Sid– What is this 'Texas friend' you got here? Doesn't he have a name? I can guess who it is, but I doubt the sheriff would want to guess. You're not saying Tompkins didn't know the name are you?"

"Well, Tompkins never would say it. He said I'd know who that was from the Ben Collins case. I asked him if he meant Jim Miller. Tompkins wouldn't say 'no,' so I guess he meant yes. He's a very cautious man, that Peter Tompkins."

"Sid. That's really curious. How about goin' back up to Tompkins' place. Tell him how much the sheriff appreciates his help. Ask him if he can remember anything else about the 'Texas friend' riding off…"

"I'll do it if that's what you want, Ben. Anyway, I'll try. Tompkins isn't much for talking any time, and he seems nervous about this. Maybe he had some kind of fuss with Miller this morning."

"Good, Sid. Ask him how the 'Texas friend' could just pay his livery stable bill, say he wasn't coming back, and ride off? Who owned the horse he wasn't bringing back, since he got here on the train Thursday. Ask if he had any equipment to stay out the night. Maybe he'll tell his name, too. "

When Sid got to Tompkins' office, a little square room in front of the stalls and hay loft–telephone, adding machine and a spindle full of receipts on a battered desk–Tompkins said there wasn't much more to tell about the "Texas friend," though he was willing to answer any questions he could. Sid reported to Ben that Tompkins never would say Jim Miller was the 'Texas friend'.

"Didn't seem to bother him when I called him 'Miller', though," Sid reported.

Sid then told Tompkins the sheriff had been advised by Ardmore police Thursday that Miller got on a train headed toward Ada. So he didn't have his own horse.

"Do you happen to know, Mr. Tompkins, whose horse Miller had Saturday morning, if he wasn't coming back?"

Tompkins then surprised Sid by saying he did remember the horse and the worn old saddle gear from last summer when Jim Williamson brought the mare in to be shod. Tompkins had known Williamson since he was a little kid, had known his father for years. Jim Williamson wasn't just another customer.

"Well, Williamson wouldn't stable his horse in Ada, would he? How did Miller get the horse?"

"Easy enough, I 'spose," Tompkins replied. "He took one of my horses out to a ranch near Allen Friday morning, then went over to Jim's farm–not far–got the mare and led her back here late. Said he needed to get up to Pottawatomie Saturday afternoon. Then he'd get back to Jim's farm late with his horse. Jim was to drive him over to Sasakwa the next morning, Sunday, to catch the Santa Fe. That's how come he had the mare Saturday morning. Anyway, that's what he said."

Tompkins' report, rewritten by Ben, was important in the sheriff's office because it involved Jim Miller, but it was nothing calling for action. There was nothing wrong with Miller being in Ada, or using his nephew's horse. Ben's report for the sheriff did underline Miller's name.

Out on the road near Lightnin' Ridge Saturday night, maybe three and a half hours after the assassination and Bob Ferguson's urgent telephone call for help from Fitzhugh, lawmen tried in a slow almost gentle way—each taking a turn nudging Bob along—to get the last detail of what the ranch hand could remember about the shooting, hoping it would provide some kind of lead.

There wasn't any doubt in Bob's mind he clearly saw the man with the gun. Something of a problem was Bob's ability to put into words exactly what he saw, to describe what the man looked like–age, features, even the color of his skin, though Bob was sure he wasn't an Indian.

After ten minutes, the lawmen stopped questioning Bob. It wasn't really a waste of time. They could be reasonably sure the assassin didn't live in Pontotoc County if Bob had never seen him before. Tracking the gunman seemed to be the only hope they had. And that couldn't be done in the dark.

Ben proposed getting Christian Harding to help, since he was not only a friend of Gus Bobbitt's, he was known all over the county for his tracking skill. Chief Culver immediately agreed and asked Ben to try and get word to Harding when they got back to town.

Ben did that by getting Bud Muller, the Frisco assistant station agent in Ada, to wire his agent in Roff and ask him to send someone out to Harding's farm at once, and tell him Gus Bobbitt had been murdered and that he was needed. The big Chickasaw got the message and rode up from Roff in the night and joined the search party at dawn.

Sid Higgins agreed to stay the night at the Bobbitt ranch with Bob Ferguson in case the assassin returned, perhaps with gang members. Ben and the police chief had a solemn ride back to Ada.

Before either of them could see the faintest glow in the night sky from the new streetlights on Twelfth Street, Ben said to the police chief trotting beside him, "Chief. I've got something to tell you...you're in charge of the investigation until the sheriff gets back. That may be late tomorrow or even Tuesday. I don't know how fast I can get a hold of him down there. The family lives out in the country east of Ardmore."

"Yeah, Ben. What is it?"

"I got to say first, Chief, the sheriff is very touchy about this kind of situation. He's bein' criticized all the time by the county commissioners, even the mayor, and the newspaper for how he's doin' the job. All of 'em want arrests and convictions right away. No excuses. Like in the Zeke Putnam case. They've been hammerin' at him for weeks.

"When we get information in the office, the sheriff wants it right away. And he doesn't want it to get out of the office until he announces it.

"We got some information in the office this morning when the sheriff was on the train goin' down to Ardmore that might, or at least it could, help us in the this case. We don't have anything else to go on, and I figure we don't have any time to lose.

"I didn't say anything about it when I talked to you early this evenin' after Bob Ferguson called the sheriff, or just now out at the ranch, because I thought, maybe hoped, we would get some better idea of what we had to do, maybe even get the name of the killer from Bob. That didn't happen. Now we've got nothin' I can see, except that tracking might turn something up.

"What I have may be nothin', too. At least there's a chance. I ask you to be mindful of how the sheriff feels, that's all. I know we got no time to lose. Every hour makes it tougher to track somebody."

"Ben," the chief replied, "I know exactly how the sheriff feels. And I know how you feel, too. You're tryin' to be loyal. I'll treat the matter with care. Now go ahead."

Ben said he didn't want to leave anything out, so he told everything he knew about the case starting mid-morning Thursday, February 25, two days before the assassination. The sheriff was in the office.

Buck Garrett, chief of police in Ardmore, a boyhood pal of the sheriff's, called on the telephone that morning to tell his old friend that Jim Miller was headed his way.

Chief Garrett didn't say he knew Miller was coming to Ada, only that he was traveling north. Miller had been seen by one of his officers coming out of Mrs. Wilson's boarding house, where he stays when he is in Ardmore. The officer tailed Miller to the train depot, where Miller bought a ticket and sat down to wait. There was only a north-bound train due.

When the train pulled in and Miller got aboard, the officer went to the ticket window and found Miller bought a ticket all the way to Muskogee. Chief Garrett told Sheriff Smith that didn't mean Miller couldn't get off in Pauls Valley and come over to Ada. He ought to be alert.

Chief Garrett knew Sheriff Smith was getting a lot of criticism and he wanted to help him in his job if he could. It was also a courtesy lawmen showed to one another when the most notorious gunman in the Southwest was moving around.

Jim Miller had been indicted for the ambush murder of Ben Collins, a former deputy marshal, August 1, 1906, and had been free on bond ever since. Witnesses for the prosecution got cold feet and the trial stalled.

Ben Collins had gone back to farming full time near Tishomingo after his lawman days. He was cut down by heavy shotgun pellets about 9 p.m. The assassin had waited behind some bushes near the gate of Collins' farm property, not far from his house.

Miller was indicted as the triggerman in a murder plot involving four old enemies of Ben Collins'. The old enemies raised the money for the assassination, then got in touch with Miller and paid him to do the dirty work. Miller didn't know Collins.

The sheriff was grateful to his old friend, Chief Garret, for telling him Jim Miller was traveling in his area, and was quick to say so. The sheriff called Ben and Sid Higgins over to his desk and repeated what Buck Garret told him. He then emphasized, "We'll handle it. Don't let one word of this get out to the politicians or the newspaper. We'll handle it."

The sheriff ordered his two deputies to make routine calls to people signed up for the community alert program without mentioning Miller's name, if the name didn't come up. He didn't want to start rumors. If anybody tripped the alert wire though, it would probably be Miller. He was better known than any other police character in southern Oklahoma since the Collins murder.

"Chief Culver, I'm still not sure what I think of the sheriff's alert program. There's something about it that bothers me. Still, I have to say it worked."

Ben then told the police chief about Peter Tompkins' call that morning, and what Tompkins told Sid afterwards. There wasn't any doubt in Tompkin's mind Jim Miller had his nephew's horse. Based on that, Ben thought it was a good bet Miller would return the horse and spend the night at Jim Williamson's farmhouse. Ben added that he and Jim Williamson had been friends since Center grade school.

Ending their moonlight ride to town from Lightnin' Ridge, Chief Culver and Ben rode around back of the court house to a barn where the lawmen kept a few horses handy, and dismounted. It was nearly four hours after the murder.

"Ben. It's been a long day, but ending up a good one," Chief Culver said, pulling the saddle off his horse. "You tellin' that it looks mighty like Miller has Williamson's horse gives us a lead. Now we got something to go on.

There was nothing at all a few hours ago. Now we got a lot of work to do, startin' at the ambush site, I'd think.

"If you want to meet here about four in the morning, we could ride out to Lightnin' Ridge together."

"Yes sir," Ben replied. "I'll be here at four. I agree we should start out at Lightnin' Ridge, and track as far as we can. That probably won't be far. Anyway, I hope we'll have Christian Harding there to help us. He knows where Gus's ranch is. It's on his way from Roff."

Chief Culver paused, holding the saddle blanket mid air; "You think we might go out to this Williamson farm right off, not go by Lightnin' Ridge? See if Miller is there? The ranch is just about the wrong way if Williamson's farm is where we want to end up."

Ben threw his saddle over a rail inside the barn, turned to look at Culver. "I've been thinkin' about that. I guess I favor stickin' together, Chief, the five of us. If it's Miller we're trailin'–and it looks like it is–we don't know if there are others in on this, or where they are.

"We know Miller will want shelter on a night like this. That doesn't have to be on Jim's farm, though. He might have spotted some deserted barn in the time he's scouted the ambush.

"My own feeling–if you're askin' me for it, Chief–is that we should track northeast just like we didn't know anything about Jim Williamson. Track fast, don't double back. If we lose the trail, we let it go and push on northeast toward the farm anyway.

"If we come to a road we know he's got to cross, we can fan out some and look for tracks, up and down. But we don't get separated. We go through pastures and prairie land with heavy grass and go fast. That's what he'd do.

"We give houses and built-up herds a wide berth. He would. He doesn't want to set dogs barkin' and cows bellowing in the middle of the night. And a horse running hard in the dark always attracts attention. We keep goin' northeast," Ben concluded.

"Ben. I think you got it perfect," the police chief answered. "That's exactly what we'll do. And what's more, I'm goin' to tell the sheriff he's got a cracker jack deputy."

Late Sunday afternoon, nearly twenty-four hours after the assassination, Chief Culver and his trackers were coming up the road to Williamson's house after a long day. Williamson was outside, getting an armful of firewood. When he saw the grim-looking men trotting down the rutted wagon road toward him, he put the wood down and shielded his eyes to get a better look.

"I guess he was happy to see someone he knew coming at him," Ben said.

The riders stopped and dismounted ten yards from Jim, who stood there quietly.

"Howdy, Ben," he said. "Howdy, Jim."

Chief Culver stepped toward Jim. "I'm George Culver, chief of police in Ada, on special assignment. Sheriff's deputy Snow here says he's known you since you were kids and knows you're a straight shooter. Good.

"I got to tell you, Mr. Williamson, we been tracking a horse all day long from a murder site southwest of town. The tracks come down that road and turn in here."

Ben remembered his old friend looked stunned.

"A murder site?" Jim asked, looking at Culver.

"Yeah. I hate to tell you this way," the Chief said. "A man named Gus Bobbitt was shot from ambush near his ranch last evenin'. The killer rode a horse we've been trackin' all the way from the ambush to here, do you have horses?"

"Well, yes, sir. I've got two plough horses and one saddle horse. A little mare…"

"That's your only saddle horse then? We'll have to look at her."

"Well, sure."

Williamson then went to the pasture gate where his mare was waiting for him, and led her into a small corral near the house. Christian Harding squeezed through the corral poles and approached the wary horse, patted her neck and then lifted her front left hoof. He quickly nodded to Chief Culver. That was the horse they were looking for.

"Where was that horse last night?" the Chief asked Williamson. He didn't bother to ask if he, Williamson, had the horse out. After Ben's briefing, and then talking to the young farmer, Chief Culver felt certain Williamson wouldn't have knowingly taken part in an assassination of anybody.

"My uncle rode up from Ada on a livery horse Friday and got the mare. Returned her last night," Williamson said.

"Did your uncle say where he went? What he did?"

"No, not exact things. He sometimes goes out in the country lookin' for cattle he might buy. Sometimes goes to the courthouse in Ada to check on leases. He brought her back pretty late."

"Is your uncle Jim Miller of Fort Worth?" Culver asked.

"Yes, sir, he is."

"Where is he now?"

"I took him up to Sasakwa to catch the Santa Fe this morning," Williamson said. "He's headed for home."

Chief Culver never did talk fast, Ben said. He talked very slow with Jim that evening. He knew Williamson was honest enough but country people were always reluctant to make trouble for kin folks.

"I guess your uncle spent what was left of last night with you. It was pretty cold. Is that right?" Culver asked.

"Yessir, that's right."

"If he borrowed your mare Friday and brought her back last night, he must have stayed somewhere else Friday night. Do you agree with that?"

"Yessir, I do. But I don't know exactly where. My uncle doesn't tell me much about his business and I don't ask," Williamson said.

"I think he was in Ada for a while checkin' leases. He might've stayed with Oscar Peeler. He's been stayin' with him lately. But I don't know that for sure."

"Who is Oscar Peeler?" the chief asked.

"Well, my uncle says he's a cousin. I never heard of him before this year. He lives on Hickory Street. I never met him."

The chief came to a critical question and asked in a casual sort of way. "Did your uncle say anything about Gus Bobbitt? Seein' Gus Bobbitt?"

"No, sir." the young farmer said. "I know the name from when he was runnin' for sheriff, but my uncle didn't say anythin' about him."

Ben described how Culver gathered his posse around him and spoke in such low tones Jim Williamson couldn't help but know he was the subject. Jim walked over to the corral to talk to his horse.

The mare had been brought back in a lather by his uncle, so Williamson put her in a shed next to the corral to get her out of the cold air while she was wet, Ben said. When the sun came up, he let her out to pasture, "No worse for the wear, as far as I could see," Jim reported.

I read in the Oklahoma City newspaper Wednesday that some town people came all the way out to the farm just to look at the horse Tuesday afternoon after the Ada newspaper story came out. Williamson didn't like strangers around so he took her over to a friend's farm.

"Mr. Williamson," Culver called after meeting with his trackers, "I hate to tell you this way, but there is good reason to think your uncle might have shot and killed Gus Bobbitt yesterday evenin' before he brought your horse back."

Williamson was always smart enough, Ben said, so he had pretty much guessed what the chief was going to say by then. He was still surprised to hear it. Maybe he shouldn't have been surprised, he later admitted to Ben. He and all the rest of the relatives knew about Jim Miller's record in West Texas and New Mexico. The family was neither proud of it or ashamed of it. It wasn't their business.

"Mr. Williamson," the chief continued, "We appreciate the way you answered our questions straight out. It's helpful to us gettin' to the bottom of this case. You are important to our investigation.

"If there's a trial down the road, you'll be an important witness. We got to know where you are, where we can talk to you, protect you if necessary. That's why I got to place you under arrest as an accomplice, no matter how innocent you are. There are procedures and rules we got to follow."

Ben remembered his old friend looked really alarmed. "Do you mean I have to go to jail, leave my family out here?" he asked the chief.

"No, Mr. Williamson. We just got to know where you are. Where we can get a hold of you when we need to. We know you aren't going to run off and leave your wife and baby.

"But you are under arrest, and as soon as you can come into town, you'll be arraigned and bonded–regular procedures. In the meantime, I got to ask you not to leave the county without permission. You stay right here on the farm so we can find you. That goes for tonight as well," the chief advised.

"It's late, gettin' cold and it's long ride into town. If you say you'll be here in the mornin,' and you say that mare will be here so we can get a shoe off her, then we can call it a day."

"Chief, I'm grateful to you," Jim answered. "I don't know anything about what my uncle might have done, except what I told you. But I don't leave my wife out here alone. I'll be right here in the mornin'. So will the mare. You can bet your life on it."

Ben said Jim admitted to him later on he was never comfortable with his hard-eyed uncle around, family or not. Betty Lou Williamson didn't like to have him around at all. You could hardly blame her with the tiny house they had.

Chief Culver's posse kept up a slow trot toward town, enough exercise to keep the evening chill off. Ben was riding alongside the chief. It was just after ten o'clock. At a rise in the road the Ada street lights made a faint glow on the horizon.

"It's been a good day, Ben," the chief said, "and a lucky one. Tompkins rememberin' Jim Williamson's horse from last summer, and then sayin' something about it. It's funny how a little thing like that would make such a big difference."

"Well," Ben replied, "like I said, I don't know how the sheriff will take it, talkin' out of the office. There wasn't anything else to do, though. We could have been searching out there for a week and never find anything."

"That's right. And it's not like the whole thing is wrapped up. Miller sure is a good suspect, but you never know. We got to talk to him," Culver pointed out. "There'some tough work ahead. Plenty for the sheriff to do."

They could see lights still on in some of the houses. Ben spoke up, "Chief Culver—tomorrow's going to be busy. I expect to see the sheriff first thing.

"I wonder if you would let me tell him about this Oscar Peeler Jim mentioned. That could be important. We shouldn't lose any time on that. I'm sure the sheriff would agree. I'll suggest we go try to find him right away."

"Yeah, sure, Ben," the Chief agreed. "You're right. Get that done fast. And the sheriff will be in charge once he's back."

The Plot Laid Bare

Sheriff Smith did return to Ada late Sunday night, or maybe it was early Monday morning, anyway in the middle of the night and hours after Chief Culver and Ben Snow got back from Williamson's farm. Before he left Ardmore, the sheriff knew from his old schoolboy pal Buck Garrett, Gus Bobbitt had been assassinated. That's all he knew.

My friend Ben understood there would be a lot of work to do that day–Monday–whether his boss, Sheriff Smith, got back or not. So he was in the office a few minutes after seven. The sheriff hurried in not long after.

"What in hell is goin' on Ben?" he demanded to know. Ben remembered he'd never seen the sheriff so het up.

"The Gus Bobbitt murder?"

"Well of course!" the sheriff shot back. "Where are we? Do we have any leads? What've you done?"

Ben remembered he said, "I think we've got a good start on this…"

"What start? Who's doing what?"

The search story was so long and so complicated, Ben remembered he had a hard time trying to tell it so the sheriff would listen and not throw in more questions.

"Sheriff, let me tell you quick it turns out Jim Miller was involved. I'll tell you how we found out about that in a minute. We thought we knew who we were tracking from the beginning, thought it might be Miller, but didn't know for sure.

"Yesterday we tracked the killer, not knowing exactly who it was, all the way from Gus Bobbitt's ranch up to a little farm near Allen–Jim Williamson's farm. It turns out he's a nephew of Miller's."

"Miller. Miller fer god's sake! I saw him at the Ardmore station last evenin'! I could've arrested him right there!"

"Well, yessir," Ben said. "But you didn't know he was a suspect then. We only found that out for sure at the Williamson farm few hours before. There was no way you could've known, nothing you should've done."

"Well, that's right, Ben," the sheriff agreed. "Arrest him for what? From what you say, I just couldn't walk up to a man at the station and put him under arrest. For what? I didn't know what happened up here. What did happen?"

Ben said the sheriff calmed down and he was able to give him the whole story going back to Tompkins' call Saturday morning. The report included the "tracking" business, how they really did it, and ended with Jim Williamson's statements about his uncle, Jim Miller.

"Well, that's good, Ben. Looks like you got a lot done. All we have to do now is get Jim Miller? Right?"

"Right, Sheriff. There's one more thing that could be very important I want to tell you about." Ben then told his boss about Jim Williamson mentioning his uncle might have stayed with Oscar Peeler in Ada Thursday and Friday nights.

"Oscar Peeler? Never heard of him."

"None of us had either, Sheriff, not even Chief Culver," the deputy replied. "But we snooped around on Hickory Street just after six this morning and an old codger goin' out back said there was a young couple from Fort Worth livin' in a rent house across the street."

"Well, I'll bet they won't be there long if he finds out what Jim Williamson told you," the sheriff said. And he was right, Ben agreed. Sheriff Smith wasn't dumb by any means, Ben always said, just not sure of himself.

"I'm goin' back south on the one o'clock Frisco and over to Ardmore to see if Miller might've gone out to check his share-crop farm," the sheriff advised. "Buck says he does that every couple of months. It's worth a try. Sure wish I could have arrested him last evenin."

Deputy Snow nodded in agreement, then suggested that he and Sid go down to the Hickory Street house the old man talked about within the hour and try to find Oscar Peeler, maybe arrest him as a potential witness if he did put Miller up.

"All right, Ben, do that," the sheriff agreed, "and some time after nine I'll go tell Wimbish what you found out yesterday and what you're goin' to do this mornin'. I'll tell him. Then, like I said, I'm goin' back to Ardmore to see if Miller went out to his farm. No point in checkin' with Wimbish any earlier. I never see him around here until nine or so."

When Ben later talked to me about the case and those hectic days right after the murder, he said it was that Monday morning he realized how little the sheriff knew about police work, not that he was fearful, just not sure what he should do next. Ben told me he didn't think Tom Smith even liked being sheriff.

Ben remembered the sheriff once told him his friend Buck Garrett suggested he think twice abut campaigning for the job. "It's not all makin' speeches and shakin' hands, Tom," Chief Garrett pointed out.

"I guess Garrett knew his old friend was better suited for other work, a job dealin' with nice people, like a school," Ben concluded.

The other thing Ben learned that Monday morning was how much Tom Smith cared what the county attorney thought, like he was really in charge. Ben said he knew a county attorney has a responsibility, being the leading government man in legal matters if not law enforcement, but he always thought the sheriff would take the lead in handling a murder case.

It didn't matter in the Bobbitt case. It was never an issue. Bob Wimbish just took over behind the scenes. Never talked about what was happening in public. Never made speeches or anything. He just called the shots. The sheriff didn't seem to mind. Maybe he was grateful.

Ben and Sid went down to the end of Hickory Street to find the old man they talked to earlier about the couple from Fort Worth. "Right over there. 'Cross the street–409 Hickory, I think it is," the old man said.

The deputies went across the street, up the porch stairs to the door and knocked. A young woman answered without opening the door.

"What do you want?" she asked.

"Ma'm," Ben answered. "We're from the sheriff's office and we would like to talk to Oscar Peeler. We're told he lives here."

The door opened a little and the young woman said she was Oscar's older sister, Ellen. She opened the door wider, seeing they really were officers of the law and not any of the drifters she had often seen on Hickory. "Come in. I'll call Oscar."

Oscar came into the little parlor from the kitchen and asked, "What is this, Ellen?"

Ben remembered he was surprised how young and innocent looking Oscar appeared to be for someone involved in such a grim business as assassination. Ben thought at the time he couldn't be much more than eighteen or nineteen years old, which turned out to be close to right. He was seventeen.

"Mr. Peeler, we are trying to get information as to the whereabouts of Jim Miller of Fort Worth," Ben explained. "We've been told he stayed here with you several nights last week, until last Saturday morning, as a matter of fact."

Young Peeler didn't blink nor hesitate. "Yes, my uncle stayed here with us. He usually does, always eats breakfast here, three eggs over," Peeler answered.

Ben admitted he was taken by surprise by the unhesitating answer to a question that could have such grave consequences. He wondered if Peeler knew Gus Bobbitt was assassinated Saturday and that his uncle was involved.

"Mr. Peeler," Snow began, "It's only right I tell you what's happened. There's been a murder and your uncle is a suspect. I'm afraid that involves you, since he stayed here. We are going to ask you to come with us down to the sheriff's office.

Ellen Peeler began to cry.

"Ma'm, I don't think it will be necessary for you to come," Snow said.

She then began to sob. "I don't want to stay alone in this awful place, the whole awful town. I want to go home," she choked out.

"Ellen, please don't cry," Oscar said, a very worried look on his face. "Everything will be all right."

Ben had no idea at that time how much Oscar knew about the assassination plan. He sensed the young fellow would be willing to answer more questions and didn't want to do anything to make him less cooperative. He could see Oscar was distressed with his older sister in tears.

There was an awkward pause, then Ben said it really was necessary for Oscar to come to the sheriff's office with him. "When things are settled down there, my partner," Ben added nodding at Sid, "will come by for your sister in a buggy and take her up to the Harris hotel."

"You mean, I'll be in jail?" Oscar asked.

"Well, the sheriff is out of town and he'll want to talk to you. So the answer is yes. If things don't work out the way you might hope, and you had to stay with us a while, we'll send your sister back to Fort Worth on the train."

The thought of getting back home to Fort Worth was enough to end Ellen's sobs and even made Oscar smile. Ben remembered he was puzzled at how almost cheerful the young man seemed to be about going to jail and wondered if he were a little teched. It didn't occur to him at the time it might have been relief, a feeling he would be safer there.

Oscar Peeler did become a prisoner in the Pontotoc County jail before noon Monday. Sheriff Smith just missed him. The sheriff had already briefed the county attorney about what his men had been doing, and had gone home for lunch before his return trip to Ardmore.

Sheriff Smith hoped to get back to Ardmore in time to ride out to Jim Miller's sharecrop farm before sundown. He just made it. By the time he arrived in Ardmore and got out to the farm, the setting sun was on the horizon. Without getting off his horse, he questioned Lem Presterman, the farmer, about the landowner, Jim Miller.

"Nope, ain't seen him," Presterman said. "Ain't seen him for a month. Don't know why he comes out here. He never says nothin' anyway."

Pete Daniels, the Ada deputy with Sheriff Smith, recalled that's all the sharecropper had to say and he wasn't very cheerful with that.

After his futile trip to Ardmore and Jim Miller's farm late Monday, the sheriff still got into the office before ten o'clock Tuesday. Ben Snow told him about Oscar Peeler's arrest and the fact that Peeler was right there, in jail. The sheriff jumped up from his desk and said the first order of business was talking to young Peeler. "Bring him on in," he ordered.

"You say Jim Miller is your uncle and he stayed with you last week up until Saturday morning?" the sheriff asked.

"Yessir," Oscar replied, "Only he's not my real uncle. We just call him uncle. He hired me and Ellen to come up here and rent a house where he could stay when he was in Ada. His wife and my mother are best friends in Fort Worth. They figured since neither of us had a job it would be some money we could earn."

"How long have you been here? How many times did Jim Miller stay with you?" the lawman asked.

"We came up last November. Been here ever since. Ellen hates it here. She's afraid of Indians. I tell her the Chickasaws are one of the Five Civilized tribes, not Comanches like in Texas."

"All right, but how many times did Jim Miller come here?"

"Well, twice before this last visit," Peeler said. "He only stays a couple of days."

"What does he do? Where does he go?"

"Well, most of the time he just goes out in the country lookin' for cattle he can buy cheap for his farm in Ardmore," Peeler said. "As far as I know that's what he was doin' this visit, the only difference was he had to return a horse Saturday and planned to go back home from Sasakwa Sunday."

The sheriff and Deputy Snow looked at one another. Then Snow asked in a quiet voice, "Last visit, Oscar. Was there anything different? Did your uncle say anything different? Look any different?"

Oscar paused and answered, "Well, no. Maybe he didn't look much like a cattleman. He had one of those little English caps on, not a regular hat. He was carryin' his shotgun. Had to get it home someway, I suppose."

Oscar paused again. He looked plainly unhappy.

"Yes, Oscar? Something more you remember?"

"Well," he started carefully, "It wasn't anything Uncle Jim said right to me. He and a man named Barry Burwell sat in our parlor in the house there on Hickory Street and talked about killin' someone, who was goin' to pay for it and how much. That happened on his second visit here, the one before this last time. They talked like I wasn't even there. I would have left in a hurry but I didn't want them to think they couldn't trust me."

Ben continued in his quiet voice, "That's interesting Oscar. Did they talk about who was going to be killed?"

"Oh, yeah," Oscar said in a sorrowful way. "They talked about a man named Bobbitt. He used to be a lawman around here. My uncle was to get $5000 from two ranchers out on the Panhandle for doin' it. They said the names, but I don't remember."

The sheriff and his deputy looked at each other again. Without saying anything, they both began thinking back over Gus Bobbitt's career, from his days as a deputy marshal up through the time he was in business on the Canadian River. The same thought popped into their heads.

"You think they might've been talkin' about two men called Jesse West and Joe Allen, Oscar?" Ben asked.

"Yeah, yeah! That's the ones. I remember now. My uncle told Mr. Burwell he never heard of either one 'em"

"What does Mr. Burwell have to do with all this, Oscar?" the sheriff wanted to know.

"Well, from what they were sayin', Mr. Burwell did know those ranchers and they gave him the money to give to my uncle, or Mr. Miller. And I even remember how much…$5000. That's an awful lot of money."

"Yes, Oscar. It certainly is," Ben agreed. "And you are doin' the right thing, tellin' us. We're goin' to have find this Mr. Burwell and talk to him. Jim Miller, too. We know something about Jim Miller. He lives in Fort Worth, right?"

"Yes, and Mr. Burwell does, too," Oscar replied.

The sheriff drummed his fingers on the table where he was sitting across from young Peeler. Then he said, "Deputy Snow is right. You're doin' the right thing tellin' us. We've got a lot of work to do…

"You're very important to us. Mr. Peeler. We're goin' to have to keep you in jail while we work on this case, more for your own protection than anything else. And Deputy Snow says he promised we'd send your sister back to Fort Worth. We'll do that tomorrow."

The two lawmen stood up and Oscar stood up, a half smile on his face. "All right," he said. He didn't know it then, but he had just saved his life.

9

The Complex Assassin

The county attorney was in court Tuesday morning while Oscar Peeler told the sheriff and Deputy Snow his surprising story. The sheriff had to wait until Tuesday afternoon to go upstairs and brief Bob Wimbish on the unexpected turn of events.

"I could'a nabbed him Sunday night," the sheriff said of Jim Miller, "only I didn't know then he killed Gus Bobbitt. You can't just arrest a man at the train station for no reason."

"No, Tom. Of course not," Wimbish answered quietly. His mind was obviously working the big problem he faced now–how to get the killing team, all Texans–back in Oklahoma jurisdiction.

After I finally did move down to Ada, I got to know Bob Wimbish pretty well. I say pretty well. We were never friends like Dwight and I were. We were just friendly enough. He was the first president of our Lions club and we worked on a number of projects together.

In all the times Bob and I were together–or maybe at the same gathering, like Presbyterian church functions–we never once talked about the Bobbitt case and what happened. It was as if a piece of history was torn out of the book. There was a blank space.

I could have mentioned very casually I knew a lot of the story, if the sad time in our town's history had ever come up in conversation. That would let him know while I didn't get to college, I manage to keep up with what's going on. Good judgment kept me from it. He probably would have stared at me and said nothing.

Some thought Wimbish was arrogant, maybe because he didn't talk about his problems with most people, including me, never said what he was going to do. He did talk to Dwight. Not only did he talk to him, he relied on him to help keep things calm in town while he figured out his strategy. Dwight was influential, certainly with the businessmen, despite his age.

It was natural enough Wimbish and Dwight would be good friends. They were about the same age. Wimbish was born in Louisiana, Dwight in Tennessee. And they came to Ada the same year–1903.

Wimbish and Dwight had young families and both were church deacons. They both had been to college and were smart anyway. Bob Wimbish had been out of the University of Texas law school seven years when he was elected the first Pontotoc county attorney.

I was glad Wimbish confided in Dwight and I was proud to warrant Dwight's confidence. It was important for me to know what was going on in a town where I was planning to move my family. Dwight made that possible. I needed to know and Dwight told me. So, besides helping me get my brick business set up in Ada, he was helping me with the personal reservations I had about moving.

Maybe you could ask how objective Dwight's advice was. It's a fair question. He was a good salesman for Ada, a strong promoter. He was totally convinced Ada had a promising future if the right people came to town and the bad ones left. He said he wanted builders in Ada, and that appealed to me, being in the brick business. I believed in him. What a mayor he would have been.

The Tuesday afternoon Sheriff Smith briefed Wimbish on everything Oscar Peeler had to say–that was March 2–the *Ada Evening News* ran the story headlined: "Where Is Jim Miller?" The *News* story didn't actually accuse Miller of Bobbitt's murder, though it sure made him the chief suspect, the only suspect at that time.

It wouldn't be right to say the newspapers inflamed public opinion. It was a big story for the town and the papers had to cover it. The more that came out–like Miller being free on bond three years before the murder–the more upset people got. The papers never did caution about "innocent until proven guilty," even-handed justice, anything that might calm people down a little.

Besides coming very close to charging Jim Miller with Gus Bobbitt's murder and pounding the drum for action, the *News* made it more difficult for lawmen to work by ridiculing them. In the same March 2 edition, the *News* ran this story:

"The officers, though they paraded that deliciously attractive 'misterious' air, and maintained a story that would make one prone to weep in admiration, either would not tell anything or did not know anything…It is suspected the latter state represented their true condition."

Most people in town knew the *News* editors had little use for the sheriff, and that's who they were talking about. The trouble was it tarred everyone working on the case with the same brush. Not only was it unfair, it wasn't true. There was a lot happening, only everything was in the first stages. Any hope of getting the four Texans back to Ada depended on plans that weren't really hatched yet. Talking about the plans openly would be the end of them.

From what Dwight said, Bob Wimbish was very much aware how difficult it would be getting the Texans back in Oklahoma to stand trial, and he wanted them all. He figured he had a pretty good chance of getting Miller extradited, despite his high-placed friends and political support, because he had such strong circumstantial evidence against him and credible witnesses. It could be a long, drawn out process, though.

Getting the two ranchers back to Oklahoma for trial would be more complicated. They had become pillars of their society out on the Panhandle–in Mobettie–and the only thing involving them in the assassination at that point was what young Oscar Peeler remembered. Barry Burwell, the bail bondsman, didn't concern Wimbish very much, one way or another, except he wanted a clean sweep.

Burwell was never difficult to locate and he was often in Oklahoma. He was a Johnny-on-the-spot bail bondsmen who operated in the larger courts throughout Texas and Oklahoma. He always let court officers know he was available. Hobnobbing with the lawyers and judges around the courthouses made him feel important, I guess.

Burwell started out as a bank clerk down in Ardmore. Standing in a little cage, handling household cash and being nice to the folks wasn't going to satisfy him though. He started arranging bail and that–dealing with people in trouble with the law–opened up all kinds of possibilities to him, nothing violent, just crafty little things like forged endorsements on checks, that level of wrong doing.

As a matter of fact, that's how he got to know Jim Miller. Miller had cut back on his old rustling schemes in West Texas and New Mexico and moved to Fort Worth to please his wife. Miller presented himself as a cattle dealer in Fort Worth and did some legal buying and selling of live stock. He also tried the real estate business.

The real estate plan that got him public notice was selling lots along the Texas coastline. He offered them as vacation homes sites to the wealthier Fort Worth citizens. That sounded all right except that some of the coastal acreage he offered was in the Gulf of Mexico, near shore and partly underwater.

Barry Burwell helped him get started financially in this enterprise by forging an endorsement on a $5000 check. Burwell got caught on that and was indicted. It didn't matter. He was quickly out on bail and never served a day in jail. He must have felt he could do about anything and get away with it, or at least get out on bail. That was a mistake.

I didn't waste much time feeling sorry for any of those men responsible for Gus Bobbitt's death, but Barry Burwell came as close I could get. He was only thirty years old when all this happened, a kind of pudgy fellow with a big nose. He could have been a county fair barker.

Burwell looked like a second stringer and that's what he was, someone just hanging around the edge, not really a bad man, not straight with the law either. Always looking for an angle or a deal. Still, you have to wonder if the punishment that lay ahead for him really fit the crime.

However you describe Burwell's role in the Gus Bobbitt case, he was part of the assassination team. A clean sweep would have to include him. Bob Wimbish took a chance and asked the Fort Worth police to arrest Burwell for questioning. They arrested him right on Main Street the first day of the Fat Stock show, a big occasion in Fort Worth in those days. Well, I guess it still is.

I'm told Burwell played it as kind of a joke with the arresting officers and said there had to be some kind of mistake, he didn't remember ever being in a town with that peculiar name. Anyway, he didn't protest extradition to Oklahoma because, he said, he wanted to clear the matter up. What could he know about the murder of this Bobbitt man? he asked.

I have been free with criticism of the newspaper in much of this, but I'll have to say, they cooperated fully with Bob Wimbish in covering Burwell's arrest and transfer to Ada's jail.

There was a little three-paragraph story back on page three saying one Barry Burwell of Fort Worth had been arrested and brought to Ada for questioning in the Bobbitt case. You had to be a careful reader to see it. The story could have been plastered all over the front page, the first arrest in the case being made when a lot of important people in town were demanding "something be done" in the investigation.

Bob Wimbish asked the editors not to make a great to-do about it because it could alert the ranchers out in Mobeetie. News didn't get out to the Texas Panhandle very fast in those days, particularly little blurbs Oklahoma editors didn't find important. Having the ranchers unaware of any developments in the case would be perfect until Wimbish was ready. It would leave every option open.

The editors were willing to cooperate to the extent of burying the story, partly because they had learned by then how much was going on and how far along Wimbish was in planning. A lot had to happen before the plans were put to the test, but at least there was a plan. The *Ada Evening News* even let up on Sheriff Smith.

Jim Miller presented a far different kind of a problem for Wimbish than Barry Burwell did certainly. The county attorney assumed Miller would know Burwell had been arrested and was in jail. That would be common knowledge around the Tarrant County courthouse. Miller would also know there hadn't been a big hoorah in Ada about Burwell's arrest, that it was treated routinely. Ada didn't seem to be a hornet's nest of revenge–if he had to go back.

Wimbish had been collecting all the new stories and official reports on Miller that he could get hold of, information that went all the way back to Miller's hard childhood. He wanted to know what motivated the assassin, what vulnerabilities he had. There was so much contradictory evidence–devoted husband and churchgoer on one hand, unfeeling, amoral killer on the other.

By now Wimbish had learned Miller didn't drink, smoke nor gamble and was faithful to his wife. You'd have to count him as a good family man.

What did Miller want in life? It couldn't be just money, though that was clearly important to him.

Dwight told me Wimbish assumed Miller would fight any extradition orders and would organize political resistance. There was no doubt he did have a number of friends in Fort Worth and Tarrant County, not just political and law enforcement types, but several ranking associates in the Tarrant County Methodist Church organization. Miller had been a devout and active church member since his days as a deputy sheriff in Pecos County, Texas. He was sometimes called "Deacon Jim" in West Texas.

From his many encounters with the law, Miller seems to have developed a theory that he had to have an alibi strong enough to convince friends and people he admired of his innocence, not just thwart prosecutors. Convincing a jury was the big thing of course, if there had to be a trial, but that was the last act. He needed support from the beginning of the trouble. Maybe there wouldn't have to be a trial.

What his friends thought of him after the murder charges were taken care of mattered a great deal to Jim Miller, if he was going to make a place for himself on the Fort Worth commercial scene, either as a cattleman or a real estate dealer. He needed his friends to believe his days as a West Texas gunman were over.

Bob Wimbish called his best friend in law school–a man named Herb LaBarre–to try and get some psychological insights on Jim Miller that weren't in typical sheriffs' and police reports. LaBarre was working for the clerk of courts in Tarrant County while he was writing a book on the history of Fort Worth. He knew about Miller, who was one of the better-known citizens frequently in the courthouse.

"He comes in here every once in a while," Herb told Wimbish. "Mr. Shelton jumps up when he sees Miller and takes care of things, so I never have talked to him.

"Sometime he comes in lookin' like an ordinary rancher, sometimes like some kind of dude from Chicago, all dressed up for what I don't know. He's different, no doubt about that. A lot of the western types you see around the courthouse look like plain thugs. Or maybe not very bright. Miller's not like that. Speaks well, very mannerly."

Herb knew Miller could be facing a murder charge in Pontotoc County. Word in the Tarrant County courthouse was that the newspaper in Ada had all but indicted him. His friend Bob Wimbish would have to be involved. Herb didn't know where the case stood legally or what Wimbish planned to do to get Miller back to Oklahoma to stand trial.

In their next telephone call, Wimbish told his old college roommate he believed he had a strong enough case to warrant extradition in Miller's case. He didn't want to do that though–the process could be strung out for months and maybe years with legal wrangling, and could be the end of his plan to get West and Allen back to Oklahoma. What he wanted was for Jim Miller to come back to Ada, if not voluntarily, at least without a drawn out legal battle, face the charges so he could uphold his growing reputation as a businessman.

"That's askin' an awful lot, Bob," Herb said. "I don't know I'd do that."

"No, you wouldn't Herb," Bob replied. "You wouldn't have to. You've been innocent all your life."

LaBarre then told Wimbish that Mr. Shelton wanted to use the telephone and he had to hang up. He promised he would try to help as best he could from such a lowly position in the clerk of courts office. LaBarre called back the next day to tell the Pontotoc County attorney that Miller was at work building his alibi.

LaBarre reported that Miller, despite the Ada newspaper story suggesting his deep involvement in the Bobbitt case, continued to socialize with his friends on the veranda of the Delaware Hotel most days when the weather was good. It was early March and the weather was uncertain in North Central Texas, bright with the promise of spring one day, grey with the dregs of winter the next. On those good days, the Delaware loungers turned out in force.

Miller took advantage of the big audiences on bright days and added to his reputation as a droll and amusing storyteller. Never did he touch upon his sinister past. He was usually an innocent victim in his stories. His yarns then–in early March–were about his February cattle buying expedition in east Oklahoma. As Miller told it, the country was full of rustic, comic people, but still too shrewd for him.

The sophisticated Fort Worth loungers were always ready to believe the worst about the mountain people of east Oklahoma and always laughed. All of Miller's first-hand reports about the remote countryside made it impossible for him to be in Ada the night of Gus Bobbitt's murder.

Miller also used props. On one occasion, he had a new hat with a bullet hole through the crown. He took it off and stuck his forefinger through the hole. "Now why would anybody want to ruin a hat like this?" he asked his guffawing pals.

Loungers on the Delaware veranda included cattlemen, grain merchants and merchants able to leave the store to underlings, most of them prosperous enough, but not the big shakers in Fort Worth. They seemed to be important to Jim Miller though. They had reached a level of success and acceptance in the community he was aiming for.

And these men seemed to genuinely like him, LaBarre said, though they surely knew about his criminal path in West Texas and New Mexico. Maybe they liked rubbing elbows with a real desperado. "Gives 'em a boot," Herb suggested.

LaBarre reminded his old friend in Ada that Miller had been a deputy sheriff, even a Texas Ranger for three months, so his cronies could make him out to be what they wanted.

"There are positive things in his record, Bob, for those who want to see that side."

When Bob Wimbish asked his college roommate if these were the kind of friends that would stick by Miller in a time of real trouble–go to bat for him politically–LaBarre said they surely were. Miller's Delaware Hotel friends had already shown they would stand by him in a pinch. LaBarre cited the Frank Fore murder case of 1904 to make the point.

Frank Fore was a detective for the American Freehold Land & Mortgage Co. who came to Fort Worth to investigate a $5000 check Miller used in his real estate business–the Gulf Coast lots. The check proved to be endorsed fraudulently and the detective was in Fort Worth to recover his company's loss. Barry Burwell would be indicted for the forgery in the coming months, but Fore didn't know that, and never would know.

The Delaware was a first-rate hotel in 1904 and Frank Fore was just the kind of self-assured man who would insist on staying in the town's best hotel. He might have heard Jim Miller frequently rocked on the Delaware veranda with his friends on a warm spring day as well.

LaBarre told Wimbish he never did know Frank Fore. The Miller-Fore encounter happened before he came up to Fort Worth from Austin. From all he heard however, Fore was no shrinking violet. He was an obnoxious fellow who said some ugly things right there on the veranda about everyone involved in the Gulf Coast land deal. Mostly though, he talked about Jim Miller, who was away at that time.

Miller's friends could hardly wait to tell Jim this out-of-town detective was saying bad things about him. They filled him in pretty fast when he got back and took his place on the veranda, two or three friends talking at once. "Even cursed you, Jim!" one said.

Frank Fore couldn't have been any more offensive to Jim Miller saying insulting things to his face than he was saying them to his new friends. Then being cursed, even though he wasn't there, was even worse. Honor was at stake. Miller was not going to put up with some mortgage company investigator cursing him.

Herb LaBarre found a copy of the May 4, 1904, edition of the *Fort Worth Record* and sent it up to Wimbish for his file on Miller. From the *Record's* front-page story, both Miller and Frank Fore were on the Delaware veranda that spring morning.

Fore got up from his rocking chair about 9 a.m. to go the men's room. He went through the hotel lobby and then downstairs one flight. Jim Miller got up and headed for the men's room going down some outside stairs.

The two met in the men's room. They both spoke about the same time. Witnesses didn't get that straight–who said what and in what order. They all agreed however–these were all Miller's friends–Fore went for his "pistol" first. It snagged coming out of his coat pocket.

Miller got his revolver out cleanly and finished Frank Fore off with one shot from a few feet away, an uncommon success for Miller. He never had been effective with a sidearm. This time it was different. In later years he relied on a shotgun from ambush.

Miller was indicted for the murder of Frank Fore and faced another jury trial. He claimed self-defense. It took the jury fifteen minutes to agree with him.

Wimbish realized he was dealing with a man whose whole life involved courts and juries and strategies to defeat them. Routine court orders across state lines weren't going to work with Miller in the Bobbitt case. As the legal procedures ground on, witnesses would move far off, or die off, or lose all interest in facing a killer in the courtroom, someone they could expect to see on the street after the trial.

When Wimbish tried to talk to Oscar Peeler about Miller's complex character and what other than the obvious things, such as money, made him tick, Oscar never seemed to understand what the county attorney was asking about. That Miller liked three eggs for breakfast was the most important thing he could think of. Wimbish gave up.

"Tom," the county attorney said, addressing the sheriff who wasn't all that sure what Wimbish was driving at either, "is there anyone around here who actually knows Miller? Who talks to him, talks to him about something other than getting a horse at the livery stable?

"How about the young farmer who loaned Miller the mare? Miller's nephew I understand–Jim Williamson. You didn't arrest him right away and you did arrest Peeler. Should we get him in here now?"

"Well, as you know, Bob, I was down in Ardmore for my father's funeral," Sheriff Smith replied. "I wasn't there on the Williamson farm Sunday night. George Culver and my deputy Ben Snow were, and agreed there was no point in haulin' Williamson into town. He answered every question straight out, including the fact that his uncle, Jim Miller, had the horse Saturday night. Besides, he's got a wife and baby there on the farm and he's not goin' anywhere.

"He told Culver and Snow he'd be there the next morning–Monday–so a couple of my men could get shoes off the mare for evidence. And he was there. Ben Snow says he's a straight arrow, always has been. They were in Center grade school together for a while."

"Well, if they're old friends, Tom, how about asking your deputy to ride back out there and talk to Williamson by himself, nobody else?" the county attorney asked.

"Maybe Williamson would tell him what Miller talked about, what interests him. They must have said something on that long wagon ride to Sasakwa."

That's how Ben Snow got the job of riding back out to Jim Williamson's farm Thursday afternoon. He expected to go to Gus Bobbitt's funeral. He decided not to ask that the visit to his grade school friend be put off until Friday so he could attend the funeral. The county attorney made it clear he wanted information without any delay. Sheriff Smith emphasized that point.

"Ben, go get this done," the sheriff said. "I don't know that a day would make all that much difference, either. Wimbish is on some sort of crusade and best we back him up. I don't know what your friend knows, but Wimbish won't stop worrying about it until we find out. Make sure you see me when you get back. I'll brief Wimbish."

Years later, when I got to know Ben, he told me about that assignment. He didn't like it much, working his old friend for information, so he just told Williamson right out his bosses back in town wanted to know what Miller talked about. They wanted to know personal stuff, like what he thought about, what he wanted to do.

I remember Ben saying Williamson wasn't at all sure what kind of information the chiefs in town were looking for, so he'd just tell about the night his uncle stayed with them, and the drive to get the Santa Fe train next day.

"First of all, it was cold up here Saturday night," Williamson said "Maybe it was cold in town, too. Not like up here in the country, though. Near freezin' toward morning.

"It must have been nine or ten o'clock that night. We'd been in bed for hours when I heard a horse comin' down the road at a fast trot. I got up out of bed and looked out the window. Saw my uncle in the moonlight pull up by that shed over there. There was no mistakin' him in that funny cap. He dismounted, kind'a tired like.

"Uncle Jim? I called from the kitchen door. He didn't say anything but started pullin' the saddle off the mare.

"I'll get it Uncle Jim, I said, gettin' a coat on and comin' out with a lantern. I pulled both the saddle and the blanket away and remember the steam comin' off the mare's back. She was about wore down but still steady. I would've liked to walk her a bit because she was so wet and it was cold. I didn't take the time though, because my uncle seemed agitated. I just put her in that shed over there for the night.

"Uncle Jim finally said, 'I'll just go back of the shed here, then I'll come in and get some sleep.'

"Sure, I told him. Everything's the same. You know the couch we got and the baby has the colic. It's still a lot better than out here."

"It was a strange night. I thought morning would never come," Jim said. "Either Betty Lou or me walked the baby up and down a half dozen times, trying to get her to stop crying.

"Uncle Jim didn't do a whole lot better. He was coughing or blowing his nose half the night. I remember that and the big gun he had out on the table beside the couch."

In the morning Jim Williamson hitched up his plough horses to a wagon he had and the two of them set out, side by side on the driver's bench, north over the rutted roads to the Canadian River and then over to the Santa Fe station at Sasakwa.

"It was a nice mornin' after the sun warmed things up a bit. And the river was down," Williamson remembered. "We got to the station in plenty of time."

"That's good Jim, havin' a nice mornin' for a long wagon ride," Ben said, "But did you ever talk?"

"Well, sure, though my uncle never says much any time. The only time he ever said a lot–for him–was when I told him ranches were startin' up all over the county and there should be plenty of opportunities for him to come back to Pontotoc for good cattle. There's a lot of good Hereford stock comin' in.

"Then I was afraid I said something wrong. He just kept turnin' around to check the road behind us, then starin' ahead. He finally said he wouldn't be coming back, the job he had was done.

"We just kept on goin' down the road and then he asked me, 'How long you been on that farm, Jim?'

"Nearly five years," I told him. "I expect to pay off the mortgage in another fifteen."

"He muttered something about fifteen years. I couldn't quite make it out."

After that Jim remembered neither of them had anything to say for quite a spell, just plodding along toward the river in the morning sunshine. Williamson said his uncle suddenly broke the silence between them in a low and kind of friendly way—"You talk about opportunity for me, Jim. You should be thinkin' about opportunities for yourself. You can work yourself down to nothin' but skin and bones on that little place and have nothin' to show for it.

"You're kin, and young, and I'm tellin' you, you got to be awake and see what's goin' on around you. Take a chance if you have to. Don't just grind your life away."

Jim said he knew his uncle was trying to help. "He just has his own way of doin' it…and our farm really is pretty small. He's the richest man in the family, you know. Got two farms, both of 'em bigger'n mine, livin' in a three-story house in Fort Worth. It would be foolish not to heed what he says. Not everybody admired what he did in West Texas, though.

"Then I thought I should let him know I appreciated his advice and said, 'I understand what you mean about opportunity, Uncle Jim, and I'll sure keep a lookout, except nothin' much happens on the farm. I still like it.'"

Jim recalled they drove on for a while, getting pretty close to the river. He remembered his uncle turned toward him just before they got to the river bank, and in about a friendly a way as he ever gets, said–

"Jim. I started out with a lot less than you've got. Didn't even know my pa. My own grandpa nearly killed me workin'.

"I moved on out west, always lookin' for a way up, doin' whatever it was to make something of myself. I don't say you should do the things I had to do.

Maybe you shouldn't, but now I've got two farms and a nice house in Fort Worth, important business friends. People come to me when they got a problem. I don't have to go out lookin' for work."

Jim Williamson paused, looked out over the pasture where his two plough horses were grazing, then added, "My uncle said two ranchers out on the Panhandle got cheated out of a saloon up here on the Canadian by a man, and didn't have the stomach to set things right. They paid him a lot of money to bring 'justice.' That's what Uncle Jim called it. 'No more to it than that,' he said. 'I brought justice. ' "

Ben remembered his school boy chum stopped right there, not saying whether his uncle told him who got the "justice." Because his old friend was being so open about what his uncle said, Ben didn't want to press him. So they stood there in the farm yard a minute.

"Look, Ben," Jim Williamson finally said. "If my uncle did somethin' wrong he's got to answer for it. He's my uncle but I don't want to get mixed up in the kind of things they say he did in West Texas.

"He never did say who the ranchers were, or what he did to anybody. And I sure didn't ask. I didn't want to hear as much as I heard. I don't want to be mixed up in things like that."

Ben asked Jim if there was anything else he could tell about. Jim thought for a second then added, "Yeah. Uncle Jim said there might be someone comin' out from town askin' about him, that some people in town knew who he was, and that I was his nephew.

"Tell 'em I stayed with you like I always do when I'm out buyin' cattle," Jim Williamson remembered him saying. Then he went on, "My uncle turned kind of cold and said, 'Don't tell 'em anything else. Don't tell 'em about family business. It could go hard for you, Jim. I don't abide people talkin' out of turn. I'm just tryin' to help you.'"

Ben nodded his head in an understanding way, turned slowly toward the fence post where his horse was tethered. Jim Williamson added one more thing–"I'm not afraid of my uncle, Ben, and I don't like to speak poorly about kin, but I don't take much pleasure in his visits. Betty Lou hates to have him around. He just seems like a keg of powder that might go up any time. I hope he hasn't done anything wrong."

"All right, Jim. I thank you for talkin' to me," Ben said. "Try and get into town for this arraignment business soon as you can leave Betty Lou and the baby for the day. Don't hold off on that. Take care of yourself."

Ben reported all this to the sheriff Friday morning. The sheriff thought Wimbish might have some questions, so he told his deputy, "Come along upstairs. You tell Wimbish what you got. It doesn't sound like much to me. Who knows what he'll think."

It is true the conversation Ben Snow had with young Williamson didn't add any nails to strengthen the case. The lawmen already knew Jim Miller rode from the ambush site to the farm on Williamson's horse Saturday night, and they already knew specifics of the assassination plan from Oscar Peeler.

Details in the reported conversation did, however, give Wimbish further insight into Miller's complex character—what was important to him, how he pictured himself and what might influence his decisions.

Getting Jim Miller to come back to Oklahoma without a legal fight was a long shot, the county attorney knew, but worth the time and risk. Any sliver of information about Miller's psychological makeup could be the key to success.

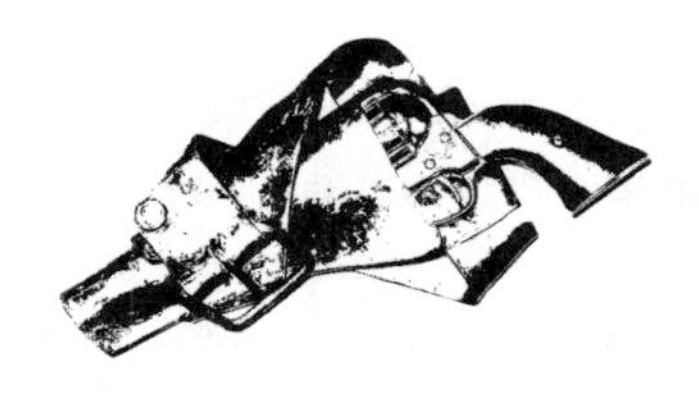

Dark Success

Funeral services for Gus Bobbitt were scheduled to start at two thirty Thursday afternoon at the Masonic Hall. Not even half the people who showed up could get in and there was a delay. I decided not to try to push my way in, being a relative newcomer in Gus's life. Others who had known him a long time weren't getting in either. Ben Snow would have had a priority except he was still out in the country after a long talk with Jim Williamson.

If there was anybody in Ada who thought poorly of Gus Bobbitt that afternoon you wouldn't have known it. Besides the overflow crowd at Masonic Hall, there was pretty much a solid line of people standing at the edge of the plank sidewalks on both sides of Main when the funeral procession went by.

"Uncle" Dick Couch led the procession down Main after services, and over to the new Rosedale Cemetery. The old one, the first cemetery down near the Frisco tracks in Old Town, was filled up; the town was growing so fast.

All the stores on Main, and on Twelfth Street too, were closed. Everyone was quiet and respectful when the hearse passed. Gus did have a lot of friends, not all of them Masons by any means.

Reverend Smootz, pastor of the Christian Church, performed the last rites at graveside. Crockett Hargis led Masonic rites. It was a very solemn afternoon in Ada.

Maybe it was the solemn funeral atmosphere, waiting for the hearse to pass, that kept people from saying angry things about Miller and the ambush. I walked along the storefronts and didn't hear any vigilante talk from the people waiting there. Nothing much different was being said about the sheriff either. I didn't hear anyone singing his praises, though. It was like a temporary truce had been called.

I'm sure Ben Snow wanted to be at the funeral. He didn't like using his friendship to get information out of Jim Williamson. More important, he and Gus Bobbitt had been good friends, despite the difference in ages.

Gus still liked to be around lawmen after he lost his deputy marshal's job at the end of Cleveland's second administration. He and his successor, good-Republican Ed Brents–also a good Mason–had been friends for a long time and Gus saw no reason to end that. He understood the political patronage game–his brother Isador was an expert on the subject–and he always called on Ed when he was in the courthouse.

Pontotoc became a regular Oklahoma county with statehood and that's when we got our first sheriff. The Chickasaws had their own sheriff before statehood but nobody ever saw him. Gus worked hard trying to win the election and become the first regular Pontotoc County sheriff. He even had his deputies lined up.

Tom Smith defeated Gus in the election and it was considered quite an upset. Tom was a good campaigner. He was also an established Republican and had the active support of local Republicans. Most important, there was nothing in his record as a businessman anybody could object to. It wasn't so simple for Gus.

Gus wasn't what you'd call a partisan Democrat. Political parties didn't seem to interest him, any of them. He didn't go in for slogans or blaming one party or the other for all the troubles in the world. I never did hear him say anything critical about President McKinley or Teddy Roosevelt, both Republicans. I don't think he was particularly interested in national affairs. People interested him. People and ranching.

More than political labels, working at The Corners saloon, and then running it, cost Gus the most votes. Ada was becoming increasingly devout–or part of it was, anyway–and the bootleg whisky business was considered a bad thing. Maybe I should say it was considered a bad thing by the citizens who would vote for a sheriff. The people who didn't think it was a bad thing didn't vote at all, such as the men down on West Main.

Gus didn't brood about his loss in the election for sheriff, mostly because he was finally in a position to buy land for his ranch. Indian severalty was abolished and he had money from The Corners. Getting the ranch operation started took most of his time and attention. Other than his pride being a bit bruised, he was a happy man.

Busy as he was at the ranch, Gus still missed law officers and the atmosphere of the law enforcement business–the heavy thud of boots, friendly guffaws and profane advice, even the smell of light oil for cleaning guns.

He would have called on the new sheriff, Tom Smith, except he really didn't like him that much. Gus didn't think he looked like a man who should be wearing a star and carrying a gun.

Gus solved that problem by avoiding Tom Smith when he came to visit in the courthouse. Instead of calling on Sheriff Smith, he dealt with his chief deputy, Ben Snow, a strapping, good looking young fellow with a mop of blond hair. Gus was going to make Ben one of his deputies. Instead, Tom Smith made him his chief deputy. Gus never came to town without calling on Ben anyway, usually passing along bits of advice gathered in the "old days."

The solemn funeral afternoon did give Bob Wimbish time to think about the information he now had in a remarkably short time. There wasn't any mystery left. It was all spelled out. The problem was how to play the hand, how to get the four men back to Oklahoma to face the charges he had already drawn up in his mind.

Wimbish didn't have any doubt, from what he'd heard, Miller could convince half the people in Texas he was one hundred fifty miles east of Ada at the time of the murder. They would be certain Miller was innocent. Miller had a remarkable way of making people believe in him, when it suited him, of course –judges, churchmen, sheriffs, Texas Rangers, about anybody.

Dwight Livingston said Wimbish's plan to get Miller to return to Ada voluntarily, or if not voluntarily, to return peaceably to a summons, didn't just jump out at him. It came to him piece by piece that the key was these same friends who would surely back up his alibi. What Wimbish needed was to get them to go one important step further and convince Miller to return to Ada and clear his name, not just support his alibi.

When Miller's Fort Worth friends heard about the unofficial charges being so openly made in Ada, they told him, with careful choice of words, he had to face the charges directly and openly, clear the record, not just avoid serving prison time. That's exactly what Wimbish hoped he would do. Miller himself wanted to do that, not only for himself, but for Sally and his three growing children, Claude, Clement and Mary Wesley.

Miller understood his friends meant well with their advice, though he told a couple of them he didn't think it made much sense to go sit in a Ada jail to prove his innocence. Most important, and he told everybody this, he didn't like to inconvenience his friends, make them go all the way up to Ada to testify on his behalf.

The Delaware regulars protested they'd be more than willing to do that for a friend. Herb LeBarre reported Miller declared, with great sincerity, he was indebted to them all. He knew how to convince people, all right, maybe from his experience preaching.

Wimbish knew he was dealing with a man as complicated as he was dangerous and any hope he had of getting Miller in the Pontotoc County jail would be a plan touching deep into Miller's wish to bury his past and become a man his family could be proud of. None of the usual ploys lawmen used to get an outlaw to come in for a "fair" trial would do. Miller was far too wary, and experienced. He'd seen it all.

Law officers in Texas and New Mexico were responsive in helping Wimbish get background information, ready to help anyone going after Miller. Both El Paso papers, the *Times* and the *Herald*, sent clips of all the stories they ever wrote about Miller and his "gang," which was a bundle. They had brave journalists out there.

Miller may have enjoyed some of the publicity in those days. One story I saw by C. W. Sorenson in particular would have pleased him. Sorenson, who called himself a West Texas humorist, wrote that Miller was no different than the rest of the bad men in the region, except that he had the best manners. Miller would have liked that.

Books have since been written about Miller. Of course they weren't available to Bob Wimbish then. Probably the best two are *Shotgun For Hire* by Glenn Shirley, and Bill James's *Untold Story Of A Texas Desperado*. They spin a good yarn and tell about all the bad things Miller did–which was plenty–but only touch on the other side of the man, the side Wimbish was trying to understand and use.

For all the talk about Miller being a Texas desperado, he was actually born in Van Buren, Crawford County, Arkansas, October 25, 1861. Everyone agrees he was taken by his parents to Robertson County, Texas, just southeast of Waco, before he was a year old.

Miller's father, Jacob, then went off to fight in the Civil War. He never returned. Maybe he got killed, maybe he just didn't want to come back. So Miller's mother took him and his sister, Georgia, to her parent's farm in Coryell County, Texas, some eighty miles further west of Robertson County. The mother, Cynthia, then left, went in search of opportunity, maybe another husband, maybe a job. Anyway, there weren't any of those things around her father's farm.

It's hard to know if the boy was really mistreated on his grandfather's farm, but even his sister, Georgia, was to say Grandpa was too hard on him. No question, young Jim worked hard. So did the grandfather. They all did.

As hard as they worked, the grandparents and the children never missed church. That's no doubt how going to church and church activities became so important to Jim Miller, at least the unshakeable routine became important. There would have to be a question of whether the church's message sunk in, or that the message applied to him, too.

None of the biographers, and none of the court and police reports I ever saw, really pinned down the widespread story that young Jim Miller killed his grandfather with a shotgun blast when he was eight years old. There were investigations, and that got in the Fort Worth papers, but because of the suspect's age, nothing ever came of it.

There was no uncertainty when Miller was arrested for killing his brother-in-law, John Coop, with a shotgun the evening of July 30, 1884. Coop was snoozing on his front porch at the time. Miller had gone to live with his sister, Georgia, on Coop's farm on Plumb Creek, just south of Gatesville, also in Coryell County.

Coop was a plain spoken man who thought Miller could have done better with some assigned chores. Offended by Coop's sarcastic tone of voice, Miller, twenty two years old, bided his time, then ended the disagreement with one shot.

Miller was tried, convicted and sentenced to life imprisonment. However, the presiding judge had some doubts and ordered a second trial. Witnesses that made the prosecutor's case in the first trial, disappeared, couldn't be found anywhere. The case was dismissed. Miller was free. He was free but you can imagine he wasn't particularly welcome in Coryell County any more. He headed west.

Miller got a job in McCulloch County in 1887 on a ranch run by Manen Clements Sr. It must have been a typical, small operation on leased land for that part of West Texas, important to Miller because it was there he met his wife, the ranch owner's daughter, Sarah Francis Clementine Clements, though she was called Sally. She was a shy but pretty girl from the pictures I've seen. Miller was devoted to her for the rest of his life.

His job on the Clements' ranch was important to Miller in another way too. There he met Manen Clements Jr. "Manny," as he was called, was sometimes called a "spirited" youth in the local papers, which in plainer language meant that he was frequently in trouble with the law.

Manny wasn't a killer but he was always a suspect when livestock disappeared in McCulloch County. Whether a truly righteous brother-in-law would have made any difference in Jim Miller's career is doubtful. He couldn't have had a worse mentor than Manny Clements in any case.

Clements Senior was not enthusiastic about Miller as a possible son-in-law when he saw Sally was much taken with the new hired hand. He had no land, no money. What he had was a disturbing past for someone just twenty-two years old.

The senior Clements wasn't a problem long. He was a candidate for sheriff to serve both McCulloch and Runnel Counties and in the course of his campaigning got into a political dispute with Joe Townsend, city marshal in Ballinger. The argument took an ugly turn and the marshal shot and killed Clements.

Jim Miller took it upon himself to avenge Clements' death on behalf of the whole family. He rode into Ballinger, found the marshal, called him down for killing Clements, then shot him. As generally the case when Miller used his revolver, he didn't kill Townsend. Fortunately for Miller, most of the people in Ballinger thought Townsend had it coming. Nothing was done.

While he might have fallen short as the avenger, Miller got full credit from the Clements family. They admired how he went right into town and took Townsend on. He was accepted. Sally and Jim were married February 15, 1888.

With the senior Clements gone, there didn't seem to be much future at the ranch. Manny didn't want to be tied down. Jim Miller didn't want to take on all the work and lease obligations starting out. His ambitions were already beyond that.

To break away from the ranch routine, Miller answered a newspaper ad run by Sheriff Alex "Bud" Frazer out further west in Pecos City, Reeves County. Frazer was trying to recruit two deputies. Deputies didn't last long out there.

Miller was fairly tall–he stood over six feet–and mannerly, something he probably got the hard way from his grandparents. You'd have to admit he was a nice looking young man, with dark hair and gray eyes. He got one of Sheriff Frazer's deputy jobs.

Miller did very well as a lawman. People were impressed with how fearlessly he handled town ruffians. The ruffians resented being bossed around by the ordinary run of new, young deputies, but Miller rose above that with soft-spoken, steely resolve. He was fearless. Established in his job, Miller sent for Sally and they began their married life together in Pecos City in 1891.

It was in Pecos City Miller affiliated officially with the Methodists. He became a church regular on his own, not on Grandpa's insistence.

Miller's first whole year as a deputy was a success, as far as the townspeople could see. He did have to kill a prisoner he was escorting from Pecos City to Fort Stockton. His explanation was that the prisoner tried to escape. Nothing ever came of that because the prisoner was Mexican anyway. That's the way citizens of Pecos City thought about it.

More important to some of the ranchers than why a Mexican prisoner got shot was Miller's growing, and quick, success as a rancher on a very few acres of leased land. These ranchers were beginning to believe Miller's herd was growing with their cattle and without a bill of sale. They demanded Sheriff Frazer investigate.

The sheriff did investigate his prized deputy and announced that Miller was innocent. It took another year with more widespread livestock rustling for doubts about Miller's innocence to rise again. Horses and mules were also disappearing all over Reeves and Pecos Counties, not just cattle.

Sheriff Frazer had to face the truth. From mounting evidence, his deputy had to be part of a gang running livestock across the Rio Grande into Mexico, either running the stock across the river themselves, or getting a dim witted ranch hand to deliver some of his employer's herd across for eight dollars a head.

When the thieving ranch hand got the cattle across into Mexico, Miller and his gang told him the price had dropped to two dollars. The thief was in no position to complain. To argue too much with that hard bunch would be an invitation to a shallow Mexican grave. He could hardly complain to law officers if he got back across the river alive, having stolen the cattle in the first place.

When the gang got a little herd built up in Mexico, they'd sell it to an American rancher and let him drive the stolen cattle back over the Rio

Grande, that, or pay some Mexican vaqueros to do it. Manny Clements was said to be a member of the gang.

The rustling problem got so bad the ranchers demanded Sheriff Frazer do something about it or quit. They insisted on a showdown, but before a showdown could be set up, the sheriff was suddenly called away from Pecos City on family business. While he was gone, his friends got word to him Jim Miller and his gang were going to kill him when he returned. The Miller gang would then take over Reeves County.

The sheriff detoured on his way home to get John R. Hughes, a famous Texas Ranger of the day, to come back to Pecos City with him and confront the outlaws. They made a good team and without anybody being killed, they got indictments against Miller and others for conspiring to kill Frazer.

Miller went to jail briefly while court orders were handed down, remanding the case to El Paso County because so many people in Reeves County had made up their minds that Miller was guilty. Then, as it was to happen many times, the principal witness against Miller and his cronies was shot and killed. The conspirators were acquitted for lack of evidence.

Sally had remained in her little house in Pecos City all this time, so Miller went back as soon as he was freed in El Paso. He was smart enough to know Sheriff Frazer was not forgiving. It was reported–true or not–Miller sewed metal plates into the front of his citified coat in preparation for the showdown sure to come. He wore that coat on Pecos City streets without fail, even with the weather turning hot.

Sheriff Frazer did originate the first encounter, coming up behind Miller on a side street and calling his name. Miller turned. Frazer shot at fairly close range and heard both the first and second bullets ricochet. They must have ricocheted right off the metal plates.

Miller was able to get off a shot before he was hit again in his right arm and lower body. He got off two shots with his left hand, one close to the sheriff, the second striking a bystander. He then slumped into the dusty street. This was the morning of April 12, 1894.

Miller was taken first to a nearby hotel and then to the Pecos City hospital. It took nearly six months for him to recover. In that time, Sheriff Frazer lost his election to stay in office. He traveled around the region looking for law enforcement work. The former sheriff came back to Pecos City once in a while. He had friends and a small house there.

On one of these visits–November, 1894–Frazer and Miller met again on the street and began firing at once, no words necessary. Miller's right arm was hit again and he tried to fire left handed.

Frazer, who must have been a pretty good shot, hit Miller's upper body twice and for the second time, heard the bullets ricochet. Bystanders said Frazer seemed to panic when he couldn't finish Miller with his good shots to the body, and just left his sagging opponent in the street, still trying to hit something with his left-handed efforts. Miller was taken back to the Pecos City hospital but in less serious condition than his first visit.

Before he got out of the hospital Miller showed he was different than the ordinary bad man all right, not just about manners in the way Sorenson pointed out though. Miller filed suit against Frazer for attempted murder, seeking revenge in the courts.

Being on the prosecutor's side of the law didn't work for Miller. After the case was remanded to El Paso, the jury there couldn't agree on the charge of premeditated murder. The case was then sent to Colorado City, Texas, where the jury found Frazer not guilty.

Both Frazer and Miller understood the fight wasn't over. They tracked one another through a network of kin for many months. Then Miller got word that Frazer had been seen a number of times playing cards with friends in a Toyah, Texas, saloon. Toyah was a hardscrabble little ranching town some sixty miles southwest of Pecos.

I used to think the country around the Triple R in Nueces County was pretty forlorn, but that was a rancher's heaven compared to the land west of Pecos. How cattle stayed alive out there was a wonder. It was also a wonder the ranchers ever found them, they had to forage so far in that rough country to find anything to eat or water to drink. No surprise, Toyah was an unruly community. Life was hard.

Toyah being a tough place didn't bother Miller and he made the long ride down there from Pecos to scout the scene. He wanted to find out if Frazer really was working out there somewhere, and if he was, he needed to know where he lived, how he moved around. He needed to pick up some pattern of Frazer's comings and goings. Then he could figure out how best to meet him again, some way without using pistols, which Miller was beginning to realize wasn't to his advantage.

You could say Miller's approach to the job in Toyah set the pattern for all of his future assassinations. Certainly it was the same in the Ben Collins ambush near Tishomingo and later here in Pontotoc County.

From the Toyah job on, Miller took his time and spent money scouting the whole thing out–where he could best lie in wait and use his shotgun from short range. He never missed with a shotgun. Hitting something is a lot easier with a shotgun, of course, particularly from a close ambush.

Maybe Miller never did find out where Frazer lived. Or perhaps he decided there was a better approach. He had learned Frazer came into town to play cards Saturday mornings, always in the same saloon and mostly with the same men. While there was no stealth involved in his plan of attack, there was an almost guaranteed reaction from Frazer which would set up a solid case for self-defense.

Late Saturday morning, September 14, 1896, nearly two years after their first gunfight, Miller was informed the card game was on. Miller walked into the saloon with his shotgun and headed for the table at the back where Frazer and his cronies were playing. About twenty feet from the table, he took aim with his Meacham shotgun and fired.

Frazer's friends scattered away from both sides of him. Miller shot again at Frazer who slumped in his chair and then fell to the floor. Miller opened the breech of his shotgun and put in two new rounds. He told everybody to stand back and then announced he never would have fired if Frazer hadn't made what he described as a "gun play."

This point, that Frazer had made a gun play, was important in the trial for murder that followed in Eastland County, some three hundred miles east of Toyah, about eighty miles west of Fort Worth.

The trial was moved that far away because people around Toyah were upset about the cold-blooded way the killing was done. Many citizens wanted to hang Miller without unnecessary legal delays.

In the first trial, the seven witnesses called could not agree on the "gun play" issue. There was agreement Frazer did see Miller come into the saloon–it wasn't very big–and did shift all the cards he was holding into his left hand. That would leave his right, or shooting hand, free. Miller's "self defense" case was based on this and it was enough to deadlock the jury. Miller was acquitted and a second trial was ordered.

Waiting for the second trail, Miller took a very strong evangelical role on behalf of his church, traveling through the countryside conducting prayer meetings. This was noted by all his defense witnesses, testimony that proved to be almost as important to his defense as the fact all the prosecutor's witnesses had disappeared. Miller was acquitted again.

However suspicious this might seem looking back, it must have looked all right out in West Texas then. Jim Miller was commissioned in the Texas Rangers August 30, 1898. Soon after his commission, he killed two men on a ranch near the Pecos River. He was sent out to the ranch to talk to them. Gunfire broke out first. Not long after that he was involved in another gunfight which the authorities thought unnecessary. By November 30, his career as a Texas Ranger was over.

All the shooting, even as a Texas Ranger, the disastrous gun battles with Frazer, then the two trials were too much for Sally. She got her husband to agree to move away from the violence of West Texas and New Mexico and settle in Fort Worth. She had traveled to Fort Worth during Miller's trial in Eastland County and the travel experience convinced her city life was what she wanted.

In 1900 Miller bought a boarding house for Sally and her mother to run at 108 East Weatherford Street near downtown Fort Worth. It was all Sally dreamed of. She had her three children and her mother in her own calm world.

Miller was happy enough with the set up. First of all, he was gone a great deal which would be natural enough for a cattle dealer. That's what he called himself. That's what he told his Delaware Hotel friends he was. His business card said "Cattle Dealer." "Real Estate" was added later. He apparently did some legitimate business buying and selling cattle. That didn't mean he had given up his earlier approach to the cattle business–stealing cattle.

Though it was a long way from Fort Worth, Miller remained active with his cronies in West Texas and New Mexico, as far west as El Paso. His "gang," as it was later called, developed about the same routine Miller used in Reeves and Pecos Counties–running stolen stock across the Rio Grande, building up a little herd, then selling everything to a rancher back on the American side.

It was in these old Southwest haunts of his Miller developed a reputation as an assassin, someone who would work on assignment. The most famous case out there was the murder of Pat Garrett near Las Cruces, New Mexico, February 19, 1908. You remember Garrett was the Sheriff of Lincoln County, New Mexico, who shot Billy the Kid in 1888.

Jim Miller had enough bad experience dueling with people face to face, out in the open. He was too smart to take on the likes of Pat Garrett who had earlier survived cattle-town violence in Kansas as a lawman. He didn't mind setting things up, though.

Miller was riding along on the wagon seat with Garrett near the famous sheriff's ranch near Las Cruces when they passed a big rock near the edge of the road. Once the wagon was by the rock, there was a rifle shot. Garrett, sheriff of Dona Ana County at that time, was hit in the back of the head and fell off the wagon, dead.

Pat Garrett was well known all over the West. He was a hero to many people. For him to be bushwhacked like that caused a big commotion. It was the heavy-bold headline story in the El Paso papers for days.

Nailing Jim Miller for the murder was not easy. He was just riding along with Garrett. So the newspapers didn't blame him. Neither did New Mexican lawmen.

That didn't stop Joseph H. Stahl, however. He was a great friend and admirer of Garrett's. He was also a very successful Houston contractor who supervised construction of the new Texas Capital building in Austin. He was much admired in Texas.

Stahl shouted to the world through any newspaper that would quote him–I saw it in the Oklahoma City papers–that Wren Brazzell was the man behind the rock who pulled the trigger, but it was Jim Miller who set the ambush up. Stahl said Miller wanted to get rid of Garrett because Garrett was on to his gang's scheme of running stolen livestock across the Rio Grande–the old routine.

Stahl kept his charges going in the newspapers for weeks, but the New Mexico authorities didn't have any luck at all. They had no evidence to move on anybody, even Wren Brazzell. Brazzell said he was in a Las Cruces bar at the time of the ambush and had witnesses to prove it. Jim Miller was questioned, of course, and admitted he knew Wren Brazzell. That's all there was to it. There were no indictments.

The last thing Joseph Stahl wanted was to do Jim Miller a favor. His hatred for Miller just kept growing. Yet his charges that Miller was a paid assassin who set up the Garrett murder was a big help for someone getting into the assassination business on a regional basis. The publicity was invaluable.

Miller also helped advance his growing reputation as a calculating killer by making threatening statements. After a court appearance in El Paso he was widely quoted as saying, "Nobody testifies against me and lives."

That statement sounds to me like somebody not very smart said it, or somebody very self confident, or arrogant. Or maybe smart and arrogant. If Miller wanted people to believe testifying against him was a dangerous thing to do, he succeeded. Looking at his record for avoiding prison, you'd have to say it worked.

The idea that danger was involved for those who proceeded against him hovered over all of Miller's later judicial appearances, including here in Ada. Witnesses for the prosecution weren't the only ones who would feel threatened, jurors came under the cloud, too. Miller didn't make any more direct, public threats, however. Didn't have to. Cautionary alarms from concerned citizens usually set the stage for him.

Pat Garrett's death was news all over the southwest, not just around El Paso. Certainly it was in Fort Worth since one of their citizens, the "cattle dealer," was involved.

Jesse West saw the stories in the Canadian, Texas, weekly, out on the Panhandle, and it gave him an idea. The thought of a professional assassin giving Gus Bobbitt what he deserved grew in his mind. What he needed was a go-between. He found that person in a *Fort Worth Record* story that reported Miller and Barry Burwell of Fort Worth, "a prominent bail bondsman," had been associates in a soured real estate deal.

Jesse West wrote to Burwell to say he would like to meet him in Oklahoma City the next time he was there to discuss a business venture. Weeks later a meeting took place. West ventured into his "business" with great care. When West finally got down to the dirty business he had in mind, Burwell thought it could be done. The way they'd work it, West would never see or communicate in any way with Miller. Burwell would be the only link between the ranchers and the assassin.

Miller was away from home much of the time in those days, as I said, out in West Texas and New Mexico. He spent a lot of time on Texas & Pacific trains running between Fort Worth and El Paso, or maybe Van Horn, east of El Paso, where he had a small ranch operation.

When Miller wasn't in the field, he was living at home in the boarding house on Weatherford Street, becoming a city man, a well dressed businessman, very much at home with the entrepreneurs at the Delaware. I have no doubt he would have liked to make that his life, and give up his old ways. He still needed money though, and opportunities to make money with his shotgun just kept coming his way, like the job Barry Burwell brought him.

With money in the bank, Miller could afford to do very careful planning, to take every precaution. He expected to do that in the Gus Bobbitt assignment, since his employers were known to be wealthy. However, he didn't find a way to guard against over confidence, or maybe it was a kind of arrogance, a grave flaw that grew out of his success cutting men down and slipping the consequences through the years.

11

Miller Taken

Just how much indecision Bob Wimbish ever suffered about anything, I don't know. Just looking at him and hearing him talk, you'd have to say none at all. That wasn't true when it came to starting the plan to get Jim Miller back to Ada. Dwight told me he really worried over that.

"Set the hook too early, you get no fish. Too late, the fish has the bait and is gone," Dwight remembered him saying something along those lines. That doesn't sound like the Bob Wimbish I know. Maybe he did say something like that to his friend Dwight. I got the idea, anyway.

Wimbish certainly did want to allow enough time for Miller's friends to convince him he should proceed like an innocent man wrongly accused, go to Ada and get the matter cleared up, if that's what it took to clean the slate. Too much time and Miller's strong combativeness would take over and it could be a legal struggle for years.

There was nothing more to do in Ada. The county attorney's office was ready. It all depended on Miller's frame of mind or mood. That would be difficult to judge anywhere. Ada, Oklahoma, certainly wasn't the place. Wimbish decided to get one more reading from Herb LaBarre in Fort Worth and called him.

"Miller hasn't been in here lately," Herb said, "so I haven't seen him. I haven't heard anything that would change your plans for dealing with him, though. Everything's the same, far as I know."

"All right, Herb. Thanks a lot. We might as well go ahead. We'll just deal with the Tarrant County authorities in a routine way. Tell 'em we have a warrant for Miller's arrest...he's wanted in Oklahoma for questioning. That's all. They've been helpful so far."

"Yeah. That's what I'd do. Miller's got friends around the courthouse. I guess you know that. They'll play it straight with you, friend of Miller's or not, if it's a regular legal procedure.

"Guess I don't need to tell you, Bob," Herb added, "whoever deals with him better be ready for anything."

Law enforcement officers in Tarrant County were very helpful in advising Wimbish where they could find Miller when he was in the county. They said he could be found in one of three places – at the Weatherford Street boarding house or the Delaware Hotel in Fort Worth, or if he wasn't in town, he would be out on his farm eighteen miles northwest of the city.

There was no question Wimbish had taken over the lead in the Bobbitt murder case. He still needed the sheriff's cooperation though, starting with having at least two deputies assigned to help bring Jim Miller back to Ada. He also needed the sheriff's agreement to have Ada Police Chief George Culver head the Pontotoc County force, whoever else was going to be part of it. Mayor King– Culver's boss – would have to agree, too.

Sheriff Smith and the county prosecutor both felt they shouldn't send a platoon of officers down to Tarrant County. Lawmen there could be offended by that, as if there was a doubt who was really in charge in the county. There still had to be enough Oklahomans to get to the three places Miller might be on a given day, without going from one place and then another, as if they were serving a warrant for trespassing. Chief Culver outlined the approach they'd take.

The chief said he would go to the boarding house and then to the hotel, if Miller wasn't at home. He reasoned Miller wouldn't cause any commotion in front of his family, or in front of his friends at the hotel. In any case, there would be support in downtown Fort Worth.

Culver said he wanted at least two deputy sheriffs to go out to the farm, since nobody knew if he would be alone out there. Also nobody could guess if Miller would accept the arrest summons peacefully and return to Ada, even if he was alone.

At the request of the police chief, Sheriff Smith assigned his chief deputy, Ben Snow, to the mission. Ben was permitted to appoint any other additional deputy he wanted. Ben selected Sid Higgins, who had been involved in the case from the beginning. Sheriff Smith agreed.

Ben told me years later it was a nervous time riding down to Fort Worth March 30. All three of them had been briefed plenty on Jim Miller and were told to be ready for any kind of reaction, even gun play, though he hadn't been doing business that way in recent years. Ben's a smart young fella' and doesn't forget much. Here's what he told me about the trip–

"Chief Culver decided we should get down to Fort Worth on the Santa Fe from Paul's Valley, and spend the night at a little hotel they got down there near the depot. First thing in the morning, we'd show up and pay respects at the Tarrant County sheriff's office. And in addition to payin' respects, Ben recalled, we wanted to find out if there had been any changes that would make a difference in our plans, such as a half dozen of his West Texas gang showing up.

People in the sheriff's office were accommodating enough about the whole thing, Ben said, mindful that Miller had friends in the office. They thought Miller had been out on his farm the last couple of days, alone as far as they knew. "He goes his own way. Watch yourself," they reminded us.

The chief asked me and Sid to get a buggy for our trip out to the Miller farm. He wanted Miller to travel right with us, if he was there and we brought him back, not on his own horse. That's why we needed a big buggy, room for all of us. Sheriff's deputies don't ordinarily ride in buggies. The rig the sheriff's office was able to get for us was old, and not much better than a wagon for ride. Springs were gone. Still, it had room enough.

Most of the trip we went along the Denver & Rio Grande tracks headin' northwest to Amarillo. Never saw a train.

I was surprised at how much farmin' there was around Fort Worth. The ploughed fields were dark brown, almost black. Fields in winter wheat were bright green. All the rest was open prairie something like Pontotoc, dusty looking but beginnin' to green. The wind hadn't started up yet–no dust in the air–and you could see a long way.

Tarrant County is maybe one hundred miles south of Pontotoc, and some west. Not far, not a big trip, but there's more of a change in the country than I thought there would be. Tarrant County must be land between the High Plains and the Grand Prairie–flatter, higher than Pontotoc. Grass is shorter, nowhere near as many trees. I can see why they call it the beginning of the West.

Tarrant County, bein' south of Pontotoc, sees spring a little bit earlier. Sid and I were lucky to get one of the bright and fairly warm mornings for late March out there. It's not always like that in springtime. Sittin' up on the driver's bench for four or five hours with a "norther howlin"around would've been miserable.

The sheriff's men told us to be on the lookout for a farm road, or maybe more of a wagon path, that went due west off the Amarillo road, about fifteen miles out of town. Jim Miller's place was three miles down that road. They said there wasn't any sign.

We finally saw some kind of road, or maybe trail with wagon tracks. There wasn't any other kind of road turnin' off anywhere else, so we turned off.

We went for a ways. It might have been a couple of miles. Then we saw this house, a small house but still two stories, sittin' out all alone. Not a thing around it. Not a tree, shrub, nothin' else.

We kept going…up to two fence posts. They might have been for a gate, 'cept there wasn't any gate. Wasn't any fence leading up to the posts either.

From the gate, or fence posts anyway, we could see a man sittin' on a rocking chair on the porch. He was in his shirtsleeves. No collar. He was wearin' a city hat pulled down to cover his eyes. He was facing right into the sun.

Nobody else around we could see. Maybe somebody in the house. We didn't know. If the man on the porch had any firearms, we couldn't see 'em. No rifle or shotgun, for sure. I nudged Sid. "Let's go."

We got out of the buggy and walked toward the house, maybe thirty yards. Both Sid and I did have our sidearms in sight. We wore our deputy badges, so we should have been armed.

About ten or fifteen yards from the house we stopped. "Mr. Miller?" I asked.

The man in the rocker didn't say anything for a bit, then he lifted his head a little. "Yeah."

"Mr. Miller. I'm Ben Snow, sheriff's deputy from Pontotoc County, Oklahoma. This here's my partner, Sid Higgins. We have a warrant for your arrest. They want to talk to you back in Ada about the death of Gus Bobbitt in February."

Miller didn't move. Then he grunted and looked up at us. He didn't look like a wild man, or a killer, or really anything out of the ordinary. He looked fit enough, like he worked outdoors. Not a storeowner or something like that.

"Yeah, I know you got a warrant. Known about it for a week. The whole thing is crazy. I never heard of that man Bobbitt before. I wasn't anywhere near Ada when he was killed. And I can prove it."

Miller sat there. Sid and I stood there, still about ten yards from the porch.

"Mr. Miller. I know you were a deputy sheriff out west and know how this works. I got a warrant and I got no choice but to serve it. That's my job. And I got to ask you to come with us."

He leaned forward, put his hands on his knees and pushed himself out of the chair, acting like the whole thing made him tired. He stood up and I saw he was taller'n than average, and strong looking. I could see if he wanted to cause trouble he could, even without a gun. I thought right then it would be nice if Chief Culver was with us. Anybody would think twice about taking him on.

"All right. I know you got no choice. Neither do I. Can't let people run around sayin' I killed somebody when I didn't. Bad for my business, crazy or not."

He turned and started for the door of his house. Sid and I both moved forward a little.

"All right, boys," he said, turning back. "You got no cause to be jumpy. You can come in. I want to put some shirts in a bag and I'll go with you. I don't want to look like a saddle tramp, even in a Ada jail."

We all went into the house, which was darn near empty. There was a table and a chair near a little cook stove, and that was about it. It had a funny smell, I remember. Not bad. Most like green lumber that didn't get much airing.

"My stuff's upstairs. Hang on," Miller said and went up the creaky stairs. They didn't creak because they were so old. It was more that they weren't very well built.

Sid and I loosened our guns and separated, Sid on one side of the room me on the other. We didn't know what to expect. In three or four minutes, Miller came back down with a little suitcase, or valise, whatever you call 'em.

"All right. Let's go. I got a pony out back I need to get back into town."

Goin' out the door, I said, "Mr. Miller. I'd be obliged if you came and got into the buggy with us. Get up on the bench with Sid, if you will. Then I'll go 'round and hitch your pony to the buggy."

Miller didn't say anything. He just headed out where we left the buggy, by the two fence posts. He still didn't have a tie on. He looked kind of funny with his businessman suit and hat, like he got dressed in too big a hurry. Other than a shirt buttoned at the top but no tie, he could'a passed as an undertaker, or a lawyer, something like that.

Sid tried to get Miller to talkin' about anything up there on the bench going back to town–the weather, crops, farm prices, anything. That got 'im nowhere. Not that Miller was surly. He just answered "yes" or "no," or "maybe" and let Sid do the talking. Sid can do that.

When we could see the first of the big buildings in Fort Worth, Miller turned to me and said, "I'm going with you because I've got no choice if I'm going to prove I had nothin' to do with that Bobbitt murder. I don't like it much, I can tell you, 'cause I had nothin' to do with it."

Miller paused, turned to look straight ahead, then turned back to me again– "You say you want to head north on the early train tomorrow. That's fine. What about tonight? You expect me to spend the night in the county jail?"

Ben told me he was thrown off by the question because that's exactly what he expected, that Miller would spend the night in the Tarrant County jail. Ben said he kind'a stammered a little, didn't come up with a quick answer. Miller had been cooperative and there was still a long way back to Ada.

Ben said Miller spoke up again. "Most of the men in the sheriff's office are friends of mine. They know I wasn't involved in your Bobbitt case. Still, most of 'em argue I should go back and clear this up. Anyway, I don't feel like spendin' a night in their jail."

Ben was hard put to answer that. People in the sheriff's office had been helpful. He didn't want them to start siding with Miller. The Oklahomans might need their help. Miller had turned back and was looking straight down the road, not saying a word.

Ben knew they were going to meet George Culver at the sheriff's office in late afternoon. He decided he would just wait and see what Chief Culver wanted to do. So he told Miller he'd have to wait to see what the chief thought about it, since he was the head of the Pontotoc County lawmen there in Fort Worth.

The Ada police chief was a smart one and he understood that it would be a lot easier getting back to Ada if Miller was cooperative if not friendly. What he proposed, and what they did, was rent a small dormitory kind of room at the depot hotel and they all slept there.

It was an odd night, Ben remembered. Nobody had much to say. It was mostly grunts. Even Sid was put off. It did solve Miller's problem about the jail though.

"We had breakfast together and then got an early train for Dallas that connected with the Frisco north to Ada. The chief didn't want to spend another night in a hotel."

Ben said Chief Culver wouldn't get it out of his mind that Miller's gang might try to get him off that train, so he arranged to have the four of them sit in the Indian section at one end of the car. The chief could see anyone coming in at the far end. The toilet bulkhead shielded them from anyone coming up in back of them unseen. Culver didn't say much to anyone really, and acted like he was involved in something he didn't like. Maybe it was Miller he didn't like, Ben guessed.

Whatever advantages there might have been traveling in the Indian section, it was a long way from the stove in the middle section where white people sat, Ben remembered. As soon as the sun came up strong they were all warm enough, anyway.

Ben told me Miller almost convinced the three of them he was innocent on the train ride back to Ada from Fort Worth, and they knew better than anyone else on earth he was the one who shot Gus Bobbitt. Ben said it wasn't that Miller was jolly, or tried to flatter anybody. In fact, he didn't say twenty words the first hour on the train.

It was mid afternoon, Ben remembered, and they were more than an hour north of the Red River, well on their way to Ada when Miller, looking out the window, said "the pasture looks good."

"We all looked at him like he said some great thing," Ben recalled. "There was nothin' to what he said, of course, but he hadn't opened his mouth for an hour and we had just about stopped trying to talk...except for Sid maybe."

Miller picked up on our surprise, and went on, "I got a farm just west of Ardmore. Like to see there's moisture this time of the year."

Ben remembered silence settled in again over the steady clacking from the track underneath. Then Miller looked straight at Chief Culver and asked, "You from around here?"

The question might have startled the Chief a little, a question about himself, like it might have been too personal from a man he didn't like, Ben thought. He looked straight back at Miller. No smile. Finally he replied, "No. I'm from Galveston."

It was Miller's turn. He looked out the window again, then, "Guess you wouldn't care much about the pasture, one way or another, if you didn't get your start around the cattle business. Guess it must have been fish, down there on the Gulf...nothin' wrong with that."

Ben wondered if Chief Culver thought Miller might be goading him, though the two of them got along all right at the hotel. Neither one said more than twenty words. Finally Culver pulled his guard down and said, "Yeah. Fish. It was a tough life on those boats."

"It would have been a tough life for me," Sid Higgins added, pleased that there was some talking at last. "I was on a boat once and got sick in five minutes. I like the ground."

Culver looked at Higgins. "It was a tough life when the fleet came in too, Sid, on the docks, and that was on the ground.

"You grow up fast. All kinds of people on those boats. Lot of them wanted by the law. They take anybody they can get for crew. No questions asked."

George Culver's suggestion that he had a hard youth seemed to stir something in Miller, maybe that he still believed working on his grandfather's farm was about as bad as slavery. "Why did you keep doin' it?" Miller asked in a way that was almost friendly. Anyway, Ben didn't think he was trying to start an argument.

Culver paused, not sure he wanted to discuss details of his past with Miller, then said, "I had to eat. I didn't know how to do anything but pull nets."

"You're not pullin' nets now."

Chief Culver looked at him, wary but not bristling. Ben said he couldn't see any mockery in Miller's question or his face. It was as if Miller was trying to relate his own difficult youth with one just as difficult, but with such a different outcome.

"No," Chief Culver answered. "…you learn to take care of yourself on the docks. On the boats sometimes, too. I decided if I was going to fight all the time, I might as well get paid for it, not count on catchin' fish. Answered an ad in the Galveston newspaper and got to be a policeman."

Ben said Miller didn't smile or make light of it. He was obviously interested. Then Miller agreed, "Yeah, I know. I answered an ad and became a deputy sheriff out in Reeves County…Pecos. They got a lot of trouble out there."

Both Sid and I looked up and smiled at the recognition of deputy sheriffs, even in Reeves County. "There's worse things to be," Sid pointed out.

The train click-clacked along, prairie and pasture outside, an occasional farm in the distance, retreating out the windows. The blue silhouette of the Arbuckle Mountains lined the horizon to the southwest.

"No offense," Miller said in a quiet way, looking at Sid. "Bein' a deputy sheriff is a good thing. Can be hard, too, I know…

"Well, I was a Texas Ranger, too. Got my commission August eight in '98 out in West Texas," Miller said. "I was proud to be a Ranger. Might have been a Ranger yet, 'cept there was a mix–up. They thought I shot a rancher when I didn't need to. They sent me out to talk to that old cuss, 'cept he didn't want to talk, he wanted to fight. I had no choice. We parted company."

"You quit the Rangers over that?" Sid asked. Sid would be doubtful because he thought being a Texas Ranger was about as high as you can go in law enforcement.

"Oh, I liked bein' a Ranger all right," Miller answered. "Cept they got more rules than the army. You got to do everything just so. You pretty near have to let someone shoot at you before you're supposed to do anything. Then they want to know where you are every minute. It's just not for me."

Ben said all three Oklahomans knew it wasn't Miller's decision to leave the two jobs he had in Texas law enforcement, and he was even indicted for conspiring to murder one former boss, the sheriff, in Reeves County. No bloodshed was involved or threatened in his departure from the Rangers. They just revoked his commission.

Ben said he didn't want to make a point of how Miller left his jobs in law enforcement. The trip was going better than anyone thought it would and it just wouldn't make sense, close to the end as they were, to set Miller off some way. He guessed both Chief Culver and Sid figured that out, too. Miller wasn't through with the conversation, though.

Looking at the chief, Miller asked, "Well, how did you get way up here? It's a long way from the ocean."

"Oh, I was in a barber shop. Saw an ad in *Policeman's Gazette*. I was gettin' tired of those boat people…

"When the fleet came in, it was like a war, everybody drunk and fightin'. It's a strange life. I didn't like any part of it, on the boats or even around 'em. Always wondered what Indian Territory was like. Thought I'd try to get the job the Ada people advertised and find out for myself. Got the job and here I am."

Ben knew Sid liked George Culver, as most of them did, and Sid added, "We're glad to have you up here, George. We need people like you."

Miller didn't look doubtful by any means, Ben remembered, but was quick to ask the chief, "You traded one war for another, didn't you? Didn't you have thirty murders in Pontotoc County last year?"

"Thirty six," Sid put in, as if it was something to be proud of, "plus more just across the Canadian River in Pottawatomie and Seminole County."

Chief Culver then looked straight at Miller. "You been up here? Been to Ada?"

"Sure. I've been all over the county, lookin' for anybody wantin' to cut back his herd–at a good price for me, you understand. That's what I do–buy and sell cattle. Have a tenant farm just outside Ardmore. The one back there a way. And I got the one north of Fort Worth. The two of you saw that one. Had one out in Van Horn for a while."

Ben said the talk kind of ran out there, the lawmen hoping Miller might say something about Gus Bobbitt, what he thought about the case, or anything that might prove useful in the coming trial. Ben could only guess what was going on in Miller's mind. He guessed he was thinking what he could say to convince three lawmen, anyway, convince them he wasn't near Pontotoc County last February 27, the night Gus Bobbitt died.

Miller broke the silence: "Bein' an old lawman myself," he said, looking at Chief Culver, "I saw that warrant you had was authorized by the county attorney and here you are, the Ada chief of police, with two deputy sheriffs.

"Where's the sheriff? Not that there's anything wrong with bein' a city chief. My brother-in-law was constable out in El Paso. You got a different kind of set up in Ada?"

Chief Culver looked annoyed for a second, Ben remembered, like he thought Miller was making fun of the country folks. Sometimes people from the cities like Fort Worth did make fun of little towns, particularly towns in Oklahoma.

"Tom Smith is our sheriff," Culver said calmly. "He was out of town when all this started, and I've been involved since the night of the murder. The sheriff asked me to stick with it, since we're all involved anyway. The mayor, my boss, said okay and I agreed to do it."

Miller nodded, looked out the window. "What do you suppose is wrong? All those murders?

"Like I said, I was in law out in Reeves County. That's when they used to say 'there isn't any law west of the Pecos.' Maybe that was left over from Roy Bean's time. Anyway, we were there. Didn't always get to do everything by the book, everything just so, but we were there. It wasn't as bad as Ada though."

The reference to Ada touched Chief Culver. "Well, it isn't just Ada. In fact, Ada itself is doin' pretty well. It's the whole rest of the county, and it's a big one.

"We're still gettin' whisky dealers and the tough drifters left over from prohibition and the Canadian River saloons. We still get Texans in trouble with the law. They just jump across the Red River and think nobody can touch 'em in Oklahoma, like we were still Indian Territory, another country."

Sid must have felt the chief was being critical. "Don't forget," he said, "we didn't even have a sheriff two years ago. I mean a real sheriff. That came with bein' a state. A few deputy marshals is all we had...as long as they lasted. And no court for a long time. Well, the one over at Fort Smith in Arkansas, then Muskogee, still a long way off."

"Sid," the chief replied. "I didn't mean to sound critical. I agree with what you say. There's a big job ahead, whatever the reason. People can't just bring their own justice however they see fit."

Jim Miller nodded his agreement. Didn't say anything for a moment, then, "I think they're lucky to have you boys. You're doin' a good thing, a job that needs doin.

"I might have stayed in law enforcement, but there didn't seem to be any future in it, at least in Reeves County. I might 'a stayed in the Rangers, if we could've worked things out. They sure got their own way of doin' things, though."

It was late afternoon, April 1, 1909 when the Frisco train from Texas pulled into the depot. The *Ada Evening News* reported the next day five hundred citizens were on hand to see Jim Miller's arrival. The newspaper wasn't always exact about things like that, but Dwight Livingston told me later there really was quite a crowd, why he wasn't sure. There wasn't any shouting or carrying on.

"The people gawked at Miller like he was from another planet," Dwight recalled. "A few said nice things to the lawmen. Not very loud, though."

The four of them–Miller, Chief Culver and the two deputies–could have walked easy enough to the court house and jail–it's only a block–except there was a buggy waiting for them, and they got in. The driver flapped the reins and in five minutes, Jim Miller was behind bars.

Ben told me later neither Miller nor any of the rest of them knew when they arrived in Ada that our sheriff, Tom Smith, got a telegram from Fort Worth earlier in the day. The telegram was signed by District Judge Mike Smith; Frank Johnson, Captain, Texas Rangers; two Tarrant county deputy sheriffs and a former sheriff. The message was:

"We know J. B. Miller. He is all right and will not give officers any trouble. We hope you will extend him any courtesies you can and make his bond reasonable."

I saw the telegram when it was reprinted in The *Ada Evening News* April 5. I understand it was reprinted at Sheriff Smith's insistence. He wanted everybody to know the kind of people who were supporting Jim Miller and why it wasn't easy just to go and arrest him, like the *News* had suggested for a month.

Ben remembered the whole experience in detail for many years. I asked him some time later what he felt about Miller, being with him that long a time, knowing he murdered Gus Bobbitt.

"He was a riddle, all right," Ben answered. "I can see why he had a lot of friends, and some of them big shots, too. Bein' with him, it's hard not to believe what he says. Good family man, good churchman. It's hard to figure.

"Yet I knew–we all knew–Miller killed Gus Bobbitt. Not only that, he shot him from ambush, like he was some sort of coward. We also knew Miller wasn't any kind of coward.

"If you'd asked me, when we got down off that train from Fort Worth, whether I thought Jim Miller would be convicted of murder in court–and would actually go to prison–or whether he'd go free again, I wouldn't have known what to say.

"So many things could happen, like they did in his earlier trials. Whether he'd scare members of another jury, or whether he would win some of them over, maybe leave shadows of doubt they'd talk about, and get a new trial, I don't know. I don't bet, but I'd say it was a fifty-fifty proposition. It would take a mighty wise man to know what to do."

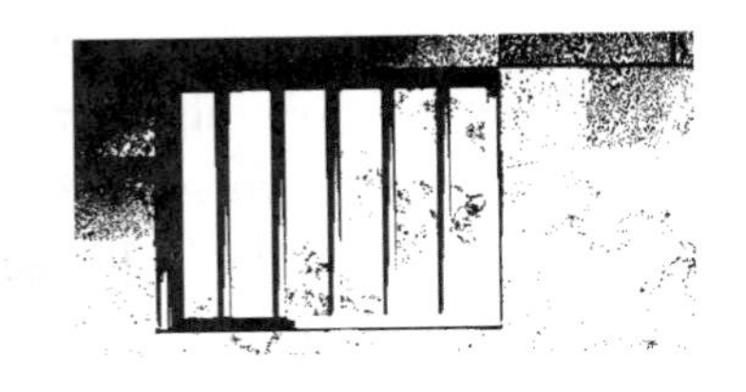

The Governor's Visit

Bob Wimbish was getting a lot of congratulations for getting Jim Miller in jail and it bothered him some. He'd say, "We've only got half those people." Sometimes he'd add, "The less said the better until we have them all," meaning the two ranchers still in Texas.

I was still in Oklahoma City trying to find a buyer with the financial backing to take over my brick plant, but several business friends in Ada told me later Wimbish was actually pretty grumpy about being congratulated, like he was resentful.

When I mentioned this to Dwight when I got back to Ada, he said, "Oh I don't think that's really fair. Keep in mind Bob's not a 'hale fellow' any time. And he's right. We've only got two of the suspects. We've got to get the other two, and then face the big problem–getting convictions in court. Long way to go."

What most of us didn't know–and I really don't think Dwight knew either–the county attorney had already started his scheme to get the two ranchers back into Oklahoma jurisdiction. If it had any real chance of succeeding, Miller's arrest would have to be played low key, even unnoticed if he could arrange it, which wasn't really possible. It was an important story.

Wimbish did get cooperation of the newspaper editors about avoiding any sensational headlines. He didn't have to try very hard. The editors weren't anxious to have Ada's biggest crime story all over the front page because Governor C.N. Haskell was coming to town April 3 on a special train from Guthrie to help celebrate the selection of Ada for the new college.

The governor made the decision to locate the new East Central State Teachers College in Ada March 25. He sent the citizens of Ada a telegram stating he signed the legislation at 10 a.m. A big celebration broke out in town–auto horns honked, church bells rang, the fire siren wailed away.

There was a Katy train at the station and they got the engineer to add his whistle. It was a celebration just about like the one in November 1907 when statehood was announced, only a Frisco engineer blew his whistle then. In any case, the *News* wrote "...it is doubtful if Ada people ever felt more jubilant" than they did about the college.

All this jubilation was without the governor, still in Guthrie. Naturally Ada officials wanted to show their appreciation, so they invited him to come to town and join the celebration, even make a speech. That usually appeals to a politician.

Any little town would be happy to have a college of course. It was something more for Ada, though. Ada's reputation was really hurt by the homicide level and it wasn't getting any better. Getting a new college could help balance all the bad publicity. People might say, "It couldn't be all that bad. They send college kids down there."

If it hadn't been for all the worrisome crime news, Ada would have gotten the new college without much question. It was known before statehood there had to be a school for teachers in the south, the last part of original Indian Territory. Railroads were bringing thousands of settlers into our part of the state from the east, and it was plain to see when they got off the train they believed in big families. Schools were in demand. There had to be teachers for the class rooms.

Competition for the new "normal" college was strong, about as fierce as competition for getting the railroads to come in. Ada had everything going for it–about the middle of the region where teachers were needed most, railroads to get here, churches, businesses, everything except for the community reputation.

There were thirty six homicides in Ada and the surrounding countryside in 1908, and while that was a record, it wasn't unusual. What made the record really bad was that it was set a year after statehood. Town leaders had been saying, "Once we're part of the state, things are going to be different." Well, things weren't different. Maybe worse.

Politicians in Guthrie who had to vote on where to put the college didn't care about the reasons for all the shooting. They had to decide whether or not to send young Oklahomans to school down here.

It wasn't an easy decision, and you can't blame the politicians for being cautious. Ada leaders spent a lot of time in the galleries and hallways of the state capital–I heard they spent a lot of cash in the hallways, too–trying to convince the lawmakers things were going to change with statehood.

Changing names–territory to state–doesn't amount to much, not at first anyway. What had to change were the people. Well, really, just some of them. Those not inclined to change made a big difference though. Kind of poisoned the air for everybody.

Most of the Ada settlers were from the very beginning what you call "good" people. I understood Ada had more churches than any other town its size around here at statehood, and it's pretty much that way now. The people who needed to change when we became a state didn't know or care much about churches. Probably most of those rough-hewn men on West Main, many of them veterans of Canadian River bootlegging, were never in one.

Statehood brought an odd kind of prohibition and it applied everywhere–odd because you could buy whisky with a doctor's prescription. Not many of people wanted to bother their doctors about getting a bottle of whiskey though. So there was still a demand for whisky and there were still bootleggers. They could be anywhere in the state. There wasn't any advantage to being north of the Canadian River anymore.

The river people who came to town to join their brethren gathered in the West Main pool halls just as they did in the old days. The "pool halls" were still there, still catering to thirsty players. There were all kinds of men in the pool halls. Many were just fairly young and boisterous, not all bad by any means.

A couple of these young men were pretty good baseball players and played on the Ada Browns when the Browns were the best team around here. Charlie Brady was a crackerjack second baseman, only he got involved in a brawl on West Main and was shot by an Ada policeman.

A number of commercial men in town–and not timid men either–didn't think most of the West Main crowd would ever become part of the community, or leave for anywhere else. Where would they go? Maybe life in some West Texas or New Mexico border town would suit them as well, but that's a long way off.

Town leaders who had to make Ada's sales pitch in Guthrie faced the community blight problem at every turn. It might not have been that grave a problem, really, except that promoters of competing towns kept reminding state political leaders of the Ada "situation." However, all the good things Ada had to offer–plus the cash, I guess–finally won the day.

Landing the college was a big step for Ada, I think even bigger than having the Portland Cement plant located here. Industry is certainly important to a small town–jobs, bigger tax rolls and all. A college is something very different. A college means smart young people coming from all over, professors, lectures, maybe sports teams later on. It adds a whole new dimension to a town, puts it on the map, really.

Selection of Ada for the college site was certainly the critical first step. It wasn't the only problem to be solved, however. The legislature provided $100,000 for classrooms and some administrative offices. Nothing in the legislation provided for the faculty payroll. Governor Haskell's continued support was important. Ada promoters wanted to make his trip really memorable, and they did.

Leaders of the 25,000 Club–earlier the Commercial Club–felt it wouldn't do to have the governor just step down from his railroad car and start his Ada visit there on the platform. They decided to have a special train–called it "The Ada Normal Special"–run up to Konawa on the Canadian River and meet the Governor's train coming south.

Ada's Mayor, Ike King, all the city aldermen and the Pontotoc County commissioners, were on the train. The trains did meet at Konawa and most of the Pontotoc welcoming speeches were made right there. Then the locomotive that started out in Ada was switched around–Konawa was a railroad town and had a turntable for locomotives–and both trains steamed on south, one right behind the other.

I don't suppose there were a lot of people to see the sight–two trains, one right behind the other, steaming along–but I would imagine anyone who was out there on the prairie would have been impressed. You have to give those Ada promoters credit. It was different.

I had never met Governor Haskell, but Dwight Livingston wrote to the governor's secretary and said there was a citizen from Oklahoma City who was moving to Ada and they might want to include him–me–on their train April 3. Dwight suggested the governor might be interested in why this one businessman, anyway, thought Ada was a city of the future. Sure enough, they were interested and I got an invitation to ride down to Ada on the governor's train.

There were people hovering around the governor for most of the trip down to Konawa like so many bees around a hive, and even more when the Ada people came aboard after the trains met. I didn't think I would get a chance to meet him, and I really didn't care that much. I didn't need anything from the government.

There was a nice young woman bustling about–one of the governor's secretaries–and she came over, looked at a notebook, and asked, "Are you Mr. Harris?" I said I was.

"There are always so many people who want to meet the governor, talk to him about some problem, that our guests sometimes don't get a chance," she said. "The governor doesn't like that to happen. So come with me and we'll get to him."

Being a lady, she could push some of the politicians and favor seekers aside, and she did. We stood in front of the governor, who was behind a little desk.

"Governor. This is John Harris from Oklahoma City who has decided to move his business and family down to Ada. You remember Dwight Livingston from the bank in Ada wrote to you about him," the lady said.

"Ah, yes, Mr. Harris," the governor replied, extending his hand across the desk. "Please sit down a minute. Dwight did write, said you had some perspectives on development of our state that might be of interest."

I knew his staff would have loaded him up on all the commercial strong points for the visit–bails of cotton, head of cattle being shipped, the new Portland cement plant, that sort of thing. He was coming to Ada to help celebrate the new college, so I wasn't sure what Dwight thought I could add.

"Well, sir," I said sitting down. "I hope Dwight didn't say too much. He might like what I say about our future down here because we agree on about everything. It's great country for ranchers and farmers, good water and soil. I'm sure you know that.

"We're getting industry, too. And we're getting the right kind of people moving in to make it a prosperous and good place to live. We've got some problems left over from Territory days, but nothing we can't handle."

The governor came alert and asked, "What kind of problems? Do you mean some of your Indian citizens are disappointed with statehood?"

"Oh, no sir," I said quickly. "Maybe some are. I don't know. Mostly our Chickasaw citizens are first rate and are doing well. Most of the land for the college you're going to dedicate–some sixteen acres–was donated by Dan Hays, one of our Indian citizens."

"I'm glad to hear that," the governor said. "The Chickasaws are a remarkable people. They didn't have the advantage of dealing with white settlers over a period of years like the Cherokees did. The Creeks and Choctaws had some of that experience as well. The Chickasaws were primarily hunters, pushed out here to survive as they could.

"Of course, they were the last to come west, except for some bands of Creeks who went to Florida and came to Indian Territory as Seminoles," the governor went on with his little lecture, like I was someone from New York.

"The Chickasaws did have one advantage being last to leave. Got the best annuities from the Federal government by far, except there wasn't any room for them on the Arkansas border. They had to go out west and deal with the Comanches."

I felt I had to let the governor know I had some knowledge of the history of our Indian citizens, too. I tacked on to his speech that I knew the Chickasaws worked out a plan with the Choctaws for the western part of their Nation, including Pontotoc County.

"You're right," the governor agreed. "It was a smart move by the Choctaws. They didn't need all that land, anyway, and it must have been nice to know they had the Chickasaws between them and the Comanches. The Chickasaws were not only hunters, they were notable warriors back east.

"Well," the governor then asked, "if your Indian citizens are accepting statehood, what problems left over from Territorial days do you have?"

I wished then I hadn't said anything like that. We did have a problem, though–Ada's reputation. Emma was not happy about moving to Ada with three young children. She was certain she'd be shot. A lot of people in Oklahoma City felt that way. I told her all the time I'd been coming to Ada, I'd never even heard a shot. It didn't do any good.

My wife used to say, "Read the paper! Helen Detweiler said she read in the *Times* Ada has become a haven for Canadian River desperadoes!" I didn't see that story but there was enough truth in Emma's argument, I didn't want to get into it.

"Really, Governor, we are going to handle our problems, which are mostly left over from prohibition days. That was a poor situation, having spirits legal one side of the Canadian River, illegal down here. That brought some difficult people into the area. They're still here."

The governor seemed puzzled about that, and asked, "Why, that demarcation line ran for something like one hundred miles or more. There are a lot of towns along the Canadian. Why did it become such a problem for Ada?"

"Well, sir, Ada was the closest town to a couple of the saloons doing a big bootleg business. Bootleggers got used to going to Ada. Now a lot of 'em feel at home. Some of those people are all right. Some of 'em aren't. We'll handle it."

"I have no doubt of that, Mr. Harris," the governor replied. "If there is ever anything I can do, I trust Ada leaders will let me help. Law and order is my first priority. Law and order will be the hallmark of my administration. Don't you have a good sheriff down there?"

"Our Sheriff Smith is a good man. Whether he is just the one to handle this problem, I don't know. He sometimes seems more like a school teacher, or maybe a good lawyer. He's a talker..."

"Why, I understand your lawmen went down to Fort Worth and got that assassin, Jim Miller," the governor pointed out. "That was a courageous act."

"Yes sir, it was. Sheriff Smith wasn't the one who did it, though. It was our Ada police chief, George Culver, and two of the sheriff's deputies."

The governor didn't know what to make of this arrangement and looked out the window at the prairie and stands of trees in the distance, turning a light green this far south. In a few seconds he turned back toward me:

"I'm sure you're aware, Mr. Harris, Ada does not have a reputation in keeping with the remarkably high goals it has set. As I understand it, Ada changed the name of their business association to the 25,000 Club because that's how many citizens they want to have in ten years? That's nearly twenty thousand more people...in ten years...quite a goal."

"Yes sir, it is. But I think they'll do it all right. People just keep coming. And the new college will help. The whole town is grateful to you, sir."

The governor turned back to the window. I could feel and hear we were slowing down for Ada. He turned to me again:

"It was nice chatting with you, Mr. Harris. Mr. Livingston said you will soon be moving to Ada. I have no doubt you will make a genuine contribution in making your new community one of Oklahoma's finest. Ada has vigorous competition from other growing towns, but there are many factors favorable you...down here in this beautiful countryside.

"I'm sure you will help promote the positive things. Concern yourself with the negative aspects, too. Ada does have to work on its reputation. It wasn't helpful in getting the college located here, as logical a place for the school as it is."

"Yes, Governor Haskell, I do understand. I think most of our town leadership understands that, too. Many people think how the Bobbitt murder trial comes out may be the key. If Miller gets what he deserves in a court trial, then we are on our way. If he doesn't, some of our rougher citizens may get the wrong message."

I thanked the governor for his time and backed away, letting the politicians work in for a last word or two. When the train stopped and the governor stepped down to the station platform, he was ushered over to the best looking rig in town–the L. T. Walters Funeral Home carriage with two matched bays in brass-studded harness. It was really something. Most of Ada had seen the rig before on sadder occasions. Nobody told the governor that.

I don't know if anybody told the Governor he almost had a ride in Bill Turner's new Buick either. He came close. There were hours of discussion in planning for the governor's visit, including a short debate on whether it would be good to show him how up-and-coming we were by having procession of automobiles, instead of carriages.

There were enough new cars in Ada, mostly Buicks and Fords, to do this but Fred McGriff, chairman of the transportation committee, vetoed the plan because, new or not, some of the cars backfired every couple of minutes and it would scare the horses going along Main. He didn't want to be responsible for some kind of "calamity."

As a further safeguard for the governor, McGriff had the delivery driver for his lumber company, George Selkirk, on the buggy bench with him handling the reins. George was known as probably the best driver in the county, with the possible exception of Barney Mott. Selkirk or Mott, one or the other, always won the driving contests at the county fair, including handling of four-mule teams.

While these two were always competitors at the county fair, they were also friends. They even got kind of famous together in the middle of a hot July night about 1900.

Ada's first separate U. S. Post Office–separate from Reed's store–was in Old Town down near the Frisco depot. All the influential businessmen wanted it moved away from Old Town and onto a vacant lot up on Main Street where commercial activity was growing.

Miss Gordie Hall, the postmaster, kept writing to Washington for permission to move the Post Office, but they never did answer her one way or the other. Miss Hall wasn't opposed to moving. She just wouldn't do it without Washington saying it was all right.

On this famous July night, the Post Office, a simple frame building, was dragged through the dirt streets from Old Town onto the chosen vacant lot on upper Main Street. The next morning everyone could see the big skid marks coming up Main, and direct evidence in the dirt that a lot of mules were involved.

At its new location, the building wasn't exactly the rectangle the carpenters built. It was good enough though, and Miss Gordie walked right to it the next morning and opened up like nothing happened. She never said a word.

Nobody ever said who drove the mule teams, either. Didn't have to. Everyone knew it had to be George and Barney. When their friends kidded them about it, they just grinned and spat. Neither one of them ever said much anyway.

Governor Haskell didn't know how skillful his driver was of course. And there wasn't much about George Selkirk, just to look at him, to suggest much out of the ordinary. He was about sixty years old, not tall, but he had powerful arms and shoulders. He could hold up a corner of a loaded grain wagon for a blacksmith changing wheels.

George Selkirk also had very strong opinions. Several young members of the Ada welcoming committee wanted the carriage drivers to wear top hats, just like the hackney drivers in England, I guess. George was so riled at that suggestion, he wouldn't even talk about it. Fred McGriff bought his delivery man a new Western hat instead and George was willing to wear that.

Besides the Governor's carriage with McGriff and Selkirk in charge, there were five other ordinary carriages at the station. I was put in the last one with Dwight Livingston. We headed east on Main and were out on the prairie in a few minutes, site of the new college. There was nothing out there, though you could see Main heading back to town, just wagon ruts that far out.

The governor got a brand new shovel along with Mayor Ike King, all the county commissioners and the city aldermen. Before they dug in for the first shovel-full of dirt to officially start construction, the governor thanked everybody for including him in such a wonderful occasion. As it turned out, none of them could get their spades down into that tough sod, but it was a nice occasion anyway.

From the college site, the procession went down Main to Rennie and the big Harris Hotel, the one with sixty rooms. I wish I could say it was mine. I didn't even know this Harris, and I stayed there many times before I found a good boarding house.

Committee members had a wooden platform built in front of the hotel where the governor was to speak. It was exactly like it was when U. S. Vice President Charles W. Fairbanks came to Ada to speak in 1906.

There must have been more than five hundred people out to listen to the governor, and they seemed to like what he said. There was clapping and quite a few Rebel yells. I don't know if Governor Haskell much liked the Rebel yells. He might have been a Yankee. I didn't ask. In any case, he said in many of his speeches it was important to move away from the past and into the future.

With the introductions and speaking going on, I was able to give Dwight a pretty good rundown on what I had a chance to say to the governor on the train. Mostly I wanted to tell Dwight the governor was concerned about Ada's reputation and thought we had better do something about it if we were going to be a real city down the road.

Dwight didn't say anything. I could see he was frowning.

"Yes. Certainly," he finally answered. "That's good advice and here we are with the biggest murder trial in Ada's history coming up. All we need is for Jim Miller to get away with murder again..."

I knew Dwight didn't expect an answer. I didn't have one anyway, nothing that was optimistic for sure.

"Well, one good thing, Dwight," I said to cheer him up a little. "Governor Haskell wants us to let him know if there is anything he can do for us. Maybe this is the time."

Dwight turned, and if it wasn't a smile, at least he didn't look so gloomy. "Well now, John. He could send the National Guard down here. That would be a big boost for our reputation."

Dwight was talking about the "Crazy Snake uprising." The week before the governor's Ada trip, two hundred Creek Indians led by Chief Crazy Snake got behind some trenches they dug on Hickory Hill, seven miles west of Henryetta, Oklahoma, declaring it was a "final stand" against white treachery.

The Creeks believed they and the other Civilized Tribes were promised specific benefits with the coming of statehood, and they didn't get them. They didn't get what they were expecting anyway. It was kind of a last straw for the Creeks.

Governor Haskell called out five companies of National Guard troopers to give white settlers in the area peace of mind. Most of the other Indians in Oklahoma thought the governor's action was a grandstand political move and didn't like it. That's why he was interested in how our Chickasaws were accepting statehood.

Dwight didn't feel any better when one of the governor's escorts, riding in the lead carriage, told him about the talk George Selkirk had with the governor driving down Main Street.

At the big celebration lunch for the governor, I cornered his young aide and asked what Selkirk really said that was so disturbing. It turned out it there wasn't any "talk." It was a remark George made, or just threw into a conversation he wasn't part of.

The aide said the governor was talking to Fred McGriff, sitting up on the driver's bench with George. The governor asked McGriff if bringing a gunman like Jim Miller to justice might help settle things down in Pontotoc County.

Fred turned back to the governor and told how city and county lawmen and the county attorney were working together to bring justice, not just to Jim Miller, but everyone involved in the Bobbitt assassination. "We'll see justice," he concluded.

It was then George Selkirk turned and growled, "Miller will walk away from our jail just like all the rest."

That wasn't a terrible thing to say, even to a governor, but it did bother Governor Haskell. He asked a couple of the welcoming committee members later if the negative attitude of his driver about law enforcement was common in Ada. I couldn't imagine these good Ada promoters saying many people felt that way, though it was true, they did feel that way. Nothing in the short history of the county court would make people think any other way.

Governor Haskell was supposed to attend a reception and banquet in Ada that evening, but he couldn't stay. Ads had been run in the *News* the week before stating that it would be a "five course affair for two dollars and at that price, tickets ...won't last long." The tickets did last though, even at that price.

To cut his visit short, the governor had to have a pretty good excuse. He did–the Crazy Snake uprising. If he expected to keep his Indian political allies in line, he had to get to the administrative headquarters for the Five Civilized Tribes in Muskogee without further delay. He needed to explain the whole "misunderstanding" that brought him to call out the National Guard.

The governor left Ada on the Frisco down at the rowdy west end of Main Street. It was mid-afternoon and kind of quiet. Nobody paid attention to who was leaving. That must have suited Governor Haskell just fine.

13

The Net Closes

The governor's visit was regarded as a success by most of the town's leaders, even though the banquet Saturday night fell flat. The governor wasn't there–on his way to Muskogee–and not selling all the banquet tickets was a disappointment. Fortunately, the mayor did disclose in the speech he made that the governor promised he would support additional funds for the college faculty. That was good news.

Another good thing about the governor's visit was that it gave the *Ada Evening News* something to write about and people something to talk about, something other than Jim Miller and whether his West Texas gang was going to come and break him out of our jail. That might have been far-fetched, but the people were ready to believe most anything about Miller.

As a matter of fact, Jim Miller was an ideal prisoner, in the opinion of Jim McCarthy, one of the jailers. This was the same McCarthy who had been a bootlegger and saloon keeper on the Canadian River before he became a jailer. Miller was a "real gentleman," he said.

Miller's friends in Fort Worth promised in their telegram Miller wouldn't give officers in Ada any trouble, and he didn't. The only problem he created, McCarthy remembered, was asking that his shirts be sent out to the Harris Hotel laundry, explaining they were expensive and he didn't want them run through the jail laundry. He also wanted them ironed just right, something he saw wasn't happening for other men there in jail.

McCarthy also reported Miller brought plenty of money from Texas, being held for him in the jail safe, and was more than willing to spend it. Miller quickly tired of jail food, McCarthy said, and ordered steaks brought in from the Broadway Café–not steaks for everybody, just for himself, McCarthy and another jailer. He didn't pay any attention to Barry Burwell, according to McCarthy. Not only didn't he get Burwell a steak, he didn't even talk to him.

I suppose you could say Miller was getting special treatment, but he was paying for it and he had all those important officials in Fort Worth asking that he get "courtesies." Most important–and some of our citizens forgot this–he returned to Ada without any resistance and was a model prisoner starting out at his Texas farm, all the way back to Ada. Ben Snow told me that was true and he was very grateful. If Miller hadn't cooperated, it would have been "one long trip."

No matter what the facts are, some people don't want to bother with them. Stories started around town, not just about the shirts and steaks, but stories saying Miller had Oriental rugs brought in because the floor of his jail cell was cold. McCarthy told me there wasn't any Oriental rug, or any other kind of rug brought in.

The *Evening News* wrote that Miller was living like a "prairie prince" in the Ada jail. What the *News* based that on mostly came to nothing, like the Oriental rugs business. True or not, stories of the favored treatment Miller enjoyed stirred up anger over the Bobbitt assassination again. That worried Bob Wimbish. He wanted everything to stay calm, at least until he could get Jesse West and Joe Allen back in Oklahoma.

Wimbish never did figure he could get the ranchers to come to Ada voluntarily. He did think he might get them to meet their Oklahoma attorney, Loren G. Pittman, in Oklahoma City if there was a good enough reason.

The chance of getting some prime ranch land down in the Red River Valley, where many young Texans, including Jesse West, started their lives in Indian Territory, would be more than enough reason, even if it was on the Oklahoma side of the river.

Both the West and Allen families were doing well on the Panhandle, the families had social standing in Mobeetie society, but water problems were beginning to break out on their Gageby Creek ranch. That problem would never go away. It could only get worse.

The Panhandle was hardly over-crowded at that time–there's a lot of marginal land out there–but the railroads kept bringing newcomers in, many of them farmers from back east determined to be ranchers. I guess they thought anything would be easier than farming, worrying about rainfall, either too much or not enough, too much wind, too many bugs, one kind or another–early spring to harvest time–the farmer's lot.

Most of these newcomers from the east didn't like the idea of an "open range." They were used to fences, believed in fences. "Makes good neighbors," some said. Most of them also believed in selective breeding and knew they had to keep half-wild prairie cattle away from the pure-bred herds they expected to have.

All the foreigners coming in felt the same way about fences, as far as I could tell. And they all seemed to have enough money to put barbed wire up. A good many of the eastern farmers did, too.

With all the fences going up, early Panhandle ranchers–Jesse West and Joe Allen among them in this case, though they were hardly pioneers–were beginning to find themselves cut off from some of their old watering holes. If you didn't have water on your own property, or you didn't have enough, or enough in the right places, that was just too bad. That's why windmills started popping up–pumping underground water for cattle.

We didn't have any Herefords down in South Texas, but I know you can't expect cows to walk more than two miles for water all the time without losing money. The cows lose fat and weight and the rancher gets paid on the basis of weight. Too much walking would be even harder on short-legged Angus or the Shorthorn breed. Cattle we had on the Triple R were all legs, bone and horn. They could walk forever and you wouldn't know they'd been anywhere to look at them.

A commercial herd can't just stand by the water–creek or lake, whatever it is. They have to eat, too. So they search for good grass. Grazing can take them miles away from the water and going back and forth means more money lost.

We were getting more fences here in Pontotoc County even before statehood in 1907, but there was usually enough water in those days, even with the fences. Enough grass, too. Land south of us in the Red River Valley had it even better. All the creeks and little rivers south of here drain into the Red River. I guess I crossed most of them in a buggy some time or other years back.

Jesse West had twice driven a small herd of Texas cattle through the Valley on the way north to his ranch in Violet Springs, and decided that's where he wanted to have his ranch one day–somewhere in the Valley, even on the Oklahoma side of the river. He told many people that, including Attorney Pittman. Water wouldn't be a problem in the Valley.

West talked about the future with Pittman once in a while because Pittman represented him in the legal scrapes he got into at The Corners saloon. Naturally they talked things over when they met, usually in Oklahoma City. Then Pittman started handling the money that flowed from The Corners. Anyway,

Jesse came to trusting him. Pittman was a good one to confide in. He was in on legal and business matters all through the Territories and knew most everybody.

While Bob Wimbish never did talk much about the Bobbitt case, I do know from Dwight Livingston he was pleased to corral Jim Miller using a psychological approach, finding the key to understanding such a complex man. That gave him real satisfaction, besides avoiding what could have been a dangerous standoff.

Even with the successful arrest of Jim Miller behind him, Wimbish never would acknowledge he had anything to do with the plan that got Jesse West and Joe Allen into jail, not even to Dwight. Nobody would call it a brilliant stroke. Maybe that was the trouble. He didn't want to take credit for anything so simple, just tricky and simple, more like a prank. Maybe the telegraph company people swore him to secrecy. Well, no matter whose idea it was, it worked and that's what counted.

The plan was to have a telegram, bearing the name of Jesse West, sent to Loren Pittman in Oklahoma City asking the attorney to meet West at the Rock Island depot in Oklahoma City April 6 when Train No. 88 pulled in from western Oklahoma and the Texas Panhandle. It was scheduled to arrive mid afternoon. The message didn't say why he wanted a meeting, any more than Jesse's telegrams to Pittman through the years ever gave a reason for what he was asking.

Jesse West didn't know about the telegram being sent in his name, any more than Loren Pittman knew about "his" message that was sent to West. Both had the same meeting instructions.

There weren't any messages to Joe Allen, though Allen and West were still good friends, their families were close and they remained ranching partners. Jesse West still made the decisions for both families, as well. Joe Allen would be where Jesse was, including on the train to Oklahoma City.

The phony Pittman message to West suggested he, Pittman, was handling an estate closing in Oklahoma City April 7 that involved ranch land in the Red River Valley and he needed to talk to West before the close of business on the sixth. Pittman suggested West get to the City on the afternoon Rock Island and they would meet at the station. The attorney would give him the details then.

Pittman also advised West to be prepared to come up with $10,000, either from his Oklahoma City account or a certified check from his Texas bank.

This exchange of phony telegrams would never have worked if they hadn't been used to vague telegraph exchanges. It was the way they had been doing business for years.

Maybe Bob Wimbish thought it was just too simple to work, that West would get to a telephone somewhere in Mobeetie and talk to Pittman, who had a telephone in his office, or one would query the other for more details, ask for another date, or something to foul it up. But nothing happened. It worked like a charm.

Bob Moore–or Robert S. Moore–was a new Oklahoma City detective at that time and he settled pretty near across the street from me. We got to be friends and he later told me he got a call from his senior partner, Bill Slaton, the morning of April 6 saying he should come to the city jail at one o'clock. Slaton told him they had to meet two men arriving from Texas on the Rock Island that afternoon.

Bob was at the jail at one and the two Oklahoma City detectives–Moore and Slaton–joined Todd Warden, a Special State Enforcement Officer. The three left the jail for the Rock Island depot to wait for the train.

On the way to the depot, Warden briefed them on the men they were going to meet–Jesse West and Joe Allen. Loren Pittman, their Oklahoma attorney, was supposed to meet the ranchers at the station as well, he understood, so there would be "three of them, and three of us," Warden advised.

The lawmen were glad Pittman was going to be there because none of them knew for sure what the Texans looked like, Bob said. They all recognized Pittman when they saw him. He ran in the Oklahoma City society crowd and had his picture in the paper every couple of weeks.

They didn't need to worry, Bob recalled. There was no mistaking the two ranchers when they climbed down from their coach and stood on the platform. They were a pair and looked like Texas ranchers–boots, short coats and big hats–and were proud of it. They were also very confident looking. Bob didn't think either one was armed.

They didn't have to guess long which rancher was which either, Bob remembered. Loren Pittman walked briskly across the platform and stuck out his hand, first to Jesse, then to Joe Allen. The three of them stood there talking while the train crowd thinned out. You could see from their expressions there was some confusion. Everyone was asking questions.

"When Todd Warden ordered, 'Let's go,' the three of us walked over and stood beside them," Bob said.

"Mr. Jesse West?" Warden asked looking at West.

"Yeah. Who are you?"

"Warden introduced himself as a Special State Enforcement Officer and the two of us as Oklahoma City detectives temporarily assigned to him," Bob said.

"What's all that got to do with me?" West demanded. Bob remembered he was a very forceful individual, kind of aggressive, just like the file said.

"Mr. West, you are wanted for questioning in Pontotoc County about the murder of one Augustus Bobbitt, a resident of that county, killed there in late February," Warden stated. He then added, looking square at Allen, "If this is Mr. Joseph Allen, county officials would like to ask you some questions, too."

About then, my friend Bob remembered, the attorney spoke up. "I am Loren Pittman, attorney at law here in the city, and I represent both these men. I can assure you my clients will obey the law and do their duty, but you, Mr. Warden, have just made an extraordinary request. Wanted by whom in Pontotoc County? On what grounds?"

"Yeah, that's right," Jesse West agreed. "Who's goin' to do all this askin'? I don't know anything about Gus Bobbitt's death. I heard about it but I was in Texas in February."

Warden fished in his coat pocket. "Yeah, sure," he said, pulling out a folded paper. "I have a warrant here for the arrest of Mr. West and Mr. Allen signed by the Pontotoc County attorney, one Robert Wimbish."

"This is preposterous," Pittman objected, "Here two distinguished Texas ranchers come to Oklahoma City to talk to their attorney and face immediate arrest because someone in Pontotoc County wants to ask them some questions!"

My neighbor Bob Moore remembered that kind of cut off talk for a moment. Jesse West glared at Warden. "That didn't put the Special Enforcement Officer off though."

"Well, sir," Warden said, looking first at Pittman and then at West. "That's about the way it shakes out. Authorities in Pontotoc want Mr. Allen and Mr. West in Ada tomorrow morning. Didn't say when exactly. We can take the first train down there in the morning–the seven o'clock Katy. That'll make it all right."

"But Mr. Warden," Pittman started, "my clients have plans here in the city, besides conferring with me. Your request is unreasonable, having them journey at dawn to Pontotoc County just after they have arrived in Oklahoma City. I will take this matter up at higher levels, I assure you, and since you are an employee of the State of Oklahoma, don't think you have heard the last of this!"

Todd Warden just looked at Pittman, then said. "My boss thinks it's reasonable enough. He thinks Mr. West and Mr. Allen can spend the night in our new jail and be ready to travel bright and early tomorrow. Let's go."

Bob recalled Loren Pittman sputtered some but then walked in our group toward a buggy we had waiting.

"Mr. Pittman," Warden advised, "you aren't involved in this as far as we know. You can go, if you want."

"No, no," the attorney protested. "I will go to the jail and start arranging bail for my clients. They can't spend the night in jail."

"Sorry to say, Mr. Pittman," Warden explained when we got to the buggy, "No authorization or time for bail. Clerk of court is about to go home. And besides, it's a new jail and not all that bad. You can ride along if you like."

Bob said they all did squeeze into the buggy. Mr. Slaton put Mr. Allen up on the driver's bench with him and the driver and off they went. Attorney Pittman was explaining to Jesse West moving along to the jail what he was going to do to arrange bail that night, despite Todd Warden's remarks. If that should fail, given the hour, Pittman said he would be working first thing in the morning "to make sense of this."

Jesse West was quiet walking into the jail, almost calm, like something had come over him, Bob said. "Resigned" might be the right word Bob added, except that he read the reports from Duncan and the Canadian River area and knew Jesse West wasn't going to just "fold up." Bob was right. West was a fighter to the very end.

Whatever Pittman was going to do about bail Tuesday evening didn't work and the two Texans spent the night behind bars. Bob said he and his partner were at the jail at six o'clock the next morning and Todd Warden showed up a few minutes later. Attorney Pittman wasn't in sight and never did come.

"That ol' Atlantic 442 the Katy had goin' south to Ada rattled us along at quite a clip," Bob recalled. "Course there were only five cars, one for passengers. Two freight cars and two for cattle came behind. After Ada, the train was going on to Coalgate, a couple more mining towns, and then Atoka.

"All five of us–the ranchers and us three lawmen–must have been sleepy. Nobody was doing any talking," Bob told me.

"We all swayed and bobbed along, lookin' out the windows at the pastures and prairie in the early sun. Mr. Warden made a few remarks about the weather and the countryside trying to be civil. Then he quit.

"Runnin' over the Canadian River trestle made quite a racket, though the engineer did slow down," Bob said. "The new noise seemed to wake something up in Jesse West. In his Oklahoma days he lived close to the river–in Violet Springs–and his saloon was right on the north bank, you know. You could imagine the river would stir up a lot of recollections for him.

"Anyway, Jesse West finally came wide awake. After studyin' the shallow river from the window next to him, then half getting up from his seat to see out the other side, he said, 'Not much water in the river for this time of year. Still, I'd like to see that much out on the Panhandle.'"

Bob recalled they all looked at the rancher, then Todd Warden asked, "Kind'a dry out there this year?"

"Well," West answered in a reasonable way, "We've been gettin' some rain, but there aren't many places for it to pond. The land is mostly high and flat. Too much of the rain just runs off and comes down here.

"The Canadian starts out on the Panhandle north of our ranch, runs through here, then joins the Arkansas, then the Mississippi and out to sea. Quite a trip. Why they call it the Canadian I don't know…goes nowhere near."

"It's a long way to Canada," Joe Allen observed.

Bob Moore admitted in later years he didn't know how he came out judging Jesse West from the hours he was with him. He knew from sheriffs' reports he had a violent temper, and maybe a mean streak, but he wasn't sure he saw the killer in him.

Joe Allen had so little to say, Bob remembered, he was even less sure what he thought about him. "No question they were partners, though. Joe Allen just seemed to go along with West without saying anything," Bob concluded.

"Of course Jesse West didn't do the actual killing in the Bobbitt case. He hired it done–that was made clear in the coming days. It wasn't that West lacked backbone, though. Nobody I ever talked to about the case through the years ever suggested West was in any way cowardly," Bob said.

West must have thought he could even up the score with Bobbitt by hiring a killer and nobody would ever know, including his wife. Maybe Barry Burwell convinced him there would be nothing to worry about as long as he provided the money. He wouldn't ever see the gunman, Burwell probably advised since he was going to do all the arranging. And West knew from the newspapers Miller had worked on contract before and got away with it, maybe after a second trial. Why not again?

What Jesse West was thinking on the train ride down to Ada, whether he had second thoughts about what had been done to Gus Bobbitt, wasn't clear, even after the rancher started talking, my detective friend recalled. West didn't pull back and said right out he and Bobbitt had been good friends in the early days, were in business together, until Bobbitt cheated him.

"Oh, I would have liked to kill Gus Bobbitt," Bob remembered him saying, "only I didn't. He cheated me in business and then stole some of my cattle. I should have settled matters with him right then and there, but I had my family to think of.

"I was away from home a lot in those days and my wife was afraid Bobbitt's gang would come up to Violet Springs and kill the whole family. We pulled out for Texas. They'll be waitin' for us in Ada. We'll never get to the jail."

Bob said they all stared at Jesse West, never having read in any report Gus Bobbitt had a gang.

"All three of us knew Gus Bobbitt had been a U. S. marshal," Bob said. "My partner, Bill Slaton, was a Mason and had heard of Bobbitt, so we couldn't believe he had a gang, or was the kind to send somebody to massacre a family.

"Yet Jesse West seemed to believe this gang business. Something was sure agitating him all of a sudden. Maybe he really did think they would shoot him down at the train station. Or maybe even in the jail.

"Our Special State Enforcement Officer, Todd Warden, said, tryin' to settle West down, 'I never heard Gus Bobbitt had a gang, and I was assigned to go down to the Canadian right after statehood to find out how big a problem all those river saloons were goin' to be. As I remember, Bobbitt got out, went to ranchin' full time'."

Jesse West sat bolt upright and declared, "Yeah. He got out all right. Made a killin' from my business before he left—

"He's got a gang all right. Couple of 'em came all the way out to Hemphill County to get me 'bout three years ago, but the sheriff spotted 'em and they left."

Todd Warden looked at the prairie slidin' by outside the window, then he said, 'Well…three years ago…Bobbitt's been out of the business at least two years now. Don't know why he'd have a gang now, if he ever did. I don't think you need to worry about that, or anything else if you had nothin' to do with Bobbitt's murder. Answer their questions and go about your business. They got a right down there to try and solve the case."

Bob recalled nobody talked very much for the rest of the trip, which was nearly over anyway. The train was slowing down. The conductor opened the door to our car and in a voice loud enough to be heard from one end to the other over the track clatter, "Ada! Ada next stop!"

Bob said Todd Warden let the other passengers get their suitcases and boxes down from overhead racks and file toward the door, then they all followed. Warden led the way, the two ranchers were next. The two Oklahoma City detectives brought up the rear.

"Two deputies from the Pontotoc County sheriff's office were on the platform waiting for us," Bob remembered. "By the time we all howdy-ed and shook, there weren't many people left on the platform. There sure wasn't any sign of a gang. A couple of people looked at us and then passed on. Mostly they seemed interested in gettin' on the train.

"The sheriff also had two buggies with drivers ready behind the depot and we split up. The sheriff's chief deputy Ben Snow, Todd Warden and Jesse West went in the first buggy, Bill Slaton, Joe Allen and me in the second.

"We went all the way down Main Street at a steady trot, past all the morning shoppers. I could see Jesse West was keepin' a sharp lookout, his head turning one way then the other.

"Anyway, we went through what must have been the busiest part of town in late morning–by most of the stores–and I don't remember anyone even lookin' at us specially. If anybody recognized West or Allen, they didn't let on," Bob said. "Whatever Jesse West thought was going to happen when he got to Ada, didn't happen."

At the jail, papers for transferring prisoners were passed between Pontotoc County officers and the Oklahoma City lawmen with a few grunts and a few heavy, inked scrawls for signatures.

"Jesse West watched the process like he was in a trance again," Bob recalled. "Didn't say a word. Joe Allen didn't say anything either.

"Both the ranchers were quiet when they went down the cell block corridor. Didn't look into the cells, one side or the other. A separate cell door was opened for each one of 'em. In they went. The doors clanged shut. The job was over for me," Bob said.

I finally decided on my own– a couple of weeks after West and Allen were arrested – the newspaper didn't know anything about the plan to arrest them, and by the time reporters did find out about it, the ranchers were in jail with Jim Miller and Barry Burwell. They were jailed Wednesday, April 7.

The next day, the *Ada Evening News* ran a story saying the two ranchers had been arrested in Oklahoma City April 6 and were transferred to the Pontotoc County jail the following day. The story went on to say:

"It is known that for many years Jesse West and Joe Allen were probably the most positive if not notorious characters in south Pottawatomie County."

What made the pair "positive if not notorious" wasn't explained in the story. Operating The Corners saloon for many years would no doubt be part of the explanation–if there had been one. The Texans were arrested, the story said, because they were wanted for questioning in the Bobbitt case. There was no mention of Jim Miller.

There wasn't then, nor has there ever been, any kind of public disclosure how it happened those particular six people ended up on the Oklahoma City depot platform at the same time. You would think newsmen would be curious about that. Well, maybe they were curious, but no lawman or public official would hazard a guess how it happened.

When you come to think about it, getting four Texans into jail–across state lines–in such a short time, was remarkable. There could have been banner stories in the paper for days crowing about the "long arm of the law" or something like that. Instead, getting the last two involved in the assassination–West and Allen–in jail was reported like two hog thieves got arrested. A routine item on the police blotter.

Looking back, I guess Bob Wimbish had a lot to do with it. He probably convinced the editors that inflammatory stories before the trial would make it very difficult to find jurors in the community who hadn't already made up their minds that the suspects were guilty. A change of venue would be ordered. The trial would have to be moved to another town. Jim Miller had exactly that lucky break in Texas and Wimbish didn't want it to happen again.

All four prisoners were arraigned before Justice of the Peace Harold J. Brown the following Friday, April 9. "Judge" Brown–people just called him Judge; he was a magistrate—determined that the charges were properly drawn, and that there was sufficient reason to warrant holding the four men for a regular preliminary hearing, when they could plead guilty or not guilty. That would be open to the public.

Judge Brown combined the cases and set the hearing for 9 a.m. Thursday, April 15, 1909, in the Pontotoc County courtroom. He said no bail would be set until after the hearing.

There was a short story in the newspaper about the arraignment, but once again, it was played way down. The story had to be pointed out to most people. It must have seemed odd to citizens following the case closely that the newspaper editors, so ready to pounce on Jim Miller, so demanding that the sheriff do something in the beginning, were all of a sudden so reluctant to print anything but the bare bones of the story.

With two whacks of his gavel, Judge Brown opened the hearing on time Thursday morning, April 15. Despite the newspaper's holding back, the county courthouse was jammed. I couldn't even get close to the courtroom door at eight thirty, a half hour before the court was to convene. I turned around and left. Some people stayed and stood in the hall, hoping to get word of what was happening in the courtroom, but I didn't have time for that.

Though I should have known better, curiosity took the upper hand and I went back to the courthouse Friday morning. The hearing was after all a historical event, and to have actually seen part of it would have been satisfying in a way, not like inauguration of the President in Washington, but important to our town.

Once again, the crowd around the door of the courtroom discouraged me and I started back down the hallway. At the very end of the hall, near the rear stairs, I saw a big Indian, hat down square on his head like they do, black braids hanging over a denim jacket. He was leaning against the wall, arms folded, one boot up and cocked back against the wall.

"Chief Harding?" I asked when I got about ten feet from him.

He looked at me. No word, no expression at all.

"My name is John Harris," I said, moving a little closer. "You saved me and our friend Gus from a long and wet night down at your farm some years ago. We got in that hay shed you had..."

You couldn't say he smiled. It was more a look of recognition, not unfriendly.

"Remember now," he said, standing straight on two feet. "Long time ago."

He was bigger than I remembered. Otherwise, he looked the same. That rainy night in his farm house was more than ten years before and he didn't look a day older. I knew Indians didn't go in for handshaking. so I stood in front of him and spoke.

"Sorry we meet again in such bad times. Are you going to testify?"

"Don't know. County lawyers say maybe today. Bailiff told me stay in building–"

"I'm sure you're an important witness for them, Mr. Harding, though I gather there's not much doubt who fired the shots at Gus's ranch. Proving it may be difficult..."

The Indian didn't say anything. You couldn't tell what he was thinking from the look on his face. Really, there wasn't any "look" on his face. It was a mahogany mask and not a friendly one. I thought Jim Miller was better off in the courtroom than he would have been out on the prairie with Harding.

I never did hear any more about Indian Police after Gus told me about them. None of their officers were in town before statehood that I ever saw, and they weren't in the news. I understood Indian Police were disbanded with statehood, but I still glanced casually to see if Christian Harding had any kind of law enforcement identification, maybe some tribal unit. He didn't.

"You're not in the law enforcement business any more?"

The Indian looked at me more like I was a friend. "No. Indian Police gone."

"Well, I'm sure you miss it in some ways. I know Gus Bobbitt did. You get to farm full time, though. Did you end up with the farm I saw in the allotment program?"

Harding answered with a little nod. "My wife is farmer. She talks to everybody about crops, when to plant, where...oldest boy reads her all the government papers. I do plowing. We all pick cotton..."

"That sounds good, like you're making a real success of your farm. Did you ever find one of the Chickasaw horses?"

"No, never. Keep looking. Not waiting though. I got horses on the farm. Breeding big ones like the Chickasaw."

"That's good to hear. You shouldn't let such a splendid tradition slip away. When I get moved down to Ada I'd like to come see your horses. Maybe I won't have to sleep in the hay shed again."

Since I never had seen Christian Harding smile, I won't claim he smiled then. He did nod agreeably, and that was enough. I'd been in the Territories long enough to know Indians generally don't use more words than necessary.

"These are difficult times for all of Gus's friends, Chief Harding–the procedures, hearings, the waiting. Maybe we'll just have to have faith in the system. It's worked well so far. We've got all the men involved. A jury might decide to hang them. Might not, too. It's justice we all want."

The Indian looked at me, then asked, "What if no court justice?"

That was the question worrying everybody, with good reason in light of Jim Miller's history, but I sure didn't have the answer. I just shook my head to admit I didn't know.

We must have both decided right then our talk had gone far enough. The mask had come back over Harding's face. He didn't move or make a sound. I said I looked forward to seeing him again in a better time, and to seeing his big horses. I turned and looked back down the hall.

The crowd was still pressing around the courtroom door and it stayed shut as far as I could tell. Nobody was getting in and nobody was coming out. So there weren't even any new rumors. I went down the back stairs to the street.

I knew it wasn't Judge Brown's responsibility to make a decision about the guilt or innocence of the four prisoners. That wasn't his job. His job was to hear how the prisoners pleaded–guilty or not guilty–and then determine if the evidence the state prosecutors had was enough to continue holding the prisoners for trial.

After a parade of witnesses presented by the county attorney–but before Christian Harding was called to testify–Judge Brown called a halt. He said he heard enough, and bound the case over to the U. S. District Court. The court was scheduled months before to convene in Ada, Monday, April 19, Judge A. T. West to preside.

Judge West and Jesse weren't related, but that didn't stop a lot of poor jokes about them having the same last name. After Judge Brown's hearing Thursday and Friday morning though, there wasn't much laughing in Ada.

The Fatal Hearing

Loren Pittman came down to Ada for Judge Brown's hearing and many people felt it was his strategy that brought on the tragedy that marks our town. He never once challenged any of the evidence Bob Wimbish presented for the state. For a day and half, witnesses told how Gus Bobbitt's assassination was done, who did it, how much they got paid—everything. And not one word for the defense.

I didn't get into the courtroom either day, as I told you, but I heard every detail of the hearing at least twenty times. That's all people talked about Friday afternoon. Loren Pittman's decision not to challenge the first thing any of the state's witnesses said, to say nothing on behalf of his clients, may have been brilliant defense tactics somewhere else, or maybe some other time, but it was a disastrous mistake in Ada.

I don't offer it as an excuse. There can't be any excuse for what happened. I'm just saying the hearing as it played out made a powerful argument for action outside the law, and gave no support to anyone with faith in the judicial system, not that there was much of that around here then.

The Daily Oklahoman had a reporter at the hearings both days. He described them as the "most interesting" in the short history of the state. His story in the *Oklahoman* Saturday April 17 said County Attorney Wimbish had presented "…a chain of evidence…that seemed hard to break."

None of the four defendants—the two ranchers, Allen and West, Jim Miller and Barry Burwell, all represented by Loren Pittman–asked for a preliminary hearing in the first place. They all waived their rights to a hearing, but Judge Brown didn't give Jim Miller a choice. He ordered one for him.

Why the defense attorney "just sat there," as the townsmen who did get into the courtroom reported, was a matter of great speculation Friday afternoon. Pittman's strategy was discussed in the barber shops, drug stores, cafes, Post Office, just about all the Main Street corners.

Most of the sidewalk experts agreed by the end of the day that Pittman was waiting to try the case before a jury starting Monday. Judge Brown wasn't going to free the defendants after the evidence he heard in a preliminary hearing. He couldn't really do anything but bind them over to the U. S. District Court. "Why "tip their hand?" was the concluding point on Pittman's strategy.

Jim Miller's remarkable success through the years intimidating juries was always brought into the discussions and became an of article of faith–if he got to stare at jury members day after day, "it would take brave bunch to find him guilty."

Probably the jury couldn't just find him innocent and let him go free in any case, since there was so much undisputed testimony on the record–the community would be outraged if they tried–but the chances of a jury deadlock and a second trial being ordered were always good for Jim Miller, most agreed. "Then the witnesses would disappear…as always," the cynics added.

The more widely-read of the town's judicial philosophers had a further explanation of Loren Pittman's strange approach for the defense–the dramatic entrance of man named Moman Pruiett of Pauls Valley.

Pruiett was a defense lawyer with an almost unbelievable record of success in the Territories and later in the state. His record for getting clients off was so remarkable, and well known, it was always assumed he would be called if a client was in deep enough trouble, and could afford it.

The Gus Bobbitt murder trial met every Moman Pruiett condition–the defendants were in very deep trouble, and might even be hanged; they had money enough to pay, and the trial would be played on a statewide and perhaps national stage. He seemed to crave that kind of attention. It was perfect for him.

I'd never seen him in a courtroom or anywhere else. Those who had seen him perform usually agreed he was every bit as good an actor as he was a lawyer. From what they say he was a big, vigorous man with strong features, starting with a prominent nose. He spoke with great force, maybe even a shout for emphasis, striding about the courtroom, arms waving, a shock of graying hair falling over his right eye. He put on quite a show and while not everyone approved of his style, there was no arguing with his success.

Pruiett had represented three hundred forty three defendants charged with murder in his long career. He won three hundred and three acquittals. Only one man not acquitted received a death sentence and Pruiett had that commuted. His reputation was so solid and well known in his later years, anyone seeking his services as defense attorney had to come up with $2000 as an advance before there was any discussion of the case at all.

Ada people who never heard of him sure got an earful Friday afternoon. I had read his name once in a while in the *Oklahoman* but it never meant much because I didn't expect I'd be needing his services.

Nobody had spotted Pruiett in Ada at that time and the more thoughtful debaters were saying, "Of course not. He and Loren Pittman would do the planning over in Pauls Valley and Monday morning, when Judge West entered the court room, there the Great Defender would be, ready to take over the defense. Bob Wimbish would get a whippin."

It was certainly true Bob Wimbish wasn't a showman. He was what you might call proper–the way he looked, dressed and talked. Still, I don't know that acting proper like he always did would make him a pushover for just any courtroom showman. He worked hard and always seemed well prepared.

Besides being careful and precise in the things he said, he gave his witnesses confidence to speak out and not stammer or hedge, not appear uncertain or fearful. That was an important part of Judge Brown's hearing–the way every witness testified with Jim Miller sitting there, like a granite statue.

Why it took a day and a half and twenty witnesses for Judge Brown to make his decision to bind the defendants over to the Federal court wasn't clear. Those who knew him explained that he was, after all, very deliberate and thorough in everything he did, even planting the vegetable garden back of his house. He sure didn't want to make some kind of procedural mistake that would spring Jim Miller. His name around Ada would be mud. Nobody would call him "Judge" anymore, that's certain.

Oscar Peeler, who was supposed to be a shy kid and maybe a little simple minded, set the tone for the witnesses. He said straight out and with no stammering who paid for the assassination and for how much; how Miller and Burwell went over dollar amounts in the parlor of the Hickory Street house, and exactly when Miller was to get the rest of his contract money from the ranchers after he killed Gus Bobbitt.

He admitted it frightened him to hear all about the assassination. Nobody would blame him for that. There was no doubting him when he said he wished he hadn't heard a thing.

"I didn't want to just get up and leave," Peeler explained. "Then they'd think I was against them."

If Peeler was worried about what Miller might do to him for spilling out all the damning information he had, he didn't show it. Maybe he really was simple minded. Or maybe he was lucky. It probably saved his life.

Peeler may have been a shy kid, but you have to remember Bob Wimbish was leading him all the time with his questions. That surely accounts for the young fellow's strong performance. In any case, young Peeler sounded like he knew what he was talking about from what everybody said. It was obvious Judge Brown was taking it all in.

Young Jim Williamson didn't falter either, though "Uncle Jim" Miller had already warned him about saying anything concerning "family business." He acknowledged his uncle had the mare in the days leading up to the assassination, and returned her about worn down the night Gus was killed.

Bob Wimbish planned to have Christian Harding testify how the horseshoe marks at the murder scene were made by the mare found at Williamson's farm. The hearing never got that far.

Of all the witnesses in the two days, Bob Ferguson, Gus's ranch hand, was the one that really set people talking. Bob had already told just about everybody in town he saw the man who rode out from behind the bush after the fatal shots were fired, so that wasn't a surprise. The county attorney asked Ferguson a series of questions that put Bob's story in the record for Judge Brown.

What was different in the courtroom was when Bob Wimbish asked Ferguson if he could identify the man now, the ranch hand slowly raised his arm, pointed his crooked finger at Miller sitting at the defense table and said in his deep voice, "That man thar."

Jim Miller didn't blink, didn't move a muscle. Attorney Pittman stared at Ferguson, then picked up a pencil, pulled his note pad closer. Bob Ferguson's eyes never left Jim Miller. The court room was dead quiet.

Bob Wimbish paused, took two deliberate steps back away from the witness stand, and asked, "You said earlier, Mr. Ferguson, the sun had gone down. How was it possible, with no sun light, for you to be so certain of what you saw? Wasn't it dark?"

The county attorney had given considerable thought to the weaknesses in his case and convinced himself the defense would jump on Bob Ferguson claiming to make a positive identification "in the dark." He could hear Pittman or Moman Prueitt say to Bob with some sarcasm, "You say the sun was down...nightfall...yet you claim you can see perfectly without the sun. Does this special power come to you in the moonlight?

"No sir, it warn't dark," Bob Ferguson told the county attorney at the hearing. "You couldn't see the sun no more, but it warn't dark ...everything was kind of reddish, but it warn't dark."

"Could you read a newspaper in that light?"

"Well sir, I don't read no newspapers. If I was to do any readin', it wouldn't be at that time 'a day anyway. Mostly I'm still workin'. There's plenty of light for workin'. It's kind'a red but you can see everything...maybe not as far."

Wimbish watched Judge Brown carefully to see if his face or his eyes gave away any doubts he had about Bob Ferguson ability to make a positive identification of Jim Miller the evening of February 29.

"Mr. Ferguson," the County Attorney started, "you acknowledge you might not be able to see as far in the twilight, when everything is reddish. Judge Brown might not understand what you mean by that..."

"Well, might not be able to spot a heifer in the south pasture. Herefords are brown, guess you know."

"So that might be a quarter of mile?"

"Oh, no sir. It's mor'in that."

Bob Wimbish paused to give the ranch hand a chance to collect his thoughts, and then asked, "The road isn't very wide there where Mr. Bobbitt was killed?"

"No sir. It's jus' a country road…'nuff for one wagon. If two wagons had to pass, both of 'em would have to pull off the road some."

"If the wagon was in the middle of the country road to Mr. Bobbitt's ranch, and you were on one side of the wagon, the rider had to pass pretty close to you on the other side. So even though the sun was setting, there was light enough for you to be sure what you saw at that distance?"

"Oh, yessir. Couldn't have been mor'in twenty feet, and it warn't all that dark."

The attorney stopped there. He didn't think the defense attorneys would be able to shake the ranch hand's recollection of what he saw, even in the twilight.

There might not have been much courtroom drama the way Bob Wimbish proceeded with his witnesses, except for Bob Ferguson's dramatic pointing at Miller, which everybody remembered. Every one of the witnesses knew what they were talking about and didn't seem afraid to speak out. Wimbish was on his twentieth witness Friday morning when Judge Brown stopped him and said he had heard enough.

Judge Brown bound the four Texans over to the District Federal Court and said he was not setting any bail. The defendants were to stay in jail until they appeared before Judge West Monday morning.

The parade of unchallenged witnesses and Moman Pruiett–that's what the people of Ada were thinking about Friday night, most of them, anyway. The men at dinner in my boarding house were mostly traveling salesmen, or businessmen in town for just a few days. They might not have been particularly interested in Judge Brown's preliminary hearing, except that's what everybody in town was talking about–the store owners and businessmen they called on, certainly.

They laughed when someone told how Bob Ferguson pointed his crooked finger at Jim Miller and said, "that man thar," making some fun of Bob. None of them knew Gus Bobbitt and none of them cared that much about Ada–just another little town in the territory.

I was in Ada more than most of them and was a "regular" at the boarding house, had friends in town, like Dwight Livingston, and was planning to move down from Oklahoma City. What happened was important to me.

"Mr. Harris," the big portly man from Kansas City said to me across the table, "You think statehood will in time, maybe in a couple of more years, help overcome the unruly frontier attitude that seems to prevail down here? Help bring law and order?"

Nothing stops the men at my boarding house from eating or talking very long, though the question from the Kansas City hardware distributor quieted most of the talk. They had made fun of the court proceedings at first but got interested in the case when they heard more about it at dinner, and heard about who was involved, the famous Texas gunman principally, "right here in Ada." Most of them knew I was planing to move to Ada and may have wondered if the hearing made me uneasy. So they listened.

"Sir—change is no easier here than anywhere else. It's never easy. We've got people left over from the wild cattle towns in the west part of your state–Kansas. We've got others runnin' from the law in Texas who think if they get to Oklahoma, the law isn't for them, like it was still Indian Territory–another country. We've also got people who want to move forward…"

"Well, Mr. Harris. I don't want to sound critical. I think Ada and Pontotoc County could be a good market for us–some day. Right now, I'm not so sure. It doesn't seem like a settled community. I have to be honest in saying that…"

The diners started back to eating, though most were looking at me at the same time.

An older man in a dark suit and vest at the far end of the table, a newcomer, spoke up– "I'm sure the citizens here will solve their problems in time, Mr. Harris. I've seen it happen in a number of new towns out here in the West. It takes time, and sometimes a crisis, for the right people to take leadership roles.

"One thing you might try to do in the short term is clean up that rough patch down by the Frisco depot. It would be pretty discouraging for a newcomer arriving from the east. There's some pretty hard looking men hanging around down there…women might be frightened."

Half the men at the table bobbed their heads up and down. Didn't stop eating though.

I certainly didn't consider myself a town leader. Hadn't even moved my family down from Oklahoma City yet, wasn't a regular citizen with a house and family. But I felt I should say something.

"The gentleman said it takes time for leadership in a new community to take the reins. I agree with that. Goes without saying, you've got to have leaders to begin with. I think we've got them here. Don't think I haven't given moving here a lot of thought. I have. The leaders are here. Time will surely tell that."

"Well said, young man," the Kansas City hardware distributor announced to the table. "I hope you are right. I'll be back here in two years and I'll check up on you, see what kind of fortune teller you are!"

Actually, I wasn't as confident as I sounded. I was really worried about what was happening. You'd think I would be brim full of confidence after a day and a half of Judge Brown's hearing, the case being so strong against Miller and the others.

Despite Bob Wimbish's fine presentation, stories about how Jim Miller cowed juries through the years, and how Moman Pruiett almost never lost a jury trial, made me gloomy, like we were doomed before the trial even started.

Emma had big weekend plans for us in Oklahoma City–both Saturday and Sunday evenings–and there didn't seem to be any doubt in her mind I was going to be there. I was away from home so much, trying to get my business started in Ada, I felt a particular obligation to fit in with her plans on the weekends. I pretty much had to leave Ada on the noon train.

In some ways I felt like I was running from a fight, like I was ducking out, though I certainly didn't know what I could do about anything if I stayed. I decided I would try to talk to Dwight Saturday morning before I left and find out what he was thinking. That's what I did. It didn't make me feel one bit better.

15

The Debate

Saturday mornings were important in Ada's business life with so many farmers and ranchers coming in from the country for stores. Meetings of the 25,000 Club weren't generally scheduled for that reason. There wasn't any meeting scheduled for Saturday, April 17 either, the day after Judge Brown adjourned his preliminary hearing. It didn't matter, the club room was half full by eight thirty, and more men kept clumping up the stairs.

I called on Dwight at the bank and an early-bird teller going in the door, told me Mr. Livingston was planning to go to the 25,000 Club for an hour or so that morning. So I knew something was up before I got there.

There wasn't any organized meeting going on. Nobody was in charge. Men were standing around in little groups. It didn't take long to know there was only one subject–the Miller hearing. Mostly the talk wasn't loud or excitable, and as usual a few men did most of the talking, the rest listening. I spotted Dwight in one of the groups, listening, and made my way over.

Dwight backed up from the group and said to me, "Mornin' John. I guess you know what we're talkin' about."

I told him I could guess and, as a matter of fact, that's mostly what I had been thinking about since yesterday.

Dwight looked at me and said, "You're a newcomer. How does it all strike you? You have any doubts about the trial, about the judge, or jury? A lot of people here do."

I looked around the room and recognized several of the more important businessmen in town. Then there were also a number of men not so far up the ladder–livery stable, lumber yard proprietors, people like that. They must have brought some of their workers from the looks of their clothes.

And there were a dozen or so ranchers in the room, again, judging from their clothes. They had to get up pretty early for the ride into town. Word of the meeting must have gone out Friday afternoon and it got out to different kinds of people. If the men in the Club room had anything in common, I couldn't see what it was, except I didn't recognize any clergymen, no law enforcement officers.

"Dwight," I answered. "I just don't know. I don't see any jury not believin' all that testimony. How can Miller scare them that bad? And what can this Moman Pruiett say to hoodwink a jury after what they're going to hear?"

Dwight didn't say anything, I remember, just shook his head slowly, frowning. He looked kind of doleful.

"John," he finally said, "I don't know the answers to your questions. That's what everybody is discussin' right now. We got some here that say Miller has been in spots a lot tighter than this one, and always got away.

"Other men chime in and say Moman Pruiett got killers off with more goin' against them than the bunch we've got. Put it together and you can see why a lot of people here don't think a jury would find Miller guilty, and if they don't find him guilty, there's nothing against the ranchers, not even the go-between–Burwell. The whole thing is lost."

That was a gloomy way to look at it, but I couldn't argue with Dwight.

"Yeah, and then Bob Ferguson and young Oscar Peeler might be in a pickle…Jim Williamson, too," I said, thinking about reports I'd heard that out in West Texas Jim Miller said nobody testifies against him and lives.

I don't remember ever seeing Dwight Livingston so downcast. You'd think the world was coming to an end. Well, maybe his world, his ideas and plans for the Tennessee Western National bank and Ada would end if Miller got away. Many of those men at the 25,000 Club Saturday morning thought that's exactly what would happen–Miller would get off, or maybe he'd get a new trial and be out on bond.

It must have been after nine when Bob Wimbish climbed up the stairs and walked into the club room. The talking stopped and everyone turned toward him. Then there were little cries of greeting, even some clapping. Bob smiled and gave a wave.

"Good morning, gentlemen," he finally said in his formal way. "I'm not sure why I'm here. I'm not sure why you're here. Maybe because somebody asked us…"

Everyone made a kind of big circle with Bob close to the middle of it. Finally, Talbert Dixon, our young druggist, spoke up and said, "Bob. Some us were at Judge Browns' hearing. Some couldn't make it, but we're all worried 'bout what happens next.

"We're all proud of you and the witnesses. You did a fine job. Seems to us the case is air tight. Yet there are things we don't understand and we're worried that bunch will get clean away with murderin' Gus Bobbitt. Why didn't they say something at the hearing? Claim 'not guilty.' Say something. We think there's got to be a trick here somewhere."

Bob Wimbish stood still, moved his head side to side slowly, as if to say he really didn't know, gave a sigh.

"Well, I guess it's plain enough these people want to go before a jury as fast as they can. That's where they expect to make their case. Nothing they might say in a preliminary hearing is going to matter. If I were in their shoes, I might feel the same way..."

"Yeah, but Bob," Dixon persisted, "that's what everybody was sayin' yesterday, 'plain as the nose on your face,' that sort of thing. It's not so plain to me. The jury is going to hear all that evidence you presented to Judge Brown and there didn't seem to be any doubt in his mind. What makes them think a jury is so different? Jim Miller goin' to scare them that bad?"

Bob Wimbish looked at the young druggist and had a smile.

"Who knows?" Bob started. "There'll be twelve of our citizens, people supposed to exercise independent judgement...without prejudice...and we don't know what they'll really hear. Or get straight. Probably they'll hear that Jim Miller was in East Oklahoma, maybe hunting in the mountains when Gus Bobbitt was killed, and has witnesses to prove it...that sort of thing.

"And keep in mind, I was leading our witnesses. Some might not sound so sure under tough cross examination, might get mixed up, contradict themselves. Doubts might spring up about what they said yesterday..."

"You mean if Moman Pruiett gets after 'em, Bob?"

"Well, it wouldn't take Moman Pruiett," Wimbish replied. "Loren Pittman can be tougher than he looks. And it only takes one juror to decide there were doubts in his mind, doubt serious enough he couldn't agree to hang four men. That juror holds out for a lesser penalty and they start to wrangle. Next thing you know they can't agree to anything and it's a hung jury and a second trial. Jim Miller has been down that road before."

The room was pretty quiet by then, except for feet shuffling. Some sat down in a chair close at hand, as if they were suddenly tired.

From the back of the circle around Bob Wimbish came a question, not shouted but loud enough for the whole room. It was Fred McGriff, owner of the lumber yard on North Broadway. "Then, what are we goin' to do?"

Pontotoc County Judge Joel Terrell in his regular black suit, vest and high starched collar, straightened up–he wasn't very tall–stuck out his chest and demanded, "Going to do? Next week we're going to see Bob Wimbish win the most important court case in his life, maybe the most important case in all of our lives–the future of our homes–of Ada.

"I agree with everything you said, Bob," Judge Terrell proclaimed, as if he were addressing a jury. "You can never be sure what a jury will do. You can rehearse your witnesses, examine and reexamine their testimony and maybe pray a little. But from what I saw last week, you have done a fine job. What you've got to do now is keep your witnesses healthy."

Everybody looked back at Bob Wimbish. "Yes, Judge Terrell. You're absolutely right. We're watchin' that. There are rumors all the time about Jim Miller's old crowd in West Texas coming in and we're on the lookout. Having Miller and the ranchers in our new jail helps. That's a sturdy building.

"We've got Bob Ferguson in town. A safe place…not saying where. We've still got Oscar Peeler safe in jail. All the other witnesses are on alert. We don't need to tell them to stay awake. We're not takin' any chances…"

The club room turned quiet again and I was surprised when Dwight Livingston spoke up in his respectful way, "Mr. Wimbish, it is apparent you have done a very thorough job. I don't know what more anyone could do. Still, others have tried to bring Jim Miller to justice through the years and nobody has been successful. I feel like Talbert Dixon, that there's a trick ahead. Could there be any irregularities in the U.S. District Court proceeding?"

"Oh, I don't think so, Dwight. I have good reports on Judge West. He might be helpful in encouraging the jury to do its duty in very strong terms, but other judges have tried that. That sort of preachment only goes so far. It sounds good in the courtroom…fades away on the street…

"Juries are reluctant to convict a dangerous man who might well get out on bail during an appeal process. I'm sure you know Miller is out on bail now for the Ben Collins murder down near Tishomingo. And that was nearly three years ago. He was indicted all right. Then the witnesses disappeared…" Wimbish stopped. He looked kind of worried

"Then what are we goin' to do?" McGriff asked again.

Judge Terrell sighed then said, "Whatever we do, we've got to proceed in a civilized manner and by the letter of the law. The reputation of Ada and our future is involved here. In trying to expunge the taint of our violent past, we can't become even more violent."

It was easy to see McGriff didn't like the dapper little judge and took the remark personally. He reddened and shot back, "We'd 'a been the horse thief capital of the world if we listened to talk like that. We put a stop to horse stealin' around here with hemp rope. Fancy words don't make it work. I know what works."

Judge Terrell was taken back and he sputtered a little bit. "I don't suggest we shrink from duty, Mr. McGriff, but how we protect our future is important, too.

"I know–we all know–you played a big part in getting the anti-horse thief group to meet here, and that it was a successful meeting. Friends from other cities have told me so. There was a crisis, and you and your associates met it head on. But times have changed. That was six years ago. We're a state now. We've got a sheriff and courts..."

Fred McGriff had settled down some, and said in a quieter way, "Judge– That was the Oklahoma and Indian Territory Anti-Horse Thief Association. If some of you weren't here then, that name might sound made up. Let me tell you, that Association was real enough and it met right here in Ada. The Association was as legal and legal sounding as we could make it.

"We were willin' to let the law work, but it didn't work. Nothin' but talk. Stringin' some of those thieves up worked. We'd a been the horse thief capital of the world..."

Fred trailed off. Tired of arguing I guess. He never did say much but people listened to him when he did talk. He backed away, turned for the door.

"I say hangin's too good for 'em anyway," Chris Laundy said, his voice rising. "Why don't we shoot 'em down like they did Gus Bobbitt. Seems to me we'd save a lot of time doin' something we all know needs doin'."

Fred McGriff stopped, turned back to the crowd. "You mean shoot 'em down in jail, in the court house?"

I didn't know McGriff very well then and I still don't. He's not easy to talk to. I do know now he's a man with very strong opinions about justice and how justice is served. I wouldn't be surprised now by his response, but I was then–

"You can't just shoot a man down in jail, in a courthouse," McGriff said. "Man's got no chance, unarmed…in a cage. You can't do that…

"Hangin' sends a message–it wasn't any accident. Anyone stealin' horses around here can expect the same. Hangin' doesn't make it legal, except that's how the courts do it. Hangin' is what those people should get."

That was quite a speech for Fred McGriff and he looked tired, or maybe disgusted, really grim anyway. He opened the door and said, "I got to get to work. If Christian Harding comes up here lookin' for me, tell him I'm at the yard…"

Someone in the back of the room called out, "Saw him an hour ago in front of the Dollar Store, Fred, talkin' to Bob Ferguson…"

"Well, tell Bob too," Fred said. "If any of you want to talk some more about this business, you know where I'll be, maybe loadin' in the back. We don't have a lot of time…" Then he was gone, George Selkerk right behind him.

Judge Terrell and Bob Wimbish looked at each other. Neither spoke. In fact, nobody said anything you could understand. Just some muttering.

"My, my," the Judge finally said. "I had hoped to be more persuasive."

Dwight Livingston spoke up. "Judge Terrell. You did well. What you said was right. We're a state now. That's true. Still, you have to admit, some things haven't changed much. Maybe worse than before…"

It was easy to see Dwight wasn't very happy. He just shook his head a little bit and drifted way from Judge Terrell and Bob Wimbish. He listened to a couple of the stern speeches calling for action and then headed for the door. I went out after him, down the stairs and out on the plank sidewalk on Main Street.

We stood there a moment and then Dwight said, "John, I wish I were going to Oklahoma City with you. I've never been so uncertain about anything in my life."

I sure didn't have any advice to give him. I wasn't any more certain than he was. You can kind of envy people like Fred McGriff in a way. There was no doubt in his mind. It was as plain as black and white.

"Dwight," I replied, taking a quick look at my watch. "I'll admit to you I'm glad I'm going. I guess Emma would forgive me for not comin' home this weekend, maybe after a while she would. But I don't know what I'd do if I stayed."

My friend looked at me in a funny kind of way. He said, "Well, sure, John. Go on home by all means. Have a good trip." He stuck out his hand.

We never talked about the Jim Miller case again. I don't know what Dwight did Sunday night, and I don't want to know.

Commitment

The pot luck supper at church Sunday evening was pleasant enough. Emma enjoyed it. I'm afraid I wasn't very sociable. I couldn't stop thinking about what might be going on in Ada, or maybe about to go on. It was still pretty early in the evening.

I'll admit I felt some guilty, too, like I ran out, leaving the others to take responsibility for deciding what to do and then doing it. I remember even now the look on Dwight Livingston's face when I left him Saturday morning. He was plain suffering.

I could never claim I had no idea what was going to happen. Nobody could have been at that powwow in the 25,000 Club room and not come away with some idea, like how they stopped horse thieves a while back. McGriff's words had an impact on those men in there. You could see it in their faces.

Even so, you couldn't be sure if the tough talk in the club room was real. Sometimes men say strong things when they're upset, particularly when there's a crowd around them. That doesn't mean they'll really do what they say. McGriff never seemed like one of those men, though. He's a strong individual.

Sunday morning, just after sunrise, I had gone to the *Daily Oklahoman* building to see if any kind of late dispatch from Ada might have come in, though I knew it was unlikely anything would have happened in Ada Saturday night. There probably wouldn't have been enough time after the 25,000 Club meeting in the morning to do any real planning–planning for whatever was decided. Still, I wanted to check.

Delivery men had started loading bundles of Sunday editions on wagons in the back and I asked if I could see one. One of the workers said, "Sure. You lookin' for a job?"

"No," I answered. "I was just wondering if you have any kind of special story from Ada."

"From Ada? Not likely." He went on loading.

They had ten pages this Sunday and I scanned all of them for an Ada dateline. Except for one story about a Hereford show and sale, there wasn't anything from Ada. I thought about telephoning Dwight at his home later in the morning, but realized he might not be able to talk about whatever happened, if anything did. Besides, I had planned a week before to be back in Ada Monday. I could wait.

All of Sunday was a difficult day for me. I knew it wouldn't be until I got back to Ada Monday before I could find out anything. The only good thing was I'd be there before noon.

Emma had been after me for weeks to spade the vegetable garden, and right after church I went at the job like crazy man, trying to work off my worries. She thought it was a new enthusiasm for gardening and was very pleased, so I didn't tell her. Fortunately, rain the south wind promised finally arrived and I had a chance to rest and clean up before the church supper.

Monday morning I was up early as usual and got to the depot in plenty of time to catch take the seven o'clock Katy down to Ada. I strolled around, being early, then spotted a stack of *Daily Oklahomans* on sale that said "special edition" at the top of the front page.

The lead story had "lynching" and "four men" in the headline– and it had an Ada dateline. I felt like a horse kicked me in the stomach when I saw it, though I half expected to see something like that.

The story was written by the *Oklahoman's* correspondent sent down to Ada to cover the Jim Miller trial, which was to start Monday at nine o'clock. He was also a stringer for the Associated Press and had the story all over the country, coast to coast, by 10 a.m. Ada was famous.

Most of the story turned out to be correct, principally that four men were taken from the county jail and lynched in a small barn near the Frisco railroad tracks very early Monday morning. So I guess it was "Sunday night" only in a manner of speaking.

I got another jolt when I read that "small barn." It must have been the barn I bought as an investment ten years before. There wasn't any other barn of any kind near the courthouse and the tracks. I read the sentence over and over to make sure the owner wasn't identified. He wasn't, though it wouldn't have mattered. He was in Oklahoma City.

The AP story said that a mob of two hundred men "broke down" the jail door and took the prisoners. Included in this mob, the AP reported, "...were many prominent men in the city, only a few of whom wore masks." It was also stated the mob "...organized in the commercial club rooms of the city." There were no names, no matter how many times I read that paragraph.

Right and wrong, the story was enough to set editorial writers all over the country railing about the barbaric act in Oklahoma and condemning mob violence wherever it might occur.

A second version of the AP story, which I saw in Ada, carried the victims' names. Jim Miller was mentioned first–a "Texas gunman"–and then the two Texas ranchers, Jesse West and Joe Allen. Barry Burwell made the last line.

The *Ada Evening News* had the two AP stories to build on for its first edition Monday afternoon, and had time to get more of the details right. I was in Ada by the time that came out. The editors cut down the size of the "frenzied mob" to between thirty and forty. They did not, however, offer any kind of reason or background for the lynching, and did not mention any names other than the victims.

Left in the updated AP story run by the *News* was that the mob "...organized in the commercial club rooms of the city." That was no surprise to me after the Saturday morning meeting.

Traveling to Ada Monday morning was a dreary experience, starting with the showery, overcast weather. It was far different than my usual pleasant trips south from Oklahoma City, watching the sun light up the prairie. I read my copy of the *Oklahoman's* special edition a half dozen times clacking along, and felt worse each time. The train was going as fast as it always goes, but it seemed like the trip took forever. I wanted to hear from my friends what happened, what might happen next, including possible arrests.

A freight agent had put stacks of the special edition on the train, so it was obvious news of the lynching didn't make the regular state-wide edition, which covered Ada. Except for those involved in the lynching, nobody in Ada would know as much as I did when I arrived. A few people would soon see the *Oklahoman's* special edition, but most of the townspeople would hear about the lynching about noon when the first edition of the *Ada Evening News* came out.

Most of the time traveling south, I was reviewing in my mind's eye the men I knew–besides Dwight–who had seen me at the meeting Saturday morning and might, under the right circumstances, talk to me about it. They knew I already had a pretty good idea how it would unfold. And I told two of the men at the meeting–men I thought might confide in me–I had no choice but to leave for Oklahoma City at noon.

I couldn't imagine Dwight would tell me what he had done. Certainly I wouldn't ask. Just to look at him Saturday morning it must have been the most difficult moral decision he ever faced. I'm sure he never had to worry long in his life about what was right or wrong. He just knew, deep inside him. He'd do whatever he thought was right, as always, and do it again Sunday night and then in the dark of Monday morning.

The two men I thought might, in time, talk to me about that terrible night were very good people, and became good friends, but weren't the kind to get all bound up in complicated moral issues. It might be these friends simply decided it was necessary and did it–no right or wrong involved. I envy people who can peel away all the doubts and worries and act, then put the whole thing behind them.

Actually, once the lynch mob left the 25,000 Club, a number of witnesses saw them and were willing to talk, and later testify about what they saw–or about what little they saw–both on the street and inside the jail. So it was only the first part of the story–inside the Club before the lynching–that I couldn't get directly. Everyone was pretty skittish about saying anything for a while, but as the months went by and nothing happened to anyone, I got most of the story piece by piece, even some things that were said, but not exactly who said them.

Everyone agrees it was raining in Ada Sunday night. I could have guessed that. A steady south wind had been blowing in Oklahoma City all day, and high clouds were moving up from the south. It would be a soaker, and a welcome one. Pontotoc wasn't dry at that time, but it's always good to get a steady, soft rain, not a thunderstorm downpour that cuts up the cultivated fields and brings flooding.

My friends agreed men started coming up the stairs to the 25,000 Club about 12:30 a.m. Monday morning. It was very dark of course, and very wet. The men hung their slickers on hooks on the wall, near the corner and front door. The Club had electric lights but they weren't on. Instead there were three coal oil lanterns giving off enough light for moving around.

Except for a few "howdies," there wasn't much talk. Everyone had a kerchief around his neck but nobody had it pulled up. Everyone knew one another. Nobody said a name though, like they had been briefed.

Well, if they had been briefed, somebody forgot to mention horses brought to town by ranchers or farmers. There were six of them tethered on Main Street, all droopy headed in the rain, right below the 25,000 Club. Having six horses tethered next to each other on Main in the middle of the night would be enough to attract anyone's attention and Patrolman Lee Masters saw them.

Our police chief, George Culver, had gotten a report that a "fast moving" burglar had left Henryetta bound for Ada. He had Lee checking all the doors along both Twelfth Street and Main. No point in letting a burglar just walk in. Some of our store owners didn't always remember to lock up.

About one o'clock, a question came out of the shadows in the quiet room. "You got your assignments. Any questions?"

There was a little grunting and a few "nahs," then:

"I heard Squeaky Nestor is sleeping in the jail tonight with the sheriff out of town. That right?"

There was a pause, then, "Yeah. I heard that...well, we'll just have to take care of 'im."

Asking about Squeaky Nestor wasn't just casual talk. Squeaky had been a deputy marshal in Indian Territory before he went to work for the sheriff and got quite a reputation for fearlessness, though he was a small man–no more than five foot six. They called him Squeaky because he had a little high pitched voice and was about as deaf as a fence post. Had measles or something as a kid.

Maybe it was to make up for his size, or maybe it was because he couldn't be sure what anybody said back to him, Squeaky was very quick with his six gun. He also carried one of those great big Winchester lever action rifles in his saddle holster, and rode about as big a horse as most people ever saw.

So Squeaky was different than the other lawmen there in the jail, including Walter Goynes, the chief jailer. It wasn't that Walter was a timid man, nor were either of the two others in the jail that night. Jim McCarthy sure wasn't. You just had to be very careful dealing with Squeaky, from all I heard of the old days. No trifling with him. He could shoot and did shoot without a lot of talk. He didn't like talking.

From the shadows, away from any of the lanterns, came: "We'll try to get in the jail door without a lot of fuss. We think we got that lined up. I suppose Walter knows Bud Muller from the Frisco...don't know how well.

"We'll just gamble he thinks Bud Muller is really outside the door with an urgent telegram from the sheriff–not our man.

"We think it's all set. If that turns out wrong for some reason I don't know about, we'll take the door down. We'll have the tools. Hate to do it, though...it'd take a lot of pounding. Even wake Squeaky up."

"Aw. I don't think even Walter would fall for that urgent telegram business. If the sheriff was in such an all-fired hurry he could use the telephone..."

"Well, I don't argue the point. What I'm telling you is, I think it's all set. Walter isn't dumb. He's no hero, either. I think it's all set. I think it'll work."

About one thirty, two men got up and started putting their slickers on. At the door one of them turned–"Guess you can look down to the corner on Twelfth to know we did the job."

They still didn't have street lights on Main. They were going to be installed on Main but a half dozen store owners on Twelfth got together and politicked the mayor to start on their street. They were very pleased with themselves and put in their newspaper ads about the lights. They weren't open when the street lights came on, so I don't see that it was much to crow about.

While there weren't many street lights in Ada, the Ada Electric Light Company worked hard to keep those first lights on when they're supposed to be on. Daryl Gilbert was a young electrical engineer who the company hired first of the year to make sure the lights worked. Daryl spent half his nights down there. The plant was across the Frisco tracks, west, about a quarter of a mile from the depot.

Years after when he got to be one of the vice presidents, Daryl told me he was there that night and everything was going just fine, all their circuits were up, rain and all, though it wasn't raining very hard. Neither were there many people still awake to use electricity, either. In any case, the system was working just the way it was supposed to.

Daryl put the time close to two o'clock when two masked men smashed in the office door at the front and came right at him in the back of the building near the switching panel, guns drawn like it was going to be a holdup.

"Pull them damn switches!" one of 'em shouted. "Be quick about it!"

Daryl admitted he was scared of these two. They hadn't even tried to get in by knocking on the door. They just smashed it and tromped on in, waving their big pistols around.

"Pull them switches or I'll shoot 'em out!"

Believing the power company was doing a fine thing–bringing electric lights to town–Daryl always got upset when his lights failed, like he was breaking a trust. And I'll have to say, though I always liked Daryl, the lights failed enough in the early days without any masked men.

"But people depend…" he remembered starting to say. One of the intruders aimed his pistol at the switch nearest Daryl and Daryl said, "Wait! Wait!" He told me he then pulled every switch on the panel and the four of them–two young electric company men and two intruders–might as well have been at the bottom of a well at midnight.

The masked men started back toward the front door, crashing into chairs and knocking over wastebaskets in the dark, and cursing.

"You leave those switches right where they are for two hours or we'll be back and level this place!" one of them shouted. Daryl remembered he didn't doubt for a second they'd do it, either, so he didn't touch them. He heard the pair mount up and ride off in a hurry. He sat in the dark, dumbfounded and a little scared.

Maybe ten minutes after two o'clock, someone pounded up the stairs to the 25,000 Club.

"They're out!" the lookout announced in a loud voice.

Silence blanketed what little talk there was in the club room, no darker with the town electricity cut off because only coal oil lamps were going anyway.

"Well, then. Guess we can get at it," came the slow, heavy voice of authority. "Any more questions? Everyone know what they're supposed to do?"

Most of the men got up from their chairs and the two sofas and headed for the wall where their slickers hung.

"One thing…I guess it doesn't matter too much…you think Walter Goynes is half expecting something, what with the sheriff bein' called out of town so sudden?"

Everyone stopped, looked back to the center of the room.

"Well, it's hard to know what he thinks might happen. For sure he knows something might. There's enough talk in town to alert anybody smarter than a nail keg. But he doesn't know exactly what or when. I don't think he'll be a problem, I tell you. He can shoot but he's no hero. None of those jailers are. Pull up your 'kerchiefs. Let's go."

The lanterns were put out. Nobody brought one along. The stairs were like in a coal mine and they creaked with all the men filing down. They went out the door and onto the muddy, dark street.

17

The Deed

Lee Masters, one of Ada's three policemen, had checked all the stores along Twelfth Street and was starting on Main near the Frisco tracks, when all the electric lights in town went out, including the new street lights on Twelfth. In a blink, there wasn't a light anywhere. It was a heavy kind of dark, though the rain had let up and it was more like a drizzle. No moon nor stars showing through.

Lee told me a long time afterwards the lights going off didn't worry him at first. They went out maybe once a week. What did bother him was that any burglar from Henryetta would have an easy time of it, running around in the dark. He didn't think about the six horses on Main when the lights first went out, then the two things—the horses and then the lights—sparked in his mind.

While he was going along, trying doors, he kept looking up the dark street toward where the horses had been, near Rennie. That was three blocks up Main and it was too dark to tell what anything was, except near buildings had some shape against the sky.

Then he thought he saw a long dark mound in the middle of the street. The mound was a good block away, up near Townsend. Lee couldn't tell what it was. He kept near store fronts, moving up Main.

With a jolt he realized the mound was moving, like there were dozens of people walking close together in the middle of the street. He guessed right. There were men in a loose column coming toward him at steady pace. He couldn't tell how many there were except there had to be dozens of them. They made no noise, no talking…had no lanterns. He had never seen anything like that before.

Lee admitted he was a little scared and didn't know what to do. He knew there were a good many men—or dark humps—coming at him, but he couldn't count whatever they were in the dark. He would have rather found the Henyretta burglar. Then he said to himself, "I'm on duty and it's my job to investigate anything unusual on the city streets." That's just about the way Lee would think.

He walked off into the Main Street mud toward the head of the advancing column. Then he saw they were men and those in front had their faces covered up to their eyes. He admitted to me he was really scared then.

"Evenin' there," he called out to the leaders. He saw three of the men had pistols out. None of them said anything but just kept coming down the street at him.

Lee stood his ground and said again, "Evenin'. What's goin'–"

The first of the masked mob walked right by him and someone said, "Lee. Get out of here. We got all the law enforcement we need."

Lee started to say something more as the column went by, all the muffled figures with kerchiefs pulled up except for a few, but he couldn't recognize those few in the dark. Several of the masked men passing were showing their pistols.

"Lee. Go on. We don't need you," he heard from someone.

Lee was in a tough spot and he didn't know what to do. The thought of stopping much less arresting anyone in that armed gang was out of the question. They seemed to know who he was, so they weren't some kind of traveling bandits. And they said they didn't need any more law enforcement. He wasn't sure what that meant. He needed help and he knew it.

Who could help him now, in the middle of the night? The smartest man he knew, someone people would pay attention to, he figured, was Judge Joel Terrell. He trotted past the last of the masked men, paying no attention to them, and headed up Main, turned south on Broadway where the town's newest houses were and where the judge lived.

While Lee was running for the judge, the first of the masked mob approached the jail house door on the Townsend Street side of the new two-story court house, around the corner from Main. Inside the jail, which was at the back of the court house on the ground level, everything was quiet, except that a drunk picked up early in the evening was snoring, Jim McCarthy, the former Canadian River bootlegger, remembered.

McCarthy and the other jailer, Joe Carter, were playing two-handed poker for broken matches by lantern light. They got the lantern going after the lights went out. They were used to the lights going out and thought nothing of it.

The jailers sat on opposite sides of a small table, one of the few things in the bare utility room between the cell block and the chief jailer's office. Walter Goynes, the chief jailer, was in his office seated behind the desk, head back, eyes closed, snoozing.

While the electric lights going out was not unusual, having the chief jailer there at night was. Mr. Goynes, or Walter, which most people usually called him, almost never spent a night in the jail, Jim said. Mostly it was Joe or him at night, and usually not both.

"Maybe Mr. Goynes spending the night in the jailhouse with Squeaky there, and the two of us already on duty, should have made me suspicious that something was going on, but it didn't," Jim recalled.

"When I said something about all of us there, Mr. Goynes said he was just being careful with the sheriff out of town and the big Miller trial about to start. That made sense to me then. Looking back, I might have been smarter. Even if I saw right through the scheme, I don't know what I could've done about it."

Squeaky Nestor was also in the utility room next to the cell block, asleep on a cot he used when he came up from his post in south Pontotoc. He usually stayed over when he brought a prisoner up to Ada.

His hat and coat were hung on nails above the cot, his boots were on the floor alongside. He slept in the rest of his clothes but had a blanket pulled up.

Jim didn't remember exactly when it all happened–some time around three o'clock. There were three loud thumps on the heavy-oak outside door. Then there were three more.

"Walter Goynes! Walter Goynes! Message down at the depot for you. Immediate delivery!" came a cry from outside.

The chief snapped awake, stood up, swaying a bit, and shuffled toward the door.

"Walter Goynes! Got a message from the sheriff!" from outside.

At the door, the chief jailer said, "Yeah? Well, who the hell are you?"

"Bud Muller. Assistant Frisco station manager. We only got one telegrapher at night. He couldn't leave the depot."

"Well, just slide it under the door," Goynes said. 'We got no lights in here.'

"That ain't deliverin' the message, Mr. Goynes. If the sheriff asks if the St. Louis and San Francisco Railroad ever delivered his message, I hope you tell 'im I tried!"

"Oh, for Chris' sake," Goynes said, sliding the big bolt away and opening the door six or eight inches.

"What in hell..." he blurted out. Six men, revolvers drawn, pushed the door open and brushed past him.

Jim and Joe Carter jumped up from the table where they were playing cards and were fumbling with their holsters when the masked men burst into the gloomy room, shadows rushing around the walls from the lantern, still on the table.

"Drop them guns! Get over there in the corner!" Two of the masked men came toward them, pointed at the corner and stood guard, leveling their revolvers at the jailers every few seconds. More masked men came pushing into the room.

"Walter! Unlock that damn cell block! Now!"

Jim said the chief jailer must have been nervous because he had a bad time finding the right keys on the big ring of keys he carried. There must have been muttered threats from the masked men near him because the chief jailer spoke up, "Hold your horses, boys. I'm gettin' it!"

About this time, Squeaky Nestor turned over on his cot. "Mor'n likely the vibrations of all those men barging around woke him up. It wasn't the shouting. He couldn't have heard it," Jim was sure.

Two of the masked men started poking around under Squeaky's blanket, looking for the big revolver which he never let get far away.

That brought Squeaky wide awake. He sat straight up and in his funny high voice cried out, "Who are ye? Wearin' a mask is a devilish good way to get in trouble!"

He reached up right over the cot where his holster and gun were hanging on another nail. The two men, who hadn't seen the gun in the shadows, reached for it, too. The three of them struggled. One of the masked men then drew away from the tussle for the gun, pulled his own revolver and slugged Squeaky over the head. Jim said he could see clear across the room black-looking blood spurt out.

"Get some of that baling wire. Make sure he stays right there," one of the men ordered. The two men then bound Squeaky's hands behind his back and straightened him out on the cot. Squeaky didn't move. Jim remembered he thought they might have killed him. Squeaky wasn't hurt too bad it turned out.

He was able to testify before the Grand Jury ten days later about the night the jail was invaded. His head was all bound up though.

The chief jailer finally got the cell bock unlocked and the barred gate swung open. Then he quickly walked down the corridor and unlocked four cells. There were shouts: "Miller! West! Allen! Burwell! Get on out here!"

Jim reminded me there weren't any lights in the cell block and nobody knew if the men were coming out or not. A long minute passed. "Get a lantern!" somebody demanded. Then again, "Miller! West! Allen! Burwell!"

"Joe Allen moved out into the corridor between the cell rows slow, like he was in a daze, working his feet down into his boots. 'What are you doing?' he asked the masked man beside him. 'The trial starts this morning.' Nobody answered. Two men grabbed his arms, pulled them behind his back and began binding them with baling wire.

"Burwell came out next into the lantern light. He looked bewildered too, not scared really, from what I could see at that distance, just like he couldn't figure what the commotion was about. His arms were wired behind his back in seconds.

"Neither Miller nor West had come out but someone must have gone into West's cell to get him and asked him something," Jim guessed. "I couldn't hear what they asked. I sure could hear what West shouted back: 'I'll tell you nothing! Leg'go of me! I'm goin' nowhere! I'll see you in hell…'

"Somebody must have hit him over the head hard because he never let out another sound from then on. A man in the cell block corridor ordered, 'Haul him out here.'

"There still wasn't any more light back there, but from what I could see there were a couple of people bending over and workin' on something on the brick floor outside Jesse West's cell. I suppose they were tying him up.

"While they were working on Jesse, a couple of the masked mob, pistols drawn, pushed Joe Allen and Barry Burwell out of the cell block into the jailer's room–the utility room–and by Joe Carter and me.

"Then I could see a couple of others, each with an arm, dragging Jesse down the passageway, out into the jailers' room. He had no more life in him than a big sack of potatoes.

"Someone called out, 'How about that kid?' "Jim said that really scared him because "the kid" would have to be Oscar Peeler and he had gotten to like him in the weeks he sat there in jail.

"I know young Peeler was supposed to have helped Miller, keeping house for him–Oscar and his sister–but I could never believe he was smart enough 'er wicked enough to have anything important to do with Gus Bobbitt's murder," Jim said. "I'da been really upset if that mob took the boy. He didn't deserve it."

Fortunately, the way Jim remembered, one of the masked men spoke up and ordered, "'Leave him be. He was a big help gettin' this case going. Leave 'im be.' And they left Oscar Peeler in his cell. How close he came to never seeing Forth Worth again, he'll never know."

Jim Miller was still in his cell while all this was going on. And Jim McCarthy was still not sure what he was seeing back in the cell block–mostly the lantern they took from the table waving around–but while they were pulling Jesse West out he heard Jim Miller's voice:

"'Wait a minute! Hold your horses. I'm gettin' my clothes on.' I remember he sounded like he was kind of in charge back there, not at all scared or whiney…kind of surprising with what was happening to him," Jim thought.

Somewhere I read Jim Miller came out of his cell that night dressed in his dark business or preacher's suit, regular shirt but no tie, his city hat square on his head. He was quoted as saying "You boys got a job to do. Get on with it." I asked McCarthy if that was really true.

"I can't swear I heard him say that. There was a lot of talking and shuffling right by me when they were dragging Jesse West out the jail door. It wouldn't surprise me, though. The last thing Jim Miller would do is let anyone think he was fearful.

"I can tell you for sure he was wearing the same outfit he came here with, and he really was wearing that black city hat.

"Another thing people wonder is true or not is whether Miller really did give me a diamond stickpin. Well, let me tell you he did. Three of those masked fellers were walking him out the cell block and they came right by me. I was still pretty much where I started out in the room after the mob broke in.

"The four of them, a masked guy on both sides of Miller and one in back, were about past me when Miller said, 'Hold up.' They did stop and Miller turned to look at me. 'Mr. McCarthy. I'd be obliged if you took my wedding ring off and made sure it gets to my wife.' That's exactly what he said.

"That kind of took me by surprise but I said 'sure' and I went behind him and took the ring off his finger. I did send it to his wife in Fort Worth.

"The masked men started pushing him toward the door. Miller turned back toward me again, 'Mr. McCarthy. There's a stick pin in my lapel. I want you to take it for the kindness you showed me here.'

"The man on Miller's left reached over and grabbed the stickpin from his lapel and tossed it back toward me. It fell on the floor but I got it. I still got it. Then they pushed him on out the door, black as ink out there.

"People also keep askin' me if Walter Goynes actually did want the lynch mob to tie him up. Well sir, he did. I heard him. When those two got through tyin' up Squeaky they went close by Walter and he said just that–'tie me up, too.' They put baling wire around his wrists behind his back like he asked, but from what I could see they were doin' a half-hearted job. It takes some effort to tie someone up with baling wire. It's not like rope."

I knew Walter Goynes many years after the lynching. He became a regular police officer and served the community admirably. No one ever suggested he lacked courage. Nobody ever said he was in on the lynch mob's plans either, though he brought it up himself every once in a while, suggesting with a kind of wry humor, if he were really on the job that night in the jail, he would have arrested all those masked men.

I asked McCarthy one time–we talked about the lynching off and on for years, every time a new story was published, anyway–whether he knew of anybody else around the jail that night, whether or not he could see them from inside.

"Well, I couldn't see outside. It was just black. Might have been most anybody out there. I still had in mind the newspaper story sayin' Miller's West Texas gang might come get him," Jim said. "But what little I saw of anybody must have been the mob and the men they took. I couldn't see faces. Once they got past the door a little way, they were gone.

"Lee Masters told me he ran uptown and got Judge Terrell after he met the mob on Main Street. If Lee said he did, he did, as far as I'm concerned. The two of them might have been out there. I don't know."

There wasn't any doubt in Lee's mind what happened to him. There was a lantern in the window at the judge's house on south Broadway and when he started up the porch stairs, the front door swung open. Judge Terrell must have been waiting for something, Lee recalled, "because he came out with a rain slicker and big hat before I said a word.

"Judge– Something bad is goin' on and I don't think there's much I can do about it. There's dozens of men walking down Main with their faces covered up, waving pistols around. They called me by name and told me to get away."

The Judge thumped down the porch stairs and started walking fast back to Main Street, not saying word. Lee walked alongside him. He decided not to say anything more or ask any questions, first because the judge was beginning to puff from the fast walking and besides, "I was the one that should have known what was happening.

"We got to the courthouse, turned onto Townsend and there the mob was," Lee remembered. "How many, I couldn't tell in the dark, and they were moving around fast.

"Well, as it turned out, it was just some of the mob, the one's still trying to get into the jail. Neither Judge Terrell or I knew there were people already inside.

"For a little while–maybe it was just seconds but it seemed a while–none of the mob took any notice of me or the judge. They were all pushing for the door and asking each other what's goin' on in there.

"Finally one of them, face covered up like all the rest, turned around and saw the Judge and me standing there behind them. He kind of jumped when he saw us. I guess he knew who I was, dark as it was. I had my police officer's hat on and we were only three or four feet apart. I don't know if he recognized the judge in his big hat, though.

"Well, this guy turned back toward the jail door and elbowed the man next to him. 'Look back there!' he said loud.

"This other fellow, face covered up to his eyes like all the rest, seemed just as surprised as the first one, but he was calmer. Maybe he could see better at night too, because he recognized Judge Terrell.

"Judge, you're not needed here. Neither are you Lee. Git!'

"That was enough to turn six or seven of the mob on the edge of the pack trying to get into the jail. There was lot of muttering until one of the mob with a stern voice said, 'Judge Terrell. It's best you leave right now!' With that, a half dozen of the people started waving their pistols around like they were shooing chickens.

"Judge Terrell was a brave enough man but he didn't have much of a chance, going back and forth with a bunch of armed men in the dark. They knew who he was but he didn't know who they were…didn't know for sure, anyway.

"I'll admit, I didn't like it very much either," Lee said. "I had my revolver, but it was holstered and these people had their guns out, waving 'em around. I wouldn't have had a chance."

"It was a bad time. One of those people could have let fly easy as not and both the Judge and me would have been lying there in the mud. Judge Terrell finally said, 'Well, boys. Don't do anything I wouldn't do.' Then he turned to walk back to Main, pulled on my coat sleeve going by and said, 'Com'on Lee.' And we left. I've thought about it a lot of times but I really don't know what we could have done different that night."

My friend McCarthy recalled when the mob left the jail with their prisoners, none of the jailers had much to say. He admitted he didn't "feel too good in the stomach" and didn't feel like going out and chasing after anybody in the dark. Jailers usually don't get involved in the capturing end of the law enforcement business. That wouldn't have been the time to start.

McCarthy went back of Walter Goynes and pulled the baling wire off–without much trouble. Walter went into his office to get a towel and pitcher of water. In a minute he came out and went to the cot where Squeaky Nestor was lying. "Squeaky hadn't moved, groaned 'er anything," Jim said.

The chief jailer put the soaked towel over Squeaky's scalp wound, rolled the little lawman on his side and took the baling wire off.

"He's got a pulse," Goynes said quietly.

McCarthy went to the oak door and opened it enough to look out into the black night.

"There was no light out there at all. There wasn't a sound. No yelling, cursing, no shouted orders, nothing…and that barn was no more'n a hundred feet or so down the street."

Why what happened inside my old barn kept bobbing up in my head like a bad dream, I'm not sure. Maybe imagining what happened with some thirty silent men going about their deadly work in the dark made it worse than it was. I'll never know.

The hanging itself had to be just as well planned as getting into the jail. The mob had to bring four lariats, or maybe long ropes, to begin with. If they weren't everyday lariats, but plain rope, they had to have good knots already tied to make strong running nooses at the ends. You can't expect to do that very well in the dark.

Somebody must have figured out which of the old rafters would bear the load of prisoners being pulled up, off the barn floor. The prisoners were all big men, or maybe heavy would be right in Burwell's case.

And just as certain, each mob member knew which prisoner was his to take care of and what he was supposed to do. There was no uncertainty about that.

I never heard if any of the prisoners tried to say anything, standing there in the dark, arms wired tight behind them, being bumped and jostled by shrouded executioners trying to finish their gruesome work quickly. Who would they say it to? Jesse West might well have shouted out his last defiance, except he was unconscious. He didn't know he was being hanged.

Joe Allen and Barry Burwell fell into a trance when the mob took them out of their jail cells. They got to the barn like sleep walkers, I was told. Maybe they didn't really know what was happening, not clear enough in their minds to say anything to the hooded, unknown executioners moving around them.

It's hard to imagine Jim Miller in a trance. He might have been resigned, facing the end as he was in total darkness, in the rough hands of angry men he couldn't see. It was against his nature to plead to anybody, much less plead to men behind masks. He wouldn't express regrets. I'm not sure he had any. Maybe the quote he's given credit for in the jail–"get on with it"–said it all for Jim Miller.

There was no need to wonder what happened– Nooses were flung over the rafters. Hands shot up in dark to capture the nooses and pull them down over the prisoners' heads. Loops were tightened against necks. Slack was drawn from the ropes. Then there was a muffled command, "pull!"

One by one, four men were pulled up from the barn floor, choking, legs jerking. Jim Miller's hat had fallen off when the noose was put around his neck. When his spasms ended, somebody in the mob put the hat back on his head.

When all of the prisoners were still and lifeless at the end of their ropes–and the white horse, Old John, was settled down–somebody said, "Let's go."

The mob, kerchiefs no longer over their faces, filed out of the barn door. The last man out pulled the barn door shut. They disappeared down Townsend Street in the dreary night, a light drizzle still coming down.

Afterward

After the mob pushed into the jail and took the prisoners to the barn down the street, Jim McCarthy told me he closed the heavy outside door and bolted it. "We didn't want them back, and we had no plans to go out after 'em."

From inside the jail, which had become strangely quiet–even the drunk stopped snoring–they never heard a sound from the barn–no shouted orders, no cursing, yelling, nothing, Jim said, and the barn wasn't much more than a hundred feet away. They thought they heard some muffled voices out on the street maybe a half hour after the prisoners were taken, like it might have been men walking up to Main, but you had to be on full alert to hear anything.

It was a few minutes after five o'clock and still dark. The electric lights hadn't come back on either, so the jailers had a couple more lanterns going just to make the place less spooky. Neither Jim nor Joe had any interest in picking up the cards again. They just kept looking around and listening.

Walter Goynes came out of his chief jailer's office in a slow pained way, walked over to the table and said to Joe, "Go on down to that barn and see what's goin' on."

McCarthy said he didn't see Joe's face in the lantern light, but Walter must have. "Well, take Jim with you," the chief jailer suggested.

"No'sir. I can take care of it myself."

Joe got up, walked over to the wall along the street where his hat was hanging on a nail, and put it on. Then he checked the cylinder of his revolver for six shots, worked the gun in and out of his holster a couple of times, went to the door and said, "I'll be back."

Joe came back in less than five minutes. "They're there all right," he reported with grave authority.

"Who's there fer Cris' sake?" Walter sputtered.

"Well, the prisoners they took, I 'spose. It's black as pitch in there. Couldn't see faces. Four men, anyway, all hangin' quiet.'

"Nobody else? No guards 'er anything?"

"Nope. Nobody."

Walter just shook his head and mumbled, not making much sense, McCarthy recalled. Then he thought he heard him say, "Somebody's got to clean this mess up…I suppose if the sheriff was here I'd get the job." He was right about that, McCarthy knew, though he didn't blame Walter for wanting to steer clear if he could.

Then the chief jailer shook the cobwebs from his head and said in a calm enough voice, "Jim, go over to the yard and get a wagon. We might as well get started."

Jim was in no big rush to walk the three blocks in the dark streets, but by the time he got over to the yard and got the stable hands awake enough to hitch a team, it was beginning to be light in the east down low on the horizon. No sun. Just the night was giving way. Low clouds were still running up from the south, though the rain had stopped, he said.

He drove the wagon back to the jail and Walter climbed up on the bench with him. Joe jumped in the back, short as the trip was. Up close to the barn they could see, even in the half light, there were people walking around.

"One of the men outside the barn–though we didn't know it then–was N. B. Stall, our town photographer," Jim said. "He had already taken a picture of the four men hangin' inside through one of the cracks in the wall. Or maybe he pushed a wall board aside. Be easy enough to do, and it let more light inside. In any case, he had enough light to take the picture you can see today as a postcard…curious way to advertise the town."

Goynes jumped down from the wagon when they got alongside the barn, walked to the creaky door, pulled it open and went inside . His head popped back out. "Jim–pull the wagon around so you get the back end as close to the door as you can."

Jim said when he got the wagon pulled around, he went inside and pulled the door closed behind him. There still wasn't much light in the barn, but more was coming through the cracks in the walls all the time. There was enough light for him to see Walter and Joe had taken off all the baling wire from the four.

"Let 'em down and drag 'em over by the door," Walter ordered.

About then a question came from some man on the outside lookin' through the cracks, Jim remembered. "That the Miller bunch, Walter?"

Walter had gone back to muttering while he was dragging the lifeless jail prisoners over to the door. He was really in a state, Jim said. “Yeah,” Walter shot back to the man outside.

“Jim,” he said to me, “Open the door. We might as well start loadin’–and get them ropes.’

While the jailers were dragging the prisoners over to the door, the crowd outside–maybe twenty or so, some of ‘em kids–moved around toward the door themselves. The four dead men were lying side by side on the barn floor when Goynes opened the door.

“‘…gawd o mighty…’ from one of the men outside.

Walter jumped up into the wagon. “Joe,” he said, “come on up here with me. Jim. Drag ‘em over. Give us the hands.’

Walter and Joe pulled Barry Burwell up into the wagon first. Jim lifted his feet. They were getting a hold of Joe Allen when this same man from outside asked, “Who done it, Walter?” The chief jailer kept pulling Joe Allen’s body back into the wagon, muttering as he labored.

“Walter – who done it?”

“How the hell would I know,” Walter shot back, next getting hold of Jesse West’s wrists and then arms.

There was a little pause and then this same man said, “Well, it’s your jail where they got ’em. Didn’t you see anything? Somebody just walk in and took four prisoners?’

“I knew Walter was just about to blow up,” Jim recalled. “He had been in some kind of shock for a couple of hours, off and on, and it was beginnin’ to wear on him.”

“No, goddam it, no!” Goynes shouted. “There was a bunch of ’em! All armed, all of ’em masked. They just about killed Bob Nestor. It was no easy thing!”

The three jailers quickly got Jim Miller’s body aboard too, and tossed his black fedora hat into the wagon after him. Walter climbed onto the driver’s bench from the back, seized the reins and geed the team ahead. Jim and Joe held hard on to the back of the bench because they went to the to the L. T. Walters funeral home at a gallop.

That’s about what Jim McCarthy remembered of early Monday morning in Ada, April 19, 1909. It took me years, off and on, to get his story because he never just started at the beginning and went to the end. He remembered different things at different times and I had to put them in some order.

Winding up their first day coverage of the lynching, the *Ada Evening News* reported that "Ada was quiet and people calm...The citizenship of the town has shown a disposition to make the best of it."

Certainly I didn't see everybody in town walking over to my boarding house from the station that morning, but the *News* was right from the citizens I did see. They seemed calm enough. Maybe it was because the early edition of the *News* had just come out and not many of these people had read it.

By early afternoon, nearly everybody older than six knew about the lynching. Well, they knew four men had been lynched, all members of the "Miller gang." They didn't know who did it, and that's what everybody was asking about. Nobody I ran across seemed outraged that it happened. They were just busting to know who did it–calm though, not in a hurry to punish somebody.

Governor Haskell up in Guthrie wasn't calm. On Tuesday, April 20, he must have corralled every newspaperman for a hundred miles around and told them the lynching was a black mark against the whole state of Oklahoma and those "...in any way implicated will be prosecuted to the full extent of the law."

I remember when I got to talk to him on the train ride down to Ada from Oklahoma City April 3–that was when the new college was officially dedicated–he said law and order was going to be at the top of his priority list. Ada was a worry for him then with all the shooting. With the lynching, he got the whole country looking at his state. To read his public statements, you'd think every human being in Ada had betrayed him.

Blasting Ada in the newspapers wasn't all he had in mind. He ordered the Oklahoma attorney general "to summon" our county attorney to Atoka, a town about forty five miles southeast of Ada, where a grand jury was to be convened. The grand jury was to investigate the lynching and then see to it those found responsible were prosecuted.

The governor was plainly upset and determined to see that justice was done. You'd think Bob Wimbish would be a little nervous about having the governor so mad. He didn't seem to be, though. He told newspaper reporters who came to see him about the governor's demand that he would get to Atoka without delay and would, of course, do his duty and prosecute anyone indicted for the crime.

Then Bob added–for the record, and printed in the *News*–there "would not likely be…any prosecution of those responsible for the lynching because…no one appeared to know the participants, and I certainly don't know any of them."

That always seemed to me a kind of strange thing to say for the county's top lawman–the county attorney–even if he felt that way. In any case, he got right over to Atoka without delay as the governor directed, to meet the attorney general and organize the grand jury proceedings.

While the attorney general and Bob Wimbish were setting things up, Jim Miller's body was sent back to his wife, Sally, in Fort Worth along with the ring McCarthy agreed to send. Miller's funeral was April 21. Services were conducted by the Rev. H. D. Knickerbocher, pastor of the First Methodist Church. "Thousands" attend the funeral, *The Fort Worth Star Telegram* reported.

Barry Burwell's remains were sent to his mother and brother in Weatherford, Texas.

Bodies of the two Texas ranchers were sent, by direction, to Shawnee in north Pottawatomie County to await the arrival of the two new widows. They were determined to accompany the remains of their men back to Mobeetie for burial. Pittman tried but failed to talk them out of their mission. He believed they would be in grave danger in Oklahoma from the Ada mob.

The widows did arrive in Shawnee at two o'clock in the morning April 21 on the Rock Island. Only Pittman and a freight agent were on hand.

Services for Jesse West and Joe Allen were conducted April 29 before what the *Canadian Record* called an "immense throng…one of the largest assemblages that ever gathered to honor the dead in Hemphill county…fully five hundred people stood in line with drawn eyes and eyes bedimmed with tears."

As sympathetic as the *Record* editors seemed to be, they chose not to speculate on the cause of the crime, or who might be to blame. However, they wrote the ranchers were "…ought we know…pure minded and innocent."

As the week went on, messages of a surprising nature–in light of all the angry editorials–began arriving in Ada. J. B. Wilson, president of the Pecos County Cattleman's Association in West Texas, sent a message congratulating the whole town of Ada for "getting rid of the coldest blooded cutthroat ever to defy the laws of Texas and Oklahoma."

Other West Texas and Oklahoma ranchers wired congratulations to Wimbish as well. Several of these careful men made telephone calls to friends in Pontotoc County to make sure Miller was really dead. Sending a telegram unfriendly to Miller wouldn't have been worth the risk otherwise.

Joseph H. Stahl, the Houston contractor, renewed his charge that Miller had set up the murder of his friend Pat Garrett in New Mexico and congratulated Wimbish for achieving "long overdue" justice.

Ranchers weren't the only ones relieved by the turn of events. The Texas attorney general told newsmen in Austin–after he got word of the lynching–that Miller was a very riled defendant in a law suit he was bringing to recover five hundred acres of public land in El Paso County. The attorney general said Miller warned his deputy in El Paso that if title to the land was cancelled, it would be the "last act" of the official who ordered it.

Journalists from out of town who came to Ada for the Miller trial stayed on for a while to see what they could learn about the lynching, since there hadn't been one word about who did it. With no real news to report they took to asking citizens on the street what they thought about Ada—"this little prairie town," the AP wrote–being pushed into the national spotlight.

I didn't see all the stories wired across the country, but I saw some and they were pretty much alike. "It's nothing to be proud of," most of the people were quoted as saying. "Two wrongs don't make a right, though some good may come of it."

Naturally the journalists also asked a number of people in town who they thought might have been part of the lynch mob. The answers all seemed to be the same—"Who knows? They all wore masks."

The grand jury in Atoka didn't do any better, even with the governor's strong support. The jury started hearing the first of twenty eight witnesses April 27. Walter Goynes and his two jailers were first among them, running through to Lee Masters. None could offer a single clue as to who mob members were because of the masks.

Bob Nestor, his head all bound up, testified as well. He said he not only couldn't recognize anybody because of the masks, he couldn't identify any voices either because of his poor hearing. None of the other witnesses claimed poor hearing, but they didn't tell the grand jury anything more than Squeaky did.

When it was obvious to the grand jury they weren't going to find out who was responsible for the hanging, they quit April 29 and wrote their official report:

"We have had practically no assistance from the main body of citizens..." they wrote.

"We deplore that this affair took place in our county and believe that in this matter the law should have taken its course...We further believe that the occurrence was largely due to the tardy administration of justice by the court."

Other than wishing the lynching hadn't happened in Pontotoc County, and laying much of the blame on the court system, the grand jury didn't seem to have any further thoughts on the matter. They certainly didn't propose anything further be done.

The Ada Evening News took about the same approach. In a short matter-of-fact story about the jury's work, the *News* declared "the community appeared ready to put the whole matter behind it."

Leaving "...the whole matter behind..." describes petty well what did happen in Ada. Bob Wimbish, the highest public official in Ada directly involved, was reelected county attorney in 1910. He beat his Republican opponent 1752 to 634. Bob served as county attorney until 1913. Then he started his private law practice. Got elected to the state legislature in 1916.

There's no doubt Bob Wimbish became one of our most respected community leaders. He was first president of the Ada Lions club when it was founded, and was active in the First Presbyterian Church all his life.

"Judge Bob," as the *News* called him, "died not long ago"–July 28, 1950. The *News* obituary July 30 started on the front page then jumped inside. The story observed that he built a "reputation of a very able attorney, particularly as a criminal lawyer skilled in alert courtroom procedure."

There wasn't one word about the 1909 lynching in the obit and Bob's critical official position at the time. The first mention of Wimbish's role in the lynching had to come from out of town–

The Daily Oklahoman ran their own obit several days after Bob's death, though it was more of an editorial. Whatever you call it, the story was written by Luther Harrison, an Ada man who went up to the City to work for the *Oklahoman*. I never did know him down here, but he seemed to know a lot about the lynching.

After a short recap of the Ada tragedy forty one years earlier, Harrison wrote, "Last week there died in Ada the attorney whose skill and courage led to the arrest and incarceration of the men who were lynched.

"The people of Pontotoc County had little hope Gus Bobbitt's murderers would ever be brought to justice," Harrison stated. Bob Wimbish, he said, "succeeded in doing what they feared would be impossible.

"It is doubtful they would have been in jail had it not been for Robert Wimbish. He showed the people of a new-born state what a county attorney should be." That's exactly what Dwight Livingston said Wimbish was determined to achieve.

Harrison never did mention any name other than Bob's, didn't even repeat that many mob members appeared to be associated with the commercial club–the 25,000 Club, which next became the Chamber of Commerce. He didn't refer to any sources he had for his story, either. He didn't have to. Everything he wrote had become part of Ada legend, things everybody who had been around for a while "knew" and believed without much question.

Looking back nearly a half century, the lynching wasn't an earth shaking calamity, though the prisoners might have felt it was important. It did, however, put a big damper on the town for a while. Lot of people went around for days after with a kind of worried look. There weren't many conversations that didn't begin or end with the lynching. People kept asking if there was something more to do, more law breakers to be taken care of. And, of course, they wanted to know who did it.

One thing I really felt bad about, Dwight Livingston told me his wife Catherine wanted to go home, back to Tennessee.

"She put up a good front for several years," Dwight said, "but she really was homesick. The lynching was just too much for her. 'I want to go back to my people,' she said.

"I can't really blame her," Dwight admitted. "She comes from a solid, respectable family–big house and all–where nothing ever seemed to go wrong.

"And it wasn't just the lynching. There was so much shooting around here the years before. And all those ruffians down on West Main. She never did like it."

Dwight didn't say anything more about that Sunday night and Monday morning, whether he went with the mob, or whether he decided not to. That's not a question I would ask anybody, particularly a friend. I was alert for any clues he might drop though, clues about his decision. There never were any.

Emma didn't mind asking me though. She was pretty upset about the whole thing and wanted to know if I had been in Ada that night, would I have been part of the mob? I had to be careful how I answered that because I was still trying to build up Ada as good place for us to live.

Besides the risk of further discouraging Emma about moving to Ada, the answer still wasn't all that clear in my mind. I remember being relieved I had to go up to Oklahoma City that fateful weekend. And I get kind of a queasy stomach to this day, fearing I might have run out, leaving the tough work to others.

I didn't have what you could call a sheltered life, particularly down in South Texas. I've been brave enough through the years I suppose, or maybe ignorant enough, but I sure never killed anybody. Never did even shoot at anybody. Guess I'm more of a talker.

There never was any doubt in my mind those four men were responsible for Gus Bobbitt's death, though hanging might have been over of the line for that bail bondsman.

The bedrock issue in my mind was–would there have been any justice if they hadn't been lynched? That's about what Christian Harding wanted to know. Based on the record–Jim Miller's and this Moman Pruiett's, if he really was going to defend Miller–the chances were pretty good they'd either get off Scott free, or else get a gutless little sentence that would be commuted.

Feeling that way then, and still feeling that way to this day, I probably would have gone to the 25,000 Club that night, to do what I'm not sure. I might have been a lookout or something. Maybe even helped get the electricity cut off. I would have been willing to be part of the group…been willing to share in the consequences, which they all knew could be very heavy.

What I don't think I could do is grab somebody, put a rope around his neck and pull 'im up. I don't have the stomach for that. Maybe I could shoot somebody if my life was in danger. Hang somebody, no. I couldn't do it. I couldn't imagine Dwight Livingston doing it either.

We know there are people in town–or were, anyway–people who did have the stomach. Not bad men. Maybe "men of action" would be the way to put it, uncomplicated men with iron-clad opinions. For years I kept looking at people I knew were around at the time, trying to imagine whether they were one of the executioners.

Another thing–there were four men who got strung up. It wasn't that some hard character was brought in from the Badlands to do the job. One person couldn't manage it all. Dozens of men had to be involved. Every one of them had to make a difficult, fateful decision.

So it's been hard for me to make a judgement. How can anyone say they approve of what happened? I guess I don't approve of it, yet I admit had I been in Ada that night, I would've joined the mob.

The years that have gone by make worrying about it a little easier. There were some changes down on West Main. Several of the roughest characters left over from the river saloon days drifted on, where I don't know. Their old Wild West days were over about everywhere.

Ada's policemen took a firmer hand on West Main. Had to shoot a couple of the really tough customers, but before long a woman could get off the train at the Frisco station and walk up Main without being fearful.

My own life changed, too. I was finally able to buy Jake Potter's brick plant and I spent a lot of time trying to make a business of it, not just a manufacturing operation. I had to miss several weekends going up to Oklahoma City and Emma decided if she wanted me for a husband, she better come to Ada. I'm glad she decided that. She likes Ada now and considers it home. The children certainly consider it home.

With three railroads coming into town for many years, the big cement plant, the college, all the ranches and cotton fields around here, and then the drilling for gas and oil in Pontotoc County starting in 1912, Ada has done pretty well. In the 1930's, the Fitts Field was brought in and we and Oklahoma City were the biggest producers in the state. Ol' Frank Byrd was right–there was oil.

A lot of drilling equipment was shipped into Ada on the railroads for developing the gas and oil fields in the early days, and it took trucks to get the equipment from the railroad siding out to the drilling sites southeast of town. The trucks made a big mess of Main Street when it rained. Mud was a foot deep. So they finally paved all the way from the college down to the Frisco tracks.

Paving Main meant they had to take down the watering trough and the seventeen foot fountain at Rennie. There weren't very many horses on Main by then, so it wasn't a hardship. I did miss hearing the running water on hot summer days though.

In some ways I also missed the town's motto the Temperance ladies put on the fountain: "Ada Not a Lady, but a Dandy Place to Live." The motto is not one I would have recommended, but there's something down to earth about it, and it sure has worked out that way.

Acknowledgements

One advantage–and maybe the only one–of taking so very long to complete a single slender volume, the author has an opportunity to know a remarkable number of helpful and pleasant people along the way. I am grateful for their contributions–

Earl Buchan, Cocoa Beach, Florida, for his early and constant enthusiasm for the project: Glenda Galvin of the Chickasaw Nation, Ada; Judith Michener, Oklahoma Historical Society, Oklahoma City; three ladies of the Pontotoc County Historical & Genealogy Society–Brenda Tollett, past President of the Society, Pat Christensen, present President, and Katherine Howry, all of Ada; Doug Poe, great grandson of Augustus Bobbitt, Ada; Karen West Scott, great niece of Jesse West, Burleson, Texas; Bill James, historian and writer, Corinth, Texas; John W. Lowry, Chairman of the Board, Oklahoma State Bank, Ada; Tish Haney Armstrong, Ada; Lemoine Blake Crabtree, Stonewall; Lucille Murphy, El Paso Public Library, El Paso, Texas; Sally Gross, University of Texas Library, Arlington, Texas; Sherry Wagner, Canadian Public Library, Canadian, Texas; Al Ritter, Editor, The Oklahoma State Troopers Magazine, Ponca City, Oklahoma; Dr. Lewis Wynne, Executive Director, Florida Historical Society; Paul Pruett, Society computer garu; and most of all I am grateful to my wife, the former Margaret Harris of Ada, for listening to the story at countless dinner gatherings with little complaint, and for her innate editing skill. Phillip Jr. was most helpful with his early enthusiasm and advice, as was Shelby, an eagle -eyed copy reader.

Historical Background: Creation of Indian Territory

President Thomas Jefferson wasn't sure he was empowered to make the Louisiana Purchase in 1803, but he put his uncertainties aside and arranged to give France a total of $27 million for 828,000 square miles of land west of the Mississippi River.

The Purchase doubled the size of the United States and assured Americans use of all the Mississippi River to the Gulf of Mexico.

There was another critical benefit of the Purchase in President Jefferson's mind: there would be enough land in the vast new territory to guarantee eastern Indians their own sovereign state far removed from encroaching white settlers. Border warfare was an increasingly nettlesome problem for him.

Where exactly this western haven for dispossessed Indians would be located wasn't decided when he left office, though removing Indians east of the Mississippi River had broad support in the Federal government. Geography, politics, both international and national, established the extent of Indian Territory in the decades following the Purchase, the same lines that shaped the state of Oklahoma in 1907.

The northern boundary of Indian Territory evolved from the Missouri Compromise of 1820, which established latitude thirty six degrees, thirty minutes north as the dividing line for new states entering the Union. It was not an extension of the Mason Dixon line which divided established eastern states. North of the Missouri Compromise line would be free states, south of the line, slave-holding states, as it was for Mason Dixon.

Kansas came into the Union as a free state with its southern boundary at thirty seven degrees. That was thirty latitudinal minutes—or sixty eight miles—north of the Missouri Compromise line. That sixty eight—mile difference between the top of the Texas Pan Handle and the Kansas state line created what came to be known as the Okalahoma Pan Handle.

The natural southern border of Indian Territory was the Red River, boundary for Spanish then Mexican lands that became the Republic of Texas in 1836.

Setting the eastern boundary of Indian Territory was uncomplicated. Congress created Arkansas Territory in 1819. The western border of Arkansas Territory became the eastern border of Indian Territory.

The western boundary of Indian Territory fell into place when Texas came into the Union and was bound by U. S. treaties, specifically the treaty President John Adams entered into with the Spain in 1819.

After Jefferson's Louisiana Purchase, the Spanish were concerned just how deeply the Americans thought they could invade their territory in the New

World. To avoid trouble with Spain, Adams agreed Americans would not go, when traveling south of the Arkansas River, farther west than the one hundredth meridian, which is the eastern boundary of the Texas Panhandle. Most land in the Louisiana Purchase was north of the Arkansas.

As a result of the treaty, the one hundredth meridian became the western boundary of American Indian Territory, except for the Cherokee Strip which runs on west over the Texas Panhandle to New Mexico. The one hundredth meridian was the eastern boundary of the Panhandle when Texas entered the Union.

Historical Background: Chickasaw Horses

Knowledgeable horse breeders do not agree on the evolution of the Chickasaw horse, though history and geography make origin of the breed clear.

Christopher Columbus brought the first horses to the Western Hemisphere on his second voyage from Spain in 1493. Spanish conquistadors brought more in the 16th century. Francisco Pizarro used Spanish horses to frighten and subdue Peruvian Incas in 1532, Hernan Cortez employed mounted troops against the Aztecs in Mexico. Hernando de Soto would not be without "horse" when he left Florida in 1539 on his ill-fated search for gold.

DeSoto personally financed an expedition with six hundred and twenty foot soldiers, and one hundred twenty three mounted lancers. For the lancers starting out from near what is now the Tampa Bay area, he provided between two hundred twenty three to three hundred horses. Historical records vary.

Fierce battles with the Timucuan Indians in northeast Florida, followed by costly battles with the Apalchee Indians in northwest Florida, cost de Soto heavily in both men and horses. His expeditionary force arrived at the Mississippi River in 1541, battered and hungry. As a result, de Soto was more obnoxious dealing with the natives than conquistadors usually were, demanding food and grain. Unfortunately for the Spaniards, they had ended up in Chickasaw territory.

Being the most dominant warriors in the region, the Chickasaws wouldn't long tolerate the Spaniards taking their food and ordering them around. After enduring the conquistadors for week, they attacked the flimsy, hurriedly built Spanish "fort" in the night and killed twelve soldiers, twelve horses and four hundred pigs. The Spaniards who survived, including DeSoto, escaped across the river.

A large number of horses were not killed and they bolted into the woods, perhaps fifty to a hundred or more. When the Chickasaws saw in the days to come the horses didn't run away, like deer, they decided to capture them and learn to use them as the Spaniards did. They became the start of the Chickasaw breed.

These horses were the Spanish Barb, descendants of the Spanish Jennet and Andalusian breeds, originally brought to the Iberian peninsula by North African Arabs in the 8th century. They were small but agile, reflecting their Arabian ancestry–not the size of cavalry horses in northern Europe whose blood lines ran back to the powerful horses armored knights needed. The Barb weighed between eight hundred and nine hundred seventy five pounds, and stood between thirteen and fourteen hands.

The Chickasaws became skilled breeders. Horses were soon a principal barter commodity and Chickasaw horses were traded to nearby tribes, including the Choctaws, when relations between the tribes were good.

Chickasaw traders quickly observed bigger horses were more valuable on the market and began their efforts to produce a bigger horse. They exchanged French prisoners of war for European horses the few times that was possible–not often–and bargained with English traders years later for use of their big horses. The Chickasaw breed emerged before the Revolutionary War and several ranking American officers rode a "Chickasaw," a horse named "Ball" the most famous.

Chickasaw horses combined with several other breeds, including draft horses. There is even a Belgian Chickasaw. The most renowned match was with Thoroughbreds on the East Coast. This combination produced what became the American Quarter Horse–fast, big enough for ranch work and herding of cattle, small enough to be agile.

There are Chickasaw breed organizations and perhaps they have established definitive criteria. As a general observation, however, the breed emerged considerably larger than the Spanish Barb, but not as big as the Thoroughbred.

The Chickasaws were usually of solid colors and do not reflect the history of Indian "ponies" in the American West, descendants of other horses brought into Mexico by the Spanish. In 1598, the Apaches became the first western Indians to get their own horses. They took them from Spanish colonists in what is now New Mexico. By the 17th century, horses had been were dispersed–by barter, Indian raiding parties and warfare–to all the tribes in the American West.

Indian ponies, as well as the wild horses of the American West, whose antecedents also came from Mexico, were generally smaller than the Chickasaw and often had variegated coloring, such as the "paint" and Appaloosa.

Historical Background: Railroads Come to Pontotoc County

Ada was first settled in 1890 but grew very slowly in the next decade. There were only about two hundred residents in 1900. A number of nearby towns, such as Center, were larger and growing faster.

The "Frisco" railroad—(St. Louis and San Francisco)—came to Ada in December 1900, missing these same faster-growing towns. By 1902 Ada had a larger freight volume than any other station between Sapulpa on the north and Denison, Texas. Cotton, cement, glass and brick were the main items shipped from Ada; merchandise, lumber, coal and later, oil field equipment, were the principle products shipped to Ada.

In just six years Ada was the trading center for the entire area with a population of five thousand, far eclipsing the towns bypassed by the railroads.

The Frisco ran between twenty and thirty trains every day on its mainline tracks in Pontotoc County during the early growth years, six of them scheduled passenger trains. American Standard 4-4-0 coal-burning locomotives pulled the early trains. They could pull up to twenty five cars on flat ground. If there was a hill to climb, the engineer might have to take only half the cars over, and then come back for the other half.

The "Katy"—Missouri, Kansas and Texas—ran tracks into Ada from the southeast in November 1903. The tracks ran from McAlester, the Katy's main north—south line, through Atoka, Ada and on to Oklahoma City. The Katy had four passenger trains, using Atlantic 4-4-2 engines, and four freight trains to serve Pontotoc County daily.

Ada's third railroad—Oklahoma Central—originally ran its tracks just south of Ada in 1906. Townsmen hadn't financially assisted the railroad coming into the community, so the tracks were run around the town. That was soon recognized as a mistake by railroad officials and tracks were laid into Ada and a depot built.

Much of this information is from *History of Pontotoc County, Oklahoma* published by the Pontotoc County Historical and Genealogical Society, copyright 1976.

Historical Background: Ada's Remarkable Water

Byrds Mill Spring is a major, natural flowing spring approximately fourteen miles south southeast of Ada. Fifteen million gallons of remarkably pure water flow from the spring every day, half of which is used by Ada and the surrounding community. What is not used goes into creeks, the Blue River and then the Red River.

The spring is fed by the Arbuckle-Simpson aquifer, a recharge area of approximately 35 square miles on higher ground south of Ada. It has been estimated the aquifer holds the equivalent of two Lake Texhomas in water volume.

The spring was well known by the Indians before white settlers came, and Indian hunting parties regularly camped there.

Grace Boeger's book, *A Story of Byrds Mill Spring: Ada's Fountainhead,* describes how the mill was designed and built in 1869-70 by the Rev. Josiah Hardin of North Texas for Frank Byrd.

Frank Byrd's brother, William Byrd, was Governor of the Chickasaw Nation at the time and asked Frank to get the mill built to help develop the area economy. Frank Byrd located and hired the Reverend Hardin, a Confederate veteran of the Civil War who had an engineering background. The Reverend started construction of the dam to impound the water, the sluice and then the mill itself in 1869.

While construction was going on, Frank Byrd ordered milling machinery from France. The entire project was completed in late 1870. Wheat farmers throughout the Pontotoc District were served by the mill for years until good roads and widespread use of trucks gave farmers other options.

The mill pond area was a picnic destination for many years after the milling operation stopped. The area is now fenced off for security reasons.

There has been some uncertainty through the years in regard to the spelling of Byrds Mill Spring—whether or not an apostrophe is called for. With the help of the U. S. Geological Survey, Mrs. Boeger settled the matter—to her own satisfaction anyway. Mrs. Boeger decreed if reference is made to the mill itself, there was an apostrophe in Byrd's. If the reference is to the spring, there is no apostrophe in Byrds.

Historical Background: Indian Territory

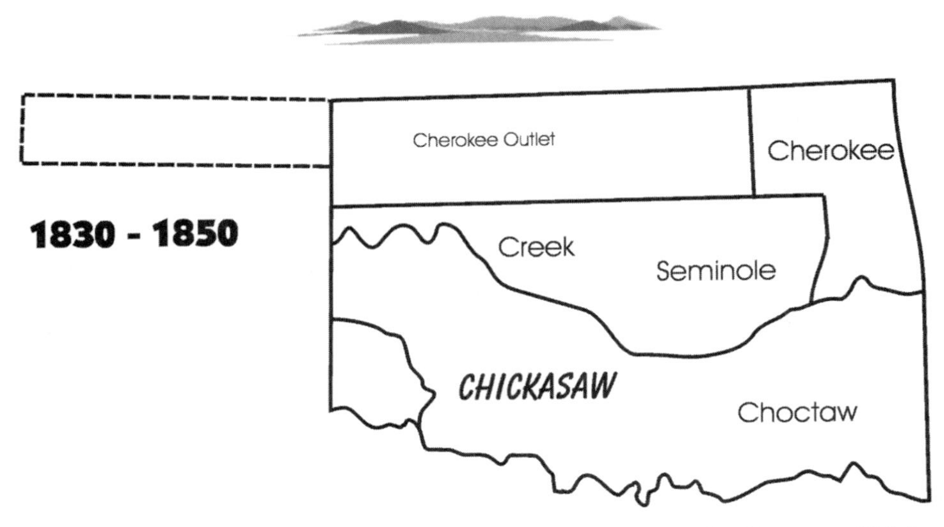

After the 1830 Indian Removal Act, The Cherokee, Creek, Choctaw, Chickasaw and Seminole tribes are confined to the Indian Territory.

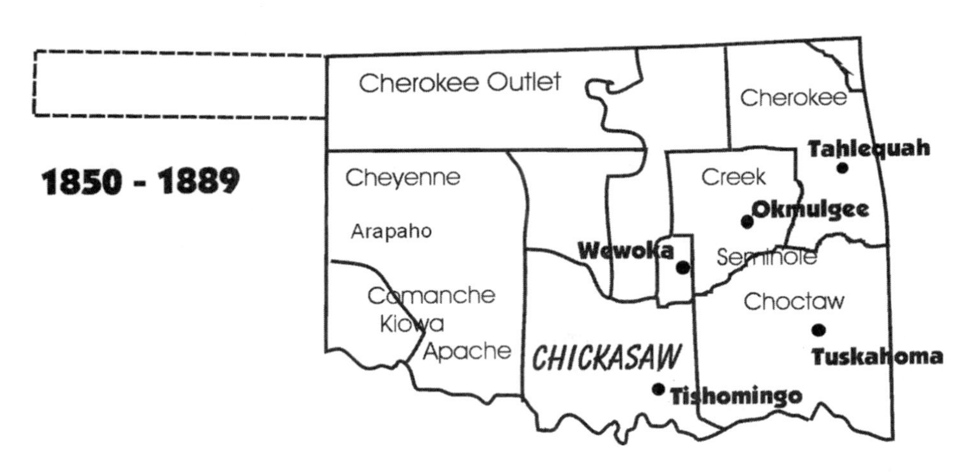

In 1851 the Indian Appropriation Act legalized reservations, and treaties in the 1850's and 1860's sent 50 tribes to the Indian Territory. In 1866 the Five Tribes ceded large tracts to the U.S., mainly for the northeastern and midwestern Indians. IN 1889 settlers rushed in for the opening of the two-million acres of unassigned land.

The creation of the Oklahoma Territory in 1890 further shrank Indian Territory by half. Under the Dawes Allotment Act, Indians had to abandon communal owning for individual plots, leaving a large surplus of land. As the land was opened for settlement, the population grew from 60,000 people in 1890 to 400,000 in 1900. In the year 1905 the Five Tribes pressed for their own state, Sequoyah, but Congress soon voted Indian Territory a part of Oklahoma State.

From 1906-1971 U.S. Presidents appointed Chickasaw governors to conduct necessary business on behalf of tribal people. That changed when Congress passed legislation in 1970 allowing certain tribes to hold elections for the purpose of choosing their own officials.

Today the Chickasaw people find themselves citizens of a triad of governments-state, federal, and tribal. Although radically changed over the years by actions of the other two, a form of tribal government within constraints of Federal and State laws serves the Chickasaw people.

The Chickasaw Nation has a website at http://www.chickasaw.net/

About the Author

Phillip Swatek was a newspaper reporter and editor in West Texas in the beginning of his career, which started after service as a Naval Aviator in World War II.

As a free lance author he wrote articles for Southwest ranch and farm magazines. It was an educational leap for a Chicagoan, who graduated from the University of Illinois.

Following the journalism and magazine-writing trail, Swatek left the Southwest and headed east. One of the articles written then is included in the *National Geographic* anthology of sea stories, *Men, Ships, and the Sea.* In 1956, he became Washington Correspondent and Chief of the Washington Bureau of the *Cincinnati Enquirer.*

Covering national political campaigns was an important part of the Washington Correspondent's job and Swatek traveled extensively with all the candidates in the Presidential election of 1960, including Jack Kennedy.

When Kennedy was elected President, Swatek was appointed Director of Public Affairs for the Federal Aviation Agency. That led to his years of work and travel as Regional Director of the FAA in Asia-Pacific, Latin America, and Europe, Africa and the Middle East.

The tragic event of 1909 in Ada, Oklahoma, his wife's hometown, and the mystery surrounding that event, had long been a story he hoped to explore. His career took him away from steady pursuit of that interest, but when he and his wife–the former Margaret Harris–and their children, returned to Ada on frequent visits he was able to continue research and interviews.

Swatek retired from government service in Brussels, Belgium in 1985. He and Margaret moved to their present home in Melbourne, Florida in 1990. In Melbourne, Swatek became an adjunct professor and lecturer at Florida Institute of Technology until writing once again became a priority.

Future Publications

Coming from the author -

FLORIDA FLYING BOATS

From the world's first scheduled airline, St. Petersburg to Tampa, 1914, to Pan American's route from Key West to Havana, 1927;

To Navy Operations of PBY's at Pensacola and Jacksonville, and PBM's at Banana River during World War II;

To flying boats operating in Florida waters today.

EXPLORE FLORIDA'S PAST
WAR
Canaveral Light
FLORIDA
The Print Shoppe
Florida Historical Society
435 Brevard Avenue
Cocoa, Florida 32922
(321) 690-0099
theprintshoppe35@aol.com
Telephone orders & purchase orders accepted.
Also: VISA/MasterCard/Discover
War in Paradise
Our Fascinating Past
Slavery in Florida
Canaveral Light
The Enduring Seminoles
Florida in the Civil War